APR -- 2018

A Dying
Note

Books by Ann Parker

A Dying Note

A Silver Rush Mystery

Ann Parker

Poisoned Pen Press

Copyright © 2018 by Ann Parker

First Edition 2018

10 9 8 7 6 5 4 3 2 1

Library of Congress Control Number: 2017951352

ISBN: 9781464209796   Hardcover
ISBN: 9781464209819   Trade Paperback
ISBN: 9781464209826   Ebook

Poisoned Pen Press
4014 N. Goldwater Blvd., #201
Scottsdale, AZ 85251
www.poisonedpenpress.com
info@poisonedpenpress.com

Printed in the United States of America

For Barbara Peters, editor extraordinaire,
who encouraged me (and my protagonist) to "go West"
to San Francisco

Acknowledgments

This book may not have taken a village to write, but the people I'd like to thank would certainly constitute a large neighborhood.

First off, thank you, dear family, especially Bill, Ian, and Devyn, for hanging in there with me. Second, I'm grateful to the friends, writers, critique partners, and beta readers/proofers who offered suggestions and support for various stages of the writing/re-writing process: Bill McConachie, Camille Minichino, Carole Price, Colleen Casey, Dani Greer, Janet Finsilver, Jonnie Jacobs, Kate Wyland, Margaret Lucke, Mary-Lynne Pierce Bernald, Penny Warner, Priscilla Royal, Rita Lakin, Trevor Lamberson, Staci McLaughlin, and Wendy McConachie. Special thanks and endless gratitude to Camille Minichino and Dick Rufer for letting me hide out in their guest room for some serious writing sprints and for their friendship over many decades. Devyn McConachie gets a super-duper shout-out for her last-minute-to-midnight reads of certain critical sections and her help with "final words." (Note to Devyn: You have the makings of an excellent copy editor!) Thanks also to the Facebook group Colorado Writers and Publishers and to the Poisoned Pen Press "posse" of authors—we're all in this together!

In the research arena, Colleen Casey deserves a tip of the hat and a dozen roses for sharing her vast knowledge of San

Francisco's history and loaning me bags of resource books, as well as for her encouragement and patience in answering my many questions and her infectious enthusiasm for the city and all its aspects. The San Francisco Public Library and particularly the San Francisco History Center and its librarians were wonderful resources and always helpful—I will be back! Stephen Parker supplied much-needed and appreciated "musical assistance." Also, thanks to Emperor Norton (aka Joseph Amster) and his insightful Time Machine Tours of San Francisco. All errors, omissions, and slips into alternate realities are mine.

And here's to the folks of Leadville, Colorado: you and your lovely mountain town and its history are always in my mind and my heart (and, as you'll see in this latest book, never far from my protagonist's thoughts as well).

Mary-Lynne "Persnickety" Pierce Bernald—thank you for lending me your name.

Maddee James and the crew at xuni.com—three cheers, a whoop, and a holler for designing and maintaining my website. (For those interested in taking a gander, www.annparker.net and www.annparker.com will both take you there.)

Janaki Yasanayake—thank you for creating the wonderful map of 1881 San Francisco for *A Dying Note*.

Last, but never least, I am grateful to Barbara Peters and Robert Rosenwald and their staff at Poisoned Pen Press for their support, encouragement, and direction. "Thanks" is too small a word for all they do, but it'll have to suffice for now.

Chapter One
San Francisco, Mission Bay
Sunday, November 6, 1881

Not my hands!

Throat crushed, blood gurgled, words choked so they screamed only in the mind.

Sight dimmed—towering bales of hay faded into gray shapes under a near-full moon.

Touch heightened—sharp pieces of straw stabbed into shaking fingers scrabbling to gain purchase on the wharf's rough planks.

Smell overwhelmed—a cesspool, an open sewer, bubbled below the splintered planks of the wharf.

Vomit rose, nowhere to go, choking further.

How did this happen? Why?

The why was clear. The how? It had only been words at first. Hot words flung back and forth like weapons, hurled like stones. Then, all that had been uncovered slipped out. The lies, the larceny, the truth. The truth had shoved them past words, into the realm of no return. A hard shove. A shove back. A wild swing that connected, yielding a yelp and curse.

A returning blow, but not by a hand. Something heavy, crushing, landing on the throat.

Even now, with breath trapped behind blood and broken

cartilage, words clamored, shouted out to be set free, to be heard:

Not my hands!

Then a command, but was it from without or within? Spoken or thought?

On your knees!

Rolling over, pain flared. Palms pushed flat on boards, trying to pull the knees up to obey the order. Limbs rebelled, juddering on the planks, no longer servants of the brain.

Hearing remained—ever faithful. Nearby, the dull thuds and creaks of anchored ships. At a distance, muffled shouts too far away to help. Beyond the wharves, clamor wafted from the saloons, cheap restaurants, and bawdy houses squatting near the drawbridge that spanned malodorous Mission Creek.

Sounds grew closer, ragged breathing, rapid tempo, from high above the fingertips, stinging and raw, above the cheek resting on the planks, wet with blood. Finally, the voice spoke, crackling with anger, aflame with a rage as intense as the fire that engulfed a hay scow a fortnight ago, burning through its mooring and sending it adrift, flaming bright, on an ebb tide out into the night-dark bay.

"Did you think you would get away with this? Destroying me? Destroying us?"

Not my hands!

This time, the trapped words must have escaped, because the voice above came closer, answering. "Not your hands? Very well. That, I can grant you."

The blow to the back of the head shattered the vision of warped wood boards into splinters. Those splinters flew up, whirling, changing into thin, stinging shards of pain. Another blow, and another. The pain spun into clamorous song piercing all thought, drowning all words, the music of life spilling out in red, red sound, before falling into darkness and silence.

Chapter Two
San Francisco Business District
Monday, November 7, 1881

The church bell cacophony began at six in the morning.

Just as it did every day.

And just as she did every day, Inez Stannert, startled awake by the clamor, rolled over and tugged her pillow over her head, damning the day she'd leapt at the chance to move into the rooms above the music store she managed.

Living quarters, gratis.

It had seemed such a good deal at the time, when the storeowner, celebrated violinist Nico Donato, had made the offer.

However, after she and her twelve-year-old ward, Antonia Gizzi, took up residence above the shop at the corner of San Francisco's Pine and Kearney streets, Inez realized that, surrounded as they were by churches of every possible denomination, the daily calls to prayer were nearly deafening. She considered it a sadistic trick of Fate—a particularly ironic variety of Hell, actually—that she should be constantly reminded of the heavy presence of Christian faith. Particularly given that her absent lover was a minister.

Pillow clutched to her ears, Inez allowed herself a moment to compare the competitive clanging of the nearby houses of worship here to that in her previous life. In the high mountain town of Leadville, Colorado, the distant sound of church bells took wing, a seductive call to soul-lifting contemplation of Heaven and the promises of eternal life. Here in San Francisco, Inez suspected a more insidious intent. It was no secret that the density of churches in the "golden city" increased in proportion to their proximity to Chinatown and the Barbary Coast, in hopes of luring lost souls into the fold with promises of eternal salvation and dire threats of eternal damnation. The D & S House of Music and Curiosities was situated close to the two unsavory neighborhoods as well as near the city's business district. Thus, Inez suffered the torments of the damned at regular hours throughout the day when the bells vied with each other.

Still, their discordant clanging served to rouse Inez and Antonia in good time on school days.

Inez had the coffee boiling on the small stove in what passed for their kitchen when Antonia finally dragged herself in, rubbing her eyes, her black hair an untamed mane. Inez brought over a mug of coffee, liberally laced with milk and sugar, set it on the table by the hairbrush, comb, and ribbons, and pointed wordlessly to the chair. Antonia sat and sipped, wincing as Inez attacked her hair with taming implements. With her locks finally plaited and beribboned, Antonia said, "I don't see why I can't cut it all off."

Inez smiled grimly. *And with that, you'd be dressing as a boy and running loose through the city in trousers, just as you were in Leadville, when I first met you and your mother. May she rest in peace.* But all she said was, "You have beautiful hair. Hair like your mother's." She smoothed it with one hand. "Treasure it as a gift from her, just as you treasure your little knife and her fortune-telling cards."

Antonia sighed and nibbled at the thick slice of bread slathered with butter. "It'd just be easier," she mumbled. Then, apropos of nothing, "I don't want to go to school anymore."

Inez crossed her arms, silver-backed hairbrush in one hand.

"What brought this on?"

A stubborn silence was her only answer.

Inez set the hairbrush on the table. "Did you not finish your lessons this weekend? Is that the problem?"

Antonia pinched off a corner of her bread and rolled it into a tight little ball of dough, before finally replying, "The kids are hoity-toities. The teachers all high-and-mighty. The school is stodgified and I'm not learnin' nothing. I can learn my numbers and letters fine helping you in the music store."

Suspecting a deeper reason, Inez pressed. "Before we left Leadville, you were looking forward to school." She let the statement hang there.

Antonia's gaze flickered to the side.

"What happened?"

At Antonia's silence, Inez said briskly, "Well then, I'll accompany you to school today, talk to your teacher, and get to the bottom of this."

Antonia's eyes widened in alarm. "No!" She clenched her jaw, then said in a low voice, defiant, hardly above a whisper, "I cut a boy."

Inez flashed on the small but deadly *salvavirgo* Antonia carried with her everywhere. At first glance, with its little blade folded away, it looked the most innocuous of weapons. Delicate little flowers were carved into the ivory at the top of the handle where the blade folded; a small inlaid figure of a fox gazed over its shoulder where a palm would naturally curl around the grip. But Inez was very aware of its sharpness and the speed with which Antonia could whip it out and open it.

"I didn't hear about this. I would have thought the principal would send me a note."

Antonia laughed, a short bark. "It was after school, last week. And d'you think that ninny'd tell anyone he was beat up by a *girl*?"

Inez briefly weighed whether a good whipping might be in order. It was exactly what her parents would have done, and *did* do, when she dared to be uppity and huffish.

One look at Antonia's face, which had something hurt and bruised about it, changed her mind.

"Why did you do it?"

Antonia looked up. Her straightforward bi-colored gaze—one eye blue, the other brown—met Inez's query without wavering. "He said only gypsies had eyes like mine and called me the bastard of a gypsy whore." The slight trembling of her mouth, which she tried hard to control, convinced Inez that she was telling the truth.

"You were not wearing your glasses?" Inez had bought a pair of tinted glasses for Antonia to keep her unusual eyes concealed.

Antonia looked down at the uneaten crust on her plate. "I was. I told him to leave me alone, but he wouldn't. He pulled my glasses off my face and threw them on the ground. At least they didn't break. He's always doing things like that to kids in the lower grades. Smashing their glasses, tossing their lunch tins into the streets, giving them a black eye."

"Well, it sounds like you taught him a lesson, then. Perhaps he will think twice before picking on someone smaller than he is. In any case, dropping school is not an option. The value of education is not simply in learning one's sums and the rules of grammar. School provides a place where one becomes familiar with the way things are done, how to negotiate one's way through life and society. Such lessons extend to how to deal with bullies without resorting to physical fights." Inez added pointedly, "Too, you know our situation here. We dare not cause any trouble for Mr. Donato, no hint of impropriety or unbecoming conduct from you or from me."

Antonia's hand curled into a fist around the compressed ball of dough.

Inez continued, "Next time, if there is any trouble at all, you will tell me right away. If I had known about this incident on Friday, I would have made sure that you were not bothered again." The steel in Inez's tone made it clear that these were not empty words, but a promise.

Inez faced the stove and poured herself a cup of coffee. "Run along now. Be sure to pick up your lunch at Mrs. Nolan's, and be careful crossing Market."

"I'm not a baby," said Antonia.

Inez turned and crossed her arms. "Excuse me?"

"Yes, ma'am," Antonia muttered.

Bonnet tied under her chin, tinted glasses masking her eyes, empty lunch bucket in hand awaiting Mrs. Nolan's sourdough sandwich and dill pickles, Antonia slung the book strap over her shoulder and headed to the stairs that would take her down and out to the street.

The door to the outside world slammed defiantly. Inez winced. She hated to be strict, but they both had to mind their Ps and Qs in San Francisco.

She carried her cup to the table, sat, cut herself a slice of bread, and buttered it, thinking. If they lived elsewhere, somewhere away from the store, it would provide them with more breathing room, less "walking on eggshells." They were paying Mrs. Nolan for board, perhaps they should consider moving into her boardinghouse. Inez immediately rejected the notion.

Mrs. Nolan was in business precisely because Inez had provided a little added financial backing to her in return for a small percent of the profits. Inez preferred to keep her various business agreements at a distance. She had made an exception when taking lodgings above the store, where they had a modicum of privacy. Living cheek-by-jowl with Mrs. Nolan, who was a notorious gossip, they would not.

She shook her head. "Too close for comfort," she said aloud. "Better to deal with the church bells here."

She sifted through a small stack of paperwork she planned to take downstairs and address before the store opened at noon. Her hand hovered over a small envelope, different from the rest. It was addressed in an authoritative masculine hand to Nico's sister Carmella, a charming young woman of twenty.

Inez knew the owner of that hand—pianist Jamie Monroe.

Jamie was one of the clique of young musicians, most of them new to town, who vied for Carmella's attention. When Carmella was not in the store, they sometimes approached Inez for advice about sheet music or where they might find a decent laundry that didn't over-starch collars. Of course, they also hung about waiting for Nico to appear and perhaps drop a casual comment about a certain theatre looking for a steam piano player, or a particular music hall in need of a flautist to fill in for a regular. If they were really lucky, the elegant violinist—so sought after, so successful—might offer a word of advice or encouragement, or even a referral. She knew they looked up to him thinking, "Someday, that could be me!"

Of all those young men, Inez suspected Carmella favored Jamie above the rest. She couldn't point to anything overt between them. Mostly, it was the subtle glances they exchanged, the way Carmella's smooth olive complexion "pinked" at the mention of his name. However, Nico kept a close eye on Carmella, especially where the young men were concerned. As far as Inez knew, none of the musicians had formally declared their interest in Carmella to her brother.

The note had been slipped under the door leading to the living quarters. Jamie knew better than to slide a missive addressed to Carmella under the shop's doors, front or back, in case Nico should spot it first.

Tapping the envelope on the table, Inez debated.

It would be unwise to become a go-between, a carrier of secret notes, even inadvertently. If Nico found out, there could be repercussions that would damage their business relationship. She could not afford that. Not now. Not after all the time and effort she had devoted to the store.

Signore Nico Donato was volatile where his sister was concerned, and well connected. His possible reactions to Antonia's playground transgressions would be nothing compared to what he might do to them if he found out Inez had encouraged an "unapproved" relationship between Monroe and his sister. He could spread stories, damage their reputations, throw them out, and dissolve their business relationship. It was possible she and Antonia could manage on the investments Inez had made, in addition to her silent partnerships with some of the small women-run businesses in the city. But if those women suspected Inez of any improprieties or financial uncertainties…

Inez shook her head.

It was not worth the risk.

She slid the sealed note to one side on the table, determined to return it to young Mr. Monroe at the first opportunity. He would have to deliver it himself.

Young love needed to prevail without her help.

Love.

After a hesitation, Inez pulled out her silver pocket watch and set it by her coffee cup. The watch ticked, invariant, reassuring. She turned it over, opened the back, and twisted it around with one finger to view the portrait of the man wedged in the circular opening.

Reverend Sands, her paramour from Leadville, stared somberly back. Justice B. Sands, the man who won her heart, held it with infinite patience and passion throughout the long, difficult year of 1880.

The last time she had seen him was a year ago, as he was departing Leadville. He had wanted to stay, to stand by her during those difficult times, but Inez pushed him away with desperate pleas for him to leave, leave, *leave* so she could focus on wresting a divorce from her recalcitrant husband. The truth of the matter was, faithless though Mark Stannert was—and none who knew him would deny that was the case—if Inez's affair with the reverend had been brought into court, all her carefully laid plans to contrive a way out of the marriage would have ended in disaster.

So Reverend Justice Sands had moved on, first taking a temporary post in Wyoming, and then another, shorter stay in the Dakotas, and then most recently…

She tried to call up the cancellation stamp on his last letter, and failed.

Montana? Minnesota? Someplace far north and far away.

Inez touched the tiny image, which captured his serious mien, the hint of danger signaled by a tightness around the eyes, an alertness in the posture. She mused how the ticking watch that accompanied the photograph, marking time, was so like the man who sent it. Constant. Present. Dependable. Never wavering. All he required was a letter now and again, a small winding, to keep the mechanism alive and moving. If she stopped the winding, stopped writing, would his letters, like the watch, slow down, and eventually just become silent? *Is that what I want?*

She rested her forehead on one hand, still gazing at the photo.

The truth was, she didn't know.

Not any more.

She snapped the watch shut and prepared to go downstairs and start her day.

Settled in the store's back office with the sign on the front door still turned to CLOSED, Inez pored over a neat stack of invoices and receipts, making payments, placing entries in the ledger books. A small parlor stove provided modest heat against the coolness of the morning, and a warm trickle of pleasure ran through her as she totaled the profits from the previous month.

When she'd taken on managing the store half a year ago, the books had been a mess. Nonexistent. Nico Donato had no idea where the finances stood and, oddly enough, didn't seem to care overmuch. It was part and parcel of his laissez-faire attitude toward the business, an attitude that only worsened as Inez took on more responsibility and he focused his attention on command musical performances for the rich and famous. Or rich and infamous, as the case might be.

If things keep moving in this direction, I shall own half the store by this time next year. After that, who knows? I might be able to convince him to sell it outright to me, lock, stock, and barrel.

The metallic slide of a key in the back door interrupted her musings. Only two people had keys besides herself and Nico, who never showed his face before noon unless absolutely necessary, so Inez made a little wager with herself.

Would it be John Hee, the purveyor of many of Nico's Oriental "curiosities" and official physician for busted stringed instruments and damaged woodwinds? Or Carmella? She guessed Carmella, who often dropped by early in the day bearing some of the Italian pastries that Antonia had grown fond of.

Carmella burst through the back door, her hat with its effervescent purple feather slightly askew, face flushed and fresh from the outdoors. With great drama and without preamble, she announced *"Zeppole!"* and deposited a napkin-covered basket atop the stacks of papers on Inez's desk. The scent of hot fried dough, with the powdered sugar on top providing sweet undernotes, was too seductive to ignore. Inez set her pencil down and lifted a corner of the napkin to examine the pastries snuggled inside.

"I made enough for you and Antonia, and any favored clients today. Antonia loves them so much, it would be a shame if I only baked them for Saint Joseph's Day."

Giving in to temptation, Inez reached for one of the pastries and, being careful not to scatter powdered sugar on her somber gray and black ensemble, took a tentative bite. A crunch through the fried exterior released the sweet dough inside. Melting in its warmth and lightness, the taste exploded in her mouth. "Carmella, you should open a bakery. These are irresistible."

Carmella beamed, then frowned. "You know what Nico would say to that. If it were up to him, I would stay at home, twittering like a bird in a cage, baking, baking, baking until I explode!"

"You are being a trifle overdramatic," said Inez. "You are hardly a prisoner. You go out and about to lectures and the theater with other young women—as is only proper. You help with the store. In addition to being a baker of irresistible delectables, you have a natural talent for creating window displays and the advertisements we place in the newspapers. Your brother may seem a bit stern, but I know he is as appreciative of your efforts as I am."

"Oh! That reminds me!" Carmella opened her large reticule and pulled out a neatly wrapped bundle. Untying the string, she spoke with words that flew as fast as her fingers. "I picked these up on the way here. They are new trade cards I designed and had printed at Madam Fleury's, to help advertise the store. Nico and I, we arranged them as a little gift for you. A surprise. We hope you are pleased."

She handed one to Inez. The large rectangle of heavy ivory-colored stock was the size of a cabinet card. One side sported a bluebird perched on an Oriental-style vase holding roses, ferns, and other greenery. A wave of notes emitted from the bird's open beak, wrapping around into a scroll. The address was at the bottom, and at the top…

Inez raised her eyebrows. "It appears the store name has expanded somewhat."

Rather than "D & S House of Music and Curiosities," the printed store name began with "Donato & Stannert." Inez flipped it over.

The reverse included the expanded name of the business, in bold, slightly Italianate script, followed by text that extolled the virtues and eclectic merchandise available in this "premiere house of musical instruments, sheet music, and merchandise, including curiosities and imports of an Oriental nature" and concluded with a reference to "repairs to a variety of instruments conducted promptly and on the premises. Satisfaction guaranteed."

"Yes!" Carmella sounded like a teacher praising an astute

student. "It was Nico's idea. You are as much a part of the business as he is. You have done so much for the store, he readily admits that. He wanted your name as clearly identified as his. In fact, he insisted. And he is even talking about changing the sign over the door."

Carmella carried the cards and the basket of pastries to the round mahogany table in the center portion of the back room. The room, which ran the width of the building, was partitioned into thirds with the office at one end and a glassed-off area for music lessons at the other. To make room for her basket, Carmella pushed aside an overflow of invoices and a case holding a clarinet with bent keys that was awaiting repair. "You are like family to us, Inez. You and Antonia. I don't know how we limped along before you came."

Inez didn't know whether to be flattered or concerned. The cards, slipped into orders and handed out individually, would enhance the visibility of the store and increase return business. But still, having her surname printed prominently in black and white, or rather in black and a robin's egg blue, made her queasy.

She had not divulged much about her previous life to the Donatos or indeed anyone in San Francisco. No one knew she was part-owner of the Silver Queen Saloon along with her ex-husband, nor that she was a silent partner of a high-end parlor house, both in Leadville. And she had most certainly not divulged that she was personally responsible for a number of deaths, all well deserved, in her estimation. But others might not see it that way. Too, Stannert was an unusual surname. Spelling it out on the trade card made her feel conspicuous when all she desired was to remain unknown.

"Very nice, Carmella, I am overwhelmed and grateful for your brother's vote of confidence—and yours too, of course, " said Inez, thinking a talk with Nico was in order.

She would have to tread carefully. On the one hand, be appreciative and acknowledge her part in making the business thrive—after all, it would only buttress her position here as time went on—but also indicate, modestly and self-effacingly, that she preferred to stay in the background. It wouldn't be hard to convince him that he should continue to occupy center stage as the "public face" of the store. If nothing else, perhaps she could forestall a change in signage, at least until her half-ownership was official.

Carmella turned her attentions back to the pastries. "Eat, Mrs. Stannert! Have another! You are thin as a rail. I *should* cook more, and be plying you with *zeppole, svogliatella, cannoli, cornetti alla marmellata*. Men, they like women with a little more to them."

Inez blinked, thinking how fast Carmella swung from being a naïve, relatively sheltered young woman to talking like she was Inez's formidable Aunt Agnes, always clucking, always plotting. And the inconsistencies! Railing against the tyranny of men one moment, then turning face-about faster than a merry-go-round to chide Inez for showing not the slightest interest in re-marrying.

Carmella persisted, "You can be so charming when selling pianos, an organette, music boxes, or even a box of woodwind reeds, Mrs. Stannert. If you put your mind to it, you could find another husband. Aren't you close to the end of your half-mourning? You have been in black, gray, and lavender since you arrived. It is time. You should be wearing vibrant colors now—green! Blue! Burgundy! Green especially would bring out the hazel in your eyes."

Inez decided to put an end to the discussion. She brought the basket to the big table, saying, "Carmella, you sound as if I should go about turning over rocks in search of someone who can accompany me to the plays or musical arias. I am quite comfortable with my life as it is. Antonia, the store, the music lessons I provide, they fill my time and are all I need right now."

There were also her side agreements with women like Mrs. Nolan, determined entrepreneurial women—laundresses, milliners, bakers, printers, dressmakers—who needed "a little extra" to improve their businesses, and who found their way, by word of mouth, to Inez's back door. But that was a part of her life she tried to keep separate from the Donatos, lest Nico think she was not giving "her all" to his store.

Inez continued, "I have no desire to, as you say, 'find' another husband."

Carmella's fine black brows swooped together, like bird wings. "Is there no one who agrees with you? Of all the men who come through here," she added hastily. "Gentlemen of fine breeding and refined tastes, do you not see how much they admire you?"

Inez turned and stared at her, dumbfounded.

The only men who came to mind were Carmella's admirers—Jamie; Jamie's boarding-roommate, cornet player Otto Klein; woodwind virtuosos William and Walter Ash; a few others. All single, all young, all obviously enamored of Carmella. Well, there was also pianist Thomas Welles, about her age, in his thirties, but he was happily married with four children. Or, it would be happily, he intimated, if the money were more forthcoming and the work more steady. Rounding out that group was Roger Haskell, forty-ish, odd man out as the publisher of a small, vociferously pro-labor newspaper, who had a special affinity for the music scene. He and Inez shared a healthy respect for each other, but that was as far as it went. Besides, Haskell smoked the vilest cigars in existence. Aside from that, there were the clients Nico sent to the store. Husbands looking for a piano for wives or daughters, or the occasional manufacturing or agricultural magnate, ushered in personally by Nico, who were interested in his Oriental "curiosities."

Inez must have looked as blank as she felt, because Carmella threw up her hands with a sigh. "Never mind. On Saturday, I noticed the flowers in the display area were wilting. I shall go clear them out." She swept out of the back room, shaking her head, apparently dismayed by Inez's obtuseness.

Inez started back to the desk and her accounts, only to jump as someone hammered on the back door with a heavy fist. Then, the shouting commenced. "Mrs. Stannert? Mr. Donato? Anyone in? Please, it's Otto. Otto Klein. It's urgent!"

Disconcerted, Inez hurried to the door. She barely unlocked it before it flew open. Otto Klein, square of face and body, stood outside, sweating in his good black suit, carrying his cornet case, and, Inez noted with alarm, wearing the black armband of a mourner.

"Mr. Klein, what is wrong?"

"Frau Stannert. It's terrible." He pulled out a black-hemmed handkerchief, removed his hat, and mopped his brow. Even though the morning was cool, his thin blond hair was plastered to his head and he was breathing hard, as though he had run some distance.

"I'm sorry, I had no idea where else to go. The others, I know not where they live." His voice cracked. "It's, it's Jamie Monroe. He's dead! Murdered!"

Chapter Three

"No!"

The scream of denial erupted behind Inez, followed by the crash of shattering glass. Inez whirled around, heart pounding.

Carmella stood in the passage between the back office and the showroom, face paled to ivory, hands to mouth as if to trap a torrent of words that threatened to pour out. Petals and stalks of withered flowers and shards of a Chinese vase were scattered at her feet, water from the huge vase now spread on her skirt and across the floor.

She removed her hands. "It cannot be." Her voice, almost a whisper, held a symphony of disbelief, a plea that it not be real.

Otto blurted, "*Verzeihung*, Fraulein Donato," then gamely pulled himself out of his native tongue. "I am sorry, Miss Donato, I did not know you were here. Perhaps it is not Herr Monroe." He looked helplessly at Inez, as if expecting her to do or say something.

Inez moved to Carmella's side, careful to avoid the broken pottery, and put an arm around the young woman's shoulders. From there, she began to recover and consider. Otto was prone to exaggeration and jumping to conclusions, then blurting out whatever was in his mind without thinking it through. "Mr. Klein, please, back up. Is it, or is it not Mr. Monroe? It must be one or the other."

He stepped over to the chaos on the floor and bent to pick

up one of the larger pieces of porcelain. "Forgive me, I perhaps spoke in haste." He retrieved one brown and dripping stalk and gathered three petals, their violet color stained brown with time. "Early this morning, a body was found in Mission Creek channel by Long Bridge. One of the longshoremen in the area, Sven Borg, who was there when the police came, saw the body and thought it might be Jamie. This Mr. Borg knows him from union meetings and came to our boardinghouse, asking for Jamie. Since Jamie and I room together, the landlady told me to talk to him." He looked beseechingly at Inez. "Mr. Borg said I should go to the police station, find where they took him, and go see if I can tell whether it is him or not. So, it may not be Jamie at all. I haven't seen Jamie since early yesterday."

Inez tried to recall the last time she had seen Jamie Monroe. It was three days ago, Friday, in the store. He had been trying to convince Otto and the others to attend some labor union gathering or other on Sunday. "We must organize! It's the only way we will ever get paid as professionals, the only way we will be taken seriously!"

Pianist Thomas Welles' short "Tried. Failed. Twice." had been followed by newsman Roger Haskell's acidic, "Sorry, Monroe. I guess you musically inclined fellas just don't have what it takes."

Rather than dousing the ardor in Jamie's light blue eyes, these responses had only seemed to set his determination afire. He'd pointed at Welles and said, "And *that's* the problem! You, Nico, all the 'old guard.' You tried and gave up! And now, you are settled, complacent. Secure. But we—" his arm swept around to capture the Ashes, Otto, and the others, all of whom were lounging and listening— "We are the newcomers. We are trying to make our lives here, just like you did, and be viewed as the professionals we all are, and be paid a living wage for our efforts."

Inez recalled that the others, who had been listening, had shifted imperceptibly as he named them, as if to duck his fervor and inclusive embrace. Otto, in particular, had looked terrified.

The memory, still fresh, released an unexpected flood of alarm. Could the union meeting have something to do with his death?

Now I'm *the one jumping to conclusions.*

Inez glanced at Carmella's stricken face, her eyes glimmering with suppressed tears. Did she believe Otto's story? In any case, those tears, her obvious distress was all the proof Inez needed that indeed Jamie was more than just "Mr. Monroe" to the young woman.

"Carmella, come sit down." Inez steered her away from the sharp bits of pottery on the floor to the table. Carmella sank onto the chair, her gaze fixed on Otto.

Inez turned to him. "I take it that since the longshoreman 'knows' Jamie but came to you, that identification is… difficult?"

"Herr Borg said the face, pardon me for saying this, got the worst of it." He gulped, a little green about the gills. "Which is why he was not sure."

"Are you going to the station today?"

"I can't!" The panic in his voice was clear. He cleared his throat and tried to explain. "I have an important job today. For a funeral." He looked guilty, furtive. "And tomorrow I must be at Woodward's Garden. Nico told me they are looking for a cornet player, he recommended me. The job is mine. All I have to do is show up. I need the money. Room and board is due for the room. We are already behind, and I have received nothing from Jamie. I may need to pay the whole amount myself."

His voice turned pleading, almost wheedling. "He did not come home last night. He was involved with a rough element, you know that, Miss Donato, Mrs. Stannert. What if it is him? I was hoping that you could ask one of the others, someone who is not working today and who comes by, to go to the police, or maybe Nico. I cannot."

Inez closed her eyes against his hopeful gaze, considering. Nico was as busy as Otto, if not more so, and his interactions with Jamie were minimal, as far as she knew. As for the others, she doubted they would do any better than Nico in determining whether a disfigured corpse was Jamie Monroe or not. On the other hand, she herself was no stranger to viewing the effects violence could have upon a human being, although not recently, not since moving to San Francisco. Could she perhaps identify him? Inez thought of his hands, beautifully proportioned with long, thin fingers, made for the keyboard. *Possibly.*

She opened her eyes, decision made. "I will take care of this, Mr. Klein. Please do not worry yourself further about it."

Otto let out a huge breath, obviously relieved. "Thank you, Frau Stannert. If by the day after tomorrow, no one has gone to view him, I will try. But I hope someone will be able to provide an answer before then." He picked up his hat from the table and turned to Carmella, still in the chair. Only her hands, which alternately gripped and released the fine fabric of her overskirt, gave any indication she was not made of stone.

He cleared his throat. "I apologize, Fraulein Donato, for causing you distress. I hope it is not Jamie Monroe." He tamped his hat down, gathered his case, and with a little bow, let himself out the back door.

As soon as he left, Carmella said, "I will go." Her voice was as calm as if someone had asked her to pick up bread at the corner bakery.

Inez stared at her. "Carmella, your brother would be horrified to hear you say that."

"He will not hear because I will not tell him. I must do this. And if I must do it alone, I will."

Inez sat down across the table from the young woman and took in her aspect. Lips compressed, jaw set, chin high. Then, all of a sudden, Carmella crumpled.

She pulled a handkerchief from her sleeve and buried her face in it. Her shoulders shook noiselessly. Stifling a sigh, Inez pulled her chair around to sit at her side and wait. After several minutes, Carmella raised her head, patting her eyes carefully. "My eyes will be red. I should leave soon, I do not want Nico to see me like this." She examined the bit of dampened embroidered linen. "Such a useless piece of cloth. Worthless, just for show. Oh, Jamie. Is it him? If so, how could I not know? Today we were to—" She pulled her lips inward, biting on them.

Inez rested an elbow on the table. "I am sorry you were here for all of this. Please, keep in mind we know nothing for certain at present. So, am I correct in guessing that your concern is more than the concern for an acquaintance, no matter how dear?" She pulled out her own, plain handkerchief and offered it, adding gently, "You have brought me into this, Carmella. I think you should tell me what you are struggling to hold inside, if only so I may forestall your brother's questions."

Carmella sat silent, her knuckles turning white around the crumpled bit of linen. She finally tucked it back up her sleeve and accepted Inez's utilitarian handkerchief. "We are engaged." She said it so faintly that Inez frowned, not certain she heard correctly.

"We plan to tell Nico," said Carmella quickly, perhaps misinterpreting the frown for displeasure. "We were waiting for Jamie to get a steady job, a good position, so he could hold his head high and ask for Nico's blessing. He had just found one that, along with his night job, would be enough. He was to start today."

"Where?" asked Inez, already wondering if this new job could have anything to do with his absence. Or his death, if it was indeed Jamie lying in a morgue somewhere.

"I don't know." She smiled, just a little. "He teased me about it. He could see how excited I was, how happy I was for him. For us. He refused to say, although I begged him. He said he would see how it went, and if it went well, he would tell me." The smile disappeared. "I hoped he could talk to Nico this week. Maybe even today."

Inez found it hard to believe Carmella and Jamie could have

been so naïve as to think that simply nailing down a good-paying, respectable position would bring acceptance from Nico. Even being hired by the eminent Baldwin's Academy of Music would not guarantee acceptance of Jamie as a serious suitor for Carmella's hand. And there were other considerations. Inez suspected Jamie of living hand-to-mouth, given the sad state of his suits, and now there was Otto's claim that Jamie had not been contributing to the rent. Nico was understanding of the penniless state of musicians new to town and struggling. But not so understanding as to embrace one into the family. Too, Nico would not be pleased that Jamie was entangled in trying to organize a professional musicians union and was hobnobbing with labor activists.

"And what did you plan to do if Nico refuses?" Inez asked. "I am certain you two must have considered that possibility."

Carmella stared at Inez, some of the indomitable Donato determination and stubbornness suffusing her face. At that moment, she was very much her brother's sister. "We will elope, tell Nico afterwards, and if he will not accept us, then we will leave and not look back on him or on San Francisco."

Shocked, Inez leaned back in the chair. What Carmella had just proposed was exactly what Inez had done when her now-ex-husband Mark Stannert had appeared out of nowhere a decade ago, whirled her around the dance floor, and wooed and won her. *I was the same age as Carmella. And just as foolish and headstrong. Left my family without a backwards glance when my father disowned me for marrying without his consent. What a strange world, or are all twenty-year-old women blind in the face of what they think is love?*

Carmella interrupted her musings. "If I don't see or hear from Jamie today, I am going to the police station tomorrow. I will not be able to live without knowing."

"And how do you propose doing this?" Inez said a trifle harshly. "Are you going to march in, present yourself as a secret fiancée, and ask to see the body? Do you think it will be so easy?"

Carmella looked down at Inez's handkerchief. "I don't know. But it doesn't matter. I will find a way."

Drumming on the tabletop, Inez deliberated. Carmella wiped her eyes, then smoothed the damp piece of fabric out on the table. Inez caught sight of initials in the corner: "MMS." It was one of Mark's old handkerchiefs that had made its way into her trunk in Leadville and from thence into her dresser drawer in San Francisco. Even after the divorce, he had found a way to wiggle into her life. *Damn his eyes!* she thought, even as something undefined contracted in her heart.

Inez took a deep breath. "Let's do this. Tomorrow morning, we shall go down to the station together. I will present myself as a distant relative. A second cousin or such." She thought it was a good thing she had had no interactions with the San Francisco gendarmes and had worked hard to stay anonymous in the large city. "You can be my daughter," said Inez. "But you should be heavily veiled. We will say we heard this might be James Monroe, and we are the only local relatives." She paused. "The body will most likely be with an undertaker. If it is a terrible death, they may not allow you to attend me."

Carmella had been brightening perceptibly during this recitation. Like the dawn of a new day, her face took on a hopeful shade of pink. "They will," she said with conviction. "They will! And as you say, it may not be Jamie at all. The longshoreman did not know for certain. He could be mistaken. And there are times I do not hear from Jamie for days. He said he wanted to be sure of this position. Maybe he needs another day or two, before he comes to tell me. He may even be living at the theater, or wherever he is working. Maybe they have given him living quarters and that is why he has not been back to the boardinghouse. He has been busy, and I know he doesn't tell Mr. Klein everything. Even though they share living quarters and friends, they live separate lives."

The scenario the young woman wove seemed to give shape to her prayers and put hope in her heart. The paleness faded from her face, and her eyes were again shining, but not with tears.

Inez herself remained unconvinced that the unfortunate victim was Jamie Monroe. Too many uncertainties. Still, she wasn't willing to commit one way or the other, so she simply said, "That may well be. In any case, you should head home, or proceed with whatever you planned to do today, and be as normal as you can. Can you do this?" She stood.

Carmella stood as well and handed Inez back the handkerchief. "Yes. You know, the more I think about it, Mrs. Stannert, the more I think it highly unlikely to be Jamie. He would not put himself in danger. And Otto, poor Otto, always jumping at shadows and to gloomy conclusions." She laughed a little then hiccupped and sniffed. "I am such a silly girl for falling apart like that. Surely I would have known, in my heart, if something happened to him. Wouldn't I? I love him." Carmella smiled at Inez, full of faith. "I have not said that out loud to anyone before, besides Jamie of course. I am glad that I can say it to you. And soon I will be able to proclaim it to the world! So, what do we do, Mrs. Stannert? About tomorrow?"

"It would be best to meet after Antonia goes to school but before the shop opens. Let's say ten in the morning at Lotta's Fountain. You know where it is?"

"At Third, Market, and Kearney. Perfect!" Carmella suddenly moved forward and embraced her. Inez found her nose buried in the frothy purple feathers of Carmella's hat.

"Thank you, Mrs. Stannert. I have had no one to talk to about Jamie. We didn't dare breathe a word, but how often I longed for a confidante. I am sure we will put this nightmare behind us, and it will prove as insubstantial as the fog come tomorrow."

Patting Carmella's back awkwardly, Inez almost added, "We shall see," but stopped herself. She reflected that despite her best intentions of a few hours previous, here she was, thoroughly enmeshed in the affairs of Jamie Monroe and Carmella

Donato. The handkerchief with her ex-husband's initials, damp in the palm of her hand, almost seemed to mock her previously unwavering determination to remain divorced from the world of love and passionate emotions.

Staring at the broken bits of vase and dead flowers that still needed to be cleaned up, preferably before Nico made his appearance, Inez tried to draw in some of Carmella's optimism. The entire incident might indeed be as insubstantial as the fog. But fog could hide a great many dangers. And despite all the arguments she lined up discounting Otto's suppositions, Inez couldn't help but feel she teetered on the verge of a cliff, unseen and shrouded in gray mist, a single misstep away from plunging into the void.

Chapter Four

Inez was on her knees, mopping up the last of the mucky vase water with the rag she usually used to polish the piano played by her students, trying to keep her dark gray skirts from soaking up the extra in the process. A key scraped in the back door lock and she looked up, half-expecting Carmella again, triumphant, with Jamie Monroe in tow. Before she left, Carmella had thoroughly talked herself into believing the longshoreman was wrong. It was a mistake, she insisted. It could be anyone who met such an unfortunate end. In fact, she ought to hurry home, because there might be a note waiting for her or even Jamie himself!

The door swung open to reveal not Jamie and Carmella, but Nico Donato, Carmella's older brother, owner of the store, violin virtuoso, and the musician most often requested to play for Signori Huntington, Hopkins, Crocker, and Stanford, and those of their ilk. Or so Nico frequently proclaimed.

Nico looked around, puzzled, before his gaze traveled down to Inez, still on her knees like a common washerwoman. In one hand, he held the key. In the other hand, a large, ornate bouquet bursting with flowers the colors of autumn: golds, reds, oranges, with green fern fronds and leaves adding highlights.

Dark eyes questioning, brows creased in a slight frown, he said, "Signora Stannert, what are you doing?" Then he held out the flowers, tilting them to bring them to Inez's eye-level. "For you," he said. Then added, "For the office."

It was only then that Inez realized that Carmella might have been subtly, or not so subtly, testing Inez's interest in her brother.

He was a handsome devil, there was no denying, what with his regal bearing, his wavy dark hair, his classical nose, and long-fingered musician's hands. It seemed Nature had also been dazzled by his good looks, for she had additionally bestowed upon him an inordinate amount of charisma. The total effect was never more apparent than when he was dressed for an evening appearance in an ensemble that, without variation, included a black swallow-tailcoat, white bow tie, white low-cut waistcoat, black trousers, a blindingly white shirt, and highly polished pumps. Even in the warmest of San Francisco evenings, not that there were many of those, he invariably topped it all off with a cloak that complemented his dramatic style—black with a white-and-black ermine collar.

Over their months of association, Inez had observed how skillfully he used his appearance, confident bearing, and dazzling charm to full effect on the wealthy and well-connected men of San Francisco, and especially on their wives and daughters.

With San Francisco's eligible and not-so-eligible women at his feet, why in the world did Nico constantly bring her flowers? Inez often wondered. The first time, Inez had been taken aback, then puzzled, and finally, suspicious. He always claimed they were for the office, so she never demurred in accepting them. However, his attitude toward her when he presented his offerings varied. Sometimes he was all charm, which put her on her guard. Other times he almost seemed to sulk or want to drop them at her feet and run away, which made her want to roll her eyes. Now, when he showed up with his ostentatious offerings—they were always huge, expensive arrangements, hardly fit for putting on the desk—Inez was bemused.

"A minor accident, involving one of your flower vases, I'm afraid." Inez tugged at her long skirts preparing to stand. Nico stuffed the key into the pocket of his morning coat and offered to help her up. She eyed his glove—spotless, immaculate—and thought of her own less-than-clean bare hands. "Thank you, Mr. Donato, but I can manage. You look as if you are dressed for an engagement."

She rose to her feet as quickly as she could to forestall any insistence on his part and brushed her skirts, which now had water stains. "The vase was from the display window. It had a handpainted scene on one side with a blue tree and varicolored flowers. I hope it wasn't one of your especially valuable curiosities."

"Ah, the Japanese Imari." He sounded dismissive. "It was flawed. Why did you not wait for John Hee to arrive? He would have taken care of the cleaning. You should not be bothering with such. I know you have other work to do." He glanced at her overflowing desk. "No matter, Signora. Do not give the vase a second thought."

Seeming to recall the bouquet, he repeated, "For you, Signora," and placed it on the table with no more élan than if he were handing off a sheaf of invoices. "I will go and find another vase."

Circling the table, he stopped suddenly and picked up one of the loose advertising cards from the stack that Carmella had left. His mouth curved up into a satisfied smile as he examined the front and back. "Ah! They arrived! And you are pleased, Signora Stannert? Yes?"

Inez opened and closed her mouth. From his tone, it was very clear that *he* was pleased. In any case, she decided, this was not the time to dive into the whys and wherefores of the store name. There were more pressing matters at hand. "They are lovely, indeed. Carmella did a wonderful job in helping design them. They should be an asset in increasing business at the store."

He shot her a measuring look. "Carmella was here this morning?"

Inez prepared to weave a story of the morning's events, most of them true, but embroidered with a small white lie. "Oh, yes, she was here early, with the cards and a basket of *zeppole*."

Nico frowned again. "Carmella has no respect for tradition. Baking *zeppole* when it's not Saint Joseph Day! Then she goes about early in the day, without a companion or a chaperone. Is she here?" He looked around, as if she might suddenly pop out of a cabinet or from under the table. "Foolish of her. Unnecessary. I am beginning to believe it was a mistake for you to introduce her to the Fleurys. They introduced her to the Women's Cooperative Printing Union. Carmella talks about it incessantly. Have you seen what this union prints? I have been too lenient. Carmella is associating with people not of her station. Her words and actions could cast doubt upon her reputation."

And make it difficult for you to find a "worthy match" for her, thought Inez uncharitably. Carmella had been right about her brother's opinion. Apparently, Nico would just as soon keep her at home, doing needlework, baking, cooking, playing the piano—but not too much, just a few non-challenging parlor tunes—until he found her a suitable husband. However, as Inez now knew, Carmella had her own ideas of a suitable mate, and had not waited for Nico to bring a parade of beaus to her door.

"She left for home soon thereafter. You did not see her in passing?" Without waiting for his response, she added, "Otto Klein then came by, with the most distressing news." She sank onto a chair by the table, staring at the bristling bouquet.

"And what news is that?"

"I should say first, there is some doubt about all this. The information comes from Otto, remember. Early today, someone, who might or might not be Jamie Monroe, was found dead. Murdered."

"*Dio Mio!*"

The shock in Nico's voice was plain. Inez looked up and saw his face was nearly as pale as Carmella's had been. "Where?"

"In the Mission Creek channel by Long Bridge." She looked back down and touched one of the fern fronds. "Whether Jamie or someone else, it was apparently a young man."

"Perhaps one of the men who work on the wharves or in the ships?"

"A longshoreman told Otto he thought it was Mr. Monroe, although apparently the face is badly disfigured. There must have been some reason he believed so. The clothes? Something else? In any case, I would think the man would have known if it was one of his kind."

"But Jamie Monroe? That area is not a place for a proper young man to be. If it was him, what was he doing down there? I wonder if anyone is asking those sorts of questions."

Inez raised a hand, palm up. *How like Nico to think of reputation and little else.* After a moment's silence she said, "Nothing is known for certain right now. Perhaps Jamie...or whoever this is...was killed elsewhere and brought there, dumped, as it were, in the sewer. Perhaps his killers thought his remains would drift out into the bay. It's horrible. Treating a human being as if he is a piece of garbage. A tragedy, all around."

She sensed Nico passing behind her and turned in the chair to view him. His face had regained its normal hue and he appeared appropriately somber. "You are correct, of course, Signora Stannert. I spoke hastily and not with compassion. It is a tragedy, no matter who it is. And it sounds as if the identity is in question. Perhaps we will never know who he is, but that does not lessen the injustice."

The back door swung open, admitting John Hee. He looked surprised at finding them there, then the surprise vanished, leaving only a polite affect. He removed his large brimmed hat and bowed to Inez. "Good morning, Mrs. Stannert." A deeper bow to Nico. "Mr. Donato."

A small, sturdy man of Chinese extraction and indeterminate age, John Hee wore his hat pulled low and a tailored American-style suit. With his long braided queue tucked under the collar of his jacket, no one on the street would give him a glance, as long as he didn't look up.

"Ah, John!" Nico seemed glad of the diversion. "The Imari vase met a violent end. I will see if I can find another for Signora Stannert's flowers. And here," he gestured at the musical case on the table, "is a clarinet that requires your attention at once. William Ash needs it for an engagement tomorrow."

John Hee opened the case and inspected the clarinet. "Many bent key."

"Yes, yes. So, if you please."

John looked from the flowers, to Nico, and, finally, to Inez. Inez wondered how much he had heard before he opened the door. Anything? Nothing? It was clear he had his own opinions and thoughts that he was keeping to himself. In any case, John knew all the young men who spent time in the store, so Inez felt she should tell him, if Nico wouldn't. "Mr. Hee, we just heard from Mr. Klein that someone bearing a resemblance to Mr. Monroe, the pianist, was grievously murdered. We don't know the identity for certain. Mr. Monroe has not been seen for a day or two, and did not return to his boardinghouse last night."

John's gaze roved from Inez to Nico and back again. "A young man, met with violence? The young, so careless. It is said, he who thinks but does not learn is in great danger."

"A platitude to ponder while repairing the clarinet," said Nico. He glanced out into the showroom floor. "I believe I see our first customer of the day peering through the front window. Has the sign been turned from CLOSED to OPEN? Not yet? I shall do so."

He strode out into the front of the store, his hard leather soles snapping briskly against the polished pine floor.

The noontime church bells began their discordant ringing, vying with each other. Inez wanted to clap her hands over her ears, but abstained. John seemed oblivious to the clamor. He stayed where he was, clarinet in hand, eyes on Inez. He finally spoke, barely loud enough to be heard over the racket. "You fond of young pianist, Mrs. Stannert?"

Inez paused, considering. It was not as though she was a stranger to violence. In Leadville, men were cut down in their prime with disturbing regularity, and women too. But since coming to San Francisco, she had grown distanced from such events, even though the nearby Barbary Coast and Chinatown had their dark sides, their secrets, their attacks, murders, and suicides. In her world within the music store, she had remained apart from all that.

Until now.

Inez sighed and stood. "I suppose so."

She picked up the flowers. As she did so, the sharp scent of rosemary stung her nose, mixing with the softer notes of moss and China roses, the color playing riot with the magnolias and maple leaves. She tried not to assign any hidden messages to the jumbled whole from the language of flowers. Most likely, Nico simply pointed to the most ostentatious, extravagant arrangement that caught his fancy and told the flower vendor, "That one."

She continued, "I'm quite fond of him, actually. Of all of Miss Donato's gentlemen callers, Mr. Monroe has, or had—oh dear, I do hope it isn't him—a certain spark about him. A certain passion and drive. So, yes, I am fond of him."

John's gaze didn't leave Inez. He remained still, as if absorbing her every word, re-forming it somewhere deep inside and pondering how to respond. His fingers moved lightly as if playing a silent tune on the broken clarinet keys. At last he said, "Some not feel as you do, Mrs. Stannert."

His words—neutral in melody, cautious in harmony, the "L's" pronounced as usual with exceeding care—caused a prickle to crawl up her neck. "Not all? Are you saying Jamie Monroe has enemies?"

The entrance door at the other end of the building squeaked and the bell overhead gave out a dispirited *clunk*.

Nico's voice echoed from the front of the store, equal parts admiration and charm, "*Buon giorno*, madam! How may I help you?"

A woman answered, "Pardon me. I'm looking for Mrs. Stannert."

That voice—lilting, flirtatious, just a hairsbreadth away from improperly bold. So familiar, but from a time so far away. Inez's breath caught, and for a moment, she was dizzy, as if the floor tilted eastward, tumbling her into her past.

It can't be.

Not here.

Not now.

Her grip on the flower stalks tightened, crushing the stems.

John silently slid from the room, case and clarinet in hand. A twin set of footsteps approached, Nico's no-nonsense tread in counterpoint to the mincing tick-tick of a feminine shoe.

Fighting dread, Inez composed her expression into one of polite anticipation and commanded her feet to move. She advanced to the door leading to the showroom, just in time to see John step behind a long counter and vanish behind the curtain hiding the repair room. She thought fleetingly that she would have to corner him later and persuade him to say more, before all of her attention focused on the woman advancing toward her.

Mrs. Florence Sweet, otherwise known as Frisco Flo, madam of one of the most prestigious "pleasure palaces" in Leadville, adjusted her gray-colored chapeau, trimmed with long ruby feathers. She slipped the looped handle of her closed, rose-colored parasol over her wrist and placed one rose-gloved hand on Nico's arm, bestowing a smile that had sent many a better man to his knees in supplication.

Inez had not seen Flo since leaving Leadville over a year ago. Yet, here she was, bold as brass. Unannounced. Unexpected. Far from her Colorado home.

Flo sashayed through the music store, where Inez had staked

her claim on building a new life. To Inez it was as if her earlier reminiscences of Leadville had conjured up a ghost.

Nico was saying to her, "It is always a pleasure to meet one of Signora Stannert's clients, Signora Sweet."

Flo smiled demurely and twisted one of the blond corkscrew curls framing her face with a finger. "Well, it certainly is a pleasure to meet *you*, Mr. Donato. Although I don't know that I would describe myself as one of Mrs. Stannert's clients."

"But that is only because Mrs. Sweet and I have yet to discuss the terms for piano lessons for her daughter," lied Inez smoothly. "Hello, Mrs. Sweet. I wasn't expecting you."

Flo didn't bat an eye at Inez's extemporization and invention. Instead, she looked at the flowers in Inez's hands, then at Nico and the empty vase he held by his side. Baby-blue eyes wide, she turned to Inez and said, "Oh dear, Mrs. Stannert. Are you otherwise *engaged*? I do hope I haven't interrupted anything. My time is limited, and I absolutely *must* speak with you regarding those...lessons."

Flo had no daughter and had certainly not traveled from Colorado to California to inquire about music lessons, but the urgency in her tone rang true.

Aware of Nico's inquisitive gaze, Inez tried to mask her unease.

A silent business partner of Flo's lucrative Colorado endeavors, Inez had always attempted to keep involvement with the madam at arm's length. Events in Leadville had not always allowed for such niceties. Since the ink had dried on their mutual contract, their lives had become considerably entangled on a personal level, with Inez coming to Flo's aid during tough times, and Flo helping Inez out on a matter of some delicacy. Even so, their secret business partnership had remained just that—secret.

Still, Inez knew far more than any proper lady should know about how Flo ruled her empire. Flo never left Leadville, not trusting her volatile employees and clientele to be governed by any but herself. It made no sense for her to come gallivanting out to San Francisco on a whim, much less make such an open visit to Inez, here, in her new life. What could be so important, Inez wondered, that Flo would risk the trip, the possible slide in profits, and the exposure of her most loyal, at-a-distance business partner?

In other words, what was she *doing* here?

"No, no, you haven't interrupted anything." The whole morning had been such a strange compilation of interruptions, sorrows, and surprises—starting small with Antonia's school woes, and progressing to Jamie's death and Carmella's reaction. Inez hated to think what Flo's arrival portended. *Trouble upon trouble.*

Chapter Five

Inez applied a matter-of-fact tone to mask her concern, as one of Flo's girls would apply a layer of cosmetics to mask her pockmarks. "You have met Signore Donato? He owns the store, and I manage its day-to-day functions."

"Ah, Mrs. Stannert, you are much more than a manager!" Nico interjected. "You saved my modest commercial enterprise, which I will admit was sadly neglected before you arrived."

Inez allowed herself a tight smile. Neglected didn't begin to describe the initial state of the original store when she first came upon it. The place had appeared run-down, almost deserted. Inside, to left and right, stacks of sheet music had slumped on top of glass cases. The cases were a jumble, holding small vases, statuary, and objects she assumed fell under the "curiosity" label of the store. The chaos abated along the plastered walls, with flutes and other woodwinds racked in rows, and a cluster of brass instruments facing off from the opposite wall. A music store selling both sheet music and instruments was unusual, and she had been intrigued by the possibilities.

In the center of the showroom floor, an exquisite Persian rug had claimed space for two dark green love seats, several unhappy ferns in vases of Oriental extraction, a trio of cellos resting against supports, and what looked to be a Chinese gong. At least all the instruments had seemed to be well taken care of. They were just about the only objects in the store that were not coated with a fine film of dust.

"You transformed this establishment," continued Nico, "bringing a feminine touch to the decor, a practical eye to the bottom line, and imposing a welcome domestic order and calm. Your attention and care frees me to pursue my own engagements and appearances, without worries. You are the muse of the music store!"

Inez wondered if Nico's extravagant praise was merely his way of making sure the ever-alluring Mrs. Sweet would indeed sign up her "daughter" for lessons and continue to return to the store.

"Thank you for your kind words, Mr. Donato." She held the bouquet out to him and said, covering her words with a blanket of entreaty, "May I please beg a favor of you? Would you help me by taking these lovely flowers and finding some place on the showroom floor for them while Mrs. Sweet and I attend to business? They are gorgeous, Nico, they should really be displayed for all to see. What a joy it will be for me to look at them while I'm on the floor this afternoon."

"Of course, of course!" Nico gallantly took the blossoms from her before turning to Flo and saying, "I hope we shall have the pleasure of meeting again, Signora Sweet."

Inez responded before Flo could answer. "You might if her daughter decides to come for lessons. Which we will determine once she and I have the chance to talk *in private*." Inez closed the door gently but firmly in his face to stop further discussion.

Inez leaned her back against the door.

"Well, well, flowers, goodness, Mrs. Stannert, you didn't waste any time once you left Leadville and settled here in San Francisco." Flo smirked. "Nico, is it? And on a first-name basis, are we?"

"No, we are not." Inez crossed her arms. "At least, not in the manner that you are insinuating." She took a moment to examine the madam. The palette was clearly rose. Beneath Flo's unbuttoned double-breasted cashmere walking coat peeked a long, slim polonaise casaque of heavy rose-colored silk, silver buttons gleaming up the front and disappearing under a fringed white silk scarf tied in a soft bow over a fluted collar. The hem of the polonaise overskirt swept up to a point just above the knee and sported piping and a wide ribbon over silk chenille fringe. The dove-gray silk underskirt flaunted rows of puffing over a knife-pleated flounce.

For her part, Flo was clearly giving Inez the once-over as well. "Mrs. Stannert, have you been scrubbing floors?"

Inez glanced down at her skirts, tellingly damp around the knees and hem. "I do what I have to do these days, Flo."

"Well, no need to tell me *that*. We *all* do what we have to do. But still. Scrubbing floors? That's a long way from lording it over the silver barons and millionaires at the Silver Queen Saloon's gaming table."

"At least it's my choice," said Inez coldly.

Flo wrinkled her nose. "And why the solemn outfit? Black and gray are good colors for you, but you look like you are in mourning. Surely you're not mourning your divorce to that charming-but-no-good husband…pardon, former husband of yours."

"Flo!" said Inez sharply, then lowered her voice. "I cannot entirely trust that there is not someone hovering on the other side of the door, ear pressed to the wood. Please, keep your voice down." She tugged on the handle behind her to be sure it was shut tight, then locked the door and stepped away. "As for mourning, it's nothing of the sort. It simply makes life far easier if everyone here thinks I am a widow, recovering slowly from the death of my dear husband, who is buried in Colorado."

"Buried is right," said Flo under her breath. "He's hardly got space to breathe these days, and certainly has his hands full with the second Mrs. Stannert. She keeps him coming and going, so to speak. And they have a little son. Did you know that? Takes after the mother."

A painful twinge thrummed through Inez, composed of sorrow and another emotion—envy?—that she didn't want to inspect too closely. In any case, the last thing Inez wanted to hear about was her former husband's new marriage and subsequent progeny.

Flo continued blithely, "And you, dear partner? Am I correct in guessing that, in some nearby boardinghouse, there is a squalling bundle of joy being fed poached eggs and Robinson's Patent Barley?"

Inez tightened her lips and said nothing.

Flo raised an eyebrow. "Are you loathe to admit that I was right in thinking that when you left Leadville you were *enceinte*? Boy or girl?"

Inez forced herself to say, "It was not meant to be." Memories from ten months previous intruded, unsolicited, unwanted. A hotel in Sacramento. Sudden pain. Sudden blood. A local doctor, unspoken questions lurking behind his clinical solicitousness. Inez, teeth clamped until her jaw ached, pushing down the moans so as to not to make matters worse for Antonia, barred from the room by the doctor. Unspoken questions dammed up behind Antonia's frightened gaze, once the doctor had allowed her in briefly as Inez lay in bed, spent and weak, after the miscarriage.

Antonia had grabbed Inez's hand, bursting out, "Don't die, Mrs. S!" The doctor had immediately called for the hotel matron to remove Antonia, with strict instructions for Inez to rest and not be disturbed. As if rest were even possible.

Understanding flooded Flo's face, accompanied by a swift, if distant, sympathy. "Oh, dear. I am sorry, Mrs. Stannert. As you know, in my business, such an event would usually be cause for relief, if not outright celebration. Fewer complications, as it were."

Inez waved one hand, as if brushing cobwebs aside. "It is past." She shut the memory and its painful emotions away, locking them up deep inside, and moved toward the table and her present concerns, gesturing Flo to a chair. "We can talk privately over here."

She raised the temperature and the volume of her voice so that it would be pleasantly audible to any eavesdroppers outside, saying, "No tea, Mrs. Sweet? Very well. Let us talk about your daughter. How long has she been playing the piano?" before sitting at the table and continuing sotto voce, "You surely did not come all this way to update me on Mark Stannert's doings, to reminisce, or to inquire about my well-being. What the *hell* is going on?"

All trace of lightness left Flo's demeanor. Her eyes narrowed, the little come-hither smile vanished as if it had never been, and her dimpled face tightened. "Nothing good, I can assure you." Ignoring the proffered chair, she paced, clasping and unclasping her hands, her lace parasol slapping her coat as it swung from her wrist on its bamboo handle. "In fact, it's a goddamned mess."

She finally sank down into the chair next to Inez. "It wasn't my idea to be here in San Francisco, believe me."

"So, why are you here?"

Flo took a deep breath. "I don't have much time. I'm supposedly out shopping for a new hat. I'm glad you're sitting down for what I'm about to tell you. I'm here with Harry Gallagher."

Inez stared, unbelieving.

Harry.

Harry Gallagher, owner of Leadville's Silver Mountain Mine, here in San Francisco?

A wealthy Eastern capitalist, Harry was one of a handful of silver barons who had extended his fortune by coming in early on the Leadville mining boom. His wealth had only continued to grow as he invested in other holdings inside and outside Colorado, as Inez knew. It would not be out of line, she reasoned, for him to have business in the West Coast's crown jewel by the bay. And to pay Flo enough that she would accompany him as his companion.

But looking into Flo's worried gaze, Inez suspected this visit was more than that. Furthermore, Inez had once, in a moment of emotional weakness, capitulated to Harry's charms, a misstep resulting in untold complications she had no desire to revisit, all of which only added a dark undercurrent to her increasing apprehensions.

"Don't look at me like that, Mrs. Stannert! I went through a great deal of trouble to come here and warn you."

Inez found her voice. "And what," she said, "has any of this to do with me?"

"Look, I know way back when you thought your husband dead and gone, before he made his surprise reappearance, you and Harry were…Well, this isn't really about that. At least, not entirely. Did you ever meet Harry's son?"

Inez blinked. "I had no idea he had a son." *But then again, I didn't even know he had a wife. At least not at the start.*

Flo nodded. "He does. Robert H. Gallagher, all of twenty-three years old. Harry brought him to Leadville a year ago, shortly after you left town, and put him in charge of Silver Mountain Mine. The son had been Back East with his mother until she died. She was an invalid, only came to Leadville once, as far as I know. Robert was devoted to her. The reason given for his sudden appearance and elevation in Leadville was that Harry was grooming him to take responsibility in the family business. I also heard rumors of certain unsavory hijinks Back East that caused Harry to think it might be best to bring him West. Well, Robert was not the least bit interested in following in his father's footsteps and has a bit of a wild streak besides."

"You would know all this how?" asked Inez.

"How?" Flo lifted an eyebrow. "How do you think? In the usual way, Mrs. Stannert. In my business, there are no secrets. At least, not many that stay that way."

She pulled at one of the curls by her ear, releasing it like a spring. Nudging aside a stack of music scores, she put her elbows on the table, and leaned toward Inez. "Apparently, Harry decided to wipe out the wild streak in Robert, plain and simple. Three months after Robert came to town he was engaged to a prim little miss who just happened to be the daughter of one of the rich muckety-mucks Harry knows. Robert was less than enthusiastic about the match."

"The match was Harry's doing?"

"The two fathers. All strictly business," said Flo.

Inez flashed on Carmella, and Nico's attempts to curb her spirit. "Let me guess. These stories seldom end well," said Inez grimly.

Flo nodded. "Robert came to talk to me, two days before the wedding. Just about six months ago. He said he was leaving town. He couldn't go through with it. He didn't love her, he said." Flo rolled her eyes. "As if love has anything to do with any of this. Anyhow, he vamoosed without a word." Flo's mouth thinned out. "Then, the stupid little fool killed herself. Poison. Rumor is, she couldn't live with the shame of being jilted."

Inez leaned back, shocked. "How awful!" following with "I suspect the elder Mr. Gallagher did not take well to this turn of events." Harry was a man who liked to control everything and everyone in his orbit.

"Oh, that's not the half of it," said Flo bitterly. "He blames *me* for Robert's bolting. I had nothing to do with it! Sure, I listened to him when he was in a talkative mood, which was most of the time. When he came to visit the girls, he never was one to screw, pull up his suspenders, and slink out the door. He liked to hang around after and talk to me, ask my advice. I swear, the boy was looking for a mother, not a—"

"You listened." Inez crossed her arms on the table top, staring hard at Flo. "What else did you do?"

"Well," she shifted in her chair a little. "I might have given him some money. Enough for a one-way ticket West."

"Flo!" Inez was aghast. This was quite unlike the hardnosed businesswoman. Oh, she could be kind to her girls and had gone the extra mile for them on occasion, but for a client?

"I know, I know," Flo looked down and straightened the

seam of one glove. "I've gone over it a thousand times, how stupid that was. I felt sorry for him, and he caught me in a moment of weakness. It's really all Harry's fault. He shouldn't have pushed Robert the way he did."

"Harry found out?"

"He found out all right." Her round blue eyes narrowed. "He threatened to close me down if I didn't come with him and find that whelp of his and drag him back by the short hairs. My words, not his. Robert will be lucky if he has any short hairs left by the time his father is done with him."

"Why San Francisco?" Inez asked. "There's New York, Chicago, St. Louis, many other cities. And why are you bringing me into this? I don't know this…Robert. Or, rather, I can think of several Roberts, all of whom have been in town longer than the one you are looking for. Trust me, my life is very circumscribed here."

"He said he was going to San Francisco. You see, it wasn't just the girl. He and Harry tangled about running the mine. Robert had this notion of 'workingmen's rights.' He believed the miners weren't getting a fair shake under his father. He tried to change things and, well, Harry didn't approve. So, it didn't happen."

"I can imagine. It sounds like Harry said, 'Manage the mine, but manage it my way.'"

Flo nodded. "And much as Robert would hate me saying this, I will say it: Like father, like son. Neither can stand being told no."

"San Francisco," Inez repeated, frustrated. "If he's got a notion to come to the aid of the workingman, he must have been drawn to the labor movement here."

Flo nodded. "But that's not all. He intended to pursue a career as a professional musician, something his mother apparently supported. Lessons from the time he could walk and all that. Music is all he has ever cared about doing. Well, in addition to the usual things young men his age care about."

Music.

Now it was becoming clear.

"Mrs. Sweet," said Inez ominously, "Did you tell Harry about what I am doing out here? About this store?"

Flo raised her hands, palms out. "I swear to God, I have not breathed a word of your whereabouts or what you are up to. But Harry knows, at least in part. He has connections, agents, working for him. He knows you are here in San Francisco. I think he knows you are in the music business, in some way or another. What else he knows, I can't even begin to guess. But he didn't learn it from me."

That sent a chill down Inez's back, but she focused on the problem at hand. "There are hundreds of professional musicians here. Hundreds! Why would he even think I might know his son? If this Robert is in the city, he's probably too smart to go by his own name."

"I know, Inez. But try to convince Harry of anything other than what he wants to believe. Anyhow, he insisted I come to San Francisco with him. He said if I don't cooperate in finding Robert, he'd see me ruined and my girls thrown out into the street."

"How could he possibly do that?" Inez asked. "You have your supporters in Leadville. Why, with the taxes and fines you pay, you probably support half the city government!"

"Leadville has changed in the year you've been gone. Every month, there is less and less tolerance for businesses like mine, or maybe I should say 'ours.' All the so-called proper women pull their skirts aside when any of my girls or I walk by." She looked furious. "It wouldn't take much for the city fathers to decide businesses like ours should be 'quarantined' in the poorer part of town or shut down altogether. And Harry is perfectly capable of nudging things in that direction. I probably don't need to point out that if Harry follows through on his threat, it'll be a disaster for you and me. As for why I'm here, warning you of all this, he knows that you and I, we have a…" she cleared her throat, "…connection."

"A connection." Inez repeated, her stomach dropping. If Flo's lucrative, high-class house of ill-fame disappeared, Inez's share of the profits would vanish as well. She could weather that. Probably. But if word got out that she was part-owner of a brothel, no matter how distant or how upscale…

Never mind her business acumen and hard work on behalf of the music store. Nico, with his rarified connections and aspirations, would immediately end their business relationship. Inez and Antonia would have to move. And it wouldn't stop there. If that and all the rest of Inez's past came out publicly— former saloon-owner, divorcée with an adulterous background, questionable morals—*and let's not forget that I am responsible for several deaths. All justifiable, but still.*

She would never live it down.

Word would inevitably get to the women in San Francisco she had formed business connections with. Inez thought of Mrs. Young—a milliner she had recently agreed to finance— the printers Fleury, Mrs. Nolan, and the laundresses Mollie and Bessie May. Such revelations would spell the end of those partnerships and others. It would be the end of her new life, and Antonia's as well.

They would have to leave San Francisco.

But for where?

"Jesus." Inez put her head in her hands. "If you didn't tell him, how did he find out?"

"I don't know," said Flo, miserably. "But he has a man with him, hired from Leadville, who came with us and is also looking for Robert."

"Who?"

"His name is a mouthful, Wolter Roeland de Bruijn."

Inez frowned. "From Leadville?"

Flo nodded. "He came to town after you left, I think. Anyhow, he, or someone else, dug up a lot of information. As I said, he's looking for Robert. He's looking for you, too, because Harry has this crazy notion that you will be able to find Robert. And there is another complication."

Inez slowly lowered her hands to the table, palms flat on the surface as if to draw strength from the warm, polished wood. "Another complication? What, then. Spit it out, Flo."

Flo sighed and the worry lines deepened, making her look older. "Phillip Poole, the father of Robert's Leadville fiancée, Vivian. He's here too. I heard Harry and de Bruijn discussing this, when they thought I couldn't hear. Poole is also looking for Robert, and he's sworn to shoot him on sight, if he gets the chance. So, we cannot waste any time."

Inez stared hard at Flo, waiting, in case there was more. She finally said, "Anything else I need to know about this convoluted, sorry situation, Mrs. Sweet?"

Flo leaned forward. "The upshot is this. We need to find Robert, before de Bruijn or Poole does, and convince him to at least talk to Harry, warn Robert that Poole is here, and that he is in danger for his life. If we don't succeed, who knows what Harry will do or think? If de Bruijn finds him first, Harry might think we lied about not knowing where Robert was, that we knew all along and helped hide his son. And if Poole finds him first and carries through on his threat, I don't even want to think what Harry might do. Neither outcome bodes well for you or for me!"

Chapter Six

Inez's mind skittered around like a trapped rat. "Back up. This agent of Harry's, what is his name, again? De Broin? Broon? Brown?"

Flo wrinkled her nose. "Mostly I hear others say 'de Brown,' but it isn't exactly that. He answers to it, or anything close."

Inez continued. "Tell me about him. Is he a private detective? A Pinkerton?"

"I don't know. All I know is he 'finds' things. At least, in Leadville, that was his service. If you, say, lost money to a confidence man, or your wife to a lover, you'd go to him." She shrugged one shoulder. "He doesn't draw a line between the paupers and the silver barons. If they are willing to pay the price he names, he'll find whatever was lost. Well, Harry lost his son, so…"

"Where is this de Bruijn now?"

"Right now? I left him with his newspaper in the lobby of the Palace Hotel where we are all staying. I told him Harry said I could go shopping for hats. He waved me away, saying I should be back before the dinner hour."

Realization slapped Inez like a cold ocean wave. "He could have followed you here! If he and Harry didn't know where I was before, they will now."

"No! I was very careful. I went to a couple of millineries first before taking a hack."

Inez was not convinced, but there was nothing to do about it now. "Well, perhaps there is nothing to worry about, but at least forewarned is forearmed." *But armed with what?* She brushed that question aside. "Describe Robert for me."

"He's the spitting image of Harry," said Flo. "Just picture Harry twenty years younger, and you'll have him."

Inez shook her head. "I need details. Mustache? Dark hair? A limp? A lazy eye? Give me something to work with, Flo."

"I don't have a likeness," she snapped, then lowered her voice again. "For what it's worth, he is about as tall as you are, dark hair, light eyes, well-formed, prone to shooting off his mouth without thinking about the consequences."

"Which describes a great many young men," Inez said under her breath.

Flo pondered a moment longer. "The only other thing I can tell you won't help one whit, unless you're planning on stripping down every likely young man. One of my girls told me he has a birthmark, here." Flo passed a hand over her left breast. "Quite large. A firemark, almost purple."

"You're right. That will not help me." Inez looked at the door leading to the showroom. Nico's voice, words indistinguishable, the tone amiable, filtered through. She thought she heard John Hee reply.

"You should leave," said Inez abruptly. "I don't like the idea of you staying here a moment longer than necessary. I will ask some of the musicians I know and see if the name Robert Gallagher sounds familiar. I'll take a good hard look at the Roberts of my acquaintance. Keep in mind, I can't go chasing after these gentlemen, I must wait until they come to me. I have a business to run, and generally stick close to the store. I am here in the office in the mornings, settling accounts, giving lessons."

Then, she remembered her promise to Carmella to accompany her on the morrow. "Except for tomorrow morning. I have a previous engagement." She stared at the door that led to the showroom. Murmurs drifted in from the other side. Was that another male voice in the mix? Maybe William Ash had come to check on his clarinet? If so, she wondered if Nico would mention the Long Bridge discovery to him, the possibility that the body might be Jamie Monroe. It was not a task she wanted to shoulder, telling Jamie's circle of friends and acquaintances of his possible demise. *I am putting the cart before the horse. Nothing need be said until we know whether the victim is Jamie or not.*

Inez continued, "I will most likely see a fair number of the regulars today. The theaters and music halls are closed on Mondays, and private fetes are rare the first part of the week. I'll ask around and do what I can to see if anyone knows a Robert Gallagher." She fought down a rising tide of panic. "Flo, it's like searching for a needle in a haystack!"

"I'll keep my eyes open, too," Flo promised. "I told Harry that I would promenade around and be on the lookout for him. I have a couple of ideas of places to try. High-class bordellos and such. I do hope he shows up and this nightmare is over soon."

Inez said, "We need to have a way to get in touch with each other, in case you or I hear of anything. If you must reach me, you can send a runner to the store, but be discreet! I recall from my earlier stay at the Palace that they are part of the telephone exchange, as we are here."

Inez silently thanked Nico for his fascination with "curiosities" of all kinds, including those of a technological variety. He had had a telephone installed as soon as they became available, although it seldom rang. Occasionally a call came through from a patron asking if Nico was available to perform for such-and-such an event on a particular date. More often, Inez used it to arrange for a Sunday drive to the coast by Point Lobos and Seal Rocks.

"You can use the telephone to ring up the store and say you want to talk further about the lessons. It's trickier if I need to reach you. I wouldn't want this de Bruijn or, God forbid, Harry, to intercept a message with my name."

Inez pondered, then went to her desk and searched for the business card she had in mind. When she found it, she brought it to Flo. "If I need to reach you, I'll send a boy with a message to the Palace Hotel that this milliner, Mrs. Young, has a hat that she thinks you might like. I would want to know that you indeed received the message. If you send the messenger back with a reply that you hope it is in purple and white, I'll know all is well and you will come as soon as you can."

"Purple and white?" Flo made a moue of distaste. "I would never!"

"Exactly. If you include the color pink, I'll know for some reason you cannot come. And we shall have to try something else."

Inez paused, thinking. "It might be a good idea for you to visit Mrs. Young's millinery on your way back to the hotel. Tell her I sent you, and buy a ribbon or something, just so you have actually met her and know where her place is. That way, if I send messages under her name, no one will think twice about it."

Flo tucked the card in her sleeve and stood.

"Now," said Inez, "we need to prepare for your exit." She rummaged through the stack of sheet music on the table, finally choosing "Better Late Than Never," thinking that the title sounded ominously appropriate.

Inez turned to Flo. "As we head out through the showroom, I will hand you this and suggest that your daughter try this piece, since she enjoys popular music. I will mention that I do not generally go to the homes of my pupils, they usually come here. I will add that we can talk further about it later, and we can set a time when I can come and observe her level of proficiency. That will set things up if you should call and someone else picks up the phone. Deal?"

"Deal." Flo smiled, a small smile of relief. "Partner."

Chapter Seven

Following Mrs. Sweet, de Bruijn discovered, had not been difficult.

After a late breakfast in the Palace Hotel's dining room, she had announced Mr. Gallagher had given her permission to go shopping. He had nodded, and said, of course, Mr. Gallagher had told him.

When, in fact, it was exactly what he had persuaded Mr. Gallagher to do.

De Bruijn settled in the anterior room of the suite and waited until she emerged, ready for the street. He'd accompanied her to the hotel entrance, much to her obvious annoyance. Once there, he had raised his hat in farewell, reminded her she was expected back by the dinner hour, and headed back inside.

At the bell station, he met the bellboy he had made arrangements with earlier. In the luggage room, he traded his black frock coat for a checked sack jacket, his black top hat for a brushed gray derby. He gave the bellboy a generous tip and proceeded to the entrance. A pass of coin from his hand to the doorman yielded not only the direction Mrs. Sweet had gone but an added bonus: she had inquired about the address of a famous millinery not far from the Palace.

He made a few other minor alterations as he walked, donning a pair of tinted spectacles pulled from an inner pocket, smoothing down the slight curl at the ends of his mustache. Mere changes of surface appearance. The trick was to also change the gait, to bring the shoulders in and down slightly, other slight variations that would encourage her eyes to slide over him, should she look in his direction.

It turned out she had not walked far, and her rose-colored parasol made her easy to spot among the late morning strollers and shoppers.

Better and better.

He waited by the hotel until the parasol was a block away, then followed her.

Now, less than two hours later, he watched from the shadows in front of the stock exchange.

How convenient that the exchange was not far up the street from the music store. He could loiter, glance at his paper, smoke, stroll up and down the sidewalk, blend in with the clusters of men—brokers, speculators, operators—who came and went from the building. It was easy to linger unnoticed with those who stood outside waiting for hacks, private carriages, the next horse-trolley. The building provided an endless stream of men, anonymous with their hats and coats. As anonymous as he was.

He waited, wondering if he'd get a glimpse of the store's proprietor.

While Mrs. Sweet's doings were of interest to his client, who had tasked de Bruijn with finding his wayward son, the "finder of the lost and stolen" was engaged in his own personal search as well. Almost two years ago, he had made a promise to a woman, Drina Gizzi, and thus to her daughter Antonia, to protect and take care of them. He had failed to fulfill that promise, and now bore the burden of being at least partially responsible for Drina's death. He hoped to do better by Antonia, once he found her. It was a search he hoped would yield results once he had the opportunity to meet the "S" half of D & S House of Music and Curiosities, a person he strongly suspected would be a woman named Inez Stannert.

He reflected again on how much easier all this would have been if Mrs. Stannert had been listed in the city directory. But she had apparently settled too recently in the city for that to be the case.

However, he was in no hurry. Now that he knew where the store was, he could visit at his leisure, when the time was right. Mrs. Stannert, if she was the manager or part-owner, was not about to vanish into thin air. She had a stake in San Francisco now.

Besides, he wanted to be certain that Mrs. Sweet had no other destination after her visit here.

At that moment, a tall gentleman opened the front door to the music store with a flourish, executing a bow of a decidedly European nature as Mrs. Sweet emerged.

Was this perhaps the "D" half of the business?

Mrs. Sweet smiled up at him, and touched her hair, her hat, flirting a bit. De Bruijn had seen this dance many times before. And what was that in her other hand? A flash of white, fluttering as she moved.

Papers of some kind.

De Bruijn casually unfolded his newspaper and adjusted the brim of his hat, watching closer.

The gentleman held up a card between two fingers, offering it to Mrs. Sweet. Too far away to tell what it was. Perhaps a calling card? Although it seemed on the large side for such. Mrs. Sweet hesitated, then nodded and accepted it, tucking it into the papers which she then rolled and stuffed into her handbag. A musical score, perhaps? But Mrs. Sweet had no musical talents, unless one counted her undeniable ability to play the men around her. She looked around, no longer focused on the gentleman. De Bruijn noted that even at a distance, Mrs. Sweet seemed nervous. He wondered again what was on the card.

The European—Italian, perhaps?—stepped into the street and hailed a passing hack, which came to an obedient stop. Mrs. Sweet entered the carriage. De Bruijn stepped forward, waved down a horse and driver heading in the opposite direction, gave him his instructions, and settled in to wait and see where Mrs. Sweet would take him next.

Chapter Eight

The empty lunch pail banged against Antonia's leg, over and over, but the stinging blows were nothing compared to the tongue-lashing and verbal bruising she'd suffered that day.

First, Miss "Persnickety" Pierce had whapped Antonia's arm good and hard because Antonia had memorized the wrong passage for recitation lessons. Then, the snickers from the class had punctuated Persnickety's equally sharp "Antonia, pay attention!" And now, she had double the number of lines to memorize for tomorrow.

She hated it.

Hated it.

Hated standing in front of the class and stumbling through some poem about a stupid skylark. Who cares? And then, at noon, she'd been forced to stay inside and write on the blackboard "I will not daydream in class" fifty times. Now, heading down Market, Antonia was ready to slug someone with her *Swinton's Reader*. Preferably one of those snotty kids who stood behind her in line and whispered, loud enough for her to hear, how *stupid* she was.

It enraged Antonia, because it wasn't true. She knew her times tables better than anyone else in the class, and could do division and fractions faster than the others. Just because her penmanship was, in Persnickety's words, "Atrocious!" and she found the reading, reciting, and memorizing downright boring, well, that didn't make her stupid.

Now, if they were reading something interesting, like "The Mutiny of the Hispaniola" by Captain George North, she'd show them all. The third installment of *Treasure Island* was in the *Young Folks* magazine she'd pinched from the stationer's on her way home from school on Friday. The same magazine she'd stuck into her *Swinton's* that morning, hoping to sneak a peek at it during the noon break.

Antonia swung the book at the end of the book strap, back and forth in time to her steps. She stopped short of the Dupont intersection, debating whether to cross and walk up Dupont so she could go past the Olympic Theater, which was always kind of fun, or go another block up Market to Kearney so she could ogle the Sherman, Clay music store that Mrs. S liked.

A horse-drawn trolley clattered by on its steel rails. She watched enviously as some boys she recognized from her school dashed low and fast to the back of the horsecar, jumped onto the stairs and grabbed hold for a free ride up Market, crouching, laughing, and hanging on.

She thought longingly of her days in Leadville, when she'd dressed as a boy and worked as a newsie for *The Independent* newspaper. All the other newsies had thought she was a boy, and treated her like one of them. They'd been her friends and called her "Deuce," because of her odd eyes, which had been fine by her. And she'd sold lots of papers, and been just as good as all of them.

If only she was wearing trousers now, and not the hot, itchy wool stockings, and her petticoats and skirts, all wrinkled and fussy, and the bonnet that kept flapping down over her eyes, she'd be out there too on the street car. She bet she'd be able to hang on longer than any of them, maybe hitching a ride all the way to—

Someone shoved past her, bumping her sore arm hard. The lunch pail clattered to the boardwalk, and her book strap caught. The leather strap ripped from her grasp, burning her palm and carrying its bound contents tumbling off the walkway and into the street.

"You no-account so-and-so!" shouted Antonia, enraged, as the older boy who had shoved her sprinted to join his mates on the car. The book strap had broken, and the *Swinton's*, along with the *Young Folks* magazine she'd hidden within its pages, were now lying in the dirty gutter.

The boys hooted at her and one yelled back, "Ooooo, savage as a meat axe!"

The commotion brought the conductor pushing to the back of the car. The boys jumped off and raced to the other side of Market, laughing, as the conductor shook a fist at them. Fuming, she grabbed her lunch pail and prepared to clamber into the gutter. She'd get it from Persnickety for sure now. That ruined book would probably result in a thrashing, more "I will not…" sentences scratched up at the chalkboard, and a note from the teacher to Mrs. S.

A shadow moved over her, and a voice from behind said, "Hold on there, Miss." An older boy—she'd seen him around at school—took a long step into the street. He scooped up her things, then hopped back up to the boardwalk, saying, "That Charlie, he's a hoodlum, heading for the lockup sooner rather than later, or I miss my guess."

"Thanks," muttered Antonia and held out her hand.

He didn't give her things back, so she finally looked up into his face. A friendly pair of blue eyes regarded her. He pushed his cap up. The sun whitewashed his freckled face and put an extra shine into his burnished red hair. "I recognize you," he said cheerfully. "You go to Lincoln, right? Me, too. I'm Mick Lynch. You are—?"

Antonia hesitated. She didn't give up her name readily. It was a habit her maman had drilled into her. "Names hold power," she'd said. "Never give your name to those you do not trust." And Mrs. S had told her, "You are under no obligation to share your name in a casual situation with people you do not know."

Still, he'd helped her. He'd told her his name. And he still had her book and magazine. "Antonia Gizzi."

"Gizzi." He grinned. "You part Guinea, then?"

Antonia reached out for the strap. Questions about her background—"Where are you from?" "What are your parents?"—made her uncomfortable, because she didn't know. Maman had never said, and Antonia had never asked.

So instead, Antonia shot back, "You Mick the Mick, then?"

He nodded, unperturbed. "Yep. Sometimes. Mostly folks call me Copper Mick, 'cause of my hair, and 'cause my da's a copper. A detective in the force. When I'm out of school, I'm going to join the force too."

"Copper Mick," said Antonia, "can I have my books?"

"Oh! Sure. Here, let me fix this first." He tucked the book and magazine under his arm, swiftly knotted the broken leather strap back together, then snugged the book and the crumpled *Young Folks* into the loop, remarking, "You like this magazine? Me, too. You must be pretty smart if you're reading this. Lots of fellows in my class, I'm in seventh grade, can't read a lick of anything. Have you been reading *Treasure Island* in there? Wish they'd do more'n one chapter at a time. It's a crackin' good story."

Surprised, Antonia responded, "Yeah! That's my favorite."

"Mine, too." Copper Mick handed the bundle to her, adding, "How about if I go with you a bit?"

She shrugged. "It's a free country."

They started walking.

He asked, "You live on the other side of Market? How come you don't go to Denman Grammar, then?"

"What's with the questions? I thought it was your pa that was a detective," said Antonia, then added, "I'm in Miss Pierce's class in fifth grade. And I can take myself home. No need to go out of your way."

He grinned and said, "Sorry! My ma says I take after him. My da, that is. Always with the questions and pestering folks. That's what she says, then my da says, 'Chip off the old block!' My da also taught me to help folks whenever I get the chance.

I've got six sisters, all younger'n me, and two brothers older."
He added, "How about I walk along, just to be sure those
b'hoys don't come back and give you six kinds of heck, if you
excuse my language?"

Antonia didn't say that she'd heard and said much worse,
instead opting for a nod. He seemed friendly enough, plus it'd
be fun to talk to someone about *Treasure Island*.

Remembering what Mrs. S always said, Antonia suggested,
"Let's cross at the corner. My aunt, Mrs. Stannert, doesn't like
me jumping into the streets."

Mick shortened his stride, apparently realizing Antonia had
to scamper to keep up with him. "You and your folks live with
your aunt?" he asked. "Us, too. We're surrounded by relatives.
Aunt, uncle, four cousins in the flat next door. My grandmother
is in the upstairs flat with my oldest brother, Danny, and his
wife. They've got a wee 'un. How many in your family?"

More questions she didn't want to answer. She always felt
queer saying it was just her and her "aunt." Antonia pushed
the tinted glasses up her nose, staring at his hands, all freckles
and knobby knuckles. "Do all coppers yak as much as you do,
Mick the Mick?"

It seemed no matter what she said, it just rolled off his
shoulders like rain off a rubberized raincoat. "The gift of Irish
blarney," he said. "We've all got it. You should see us around
the supper table. Everyone talking at once, Ma yelling, 'One at
a time, one at a time!'"

They stopped at the corner of Dupont and Market, joining
a cluster of adults—women with shopping baskets over their
arms, men with their newspapers, canes, and cases, and a few
other kids. Antonia thought they might be Mick's schoolmates
the way the boys nodded at him and the girls looked slantwise
at him and giggled in that silly way girls did when they wanted
a boy to notice them.

A traffic copper standing in the middle of the street was
waving his white-gloved hands this way and that like he was

conducting a band. He blew his whistle and gestured for the group to cross. As Mick and Antonia approached, the policeman saluted, saying, "Well, now Master Michael Lynch, does your ma know you're taking the long way home from classes today?"

Mick touched his cap in response. "Afternoon, Officer Daniel Lynch. Just making sure the little lady doesn't get further bothered by the local hoodlums."

"Ah. Good boy." The officer winked, whether at Mick, her, or both, Antonia wasn't sure.

Once they'd crossed the street, Antonia said, "I'm thirteen." The words just slipped out. She wasn't sure why she'd said anything at all, except that "little lady" made it sound like she was one of those first grade girls who wailed and sobbed when their pigtails were pulled.

She didn't really know how old she was. Her maman had said she was twelve in Leadville. Mrs. S said Antonia seemed small for her age, so maybe she was younger, "Although your extreme precociousness would argue against that," Mrs. S had said. After listening to Antonia recite, watching her do her numbers, and wrinkling her nose at her penmanship, the school principal had suggested Antonia had some "catching up to do" and plunked her in grade five, much to Antonia's frustration.

She tipped her head up to see his expression from beneath her bonnet brim.

"Thirteen?" His red eyebrows shot up. "You *are* a pipsqueak, aren'tcha?" But there was nothing mean in his face or in his tone. Or suspicious. He seemed more amused than anything.

"That copper back there. Officer Daniel Lynch," she tried to imitate his brogue. "Is that your brother?"

"Surely 'tis. And you can believe that I'll be getting nothing but the third degree from my family tonight. You think I ask a lot of questions." He shook his head. "Well, now, Miss Antonia Gizzi, how far do we go up Dupont?"

With a start she realized they had walked nearly five blocks and stood even with Pine Street. "I turn here." She glanced down Pine toward the waterfront.

"I might as well walk with you one more block and turn right on Kearney. I'm not going to cross Danny's corner again. He'll make me stand with him in the middle of the street until I tell him everything."

"Everything" was left undefined, but Antonia felt her face burn under the bonnet's wide brim.

"I'm fine from here," she said. She really didn't want him to know where she lived. Up above the music store, with no one but Mrs. S for family. It seemed sad, somehow. "Thanks, Copper Mick," she added.

"Well, sure." He grinned. "Maybe I'll see you at school, yeah? At noontime."

"Maybe." *If Persnickety doesn't have me writing a million lines on the board and missing the lunch hour again.* Antonia could almost smell the sharp scent of chalk and hear the squeak of it on the board.

After they said good-bye and parted ways, Antonia continued to the store, thinking about family. Thinking about Maman, dead and buried in Leadville. How up to the very end, Maman had believed there was a "knight in shining armor" who'd ride to their rescue. Who'd pull them out of the shack in Leadville's Stillborn Alley where they had lived after being thrown out of the hotel, and they'd all live happily ever after.

But he'd never shown up.

Remembering her mother made Antonia sad again. She tried not to think about her all the time, but sometimes she couldn't help it.

Rain began, warning spits darkening the wooden sidewalk. Looking up, Antonia recognized the unmistakable form of Mrs. S with her black umbrella ahead of her on the other side of the street, walking toward the store about half a block away.

Antonia began walking faster, looking for an opening on the street to dart across and catch up.

Antonia!

Antonia jerked to a stop as the urgent whisper surrounded her. The familiar voice, the voice of her maman, echoed in her head.

It had been so long since she'd heard her maman's voice talking in her mind like that.

That's what it was, right?

Just all in her mind?

It couldn't really be her maman.

She was dead.

And the dead couldn't talk.

Could they?

An uncontrollable shiver ran up Antonia's back and breathed ice on her neck. Rain pattered on her bonnet, making small *pick-pick-pick* sounds.

She looked around, trying to see if someone else had called her name. Maybe one of the jokers from her class had followed her this far and was trying to get her goat.

Her gaze snagged on a man across the street from her, some ways behind Mrs. S, walking and also carrying an umbrella. He wore a checked jacket, gray derby hat. She caught the flash of a dark, short beard before all she could see was the back of his jacket and his umbrella, moving away.

Antonia's fingers and toes went cold and numb, as if she were back in Stillborn Alley after dark, making her way to the shack where Maman waited.

Antonia began to walk again, no longer trying to catch up. She watched Mrs. S, who had almost reached the store, and the man in the gray derby who followed her.

Mrs. S slowed.

The man in the gray derby slowed.

Mrs. S. stopped in front of the door and closed her umbrella, glancing up the street.

The man in the gray derby with the umbrella stopped and pulled out his watch.

Mrs. S opened the door and went inside.

The man tucked his watch away. He turned around and began heading up the street in Antonia's direction.

She could see he had a small neat beard and mustache, and glasses.

A roar filled Antonia's head, like the voice of the wind. Her maman's voice wove through it, whispering: *He is here.*

Thoroughly spooked now, Antonia ducked into the nearest store—A. C. Robison, Importer and Dealer in Birds and Cages. The door slammed shut behind her and she was engulfed in an explosion of squawks, screeches, twitters, and coos. Wings beat against wires, and feathers floated to the bottoms of cages, with some escaping to land on the floor. A man wearing an apron and holding a sack of sunflower seed looked up, first hopeful, then annoyed. "Can I help you?"

The chill had disappeared, and now she was suffocatingly hot in the store. "My aunt's birthday is soon and she wants a bird. I heard you have lots of birds." Lying came easier to Antonia than telling the truth.

He perked up. "What kind of bird?" he asked. "Does she want one that sings? Talks? We have canaries, finches, nightingales, parrots—including Cuban parrots—but I would recommend the yellow-headed Mexican first, as a talker, with the gray African as a whistler."

She looked around at the winged prisoners, some hopping on their perches, others knocking against the bars, others with beaks lowered and feathers fluffed, like they'd given up and were just waiting for whatever life decided to drop next on their little heads. "Uh. I dunno." She backed toward the door. "I'll bring her back with me. Later."

With that, she slipped out and, holding her breath, scanned the street.

No gray derby in sight.

No dead voices whispering in her ear.

Antonia clutched her lunch pail and book strap tighter, and dashed across the street, heading to the store.

Chapter Nine

Rain pattering atop her open umbrella, Inez strode down Pine, thinking about her just-completed visit to Mrs. Young's millinery shop. She had been pleased at Mrs. Young's positive response to an offer of buying a twenty-percent share of the business in return for financial stability. "It's been difficult since my husband passed on, some years ago," said Mrs. Young.

Inez had nodded. "I quite understand."

"Yes, I'm certain you do." Mrs. Young had passed her hand over the black grosgrain ribbon on the counter, destined to grace a half-completed widow's bonnet. Black net drifted over the polished wood.

Inez had also mentioned, as if in passing, that she had recommended the establishment to a friend of hers, Mrs. Sweet.

"Oh, yes." Mrs. Young beamed. "She was here earlier. Very charming, and her husband no less so."

"Her husband?" A vision of Harry Gallagher rose unprompted in her mind. But that made no sense. Harry was not the type to care about such trivialities, nor to pretend to be anyone other than who he was.

Unless it wasn't Harry.

Inez said cautiously. "So, Mr. Sweet, he was with her?"

"Oh, no. He came in later. Wanted to know if she had shown interest in any particular bonnet. Obviously, he dotes on her, he was so solicitous!"

Definitely not Harry.

And if not him, then it had to be the mysterious de Bruijn.

Inez regretted that she couldn't demand a description of the impostor, since she'd presented herself as such close friends with Flo.

Unease darkened her mood. On the walk back, Inez pondered if, perhaps, the elusive detective had first followed Flo to the music store, despite Flo's maneuvers. In that case, it might be that "the jig was up," and she should steel herself for a visit from the as-yet-faceless de Bruijn or perhaps even Harry himself. Neither was a pleasant prospect.

Inez stopped in front of the store and tilted her umbrella to protect her hat from a sudden gust. The lively notes of a popular parlor tune drifted out to her. Through the glass, she saw the "Monday night regulars," including Carmella's admirers, clustered around the centerpiece grand. Welles was at the bench, playing, while Nico stood off to one side, deep in conversation with John Hee.

The rain intensified. She looked up and down the street, wary.

Nothing in particular caught her attention. The usual gentlemen of leisure and business hurried by. A few women, baskets over their arms, hastened home to prepare for family and suppers. No one stared at her. No one suddenly turned away. Jostling umbrellas hid faces for the most part. And even if they didn't, she had no idea who she was looking for. She closed her umbrella, and went inside the store.

"Ah, good," said Nico in an uncharacteristically shorthand fashion. "Mrs. Stannert, John and I have some business at the warehouse. Now that you are here, we can depart."

Welles segued into a salacious tune more appropriate for a battered upright in a deadfall on the Barbary Coast than the elegant keyboard in the middle of an upscale showroom. The others laughed uproariously. Although no one burst into song, it was clear they all knew the lyrics.

Nico coughed, a small sound of disapproval, and turned to Inez. "You will stay on the floor, no lessons this afternoon?"

Inez said, "No lessons, however, I have a question for you both."

They leaned in toward her, and she lowered her voice so no one else would hear. "Have you told anyone about Mr. Monroe?"

Hee shook his head. Nico frowned. "No." He glanced at the merry band by the piano. "I would guess no one has."

"Good. Since there is a chance that it is someone else, it seems best if we keep this to ourselves for now and not spread rumors. Wouldn't you agree?"

At that moment, the door banged open with a vengeance. Welles stopped mid-refrain and everyone turned to look at Antonia in the doorway. She closed the door carefully, as if to make up for her noisy entrance. Violinist Giotto Laguardia smoothed back his dark hair. "Antonia, you are all wet! Did you forget your umbrella again?" All the young men doted on and teased the girl, but Giotto seemed the most eager to please, perhaps thinking that by endearing himself to Antonia, he would eventually worm his way into Carmella's heart as well.

Ignoring him, she headed for Inez, leaving a line of wet footprints on the polished floor. "Mrs. S, I have to talk to you." She lowered her voice. "It's important."

Inez turned to Nico. "Give us a few minutes?"

Nico fidgeted, glancing at John Hee, who shrugged. "Very well," said Nico, grudgingly.

Inez put an arm around Antonia's shoulders and guided her into the back area. As soon as the door closed, Inez asked, "Did something happen at school?"

"No." Antonia looked a little shifty-eyed and crossed her arms.

Inez mentally filed away a reminder to pursue the school issues later. "What then?"

"Someone was following you. I saw him."

Inez's breath caught, and it was her turn to cross her arms. "Where? When?"

"When you were walking down Pine. To the store. I was across the street. When you went inside he turned around and went back the way he came."

"Have you seen him before, that you recall?"

She shook her head.

"Can you describe him?"

Antonia mentioned the umbrella, gray hat, checked jacket, spectacles. No help there, Inez thought, it could be one of thousands of men.

Antonia finished with, "He had a little beard."

"Was his beard dark? Light?"

"Dark," she confirmed.

Inez clenched her teeth, wondering what to do with the information. It wasn't much to work with.

"Are you certain he was following me?" she pressed. "It could have been just a coincidence."

Antonia took off her glasses, and polished them with a fold of her dress, finally looking up at Inez. Inez was struck again with those disconcerting eyes—one blue, one brown. Much like those of Antonia's mother, but less intense in hue.

"I heard my maman."

The words filled the room, drifting about like a conjured spirit, while Inez carefully composed a response. She knew Antonia was sensitive about these odd auditory apparitions. "It's been quite a while since you've heard your mother's voice, hasn't it?" she asked gently.

Antonia nodded. She looked miserable.

"When was the last time? In Leadville?"

"Uh-huh." Antonia's mouth trembled. "I thought she was gone. Once we buried her in the cemetery, with the angel statue watching over her and all."

Inez gave her young ward a moment to compose herself. "Your mother loved you with all her heart. She will never be 'gone.' She watches over you, in your heart, and in your mind. Always."

"Yeah, well…" Antonia put the glasses back on. "She spoke to me. She warned me about the man following you."

"Really? What did she say?"

Antonia stared out the back window, rubbing one hand against her skirt. The rain had changed into hail, which sounded like gunshots against the brick wall.

"She said my name. And then she said, 'He is here.'"

Chapter Ten

The client was the client, de Bruijn thought.

The client paid for information, and when information was uncovered, it perforce was delivered.

However, there had been times when de Bruijn held back certain facts and discoveries, if disclosing them would hamper his search. Thus, he had mulled over whether it was wise to impart what he had discovered that day to his client, Harry Gallagher, or whether he ought to wait a bit. After all, he had been hired by Gallagher to find the son. That was the primary objective. Yet, he had decided to go against his better judgment for the time being. Now, he wondered whether he would regret doing so.

De Bruijn contemplated Gallagher's thunderous countenance, saying, "This is, of course, good news. Mrs. Sweet's actions prove we were correct in thinking that she was in contact with Mrs. Stannert and had knowledge of her whereabouts."

Gallagher shifted, obviously irate. "I anticipated uncovering her whereabouts would be easier."

"She is too recently arrived in town to appear in the annual city directory or other records," de Bruijn pointed out, yet again. "So, yes, this took somewhat longer, but we have the same results."

Gallagher gestured impatiently, silver and diamond cufflinks glinting in the chandelier's brilliant gaslight.

De Bruijn complied with the unspoken command. He set on the table between them the advertising card he had removed from the sheet music concealed in Mrs. Sweet's purse. She had been anything but sweet about it when, once she had returned to the hotel, he had insisted she hand over her purse to him.

Gallagher stared down at the card.

"Donato and Stannert," de Bruijn pointed out, somewhat unnecessarily.

"Who is this Donato?"

It was not the question de Bruijn would have asked first if he were in Gallagher's position.

The client is the client, he reminded himself again. "He appears to be Mrs. Stannert's business partner. I made a few general inquiries. Nico Donato is a violinist of some local renown. Performs at gatherings of such notables as Collis Huntington, Leland Stanford—"

"Yes." Gallagher cut him off again.

De Bruijn waited to see if Gallagher had more to say, and continued when he did not. "Mr. Donato is in a quartet performing at a private party tonight, at the Flood residence."

"It so happens I will be there."

De Bruijn nodded.

Finally, Gallagher asked the question that de Bruijn thought he would pose first. "Are you certain this is Inez Stannert?"

"Not only did Mrs. Sweet visit the music store, she went to a milliner's afterwards, which Mrs. Stannert also visited later." De Bruijn decided not to mention the large part that serendipity and luck had played in his discovery of the connection between the milliner and Mrs. Stannert. How he had, after "acquiring" the advertising card and locking Mrs. Sweet in her room as a guard against further unaccompanied wanderings around town, gone to Mrs. Young's and led the woman to believe he was Mr. Sweet. An unfortunate deception, but necessary. How, during an innocent conversation of hats, bonnets, and chapeaus of various styles, materials, and decoration, he had managed to slip in Mrs. Stannert's name in connection with Mrs. Sweet, to see what might come of such a fishing expedition.

Mrs. Young had leapt at the bait, her response instant and enthusiastic. "Oh, yes, Mrs. Stannert! Such a remarkable woman! In fact, she is due here shortly to discuss a business proposition with me. I hope to expand my spring offerings, you see. If you and Mrs. Sweet are in San Francisco over the New Year, she should come by. I expect to have all the latest fashions in stock."

Such confluences of events occasionally happened in his investigations. Even better, he had had to wait in the stand-up bar across the street less than an hour before a woman answering to Mrs. Stannert's description had walked into the millinery shop without a single glance around. At least she hadn't arrived while he had been in discussion with Mrs. Young.

He continued his report, "Mrs. Stannert was not there for the hats. It seems she and the milliner Mrs. Young are in business together. I did not have time to pursue the details." Privately, de Bruijn thought that Mrs. Stannert seemed quite the enterprising woman. He was curious as to how far and in what directions she was casting her net.

"I had hoped that, given Mrs. Sweet's visit to Mrs. Stannert, that Mrs. Stannert might then proceed to your son's current location, to warn him, or encourage him. However, she returned to the music store. I followed, and made it a point to get visual confirmation. She is as you described her."

He forbore to add Mr. Gallagher had described Mrs. Stannert to him most thoroughly. That description had also been delivered with a familiarity that had raised several questions in de Bruijn's mind—questions he had decided were best left unasked.

"Good," said Gallagher, although his tone had nothing good about it.

De Bruijn said, "I would suggest we hire a lady Pinkerton of my professional acquaintance, a Miss Elizabeth O'Connell, to keep Mrs. Sweet company tomorrow. That will give me the time I need to pay a visit to Mrs. Stannert and extract what she knows about your son."

Gallagher swept up the trade card. "As you wish. I'll pay her a visit this evening before the dinner party at the Floods and question her myself."

"I would not advise that." The words slipped out before de Bruijn had time to consider them.

Gallagher stood, adjusting the silk vest of his black dress-suit, pale eyes cold as ice. "When I want your advice, I shall ask, Mr. de Bruijn. With Poole also looking for Robert, there is no time for niceties, and I am disinclined to wait until morning and make a formal visit, calling card in hand. For now, arrange for the lady Pinkerton you spoke of, and then arrange to keep Mrs. Sweet off the streets and out of trouble for the rest of the evening."

Chapter Eleven

After Nico and John Hee left, Inez shooed the lingering musicians out, saying, "Suppertime, gentlemen, time for me to close the store. I will be back for our usual evening gathering, of course."

She knew they looked forward to the Monday night round of cards that she allowed—and subtly encouraged—in the back room. Being that Monday was when the theaters were closed and many of the musical folks were at loose ends, it proved a good time for them to all relax and catch up.

"Good," said William Ash. "Had quite a good run at Woodward's Gardens last week and actually have a few pennies to rub together for tonight's game."

"Which you will no doubt promptly lose," grumbled his brother Walter. "Just remember to hold enough aside for next week's room and board. I'll not float you again."

They all left in a gaggle, no doubt to carry on their discussion at one of the many elbow-bending establishments on the edge of the Barbary Coast district that catered to musicians.

Inez elected to take Antonia to the nearby Russ House, eschewing Mrs. Nolan's cold boiled ham and gossipy boarders. There, over consommé, broiled mutton chops, mashed potatoes, and apple pie, Antonia poured out her sorry day at school, concluding with when her *Swinton's* went spinning into the street.

Inez tried to listen. Part of her mind remained distracted, torn between the morrow's visit with Carmella to the morgue, the man who had been following her—at least, according to Antonia—and Antonia's deceased mother.

"So, you heard her voice after all this happened, correct?" Searching for pragmatic explanations, Inez surmised that perhaps the strain of the day's events at school had brought Antonia's mother "back." Although she respected the beliefs of others, Inez did not believe in connections between the earthly and less corporeal realms. What she'd seen of the activities of spiritualists, mediums, and various brethren of the table-knocking fraternity reminded her of nothing so much as the flimflam and cagey doings of those employed in the confidence trade.

Antonia stabbed the remaining crust of pie and flattened the fork, crumbling the flaky pastry into bits. "Yes'm. But I wasn't thinking about school when I was walking. I wasn't thinking about Maman. Just all of a sudden, she was there. Inside my head."

Antonia was shaken and upset enough that Inez kept her suspicions to herself. She said simply, "Well, no matter. You do realize that you lost your mother just about a year ago, yes? Perhaps that has something to do with this."

"Maybe," muttered Antonia, sounding unconvinced. Her fork chased the crust crumbs around the plate, gathering them and driving them into the sticky puddle of syrup in the middle.

The two of them finished their evening meal and walked home in the unrelenting rain. As they approached the store, Inez slowed at the sight of two hacks waiting at the curb. One would be for Nico, but the other...?

Holding the umbrella to shelter both herself and Antonia, Inez approached the glass-paned door to the store. There inside, readily visible in the well-lit interior was Nico in his evening clothes. Standing with Nico was a man she had no trouble recognizing, despite the passage of time.

Harry Gallagher.

The lamb and pie in her stomach settled like a lead weight, and she took as deep a breath as she could, given the meal and the suddenly much-too-tight corset. Inez had suspected she would eventually have to face this particular ghost from her disreputable past, just not so soon.

Both men had cigars. Nico, who seemed to be doing most of the talking, gestured with his, sweeping his arm grandly around the store as if showing off the extent of their wares. The smoke drifted up and curled in the air above their heads, like a vengeful wraith.

"Who's that with Nico?" Antonia leaned close to the glass for a better look.

Inez swiftly guided Antonia away from the storefront and toward the door leading to their living quarters. "A gentleman I've been expecting. Business. You shall have to see yourself upstairs and memorize those lines Miss Pierce set forth for you. You can recite them to me over breakfast tomorrow."

"Aren't you going to play anything tonight?" Antonia didn't hide her disappointment. One of their after-supper rituals on Mondays was for Inez to play the grand piano. Antonia liked to crawl under the instrument, lie on the rug, and dream to the music. Inez always saved Antonia's favorite, *Für Elise*, for last.

Inez unlocked the door, and they entered the dark entryway.

"After I'm done talking with the gentleman there, I shall have to prepare for the usual visitation from Carmella's beaus and the rest." She had never made a secret of the Monday night gatherings for cards and conversation in the back room.

"Tomorrow night, I promise." Inez added. She hated to let Antonia down, but it couldn't be helped. Inez lit one of the oil lamps waiting at the bottom of the stairwell, helped Antonia hang her wet mackintosh on a peg by the door, and hung her own alongside. After giving Antonia a quick hug and handing her the lamp, she continued, "Now, go along."

Antonia dragged herself upstairs, her heavy tread expressing her disappointment.

Inez stifled a sigh, thinking that she would much rather play for Antonia than deal with what was coming next, then gave herself a shake. *I can handle Harry. I have in the past, and I will now. I must remember: the focus of his visit is his son. He wants information. I need only convince him that I have none, and he will look elsewhere.* She closed and locked the door, returned to the store entrance, grasped the doorknob, twisted it harder than necessary, and entered, head high.

The two men turned toward her. Inez placed her umbrella in the elephant-foot stand by the door, eyeing Harry in his bespoke eveningwear. The obligatory swallow-tail coat and black low-cut waistcoat—both of a black so deep and rich it seemed to swallow all light—and the blinding white cravat and shirt said plainer than words he was on his way to an important event. The lid of the nearby grand piano held his overcoat and a silk hat. The two men were dressed almost identically. With their similar heights, the casual way they held their cigars, the equally intent manner in which they attended to her entry, they could have been matching bookends.

Inez said, "Good evening, gentlemen," as calmly as her racing heart would allow and walked forward, pulling off her gloves as she approached.

"Good evening, Mrs. Stannert." That was Harry, polite to a fault. The years since they had last spoken faded away, leaving her almost dizzy.

"Ah, Signora Stannert. It appears you have a very wealthy admirer who has traveled all the way from Colorado to see you." Nico's obsequiousness oozed as sticky sweet as the apple pie filling.

Inez wondered what Harry and Nico had been discussing. She was willing to bet it wasn't pianofortes or Oriental vases.

However, all Nico said was, "Signore Gallagher was telling me he's heard you perform in Colorado in the past, and was praising you for being an accomplished pianist. I, of course, readily agreed, having known this since the day of our first acquaintance." He sounded grudging and dazzled at the same time.

"Thank you, Mr. Donato, for your kind words on my behalf." She turned to Harry. "Welcome to San Francisco, Mr. Gallagher. What a surprise to see you here." She couldn't force herself to add the adjective "pleasant."

"The pleasure is all mine, Mrs. Stannert," Harry responded.

Nico cleared his throat. "Well. I must be off. I am to perform at the Floods' tonight and need to gather the rest of the quartet."

Harry diverted his gaze to Nico. "I shall see you there, Mr. Donato."

"I look forward to that, Signore." He executed a deferential bow.

Inez thought sourly that Nico probably hoped to cultivate yet another wealthy patron, even a visiting one. Perhaps he was angling for employment at a soirée or some other private, high-toned function hosted by Gallagher while he was in town.

Once the door closed behind Nico, Harry said, "Is there someplace private we can speak, where we are not on display to the world like a case of dry goods?"

The last thing Inez wanted was to be enclosed somewhere private with Harry Gallagher. She glanced at the plate-glass windows facing the rainy, dark streets, considering her response. At that hour, pedestrians, carriages of all kinds still filed past. With the lights inside, the two of them would appear as actors on the stage to those outside. Also not what she wanted. "There is an office in the back. But I only have a few minutes. I am expecting other visitors." She took an almost childish pleasure in withholding an explanation of whom those visitors might be.

He gathered his hat and coat and accompanied her. She was acutely aware of him surveying the store and its "curiosities," his expression unreadable. He moved through the showroom as all wealthy men did, as if they owned the walls, the floors, the contents, the very people in the room, as well as the air they breathed and the light that illuminated all.

Inez set her hand on the door, but Harry reached past her and pushed it open so she could pass. His arm brushed hers, igniting memories and a flicker of emotions she did not wish to rekindle.

She moved quickly away, gathering a box of lucifers to light the paraffin lamp on the round table. "Leave the door open," she said.

Harry leaned against the doorframe, smoking, watching her, his ice-blue eyes tracking her movements, intent. "I didn't think to find you in such a place as this."

Inez paused, burning match in hand. "And where did you expect to find me?" Any shakiness in her voice was concealed by sharpness. "On the Barbary Coast, perhaps? Ruling over some dank whiskey mill?"

Strangely enough, Harry smiled. It was small, almost invisible under his mustache, but definitely there. "Not at all." He straightened up as the wick took the fire, shedding light into the gloom. "I expected to find you a minister's wife."

Inez pushed a crystal ashtray in his direction and shifted to the other side of the table, putting the wide wood expanse between them. "That's not what you came here to talk to me about. Let's not play games or mince words. Clearly, you were looking for me and you have found me. No doubt you twisted Flo's arm and applied some not-so-subtle pressure."

Harry ground out the cigar in the ashtray before pulling a card from his overcoat and spinning it toward her across the tabletop. It slid over the polished surface, coming to rest an arm's length away. The printed words "Donato and Stannert" blazed up at her from one of the store's new trade cards. Well, *that* horse is out of the barn, Inez thought grimly, wishing she'd followed her first instinct and insisted the card be reprinted with the anonymous "D & S."

All Harry said was, "You were not hard to find."

She pushed the card to one side and decided to forego further digressions or palaver. "Flo told me that you are looking for your son. I'll tell you straight away so we do not waste time here, I have not heard of nor do I know a Robert Gallagher. Harry, you are on a fool's errand. Trying to find one young man who doesn't want to be found, in a city of two-hundred-thousand-plus souls? Who is to say he is even using that name, assuming he is in the city at all?"

The half-smile vanished. He reached again into the overcoat's inner pocket and extracted another, slightly larger pasteboard, walking around the table toward Inez. She forced herself to stand her ground as he approached. Without a word, he held the object out to her—a *carte de visite* of a young man. Inez reluctantly took the studio portrait, and studied it.

Harry's son. Obviously.

Robert was handsome, Inez gave him that. In the photograph he sat in a low-backed chair and was dressed in a well-tailored sackcoat and checked trousers. With one ungloved hand, he balanced a silk top hat on his knee, while holding a walking stick loosely in the other hand. He had the long slender fingers of a pianist. Along with a head of smooth dark hair, brushed back and cut short and business-like, that came to a widow's peak in front, he sported a mustache and beard, effectively disguising his mouth and chin. The younger Gallagher gazed to one side, in three-quarters view, pale eyes turned away from the probing camera lens. His face held a pensive, guarded expression, as if he wished himself far away.

Glancing up at Harry, Inez realized that the son did indeed resemble the father in face and form, sharing the same striking pale blue eyes. She returned to the portrait. *Those eyes. The widow's peak. Have I seen them before? On two separate men, or all on one?* A prickle raced down her spine.

Her unease at having Harry so close, his attention so focused on her, made it impossible for her to chase the thought any farther.

She handed the photograph back. "I'm sorry, Harry. I've not seen him."

The lines around Harry's eyes tightened and his dark eyebrows drew together.

"I swear it," she added hastily. "These young musicians, they come and go all the time. If they stay for any period of time in the city, they often show up here." The minute the words were out, she wanted to bite her tongue.

"Then I am correct to think he has probably been here, and you may have seen him."

She shook her head, in annoyance at herself as much as in denial. "I told you. He does not look familiar to me. Honestly, they come to see Mr. Donato, for the most part. He draws them in and encourages them, the new ones in town. You might show Signore Donato your *carte de visite* and see what he says."

"That popinjay." Harry sounded dismissive. "It's clear he only has eyes for the mirror and for himself."

"That's not true!" Even though she secretly agreed, Inez came to Nico's defense, stung by the critique of her business partner. "Mr. Donato is extremely talented and well-recognized and admired locally. He works hard at bettering his professional reputation and never shirks from helping those who are talented but less fortunate than himself."

Harry pocketed the photograph. "In that case, I'll make a point of speaking with him tonight at the Floods'." He started toward the door leading to the showroom. "I am staying at the Palace Hotel, Mrs. Stannert. I expect you to send word if you catch sight or hear any mention of my son. Even the slightest of rumors or whispers. Robert is here. Sooner or later he will surface, and if this is where musicians new to town assemble, he will show himself. Robert is not one to hide in the shadows."

Relieved their meeting had not involved much drama, and they had skirted discussion of their shared, volatile past, Inez hurried to catch up and lead him out of the store. However,

Flo's warnings nagged at her, and she had to ask. "Flo said you threatened to ruin her and me should we not succeed in helping you find your son."

Harry stopped so abruptly that Inez collided into him. He turned to face her, taking her arm. Inez assumed he was just trying to help steady her after she'd nearly been knocked down. When he didn't let go, she began to reconsider.

"Mrs. Sweet's mind jumps to dime novels and melodramas." The tightening grip on her arm, the way he pulled her closer, just the slightest bit, belied his calm words and tone.

An electric jolt ran down her spine as he continued, "I cannot imagine a scenario in which you or Mrs. Sweet would elect to hide any information you might have about my son from me. Therefore, you have nothing to worry about."

Inez's breath caught in her throat. She managed to blurt out, "Harry, I'll tell you exactly what I told Flo. Looking for your son will be like looking for a needle in a haystack."

He leaned toward her, his hold steady. She drew back as far as his grip would allow.

"You have a son, Inez. I know the lengths you went to ensure his safety and well-being, even sending him away to live with relatives. If he were a grown man, but young and foolish, and disappeared, leaving no word, and he was traveling down a wrong road, a road filled with dangers he knew nothing about, what would you do to find and protect him?"

She didn't reply. The answer that she bit back behind closed lips was *I would do whatever I had to do. Whatever was necessary.*

He must have read it in her face, because he nodded once and released her arm.

She stepped back one pace, then two, before she rallied. "What do you mean dangerous? *How* dangerous? And how do I know he would not be in more danger if I learn something that led to you tracking him down? I heard about his Leadville fiancée, Vivian Poole. I heard her father, Phillip Poole, is out for blood and that he is in the city as well."

"Where did you hear this?" The question was mild, the tone was not.

Too late, Inez remembered that Flo had come by that bit of information through stealth. She sidestepped a direct answer, countering, "If it's true, doesn't that concern you? Maybe Robert disappearing is best, if you fear for his safety."

Inez caught an unmistakable ripple of worry surge across his face before it vanished, leaving his expression cold and distant. "Inez, you are meddling in family matters that are none of your business."

He pulled out his pocket watch, clicked it open, and glanced at the face. "I've tarried long enough. I said what I came to say, except for this." He closed the cover with a snap and surveyed the back room slowly—the office, the gathering area with the round table, the practice room with the pianos. "You have a new life in San Francisco. One you have obviously worked hard to achieve. One clearly divorced from your past in Leadville. Far from State Street, the Silver Queen, various unsavory escapades, and your shared 'business endeavors' with Mrs. Sweet. I understand your desire to keep it that way."

The implied threat could not have been plainer.

Her fear shifted into anger. "If you think to frighten or blackmail me—"

He moved into the showroom and away from her. "I am certain you and Mrs. Sweet will do all you can, using your considerable talents and connections to help me find my wayward son. I have others looking for him as well, so I do not expect this to take long. In the meantime, keep me apprised of any developments, particularly if you hear any news indicating where he might be. I will let myself out, Mrs. Stannert."

Chapter Twelve

"Ante up, gentlemen." Inez watched the six men at the round table pitch in their pennies for the next hand, rubbing her arm absently. The memory of Harry's hand on her arm, pulling her close, still burned.

The copper bits plinked onto the table, sounding like a miniature version of the rain that dripped onto the wood porch outside the back door.

She dealt the cards.

To her left, violinist Giotto Laguardia swirled the brandy in his goblet as he examined his cards, mouth turned down. His unhappiness, she suspected, was probably not with the cards but with the fact he was not part of Nico's quartet that evening. Her suspicion was confirmed when Giotto said to the table at large, "So, Nico is playing at the Flood mansion tonight. A quartet. Anyone know who the other three are?"

The Ash brothers, Walter and William, looked at each other. They often appeared to communicate with a glance, as if an invisible telegraph wire was strung between them. They shrugged simultaneously. Walter said, "He didn't ask you to be second violin?"

Giotto glared. "I'm here, yes? That should answer your question." His voice clearly communicated his displeasure at being left out. He downed the last of his drink. It had disappeared quickly, Inez noted, as she pushed the bottle toward him.

To her right, the labor newspaperman, Roger Haskell, grumbled and shifted his foul-smelling cigar from one corner of his mouth to the other. "Better luck next time, Giotto. I gotta say, hope my luck at the table tonight is better than this weather. And the news. It's been dreary, all around."

Inez raised an eyebrow. "Bad news on the labor front, Mr. Haskell?"

That was all the encouragement he needed; the floodgates opened.

"Is there ever anything good?" he asked. "The disgrace in the Hawaiian Islands. Heard about it? It's all about sugar, kinda far removed from the music world, but strikes at the heart of the workingman's plight. *The Chronicle* today had a piece on the Reciprocity Treaty with the Hawaiian Islands. All the treaty's done is hand a couple of sugar producers a virtual monopoly. You like sugar in your coffee or tea? Well, you're supporting slavery or worse for the plantation workers. And our local sugar baron, you all know his name, sells the sweet stuff for more here than on the East Coast. He pays the railroad forty dollars a ton for two thousand-five hundred tons of freight from New York to San Francisco, but the railroad doesn't even carry the cargo! This hundred-thousand-dollar per annum subsidy keeps Eastern sugar out of the market, see? As a result, he charges two cents a pound over the New York price for all the sugar consumed on this coast. Think about that."

He drew hard on his cigar and expelled a noxious cloud. "That's just a drop in the bucket of the tribute daily exacted from the people by the giant corporations of this country. There's no competition as far as the manufacturing industries and the railway systems are concerned."

Haskell sounded almost cheerful after his recitation of the sad and sorry state of labor affairs. His attitude was no surprise to Inez. She had pegged him early in their acquaintance as the sort who was most happy when miserable. Perfect for a union-leaning publisher of a small labor newspaper.

Of course, his cheerfulness could indicate he had been dealt a strong hand.

Time would tell.

"Mark me," he continued, "there will come a time when the oppression by the moneyed powers of this country will be so great it will no longer be endured. The people will demand the government adopt radical measures for eradicating the evil. The sooner this work begins, the better it'll be for us. In my opinion."

Otto groaned.

Percussionist Isaac Pérez nudged Otto with an elbow. "Mourning the future loss of Miss Donato's sugar-laden pastries due to market manipulations?"

"Just mourning the waste of a cent." Otto tossed his cards down. "I'm out."

Inez knew a bad hand wasn't the only reason for Otto's uncharacteristic dolefulness. When he had arrived to the gathering late, still wearing the black armband from his day's employment, she had pulled him aside for a quick word. "Have you told any of the others about the longshoreman's visit to your boardinghouse this morning?" she murmured, handing him a glass of whiskey.

Otto had glanced at his companions, chatting and smoking at the table, out of earshot. "I have not seen them. I was working all day. I have not talked to anyone of this." He looked down at his tumbler, gave the liquid a tentative swirl. She suspected he was barely controlling the urge to toss it down in one gulp.

"Good. No need to stir the pot any more than it has already been stirred. At least until we know what is what. Or who is who. It is being taken care of, and we should know soon. If the conversation allows, I will ask if anyone has seen Jamie out and about today. *Verstehen Sie?*"

He'd understood.

That was two games and six refills ago. And rather than

increase his joviality, all the liquor had done was to carry him deeper into his funk.

"Not even staying in for the first round of betting?" Welles asked, eyeing Otto's slim stacks of pennies and nickels.

"Not even," Otto responded, and leaned back in his chair, fingers clasped over his checked waistcoat. "Landlady has been at the door. Rent is overdue."

"Well, you're not the only ones in the city scrambling to pay for lodgings right now," continued Haskell cheerfully. "The city's school fund has officially been declared exhausted as of yesterday and is short by seventeen thousand bucks. Teachers who didn't present their warrants for payment before ten-thirty Saturday are now going to have to wait until the middle of December to get paid. Pity the school marm who's got nothing saved up for room and board. It'll be a long time until the next meal."

With a twinge of sympathy, Inez thought of Miss Pierce and her snappish attitude toward Antonia. Perhaps she was one of the unfortunate teachers.

Haskell settled comfortably into his seat with another smoky exhalation. She debated the wisdom of buying a different brand of cigar and offering them all around at the next gathering, with the intent of switching Haskell off his current highly unpleasant favorite.

Welles said, "How about the music world? Anyone know of any leads?" He had dark circles under his eyes as if he hadn't slept in days.

William Ash said, "Jossefy's looking for a harmonium player, I hear."

"No use to me," said Welles glumly. "I'm not an organist. But maybe I ought to take it up. Could maybe pick up work in churches or for ladies' clubs."

Inez wondered why he was sitting in the game. His wife could no doubt make good use of the penny he'd just tossed into the pot. Inez decided she might see if she couldn't arrange it so he left the evening richer than when he had arrived. She never engaged in card mechanics such as false shuffling and culling when the pots were small. If she did decide to try and better Welles' lot, she would have to be careful. Despite the meager size of the winnings, the musicians were cutthroat, often reacting as if they were betting gold eagles when only raising nickels. For a moment, Inez drifted off into memories, reminiscing about evenings at the Silver Queen when hundreds, even thousands of dollars sometimes rode on the single turn of a card.

Giotto opened the first round of betting with a penny.

Everyone called.

With a pair of sevens, Inez decided to let the game play itself out naturally and instead focus on finding an opening in the conversation to ask if anyone knew a "Robert Gallagher." She also hoped she could slide in a query about Jamie. If someone had seen him earlier in the day, it would mean it wasn't Jamie who was pulled out of Mission Creek that morning.

Haskell said, "It's tough out there now, Welles. All the new-comers of summer are fighting to find winter work. Thought you were keeping busy with California Theater."

Welles looked down at his meager pile of coins. "I got the boot from the California."

Sympathetic murmurs rippled around the table.

Walter Ash, a cigarette held casually in one hand, squinted through the smoke. "How so? You never miss a beat, Welles. Or a note."

"Someone offered to play for less." He set his jaw. "I had another position lined up, but it didn't work out."

Haskell pointed his cigar at Welles. "And *that's* why you fel-las got to form a union."

"We tried," said Welles testily. "You were there, Haskell. You remember what a mess it was."

"What happened?" asked Giotto.

Welles just shook his head.

Haskell said, "Way I heard it, there was infighting, different fellas thinking they oughta be king. Some thought rival organizations were conniving to make sure the union failed. Others claimed the leaders were out for themselves and not for the common good."

"The union was a sham," said Welles. "Just like now, every man for himself."

"We're artists!" interjected Isaac Pérez. "Not dockworkers or sailors. What use is a union to us?"

Walter and William nodded in synchronized agreement.

"Cards, gentlemen?" Inez prodded.

Haskell tossed a couple onto the table. "Two."

Inez obliged.

Welles held up three fingers, and pushed his discards toward Inez. Replacements sailed his way.

Giotto rapped the table with his knuckles, standing pat.

Pérez discarded three.

The Ash brothers each took one.

Welles shifted in his chair as he examined his updated hand. "The missus and I, we had one in diapers and another on the way. I was trying to save up every penny I could, and wasn't crazy about paying union dues. It seemed like all the plum jobs went to the officers and their cronies anyway. Soured me on unions."

Haskell added, "Plus, after the union disbanded, the treasury funds were supposed to be divvied up among the members. Before that could happen, the treasurer disappeared."

Curiosity piqued, Inez asked, "The treasurer absconded with the funds?"

Welles grunted and didn't answer. Haskell responded, "Who knows? All anyone could say was that a big chunk of the money disappeared along with the guy who was supposed to keep track of it. A black day for the members, I remember that. Reported on it and hated doing so. Shenanigans like that give unions a bad name. Welles doesn't want to talk about it, but you could ask Nico for details, if you want. He was part of the union, too, back then."

Haskell leaned back in his chair and blew a smoke ring at the ceiling. "On second thought, you probably shouldn't ask Nico. He's kinda sensitive about the subject, like Welles. It was just after the Donato parents had died, and he was taking care of Carmella while hustling for work. Not a good time for anyone."

Welles threw in a nickel. "Let's get this game rolling."

Eyebrows raised. Murmurs circled the table. Pérez peered at Welles. "*Madre de Dios.* Luck finally breaking your way, Thomas?"

Welles looked at the Spaniard with a stony expression. "Guess you'll have to pay to find out, Isaac."

Inez winced. Welles seemed uncommonly testy. Perhaps due to the loss of his job and then having a replacement position slip through his fingers. He was usually implacable and hard to read, particularly at the poker table. Rather like Harry Gallagher, who had been one of her regulars at the Silver Queen. Harry had been an enigma from the start. No more so than during their brief affair, which had flared into existence soon after her then-husband Mark had disappeared and she'd believed him dead. The liaison had been quickly extinguished once she had discovered Harry was a married man.

Haskell still seemed to be ruminating over Welles' misfortune. "I'll keep my ear to the ground for someone needing an experienced domino thumper," he said. "Competition's fierce in that area right now. More talented hopefuls pouring into the city every day."

As good a segue as any.

"By the way," Inez nonchalantly rearranged her hand of cards, "does the name Robert Gallagher ring a bell for anyone? New to town?"

She scanned her visitors.

Blank-faced, the lot of them.

"What does he play?" asked Walter Ash.

Inez realized that neither Flo nor Harry had said and she had neglected to ask.

"I don't know. He would be fairly new to town, though. Six months? Less?"

"Why are you asking?" said Otto, taking a cigarette from his case and hunting his pockets for a match.

"Someone from out of town queried me about him today. It was not a name I've encountered, but I thought one of you might have heard of him."

Shakes of heads and shrugs of shoulders were the only responses.

She relaxed. At least none in her immediate circle recognized the name. *Now, to find an opening in which to inquire about Jamie Monroe's whereabouts.* She returned her attention to her pair of sevens, which had not been bettered a whit despite three new cards.

Haskell started the next round of betting with two pennies. Welles raised one more cent. Good-natured grumbling followed. All stayed in, except Walter Ash, who decided to fold and hang tight to his three copper coins.

"Call," said Giotto after nudging his contribution to the pot.

Welles had a full house, queens and nines. A flicker of approval curled through Inez when the hands of the other players fell short. Haskell examined his three-of-a-kind jacks and shrugged. "Thought I had it sewn up. Good show, Welles. Maybe your luck *has* changed."

Welles, looking less gloomy, merged his winnings with his remaining coins.

Haskell tipped his chair onto its back legs. "Mrs. Stannert, did you hear that the city is enforcing that gambling ban I told you about last week?"

Inez raised an eyebrow. "Is that so?"

"All gambling-houses in the area bounded by Larkin,

Market, Church, Eighteenth, and Channel streets and the waterfront. Guess we're all breaking the law here."

Inez gathered the cards and began shuffling. "I suspect the ordinance is directed at Chinatown, Mr. Haskell. And, in any case, if an occasional friendly game of penny poker provokes the attention of the local constabulary, the entire city will be in trouble."

Isaac Pérez pulled out his pocket watch and examined the time. "Monroe must have landed a last-minute job somewhere. When we talked yesterday, he'd said he'd be here."

Otto reached for the bottle.

Secretly blessing Pérez for mentioning Jamie, Inez pasted a look of mild interest on her face. "I was expecting Mr. Monroe today as well. Have any of you seen him?"

Pérez turned to Otto. "Herr Klein here would have heard him snoring last night, yes?"

Otto slopped some of the liquor onto the table. "Not there last night."

Pérez grinned. "Ah! Who is the lucky lady, Klein?" At Walter Ash's cough, Pérez turned to Inez, abashed. "Apologies, Señora Stannert, for my crude remark."

"I was home," said Otto gruffly, keeping his gaze on the table as he mopped up the spill with his handkerchief. "It was Jamie who was not."

Haskell volunteered, "I saw him on Sunday at one of the sandlot meetings, talking with Frank Roney. Roney's a real force for labor. He pulled together the Seamen's Protective Association last year. Monroe is getting in pretty deep with Roney and his type. I gotta hand it to the kid, he really cares about the movement. And he wants to see a musician's union succeed." Haskell picked up his cards. "He stopped by the paper's office last Friday, looking for information on the last merry-go-round in '74. I gave him what I had, then pointed him to you, Welles. Didn't he talk to you?"

Welles' expression darkened throughout Haskell's remarks.

He picked up his cards, and with barely a glance at them, tossed them back down. "Yeah. He came by." He opened his mouth like he was going to say something further, then stopped.

He scooped up his winnings, stood, and grabbed his hat off the hat rack. "The missus is going to have my hide if I'm not home soon. See you guys around. G'night, Mrs. Stannert." He opened the back door. The sound of heavy rain rushed into the room on the wings of a cold, wet gust. The players pinned their cards to the table to keep them from flying into the breeze. He left, slamming the door behind him.

Mystified, Inez turned to Haskell. "What was that about?"

"No idea, Mrs. Stannert. He's a man of many moods. And obviously under pressure."

"So it seems." She tried to refocus on her hand, but Welles' anger and its possible origins lingered over the table and cast a dark shadow over her thoughts.

Chapter Thirteen

Antonia awoke with a snort, the routine clamor of bells smashing her dream. She wiped at the drool that dampened her cheek and turned one ear into the pillow, clapping a hand over the other ear. The words from a remembered poem beat along with the muffled noise: *Hear the tolling of the bells—Iron bells! What a world of solemn thought their monody compels!*

What was monody, again? Then she remembered what Mrs. S had told her.

"It can refer to poem or music," she'd said. "In music, it's a song for a solo singer accompanied by some instrument or other. It defined a particular musical style in seventeenth century Italian song. Where did you hear that term? From Mr. Donato?"

Antonia showed Mrs. S the book she'd purloined from the public library.

Mrs. S had looked at her strangely. *The Works of Edgar Allen Poe?* "You're reading this but having trouble with your *Swinton's Reader?*"

Antonia had shrugged. "*Swinton's* is boring. How do you know all this stuff anyway?"

"I went to school. And I listened to what my teachers said."

Cheek against the pillow, eyes closed, Antonia sniffed experimentally. Her plugged nose gurgled. Maybe she was coming down with a cold. Maybe she could talk Mrs. S into letting her stay home today....

Her bed jiggled. Antonia's eyes popped open. The bells were quiet, but she could hear the traffic in the street outside her window.

Mrs. S stood there, a shawl over her shoulders, dressed for the day. "Get up, Antonia. It's already half past. I can't understand how you slept through the racket."

"I'm sick." She snuffled to demonstrate.

Mrs. S moved to the side of the bed and put a hand on her brow.

"No fever." Mrs. S gave her the once over. "You'll be fine. Wear your flannel petticoat and your wool stockings. I'll give you an extra handkerchief to carry."

Antonia grumbled and swung her feet out of bed onto the braided rug, pulling off her nightcap.

"And be sure to take your umbrella." Mrs. S moved toward the door. "It's not raining at the moment, but who knows about later? I'll fix your breakfast. Hurry up now."

Antonia got dressed, feeling as if her limbs were struggling through molasses, and dragged herself to the table. Two round *zeppole*, white with powdered sugar, waited for her. "Carmella?" she asked, delighted.

Mrs. S nodded, busy at the small stove. "She made those yesterday. I warmed them for you this morning." She brought over Antonia's heated, coffee-laced milk. Antonia took it and got a good look at Mrs. S, who looked like she hadn't slept much.

No surprise there.

Antonia lowered her gaze to the fried dough balls, picked one up and took a bite, focusing on the taste. Antonia didn't want Mrs. S looking into her eyes and figuring out that she had heard what that man, Mr. Gallagher, had said last night, and what Mrs. S had said back.

She knew she shouldn't eavesdrop. Mrs. S would tan her hide if she found out, but Antonia took great pains to keep her sneaky doings secret. Her little bolthole was in the second-floor storage room, among the trunks and boxes and dust, where no one ever went. Even if they did, they'd never realize one of the knots in the floor planks could be pulled out. This peephole was above the chandelier. No one ever looked up, but she could look down, directly into the back room and see the office and all. Antonia had been pleased as all get-out when she'd managed to pry out the cylinder of wood and had set it up so she could easily pull it out and plug it in whenever she wanted.

And now she knew Mrs. S was in trouble with that silver baron Mr. Gallagher. He'd been all smooth and swank in his topcoat and tails, just like all of the rich folk in San Francisco and Leadville, all those places with money.

Antonia had had a bad feeling about him from the start. She didn't remember ever hearing about a Mr. Gallagher when she had been a newsie running with the other newsies in Leadville. And they knew everyone, especially the bigwigs, the ones who were flush and tipped big when buying a paper. Mrs. S had never mentioned him either, not in Leadville or here. But from the words they threw back and forth down there and the way he grabbed her arm, it looked like he knew her and she sure as shootin' knew him.

Back in Leadville, as far as men went, Mrs. S mostly swore at Mr. Stannert, who she finally left, or canoodled with Reverend Sands, who seemed to have left her. Antonia couldn't figure it, because they had seemed sweet on each other in Leadville. But he had been there, and then he was gone, leaving Mrs. S to take her mister to court and get free of him all by herself.

Antonia didn't ask about the reverend, where he was or what had happened or any of that. Mrs. S didn't talk about him, so the only thing Antonia could figure was something sad must've happened between them, something Mrs. S kept to herself.

Antonia could understand that.

So, who the heck was this Mr. High-and-Mighty-Gallagher who acted like he was one of the society folk living up on Nob Hill?

Well, whoever he was, he was looking for his son. And Mrs. S had told him nope, she didn't know him, but it had sounded like Gallagher didn't believe her. It had sounded like he might even do something nasty if Mrs. S didn't do what he said. Someone like that—who was rich and knew other rich folks, and who could scare Mrs. S—was someone not to cross.

Seems like he thought he could come in and push Mrs. S around and tell her what to do, just like the bullies at school did to Antonia. Well, she was going to help Mrs. S out, and see if she couldn't draw a bead on this Robert Gallagher and get that toff out of their lives.

But how?

Antonia's wandering mind settled on Copper Mick. *His da's a detective. Maybe Mick can help.*

"Are they stale?"

"Huh?" Antonia realized she'd been holding the *zeppola* up to her lips but not eating while all this rumbled through her mind. "No, they're great. I just can't taste very much 'cause my nose." She took another bite and polished it and the second pastry off.

"The day you turn down Carmella's *zeppole* is the day I know you are sick," said Mrs. S. "Brush the sugar off your collar, and gather your things. You'll need to hurry."

Antonia grabbed her glasses and her bonnet, stuffed the extra handkerchief lying by her bookbag up her sleeve, and hoisted her lunch pail to her arm and her book strap with the *Swinton's* over her shoulder. "Too much stuff," she muttered, clattering down the stairs with Mrs. S close behind.

Mrs. S draped Antonia's coat over her shoulders and handed her an umbrella. "You'll have to be quick as a bunny to get your lunch from Mrs. Nolan," she opened the door, "and get to school on time—Oh!"

They both stopped short. Mr. Donato stood right outside, hand gripping the bell twist, prepared to ring the doorbell. "Ah! Good morning, Antonia, Mrs. Stannert. Signora, I'd hoped to have a few words with you before you start your day."

"I have an appointment this morning, Signore. One I cannot break. We shall have to talk later."

Antonia blinked. Mrs. S hardly ever refused Mr. Donato, even when he made ridiculous requests. Hearing her say "no" like that reminded Antonia of what Mrs. S had been like when in Leadville. Back then, Mrs. S was almost scary, always carrying her pocket pistol and not afraid of anything or anyone. But plenty of folks were afraid of *her*. It was like she was invincible, and no one dared cross her. She made Antonia feel safe. But since Sacramento, Mrs. S had been… different. Not weak, exactly, but more wary. Quiet. Like she was trying to be invisible. And now, Antonia didn't feel as safe as she once did.

Donato seemed as surprised as Antonia at Mrs. S's response and sputtered out, "But, I—"

"I'll be back in time to open the store." Mrs. S took Antonia's shoulder and marched her down Kearney toward Market.

"Where are you going?" Antonia had the terrifying idea that Mrs. S was coming with her to talk to Miss Pierce or maybe the principal.

Mrs. S squeezed her shoulder. "As I told Mr. Donato, I have an appointment. One that I must keep. And I wanted to tell you something first. Mrs. Sweet from Leadville is in town. Do you remember Mrs. Sweet?"

Antonia wrinkled her nose, which only caused it to run. "Mrs. Sweet? You mean Frisco Flo, the madam who runs the whoreh—"

"Ssssst!" Inez cut her off. "None of that here. I wanted to warn you that she may come by the store at some point to talk to me about a business matter. If you see her, I want you to pretend that you are meeting for the first time. I will introduce you, and you will address her as Mrs. Sweet."

Antonia noted how the lines tightened around Mrs. Stannert's eyes as she talked about Madam Flo. "What's she doing here? In San Francisco?"

"It's a business matter, as I said." Mrs. S paused. "There may be other people from Leadville who will be in town as well. Things could become a bit delicate. I don't think you would know them, but if it happens someone drops by the store and you recognize them from Leadville, don't be startled. Just follow my lead. I wanted to let you know, so you would understand."

Antonia wanted to say she didn't understand anything. Or rather, because she'd been spying on the goings-on last night, she understood some, but not everything. But she couldn't say that.

Mrs. S continued, "To reiterate, because this is important, I want you on your best behavior if you are in the store when Mrs. Sweet arrives. Just say 'Good day, ma'am,' and absolutely no words about the Silver Queen, State Street, 'pleasure palaces,' and so on."

"I know," said Antonia. "You don't have to keep telling me not to talk about Leadville."

Mrs. S nodded, but she didn't seem to be really listening. "Good. Now, run along. Be quick or you'll be late!"

Antonia obediently quickened her stride, leaving Mrs. S behind. However, she couldn't help but wonder where Mrs. S was going.

Antonia glanced back. Mrs. S wasn't hailing a hack. So, she was walking somewhere close by.

Was she meeting Frisco Flo?

Mrs. S headed toward Market, but so slow it almost seemed on purpose, like she didn't want Antonia to know where she was going. Antonia kept up her pace, beginning to sweat in her woolen stockings and warm petticoat. As she turned the corner onto Market, she glanced behind her again. Mrs. S was still coming and had opened her umbrella because it was starting to sprinkle. Antonia ducked into a bakery and went up to the shelves, examining the rows of bread with great interest. A few minutes later, Mrs. S walked by, clutching her coat closed at the throat, head bowed under the umbrella.

Antonia waited a few heartbeats, dashed back out, and opened her own umbrella. The ocean of dark umbrellas on Market confused her until she picked out Mrs. S, taller than the other women and even some of the men. Antonia hung back, sliding along the storefronts in case Mrs. S turned in her direction and she needed to duck inside somewhere.

Mrs. S slowed and stopped by the tall fountain they called Lotta's Fountain at the corner of Market, Kearney, and Third. A veiled woman also with an umbrella approached Mrs. S. They talked, then started walking in Antonia's direction, the edges of their umbrellas touching, heads bent toward each other.

Antonia ducked into a basket store, lowering her umbrella so as not to incur the wrath of the storeowner, who stared curiously at her. Antonia waited until the women swept past and followed, cautious.

Was this the important appointment Mrs. S mentioned?

Who was the lady with her? Could it be Madam Flo? With the veil, Antonia couldn't tell. The other lady wasn't very tall, and Antonia remembered the whorehouse madam as being pretty short, so maybe.

And where were they going?

The two women turned up Kearney. Antonia followed.

Were they heading back to the store?

But no, they walked past Pine.

They were getting close to the edge of Chinatown.

Antonia walked behind a gaggle of Chinese men talking softly to each other in their singsong language. Antonia's mind wandered. She wondered why John Hee never seemed to talk to any of his kind. Come to think of it, she never saw him anywhere but in the store, mostly in the repair room. He was nice, though. And he had showed her once how to replace a bridge on a violin and how to string it correctly.

She suddenly realized that it was WAY past the time for the start of school.

Never mind.

She wasn't going to school that day.

Instead, she'd hole up in the storage room upstairs. Mrs. S would be in the store all day, so she'd most likely not come up to the second floor anyway. Antonia decided she'd stop at Mrs. Nolan's on the way back, once she knew what Mrs. S and the mystery woman were up to, grab her lunch, and have a picnic all by herself upstairs. Just her and her copy of *Young Folks*. She could finish reading the *Treasure Island* installment and see if anything more happened in the office below that would explain what the heck was happening.

Intent on plotting her next steps and what she'd do upstairs once she got home, Antonia almost missed it when Mrs. S and the mystery woman turned to enter a large brick building just past Merchant.

Staring at the building, Antonia slowed and came to a dead stop, then turned around headed back down Kearney.

She told herself that if she wanted to pick up her pickles, cheese, and bread from Mrs. Nolan's boardinghouse and avoid questions, she'd better move fast.

But there was one question she couldn't outrun, and it burned in her brain as she hurried away.

What were Mrs. S and the other woman doing in the police station?

Madam Flo wouldn't have anything to do with the law. It had to be someone else.

What was going on?

Antonia figured if she hung out in the storage room above the office that day and kept her ears and eyes open, she just might find out.

Chapter Fourteen

At the top of the steps, Inez turned to the heavily veiled Carmella Donato. "Let me do the talking," she said, laying a hand on the young woman's arm. She could feel the tension radiating through Carmella.

"It can't be Jamie," she whispered back fiercely. "It is not possible, I am certain."

"First, we must find out where they took the remains." Inez couldn't quite bring herself to say "the deceased" or the word "corpse." "I am certain it would not be here," she added. "But the Central Police Station seems like the best place to start."

She stopped talking as a derby-hatted gentleman exited the building and held the door for them to enter. Inez asked him for directions to the Central Police Station. "I understand it is inside somewhere," she added.

The man pointed to a set of stairs leading down. "In the basement."

She thanked him and they moved toward the stairs. This time, as they descended, it was Carmella who grabbed Inez's arm. "Surely not here? He wouldn't be here?"

"I doubt it," Inez assured her. Downstairs, they paused. In one direction was the City Receiving Hospital. Doors swung open, emitting a weeping woman leaning heavily on the arm of a man. Behind them Inez glimpsed a seething mass of people, standing, sitting, lying on gurneys and even on the floor.

Sounds of pain and fear rolled out before the doors swung shut. Inez spotted the sign to the police station offices in the opposite direction. "There."

Once in the station, they approached an officer behind a tall wooden desk. He listened more or less patiently as Inez said, "We were notified that an unidentified man was found by Long Bridge yesterday morning. It may be we can identify him."

"Well now, Long Bridge, is it?" He scratched his bristly mustache. Inez detected bread crumbs of some kind tenaciously entrenched in the upper lip foliage. "Let me see what I can find out for you, ma'am."

He disappeared down a hallway. They waited, Carmella's fingertips digging painfully through the wool of Inez's coat sleeve. He reappeared, his mustache more orderly, crumbs gone, obviously having taken the moment to neaten up. "The unfortunate fella dredged up from the Mission Creek channel, is that right?"

Inez nodded her affirmation.

"Turns out he's with one of the city's deputy coroners, Mr. W. T. Hamilton."

"And where might that be?" inquired Inez.

He gave her the address, 1112 Broadway, then paused. "Surely you ladies have a gentleman with you who will perform the visual identification of the unknown?"

Inez gave him a tight little smile. "Thank you for your help, Officer. And for your concern."

She hustled Carmella up the stairs and out the doors, hailed a passing hack, gave the address to the driver, and asked him to wait once they got there. She was becoming concerned about her time away from the store. Too, if worse came to worst, and the victim was, indeed, Jamie Monroe, she didn't want to subject Carmella to a long wait for another carriage.

They pulled up to a neat building that appeared to be both residence and office, commanding the corner of Broadway and

Jones. Inez gave him a coin with the promise they would not be long. He tipped his hat, and went to the boot to pull out a feedbag for his horse. They were on the shoulder of Russian Hill, bay and ocean stretching to the east and north. Carmella pulled her veil back down and faced east toward the bay. The clouds had cleared, leaving the air cool but gentle. Sunlight sparkled on the distant water. Inez joined her, and they stood looking out over the wide-open view. Inez inhaled, tasting the softness of salt.

Finally, Carmella said, "We have so many plans, Jamie and I. So much to look forward to."

Inez said, "Would you prefer to wait in the carriage? I can take care of this."

The dark veil shimmered as Carmella shook her head.

They walked up to the door. Carmella reached for the bell twist, and Inez said, "Wait." She rummaged in her reticule, finally handing Carmella a lace-edged linen handkerchief. "Hold it to your face if the smell is overwhelming," said Inez.

Carmella took a sniff through the veil. "Cloves?"

"The best I could do on short notice," said Inez, reflecting she was lucky to find that much in her meager kitchen. Inez pulled out her own clove-scented cloth and tucked it into her coat pocket. Carmella turned the bell twist. A metallic ring answered from inside. Soon thereafter Inez detected a tread, and the door opened partway. A giant of a man with the pitted complexion of a long-ago encounter with smallpox looked down at them.

They looked up.

Standing there in his shirtsleeves, he seemed to have been caught unprepared for visitors

"May I help you?" he asked, his voice so soft Inez had to bend forward to hear him.

She cleared her throat. "We are looking for Mr. Hamilton."

"I'm sorry. He is not in at the moment." Inez experienced a wave of disappointment mixed with relief.

Carmella spoke up from behind her veil. "We are here regarding a young man found by Long Bridge yesterday. We might know who he is."

"Oh." His quiet exhalation was followed by a long hesitation. "It would be best if you returned when Mr. Hamilton is here. I am his assistant, you see. He was called out but will be available tomorrow morning."

"We have come a long way," said Inez. Submitting Carmella to another long night of not knowing was not going to happen if she could help it. Besides, if Hamilton was not there, perhaps that was a good thing. The coroner might ask far more questions of them than the assistant. They could see what they came to see, then vanish, anonymous as the fog.

Inez continued, "This has been a big strain on my niece." She turned pointedly to Carmella, who clasped her gloved hands before her as if in silent prayer.

She turned back to the assistant. "We only need a moment with the deceased. He may be my nephew. Her cousin. He has not been heard of for some time. If you could see it in your heart to let us in, I promise we will not take much of your time."

"The deceased's face is…" The assistant paused again. "He may be difficult to recognize. The police surgeon said he was beaten with a heavy object. And he was in the channel for a while. He has been examined, washed, and cleaned. We did the best we could, but….You must know all this? You were told by the coroner? That is how you knew to come here?"

Inez thought of agreeing with all he said, but was loathe to lie outright in front of Carmella. To her surprise, Carmella said, "That is right. We know about the condition. And we are prepared." She pulled out the handkerchief and waved it, as if it were a magic wand to banish death.

The assistant retreated a step, beaten back by the strong scent of cloves. In the process he pulled the door further open.

Inez set a foot over the threshold, repeating, "We will not

take much of your time." She tried to mix the determination in her tone with notes of gratitude and reassurance. "And we are ever so grateful."

He retreated further. "Please come in, then, Mrs. and Miss…?"

Inez had not considered whether it would be wise or not to give their real names. She mumbled "Stanfort." If it caused problems later, she would claim she had been perfectly clear.

"Stanfort," he repeated. "Please, come in." He directed them into a pocket-sized parlor to the left of the door. Inez spotted a much larger, more formal room on the right, before he said, "A few minutes, please. Please make yourselves comfortable," and closed the door.

Inez sat. Carmella lifted her veil over her hat and commenced pacing.

"It cannot be Jamie," she said, twisting the handkerchief in both hands. "I thought about this, all last night. Otto is always jumping to conclusions. And Otto said himself, the longshoreman did not know for certain. And how well would a longshoreman know Jamie, anyway, if they only met at a few union meetings?"

"That does seem possible. Please, Carmella, come sit." Inez moved a few needlepoint pillows aside on the sofa.

Carmella continued her restless back and forth. "I am certain it is not him. We will see, then we will go home. And Jamie will show up today or tomorrow. The scolding I will give him! I will tell him what happened, and he and I will laugh, and he will reproach Otto for causing us so much worry."

The door opened. The assistant, now be-jacketed, beckoned to them. "Follow me."

As they walked down the hallway, he said, "I covered the head separately. That way, you need not look at the face. We washed his clothes. They are to one side. We do not have any of the items or money the police found in his pockets."

"He had money on him?" *Not a random robbery, then.*

He nodded. "The coroner can give you more details."

He veered left and opened a door, "Usually, Mr. Hamilton stays present for the identification."

"We would like a few private moments," said Carmella. "You needn't worry about us, truly."

"I am not certain Mr. Hamilton would approve," he said plaintively.

Inez herded him out the door. "If you would, just wait outside. If we need you, we will call."

"We have smelling salts," he said as she shut the door.

"Thank you, if we need them we shall call you," said Inez on the other side.

The two women turned to face a simple casket with a figure under a cloth inside. A separate square of material covered the face.

The faint, sweet stench of death wafted toward them. Both women pulled out their clove-scented handkerchiefs.

Inez said, "Let me, Carmella." Holding her linen to her nose, she moved toward the body. She lifted one side of the cloth exposing a hand, wrinkled as a washerwoman's. If the body was of the young pianist, the hand provided no clue. She dropped the sheet and moved to the head, pinching her nostrils closed.

Carmella crowded her shoulder as Inez peeled the cloth back and almost choked.

Inez dropped the cloth over the face. Or what had been a face. She turned to Carmella, wide-eyed above her handkerchief. "Carmella, I cannot tell whether that is Jamie or not. I hoped the hands…but no, they are too changed. Perhaps the clothes or personal effects will tell us something."

Inez moved to the neat stack of clothes on a nearby chair. She picked up a flowered waistcoat on top. "This looks new. I don't recall seeing it on Jamie before, do you?"

Carmella stared at the covered body, her face twisted with indecision, one black-gloved hand clasping the opposite wrist as if to pin it in place. She looked at Inez and the waistcoat. "I've not seen it before."

She released her wrist and reached into the casket, saying, "Mrs. Stannert, please, I hope you do not think less of me. But I must know, and this is the only way I can be sure."

She proceeded to draw the material down from the neck, exposing collarbones, then sternum.

Inez gasped, shocked. "Carmella! What are you doing?" She had always assumed Nico's sister was a proper young woman who, despite an occasional defiant kick against convention, followed the sensibilities and mores of her class. Now, that appeared to not entirely be the case.

A birthmark emerged from beneath the cloth. Large, purple, violent against the dead white skin. Inez watched, speechless, as Carmella revealed a firemark extending over the left side of the chest.

Carmella's voice shook, almost inaudible. "Oh, Jamie." She twisted the sheet back up and turned to Inez, tears spilling down her cheeks. "It's him."

Inez closed her eyes, as if blocking the sight would deny what she now knew was true. *Robert. Jamie is Robert Gallagher.*

Chapter Fifteen

Back in the carriage, Inez listened with half an ear to Carmella's heartfelt outpourings while she wrestled with her discovery.

How had she not seen Jamie Monroe and Robert Gallagher were one and the same? Regardless, there was no doubt now. Now, the immediate question was how much, if anything, to tell Carmella about Jamie's double life.

"He was a good man," Carmella was saying. "Nico couldn't see that. When he saw us talking, even in passing at the store, he would frown. And one time Jamie called on me at home. We were just sitting in the parlor, nothing improper—"

Inez thought of Carmella identifying Jamie by the birthmark. If nothing "improper" happened in the parlor, something most certainly did at some phase in their courtship.

"—and Nico came home. He wasn't supposed to return, not for hours! He was so cold to Jamie and afterwards gave me such a lecture. He said Jamie was ruining me, my reputation, and said he was not the proper young gentleman he portrayed, but a ruffian. He insisted Jamie was an opportunist, a gold digger, only interested in me because I am the sister of the *famous* Nico Donato." She sounded almost hysterical.

"What do you mean?" Inez asked.

"Nico insists I can do better. He wants me to marry someone 'socially acceptable,' rich, someone from Nob Hill. Oh! It is ridiculous. Someone like that would never even look at me, the daughter of a fruitmonger, no matter how much they might call on Nico for his violin. And it wouldn't matter if they did, because I only wanted to marry Jamie!"

Carmella covered her face.

Inez laid a comforting hand on the young woman's shoulder and kept her peace. There was nothing she could say to ease Carmella's grief or shock. Only time would help her to come to terms with her loss.

The carriage rocked on, the squeaks of the harness and rattling of the wheels filling the space. Finally, Carmella's muffled voice emerged. "Have the driver take me home. I cannot bear any more right now." She added, "Please, don't tell Nico any of this."

"I understand. I will not compromise you. However, at some point, the news about Jamie's death may come out. You should prepare yourself. You can talk to me anytime, Carmella. You know where to reach me."

After the carriage dropped Carmella in front of the Donatos' tidy three-story home in the Western Addition, Inez pondered her next steps. No matter how she looked at the situation, it didn't look good. She dismissed her first impulse, which was not to tell Harry. He would tighten the screws until one of two things happened: he either accepted that Robert was unfindable or he found out that Robert was dead and had been living under an assumed name.

No.

She dare not chance that he uncover the connection between Robert and Jamie through his detective or through some other means. She would have to tell him. But when? And how?

And what of Jamie's friends and Nico? They would have to be told at least some of the truth. Once Harry claimed his son's body, perhaps she could simply tell them family had taken Jamie away for a proper burial, which would be true. The focus would then switch to how he died, and why, and who killed him. Inez closed her eyes for a moment. *What a sorry mess.*

She let the sounds of traffic flow over her inside the womblike closure of the carriage.

Now, of course, she could see the resemblance of the son to the father. The way Jamie leaned against the door, his almost colorless light blue eyes, the angular planes of his face, even the studied casualness in his tone and the cold anger that could grip him in a flash. Stance, cadence of speech, physiognomy— all of it was familiar. *Too* familiar. Replace the cigarette with a cigar. Replace the worn overcoat with an elegant, expensive tailcoat. Add a mustache.

Harry.

She shook herself out of her reverie. She couldn't blame herself for not seeing it before. Robert had facial hair in the Leadville photograph, but had been clean-shaven as Jamie in San Francisco. Then, there had been the distraction of having Harry loom over her in close quarters while she examined the image. Even if she had identified Robert from the photograph, it would have been too late. He was already dead.

So, first things first. She would have to meet with Flo and they would have to come up with a plan.

The carriage bumped to a halt in front of D & S House of Music and Curiosities. A window painter was crouched at the large front display pane of glass, methodically scraping off the "S," his cans of white and black paint close by.

For a terrified moment, she thought that Nico had some-how got wind of her past vocations and less savory Leadville investments, and was erasing her from his life and the store name.

Inez disembarked, paid the driver, and hurried over, demanding, "What are you doing?"

He looked up startled.

"I am the manager. What is going on here?"

"Mr. Donato hired me to spell out the store name," he said, and wiped a hand across his forehead. Inez noticed that the creases in his hands and knuckles were traced in white. "Since you're here, I can ask: Stannert is with a double n, right?"

So. Nico was moving forward with the change in name for the store. *That must be what he wanted to talk to me about this morning.* Inez didn't know whether to be relieved or alarmed. In any case, she had more pressing things on her mind, so she let it go.

She looked at her pocket watch. There were only minutes before the infernal noontime bells began their chorus. She stepped to the corner and glanced toward the stock exchange. There were any number of street urchins hovering around, who should probably have been at school but weren't, opting instead to earn pennies by delivering messages to downtown businesses and offices. She hurried up the block, just as the church bells began to ring, and nabbed a boy who looked clean around the ears and therefore perhaps a little more responsible than the rest.

She held up a dime. "I have a very important message that must be delivered in person to a guest at the Palace Hotel. Can you do it? There will be another like this one when you bring back a reply."

He brightened at the sight of the coin. "Sure!"

"It's not a written message. You'll need to commit it to memory, but it's short. I need you to ask for Mrs. Florence Sweet. When you see her—face-to-face, mind—tell her that you have a message from Mrs. Young. The message is this: Mrs. Young has a bonnet that she thinks Mrs. Sweet would like. A very special bonnet. Add that it is urgent that she come as soon as possible. Emphasize 'urgent,' please. And the message goes only to her, you understand?"

He looked at her curiously. "This important message is about hats?"

Inez moved the coin closer to his nose. His eyes almost crossed to keep it in focus.

"Repeat the message back to me, please."

He did.

She nodded her satisfaction. "If she is there, she will give you a message for me. It's important I receive her reply, word for word. If she is not there, come back in any case and let me know that as well. I shall be in the music store over there." She pointed.

Inez returned to the store, switched the sign to OPEN, and retreated to the back. She left the connecting door ajar so she could hear and see if anyone came into the store. Tuesdays were usually quiet, leading her to hope for time to herself until Flo's arrival.

Inez planted herself at the desk but couldn't sit still. She got up, paced around the office, went into the lesson room. Sitting at the student piano, she ran through a few scales and marched perfunctorily through Bach's *Prelude to the Well Tempered Clavichord*. Even the easy, flowing music didn't serve to calm her nerves.

She got up, paced some more, and noticed there was still a pot of coffee on the small stove. Perhaps brewed for her return by John Hee, who did so now and again. No doubt very strong by now.

She grabbed her cup and poured in the dark liquid, pleased that it was still warm. The bottle of brandy in the locked cabinet whispered seductively—*you need me*. She agreed. Inez unlocked the glass doors and added a generous tot to the coffee, wishing she had something more substantial in size than the dainty teacup. Pacing past the desk, she recalled the note to Carmella from Jamie. She supposed she should start thinking of him as "Robert" but just couldn't.

She pulled out the envelope from one of the many cubbyholes and stared at the handwriting on the front.

I shouldn't do this. I should give it to Carmella, sealed.

After a swallow of the laced coffee, she sat at the desk. Placing the cup to one side, she slid the sterling silver letter opener out from a drawer, slit the envelope, and pulled out the single sheet of paper. Inez held the note up and away to put some distance between her prying gaze and his passionate words. Words promising love forever, promising Nico could not keep them apart. *...I am close, dear heart, close to having what I need to win Nico over. I know it means very much to you, to have your brother's blessing, and, upon my life, you shall.*

She set the note down and picked up her coffee.

Upon my life.

What an unfortunate choice of words.

The brandy instilling a comforting glow within, Inez returned to the note and read the rest of the words from the dead man in a rush. *...And please, my sweet Carmella, do not think for a moment I am in danger from this union business. Any threats are toothless, groundless, from cowards who dare not show their faces. I wish you had not heard of them, for I would never in a thousand lifetimes cause you worry on my account. I am close to an answer, I know it. Nothing can happen to me for I am shielded by your love and the truth.*

Love. Truth.

In the end, just how truthful was he with Carmella? He was honest about his philosophy and beliefs, but not about the most basic facts of his life and who he was. Dissembling and wearing a false face to the woman he professed to love.

And what was this about threats? What had Jamie been up to that he felt the need to reassure Carmella that he was not in danger? Did it have to do with his efforts to organize the musicians, or was it something else?

The doorbell clunked.

Inez stood up, hastily shoved the note into the drawer, tossed the empty envelope on top, and went to the entrance of the showroom, expecting the messenger boy. Instead, Frisco Flo Sweet bustled toward her, a gray and rose paisley shawl around her shoulders, a dainty gray hat slanted atop blond curls that looked as if they took hours with a curling iron to get "just so."

"Flo! What are you doing here?"

"You said it was urgent. I decided rather than send a reply, I'd just come myself."

"But…" Inez looked toward the entrance in trepidation.

"Don't worry. Harry and his personal fly-cop are gone for the day. It's been just me, coffee, and the morning paper. Today, I'm planning to visit a few of the more elevated madams that I know. I figure Robert might be an occasional or regular visitor." She stopped. "What is it? What has you in a dither?"

"Come." Inez led her toward the office. "I don't think John Hee is around, but he could be in the repair room. I haven't checked, and we need privacy for this conversation."

"What is it?" Flo repeated once they were in the back room.

Inez put her fingertips to her temples, gazing at Flo. "I know where Robert is."

"Well, where?"

"At the undertaker's." Inez took a deep breath. "He's dead."

Flo stared. "Hell and damnation."

"It gets worse. He is someone I know, or knew. He went by the name James Monroe. Why didn't you tell me he was a pianist?"

"You didn't ask, and I didn't think to say!" Flo sank onto a chair by the round table.

Inez went to the cupboard, tipped a generous portion of brandy into an extra tumbler, and brought bottle and glass to the table. Flo took the glass, almost absent-mindedly. "Was it an accident? Oh please, let it be a runaway horse or streetcar."

Inez shook her head.

"Suicide? Opium overdose? What?"

"Murder."

Flo's wide blue eyes got wider. "No."

"Yes. He was bludgeoned to death, then dumped into the Mission Creek canal."

"*Merde.* Was it a robbery? Or maybe Poole caught up with him first, and carried through on his threat to kill Robert for jilting his daughter." For a moment she looked terrified.

"Perhaps it was completely random," said Inez. "He was down by the waterfront, in a part of town where he had no business being." Jamie's note, the words in a strong angular script, appeared in her mind's eye. "Or maybe it was connected with his union activities. He was trying to form a professional musicians union. I gather there were threats."

Flo said tentatively, "Any chance you're wrong, that this Jamie isn't Robert?"

Inez shook her head.

"So, you *did* know him." Flo looked troubled. "This is very bad. What will Harry think? Was it just a nodding acquaintance? Maybe Robert came through your store once or twice, with others. You could hardly be expected to recognize him from a photograph then."

"Jamie—that is, Robert—was secretly engaged to the sister of the owner of this store."

"Mr. Donato has a sister?"

Inez nodded. "And he was none too happy about the two of them even conversing. Nico should have known better," she said under her breath. "The more he tried to push them apart, the closer they became."

Flo finished off her brandy, poured another, and tipped the bottle toward Inez. Inez held her empty coffee cup up for a refill.

"So," said Inez. "How are we going to explain to Harry?"

"We? Oh no, Inez. I can't. It has to be you. You're the one who figured it out. You're the one who found him."

"Found him too late. Jesus." Inez set her cup down hard, sloshing brandy. "Telling Harry is going to be difficult. And I can't today. I'm alone in the store, I have pupils coming in, meetings lined up. I have to consider how to break the news so he won't turn on me when I do."

"Why would he do that?" Flo asked. "You didn't know you knew Robert. And you *did* find him. Too late, but still. Harry has to know that you did what he asked you to do. It's the only way we'll get out of this mess. It's probably best not to bring up the fiancée. You should mention the union involvement, though."

"I suppose you're right," Inez said bleakly. "I'll have to tell Harry that his son, Robert Gallagher, was going by the name of James Monroe. He was following his dream to be a musician and was involved in the labor movement. The information should come from me. Not the detective he's got sniffing around, nor anyone else. It has to be me."

Chapter Sixteen

Kneeling upstairs in the storage room at her "listening post," Antonia nudged the wooden knot back into the hole in the floor. She sat back on her heels, and pinched her nostrils shut to stop an explosive sneeze.

That was a close one.

She hated to think what would've happened if Mrs. S and Madam Flo had heard a big *ah-choo!* blast through the ceiling above their heads.

But that worry was overshadowed by what she'd heard.

And she'd heard everything.

So if High-and-Mighty Gallagher was in a position to "ruin" Mrs. S and Madam Flo, why weren't they both hightailing over to the Palace Hotel right now to spill the beans to Gallagher about his son being Jamie Monroe and being dead as well?

Jamie.

Dead.

And he and Carmella were engaged? And Mr. Donato didn't know?

Antonia tiptoed to the storeroom door and leaned against it. She pulled out a handkerchief and blew her nose, trying to be quiet about it and thinking about Carmella and how sad it all was.

Did Carmella know about Jamie being dead and a Gallagher and all? Mrs. S didn't say.

Antonia stuffed the handkerchief back into her pocket. It sounded like others were on the prowl, and Mrs. S was worried what would happen if they found out what's what and told Mr. Gallagher first.

Mrs. S said she had to think about what to say and that she couldn't get away from the store. And Madam Flo was too chicken.

So she, Antonia, had to do something to help Mrs. S get out of trouble with Mr. Harry Gallagher. Make him leave them alone and go back to wherever he came from.

There was only one thing to do.

She'd have to go tell Mr. Gallagher herself and make sure he understood that Mrs. S hadn't been keeping anything back from him.

It was up to her.

She had to help Mrs. S out of this jam.

Antonia tiptoed into her room, wary of the creaky floorboards in the hall, and watched from the window until she saw Flo leave. The whorehouse madam got into a hack and headed toward the Barbary Coast. Antonia wondered if the madam was really as desperate as she made out to be. Maybe she just fed Mrs. S nonsense to get Mrs. S to do all the dirty work.

Antonia waited a bit, watching to be sure that Mrs. S wasn't coming out for any reason.

After that, sneaking down the stairs, out the door, and around the corner was easy as pie. Once out of sight of the storefront, Antonia relaxed. She made a beeline for the Palace Hotel, and walked in like she lived there. Which she had, at least for a while.

When she and Mrs. S had first come to the city, Mrs. S had set up shop in the Palace and Antonia had the run of the place before she was forced to start school. And the Palace Hotel was huge, the biggest building Antonia'd ever seen. A bellboy had told her there were more than eight hundred rooms and more than four hundred bathtubs! And it was built with more than thirty-one million bricks! Antonia thought maybe he was trying to pull the wool over her eyes on that last figure. For one thing, who'd count all those bricks?

Entering now, she was again struck by the courtyard where the carriages drove up. The courtyard was surrounded by floor after floor of arcaded galleries, all looking down on who was coming and going. Antonia remembered the days when she'd spend hours peering over the railing outside their room, watching the activity far below.

She'd liked the Palace Hotel. Lots of places to explore, hide, and spy. No one nattering at her to work on her penmanship or memorize lines of useless poetry.

But no more remembering.

She had a mission.

Antonia marched through the main entrance, into the lobby, right over the fancy tiled floor, right up to the desk, gaining a few stares from the toffs who probably wondered why she was walking in, bold as brass, rather than coming in through the ladies' door. As she'd hoped, the nob with the over-starched stand-up collar standing behind the desk hurried over, saying, "Excuse me, miss, can I help you?"

"You can, my good man." She used a haughty, high-toned voice, like the one that Mrs. Stannert had used when talking to the Palace "staff." For good measure, she tilted her nose in the air so she looked high and mighty herself. Good thing she was wearing her school clothes and they weren't all mussed up. "I must speak with Mr. Gallagher. Please tell him I have an important, private message for him from Mrs. Stannert."

"Certainly. Why don't you wait in here?" Starched-Collar Nob marched her out of the lobby and into the ladies' reception room.

"And tell him," Antonia continued imperiously, "that it is a matter of some urgency, about his son." *That'll get his attention.* "But I must speak with him privately," Antonia admonished.

Nob did a small bow, so she must've done it right. "Of course, Miss. May I tell Mr. Gallagher who is calling?"

She hadn't expected *that.* "I am Miss Gizzi, a ward of Mrs. Stannert's. However, my name will not mean anything to him. Just tell him, please, that it concerns Master Robert Gallagher."

Now the nob seemed a little suspicious, but he inclined his head and said, "Please wait here, Miss Gizzi."

The waiting took longer than she thought it would. At first, she thought maybe Gallagher wasn't in and she'd end up cooling her heels until he returned from wherever he was. And then, she started to wonder if maybe Gallagher hadn't gone off to see Mrs. S. Maybe even now he was demanding what did she think she was doing, sending a messenger girl when it should have been the missus herself coming to tell him whatever it was that was so urgent?

She started to seriously sweat in her flannel petticoat and woolen stockings. It was because it was so warm inside, she told herself, not because she was nervy or anything like that. She'd just taken off her glasses to clean them—they were all fogged up—when a bellboy came into the reception room and looked around. His gaze stopped on her. She hastily stuffed her glasses in a pocket as he walked over. "Miss Gizzi."

"That is I," she said primly.

"Mr. Gallagher will see you now. Please follow me."

They headed for the elevators, and Antonia silently rejoiced. When she and Mrs. S were staying at the hotel, Antonia'd loved going up and down in the elevators. She could've done it all day. The grille closed, and the operator pulled levers, pushed buttons, and the elevator rose silently, giving her that special thrill in her stomach.

They rose higher and higher. "Seventh floor," announced the operator.

That was when Antonia began to wonder if she'd made a mistake.

The seventh floor held some of the grandest of the grand rooms. The ones with really tall ceilings and windows that looked out over the city, making you feel like you were living in the clouds. Antonia knew this because the bellboy who'd fed her the bosh about millions of bricks had once brought her up here and opened a door to let her peek inside.

And now, she was being led right to one of those doors! For a corner room!

Antonia began to sweat more.

The bellboy knocked. A voice inside called "Enter."

He opened the door, said, "Miss Gizzi, sir," and turned to Antonia giving her that head-wag that said, "Go on, get in there!"

Knees quaking, Antonia entered. The bellboy closed the door, nearly clipping her heels. Her feet sank into the deep carpet as she looked warily around. The far windows, curtains drawn back, gave her the view she expected—a view of the city, fit for gods, letting in light that almost blinded her.

The man standing in the middle of the parlor was dressed like he was going to some swank party on Nob Hill, even though it was only afternoon. He was older and taller than Antonia thought he would be, with silver hair, and a dark mustache and eyebrows. But then, she'd only seen him from above through the knothole. His eyebrows were drawn together in a frown, although all he said was "Miss Gizzi, is it? You told the front desk officer that Mrs. Stannert sent you. Is that true?"

He didn't invite her to come in, have a seat. And Antonia was glad, because she wanted to stay right where she was, with the doorknob close at hand for a quick escape.

She'd originally intended to quiz whoever claimed to be Mr. Gallagher to be sure she had the right gent, but she'd abandoned that idea the minute she'd stepped into the room and saw him.

This was Mr. Harry Gallagher, for sure.

And now, all she wanted to do was say what she'd come to say and get out as fast as possible. "I have a message for you. From Mrs. St-Stannert," she stuttered. "About your son, Robert Gallagher."

The frown deepened. His words were "And that message is?" but his tone said things like *I am a busy man* and *don't keep me waiting* and definitely *I doubt you are who you say you are.*

The speech Antonia had worked up on the way to the hotel now came out in a nervous jumbly rush. "Mrs. Stannert wants you to know, he, uh, your son, he's in the city. He changed his name to Jamie, uh, James Monroe. He's a pianist. And, I'm sorry sir, I really am, but he's dead."

Mr. Gallagher didn't move, but Antonia got the distinct impression that her confused recitation had hit him like a hammer, a hammer that froze something inside him, turning him into a statue of ice.

"What?" he said. He said it quiet, but all it did was make Antonia wish she'd never ever set foot outside the storage room on the second floor above the music store.

"He, he died over by Long Bridge. That's where they found him. The police, that is. He was beaten pretty badly. It was hard to tell it was him."

"Who are you?" He boomed.

Did he think she was lying to him, making it all up?

"It's true!" she burst out. She reached for the doorknob behind her back, grasped it.

He started walking toward her. "And why would Mrs. Stannert send someone like you, a mere child, to tell me this?"

Now she was *really* in for it.

He reached for her, as if to grab her shoulder.

She twisted the door open, tumbled out into the hallway, and ran faster than she thought she could, heading for the nearest iron staircase. *Use that staircase only in case of emergency, if there is a fire*—that was Mrs. S's voice reminding her. And well, this wasn't a fire, but it sure was an emergency.

Antonia yanked the iron door open and pounded down the flight of stairs, the iron ringing as loud as any of the church bells in her ears. On reaching the sixth floor she burst out into the hallway, hurtled past startled guests, and, flying on memory and instinct, zigzagged through a maze of hallways and corridors to one of the servants' staircases. In this manner, she made her way down floor after floor, moving between wings and various staircases. Between the third and second floor, she finally slowed down, gasping, and used her sleeve to wipe her nose, which was full of snot from the stupid cold, leaving a wet streak on the blue plaid fabric.

Hand on the door to the second floor, she pushed it open slowly. Nothing unusual. No horde of bellmen or cops waiting to nab her and haul her back up to the seventh floor to face Gallagher for questioning.

She slid out into the hallway. Keeping her pace sedate, she headed for an obscure staircase, far away from the lobby and the grand courtyard, which led out to a side street.

It was only then Antonia realized that Gallagher hadn't chased her or shouted at her to come back or stop. He hadn't even, it seemed, alerted the desk to have her hunted down and hauled back to him for further questioning.

So what was he doing?

The probable answer only made her knees—already shaking from all the stairs and the running—feel like they were going to give way entirely.

He's gone to see Mrs. S.

She's gonna murder me.

Chapter Seventeen

Inez listened with half a mind as Patrick May, son of laundress Molly May, hunched over the upright piano in the lesson room, doing a very credible job on Clementi's Sonatina in C, Opus 36, Number 3. Patrick's kinky red hair, pomaded into submission when he first sat down to the lesson, was now in disarray. He focused on his hands, his face with its café-au-lait skin sprinkled with freckles and acne, twisted in concentration.

When he was done, Inez said, "Very nice, Patrick. Your fingering for the scale passages is good, and in general you are handling the different tempos well. Watch the small ornamental note in the fourteenth measure. Begin slowly and gradually increase the tempo."

He nodded, green eyes as focused on her now as they had been on his hands earlier.

"And watch your posture. Sit straight, near the edge of the stool. Keep your forearms parallel to the floor. Pay attention to your shoulders. When they are raised up around your ears, it causes unnecessary stress. Playing well requires a balance between focus, a certain amount of tension, and free, flexible movement. Again, please."

He straightened his back, shook out his hands and rolled his shoulders, then placed his fingertips on the keys and closed his eyes. Inez recognized the pose. She often did the same thing herself, gathering her wits and awareness before launching into a piece. In the quiet pause, she reflected briefly on the Mays. Patrick's mother, Molly, and his aunt, Bessie, were two of her business clients. The Mays were the hardest working, most determined women she knew, which is why she had advanced them a sizeable loan to rebuild their small laundry recently ravaged by fire.

Always on time with their payments, they were building a loyal clientele, slowly, over time. Bessie took care of the heavy laundry work, channeling her ire at the unfairness of the world and their lot into the vigorous washing, bleaching, wringing, and drying. Molly was in charge of the more precise tasks of ironing and sewing. A skilled seamstress, she could repair a silk stocking such that you never saw the run, a man's fine shirt such that you never detected the tear. Impressed, Inez sent her and Antonia's things to the Mays for cleaning, knowing that they would come back looking as if they were new bought.

When Bessie first came to Inez's office looking for a loan on behalf of the sisters, she had spilled out far more of their convoluted family history than Inez had cared or desired to know, invoking God's name only when she railed against him and her sister.

"That Molly, my sister, she brought disgrace upon our family. If you don't know that already, well, you will soon enough, so I'll tell you now. Disowned by mother, father, uncles, aunts, everyone. I stood by her. The only one. I'm her sister, and I told them, they could throw me out too. I'd not see my sister and her baby starving in the streets. God will see them all in Hell for their lack of charity. Molly having a bastard child, well, that's bad enough, but when the child's of tainted blood, they couldn't spare a Christian thought on them."

She had wheeled around pointing a finger accusingly at Inez, as if Inez had said the words, and not her. "It doesn't matter who or what his father was. Patrick, he's better than all of them that turned their backs on us. Better than his mother or me, and I dare anyone to say otherwise. He's a smart boy. A courteous boy. Works hard. A good heart."

The "boy" Patrick, actually fifteen or so and well on his way to being a young man, possessed a polite demeanor and an uncommon musical talent. He had been at one of the Mays' first meetings with Inez, had drifted over to the student piano, and asked permission to play. Upon hearing him sound out a skillful two-handed rendition of "I'll Take You Home Again, Kathleen," the sisters and Inez were astonished. When Patrick was asked for an accounting, he'd ducked his head and said, "I hear music on the wharf. The tunes go in my head and out my hands."

Inez had offered him free lessons on the spot.

He was prompt and confided he had access to a piano in a bar close to home. "They let me practice sometimes. My ma doesn't know, auntie neither, but I don't get into trouble, and the owner says as long as I play for free, he doesn't care." Inez was impressed with his progress, but sorrowed that as a mulatto and of poor birth, Patrick would find his employment opportunities limited.

When Patrick finished, she said, "Much better." She stood, saying, "Next week, then?"

He nodded and rose.

Even through the ordinary routine of lessons and business, Inez found that the conundrum of Jamie's death and the looming confrontation with Harry weren't far from her mind. She had been wracking her brain, trying to think of something she could do, something she could offer to ease the blow.

She kept coming back to the same questions.

Who killed the young musician?

And why?

Was it strictly a random attack?

If so, why did he still have money in his pockets when his body was rolled into the canal?

Perhaps by visiting the area by Long Bridge, the scene of his demise—or at least where he was found—she might make some sense from what seemed a senseless situation. It wasn't a bad part of town during the daylight hours.

Then, she remembered. "Patrick, do I recall correctly that your laundry is near Long Bridge?"

He nodded.

"How is the rebuilding coming along after the fire?"

He ducked his head and passed his hand over the tight curls. She resisted the impulse to hand him a comb. "We's got a load of bricks t'other day. I have to work on the wall when I get home."

She winced at the thought of his expressive pianist's hands wielding a trowel and mortar. "I should come down and see how things are progressing."

He looked alarmed.

"I just want to be certain your aunt and mother are getting the assistance they need," she assured him. "You can't rebuild it all by yourself! Perhaps hiring a laborer would make sense, hurry up the process. It can't be easy running a laundry in a place that is still under construction."

"No'm. My ma and aunt, well, they work all the time, and there's plenty of business, but like you said, it's hard."

"That settles it then. Please tell your aunt and mother I will be coming around tomorrow."

"Yes'm."

After Patrick left, she returned to her desk and picked up the agreement she was to go over with the milliner, Mrs. Young, later that day. Her mind kept going back to Jamie's death. The discovery that Jamie was Robert Gallagher. Carmella's reaction. The dreaded meeting she would have to have with Harry.

Perhaps she should call the Palace Hotel now and ask him to come to the store.

No.

That was a bad idea.

In addition to the visit from Mrs. Young, she was expecting a buyer that afternoon for one of their upright pianos. He had brought his wife in the previous week, and the missus had given the nod for buying a compact, sound-worthy Steinway.

The sale would add a tidy sum to the month's income. Inez certainly didn't want to be embroiled in a conversation with Harry about the death of his son and have someone walk in. It would be best to talk with him after hours. Perhaps, if the store was slow at end of the day, she could close early and arrange to meet him at the hotel.

Damn Flo for gallivanting off to the Barbary Coast that afternoon. "I might be able to find out what happened to Robert," she'd said. "Besides, I have friends in that quarter of the city and elsewhere to catch up with. Best to do so before business hours."

"You know madams in San Francisco?" This was news to Inez.

"Oh, I never told you? Before I came to Colorado I spent a few years here. Hence, the 'Frisco Flo' moniker." She winked. "Being from the Paris of the West adds a little exotic allure."

The entry bell clunked. The door squeaked open and slammed shut, with violence. Inez glanced at the pocket watch she'd put on the corner of the desk, surprised to see the time. The day was fleeing away. She stood and walked toward the passage. "Antonia, is that you?"

She was greeted by the sight of Harry Gallagher storming toward her.

Inez involuntarily retreated a step. Part of her wanted to slam the passage door in his face and escape out the back into the alley. Instead, she stiffened her resolve and moved forward to meet him, trying to control the shakiness in her limbs. "Mr. Gallagher, what—?"

He seized her by the arm and without a word propelled her into the office area. He was dressed as always—impeccably, expensively—but there was something wild and alarming in his eye.

He banged the door shut behind them, saying, "Did you send her with that message?"

Inez's first thought was maybe Flo had had a change of heart and screwed up her courage to tell Harry about his son. That hope exploded when he said in barely controlled rage, "Little Miss Gizzi. Did you send her to tell me of my son's death? My son's *death*. You couldn't do me the courtesy of telling me to my face or even writing a note, for God's sake? You handed over the responsibility of relaying information of such a nature to a child?"

"What? No!" Inez, alarmed, was caught off guard. "Antonia? Antonia Gizzi came to see you? And she, she told you, about—"

He shook her arm, cutting her off. "About Robert masquerading as someone named James Monroe while playing out his fantasy of being a musician in San Francisco. Yes, she did. Albeit very poorly. She told me he was dead, then scampered away. It took me a trip to the police station, a talk with the Police Chief and the Police Surgeon, to find out where Robert was and—" Harry stopped. It was as if a train barreling down the track had slammed into a granite wall.

He shoved Inez away. "This. This was beneath you, Inez." Fury mixed with his despair.

Inez staggered a little, then recovered. "I grieve for your loss, Harry, but I assure you, I did not send Antonia to you with such a message. Do you truly think I would stoop to that? I have no idea, *none*, how she even knows about your son. I only worked it out this morning."

"You *worked it out*," he said. The anger vanished and a mask settled over his face. "I was told by the undertaker a Mrs. Stanfort came by to identify him. Clearly that was you. And you had your niece in tow. Miss Gizzi?"

Inez decided to sidestep that one. "Antonia is my ward, but she calls me aunt. Honestly, I had no idea he was your son. I knew him as James Monroe."

"How did you identify him, then?" Harry's eyes bore into hers. "He was unrecognizable."

She cleared her throat and looked away. "Your son has, had, a distinctive mark." She looked back at Harry and hastily added, "Flo knew about it. She told me."

He closed his eyes. "She would," he muttered.

"I didn't know your son was using a false name. I swear, Harry, I had no idea until then."

Only his compressed, downturned mouth, the sudden age that weighted his shoulders, showed the burden he now carried.

He pointed to a nearby chair, indicating she should sit.

Inez did so, her heart pounding like a fist on a door. She heartily wished she could vanish on the spot.

Standing above her, he reached into his waistcoat pocket, pulled out his pocket watch—silver engraved and attached with a silver chain—clicked it open, glanced at the face, clicked it shut, and put it away. The process was mechanical, more as if he had wanted a space of time to collect his thoughts and contain his emotions rather than check the time.

He began. "This is what will happen now, Mrs. Stannert. I am going to have my son prepared so I can take him Back East for a proper burial as befits his station. In the meantime, I have business in Virginia City. While I am gone, you, Mrs. Sweet, and Mr. de Bruijn—whom I am certain Mrs. Sweet has told you about—are going to *work out* who killed my son. When I return, you will tell me what you have found. You have a week."

"What about the police?" Inez managed to croak out. "Aren't they investigating? Whatever information we uncover, surely we should tell them."

His laugh, short, bitter, cut off as if with a hatchet. "The police? The kind of justice my son's killer deserves will not be meted out by the law. For suspects, I suggest you start with Phillip Poole, the man who accused my son of driving his daughter mad with despair and causing her death."

She tried to reason this through, give him the benefit of the doubt for what he was saying. He was crazy with grief, surely. But with someone like Harry, it didn't matter if he was thinking straight or not. He would do what he set out to do. And if he commanded you to do something, whether it made sense or not, whether it was foolhardy or not, you did it, or there would be hell to pay. She softened her voice. "Please, be reasonable. I did not lie to you. I did not betray you. I will do what I can, but—"

The muffled clunk of the entry bell penetrated the closed door. Off in the distance, from another part of her life, she heard the gentleman who had promised to return with check in hand for a piano for his wife call out, "Excuse me, Mrs. Stannert? Is anyone here?"

She stood, bringing herself closer to his level. "How am I supposed to do this? I cannot go gallivanting all over the city. The police and your detective are better equipped to do this than me. I have a business to run."

"You have connections in the music world that they do not. You *knew* my son. If you had only told me this when we first talked." His hands opened and closed by his sides, as if grasping for something, anything, that could change what was, turn back time.

He finally turned and opened the door for her to pass, saying, "I have said what I came to say. If you do not get busy and find who murdered my son, I swear to you, your business will be the least of your worries. I will make sure you rue the day you ever set foot in San Francisco."

Chapter Eighteen

De Bruijn returned to the Palace Hotel after a long day spent trying to determine the lot of San Francisco's musicians, whether there was a musicians union formed or forming, and if so, who was involved. He suspected if young Gallagher was in San Francisco, he would surface in a labor movement, given his leanings in that direction. From what de Bruijn had learned, the young man was as determined to bring "rights" to the workingman as a moth was determined to destroy itself in a flame.

He had made tours of union haunts, musical venues such as music halls, theaters, public gardens and parks, and newspaper offices. Journalists, he knew, were always willing to talk about local doings for the price of a free drink. Musicians were much the same, more than happy to dissect the current state of affairs of their particular world.

De Bruijn had limited his own intake. He had to stay coherent and sharp, otherwise it would be difficult to determine who was telling the truth and who was dissembling in hopes of caging an extra drink.

All his efforts had provided but one slim lead: a young man by the name of James Monroe. Recently settled in the city, a pianist, he had been seen at rallies and sandlot gatherings, talking up the creation of a new musicians union. From what de Bruijn gleaned, there wasn't much support from the musical rank and file, but that hadn't dampened Monroe's ardor.

When shown a photograph, some thought Monroe bore some resemblance to young Gallagher. Others shook their heads.

Monroe, it turned out, was one of a larger group hanging around the D & S House of Music and Curiosities. An odd coincidence, given that Mrs. Stannert was involved with the store in some capacity.

Only, de Bruijn didn't believe in coincidences.

He planned to pay Mrs. Stannert a visit early tomorrow and see what she had to say.

Right now, however, he had one more person to see before reporting to his client.

He found Miss Elizabeth O'Connell, part-time Pinkerton and occasional freelance personal agent, enjoying a cup of tea in the tropical garden off the Palace Hotel's central court. De Bruijn sank into the chair opposite hers. "Are you enjoying your tea, Miss O'Connell?"

"Indeed. The scones are superb. My thanks to you and Mr. Gallagher." She gave him a tight, thin little smile, which for Miss O'Connell passed for approval. In her late twenties or early thirties, of middling height, auburn hair, light brown eyes, and fair complected, Miss O'Connell could have passed for a primary school teacher, or a private elocutionist. Or some other profession suitable for an as-yet-unmarried daughter of a middle-class father who came from the Emerald Isle in '49 with a lust for gold and settled for a comfortable living as a shop owner. But that was just what he had managed to discern from occasional conversations and a preliminary search he had conducted before hiring her some years ago when he was in San Francisco for a different client.

In truth, he knew little about her, except that Miss O'Connell was thorough, observant, punctual, well-regarded by Pinkerton himself, and didn't mind taking on a "side job" now and again when the pay was right. He also knew from past experience that she possessed an iron will and nerve, seldom on display, swathed underneath impeccable manners and a soft voice, much as he envisioned the steel stays of her corset were swathed by layers of sensible linen and wool.

Not that he had personal knowledge of what sort of unmentionables Miss O'Connell preferred. He simply suspected they were of the no-nonsense, no-frills variety.

Quite the opposite, for instance, of those Mrs. Sweet displayed in such a casual, some would say "shocking" manner—tossed about her room, on the rug, on the chairs, even hanging from the harp in her parlor.

And that brought him to…

"What did our lady of dubious reputation and indefatigable energy do today while I was exploring the lot of the working-man in your fair city?" asked de Bruijn.

Miss O'Connell pursed her lips for a sip, then set the china cup down carefully on the saucer. "Mrs. Sweet didn't arise until almost eleven. Much time was spent in front of the mirror at that point. Shortly thereafter, an urchin showed up with an 'urgent' message. Something about hats."

"Really?" He was impressed. "How did you come by this information?"

"She asked for a maid to come help her dress. The maid was happy enough to provide details for a modest tip."

He nodded encouragingly.

"After the message was delivered, Mrs. Sweet took off like a bat out of…Well." Miss O'Connell smiled demurely. "I followed her, as you instructed. She went to the music store you had mentioned and spent quite a while inside. When she came out, she seemed distressed. That is just my opinion, you understand. She then took a hack through the Barbary Coast, dawdled through Morton Lane, and stopped in at three of the higher-class 'disorderly houses,' the last being Diamond Carrie Maclay's at 205 Post." She sighed. "During those visits, it was a lot of waiting around, Mr. de Bruijn. I can't tell you what transpired inside for obvious reasons. She kept her hack waiting, which certainly cost her a pretty penny, as you will see when you get the bill for my own transportation."

"No matter," assured de Bruijn. "Mr. Gallagher will cover it."

She tilted her head a little, her gaze drifting upward, as if recalling the timing of events. "It was almost five when she finally emerged, took the hack back here to the hotel, and proceeded to her rooms. The maid was called up. She has instructions to contact you with any further developments." Miss O'Connell glanced at de Bruijn. "For what it's worth, I do believe the visit to Carrie's involved heavy imbibing, for she was not altogether steady on her feet once she returned."

"Thank you." De Bruijn pulled an envelope with the agreed-upon payment from his jacket and placed it at her elbow on the damask tablecloth.

She slid it into her satchel. De Bruijn glimpsed a book and the nickel-plated flash of a revolver inside before she closed it tight, saying, "Thank you for your patronage and the tea. As I said before, it's good to see you again, after all this time. Should you have further need of my services—"

"I know where to reach you," he finished.

They both stood, shook hands, and she left, pulling the modest collar of her sensible brown overcoat up high around her neck.

From there, it was up the elevator to the seventh floor.

He stopped outside the door to the suite and listened. All was quiet.

So, according to Miss O'Connell's report, it seemed that Mrs. Sweet had spent her afternoon checking some of the higher-class brothels for signs of Robert Gallagher, just as she had promised she would.

But why stop at the music store?

He tucked that question away for later and knocked on the door.

"Enter," came the voice from within.

De Bruijn obliged.

He was shocked, but only briefly, at the sight of Mr. Gallagher sitting in one chair, dressed for the evening, while Mrs. Sweet slouched, her face full of sullen storm, in another chair, dressed for…Well, the silk dressing gown was a fit prelude to retiring, although the hour argued against it.

"A change of plans," said Gallagher, and motioned de Bruijn to a third, nearby chair.

"A change of plans?" De Bruijn took the indicated seat. The arrangement of the chairs placed him at the apex of a very sharp triangle.

"Robert is dead," said Gallagher. "Through violent means, in a part of town he had no business being in."

De Bruijn sat back in the chair, stunned.

Mrs. Sweet shifted uneasily, the fabric of her dressing gown shimmering.

Gallagher stared at him, his face a mask. A half-smoked cigar held between two fingers sent a languishing curl of smoke up toward the high ceiling.

It occurred to de Bruijn that this was how so many of the men of Gallagher's standing responded to the death of those close to them—at least publicly. They continued as they were, the clues to their grief small but detectable, if you knew what to look for. They buttoned their jackets more slowly. Polished their spectacles more thoroughly. Checked their pocket watches more often. Spoke in careful, mechanical monotones.

De Bruijn finally said, "This is terrible. My condolences, sir."

Gallagher drew on his cigar, then exhaled, waving de Bruijn's words away with the smoke. "He was living in the city under an assumed name.

Mrs. Sweet covered her mouth. She was, de Bruijn noted, uncomfortable with the turn of conversation. He looked back at Gallagher. "How—?"

"How did I find out?" A bitter smile escaped, then vanished. "A young girl came to the hotel early today, demanding to speak with me. Said she had a private message purportedly from Mrs. Stannert. Little Miss Gizzi."

Gizzi!

De Bruijn lost track of what Gallagher was saying. It was as if having been delivered one blow in the boxing ring that made him stagger, he received a second that sent him to the mat.

He dragged his attention back to Gallagher's voice. "After telling me Robert was dead and directing me to the police, she took off like a jackrabbit."

"What did she look like, this girl?" de Bruijn asked.

Gallagher paused. "Small. Dark." He frowned. "Unusual eyes."

De Bruijn tensed. "Unusual?"

"One was noticeably dark, brown, perhaps. The other a light blue."

A chill, almost electric, ran through him. Could finding Antonia Gizzi at last be as simple as finding Mrs. Stannert? Could he dare hope? She had been elusive for so long.

Gallagher continued, "I leave before dawn tomorrow for business in Virginia City. My son's body will remain in San Francisco for preparation for his final journey East. I met with Mrs. Stannert earlier today. I am telling you what I said to her and, just now, to Mrs. Sweet. You three are going to find who killed Robert. I expect you to work with Mrs. Stannert and keep Mrs. Sweet here from running wild. Use whatever resources you have at your disposal. This is your expertise, Mr. de Bruijn, finding what is lost. I needn't tell you how to conduct this business. I will return in a week, expecting that you will have an answer for me."

"And if we don't?" Flo sneered.

Harry looked at her, emotionless. "I believe I've made it clear what I am prepared to do, Mrs. Sweet."

The silk quilted dressing gown hissed on the upholstery as Flo slid to the edge of the chair, puffing up in defiance like one of the pigeons that strutted the city avenues. She bounced to her feet, grabbed the ends of the braided cord belt looped loosely around the gown and tugged the ends tight, cinching it closed. "Screw you, Harry!"

De Bruijn wondered if he would be called upon to keep the madam from attacking his client.

Gallagher simply said, "Mrs. Sweet, you're drunk."

"And to think, I actually felt *sorry* for you, because you lost your son." The slur in her words was pronounced. "But you lost him long ago. And you're still the same bastard you've always been." With that, she stormed across the parlor into one of the two adjoining apartments, and slammed the door behind her.

Harry set his cigar down in the ashtray at his elbow. "She'll come to her senses in the morning." He stood. "I have arrangements to make for the morrow."

"Of course," De Bruijn took the hint and rose, glancing at the ornate ormolu clock on the parlor mantel.

Still early.

Plenty of time to put his own change of plans in effect and pay a surprise visit on Mrs. Stannert and, with luck, Antonia Gizzi.

Chapter Nineteen

As soon as Harry departed, Inez stormed up to the apartment, ready to whip the living daylights out of Antonia. She couldn't fathom what had compelled her ward, first of all, to skip school, and then to eavesdrop and take the information directly to the one man who could cause their lives to tumble about their ears.

What the hell was she thinking?

But Antonia wasn't there.

Inez grabbed her silver-backed hairbrush and brought it with her to the store, ready to mete out punishment when the truant finally appeared.

But as the hours ticked by and there was no sign of her, anger began to darken into worry.

Where was she? Could something have happened to her? Surely she didn't run away. Most likely, she was somewhere in town, reluctant to come home. Inez knew that, as often as she admonished Antonia to avoid the Barbary Coast and Chinatown, those areas were like a magnet for youngsters of an adventurous turn of spirit. And Antonia, chafing in her petticoats, was nothing if not adventurous.

Inez paced from the office to the lesson room, ears attuned for the clank of the entry bell. Instead, she heard the sweet strains of a violin coming from the front of the store. Curious, she ventured into the showroom. The music was coming from the repair room.

John Hee?

He must have come in while she was upstairs looking for Antonia. Inez headed to the repair alcove and twitched the curtain aside. John Hee stood, his back to her, playing to the brick wall and the counter where he did repairs. She waited, hating to break the flow of music. After about a minute, she cleared her throat. Hee lowered the violin and turned around, "Mrs. Stannert," he said, seeming not at all surprised to see her there. "Testing the tone," he added, as if by way of explanation. "To see if soundpost in correct place."

"Lovely music," said Inez. "I didn't want to interrupt you. However, I am wondering, have you seen Antonia?" She surveyed the room. A partially disassembled brass instrument along with bits of brass tubing, springs, and tools occupied one side of the counter. On the far end, some small Oriental curios were half visible in a rucksack.

Hee returned to the counter, closed the satchel, and shut the violin in its case. "She not upstairs?"

"No." Inez's throat constricted. "It is close to dark. She is never this late."

"Time for me to go," said Hee. "I will look for her on my way."

"If she is in Chinatown this time of night…" Inez couldn't finish the sentence.

Hee shrugged into his jacket and picked up his wide-brimmed hat. "She has much common sense. Do not worry, Mrs. Stannert. She take care of herself."

Inez hoped so. She turned and opened the curtain. Startled, she stepped back, inadvertently treading on the toe of Hee's boot.

A strange gentleman stood on the other side of the display case of music boxes. However, he wasn't looking at the merchandise, but at her, as if he had been waiting for Inez and John Hee to appear.

Inez's first thought: *Why didn't I hear the bell?*

Cantankerous though it was, it had been, up to now, reliable, and she was well attuned to its metallic note, hearing its alert even from the back rooms.

Her next thought: *How long has he been standing there?* Followed by: *Who is he?*

Her initial impression of him was that, whoever he was, he was a neat and careful man. From his brushed dark gray derby to the muted checked overcoat in somber browns and grays to his polished black boots, he appeared no different from the city's multitudes of businessmen. A bamboo walking stick with an L-shaped, elegantly carved ivory handle provided the single mark of distinction. He had straight dark hair, a short, well-groomed Van Dyke beard, the mustache curling up a bit at the ends. His large brown eyes focused unwaveringly upon her. In a voice as careful and neat as his appearance, he asked, "Do I have the pleasure of addressing Mrs. Stannert?"

John Hee moved to stand by her side. Her hand automatically slid into the hidden pocket of her skirt before she recalled it was empty. The small Remington Smoot pocket revolver she had always carried with her in Leadville was not there but tucked away in her nightstand upstairs.

The gentleman's gaze didn't shift, but Inez sensed he was quite aware of Hee's movements and her inadvertent hand-to-pocket gesture.

She didn't see any reason to deny who she was. *My bloody name is now writ in black and gilt on the store's window right beside Nico's.* "Yes, I am Mrs. Stannert. And you are?"

He tipped his hat. "De Bruijn. Wolter Roeland de Bruijn."

Inez sucked in her breath. "From Mr. Gallagher, yes?"

"Correct."

Inez set her jaw. *Harry certainly wasted no time. First, he tells me that I am to work with Flo and his henchman de Bruijn to find his son's murderer. Then, he sends de Bruijn to dictate how we are to do his bidding.* Inez turned to John Hee. "Thank you, John. You may go."

"I stay, do more repairs."

Inez was grateful to him for offering to stay so she would not be alone in the store with a stranger.

"It's quite all right, Mr. Hee. I was expecting Mr. de Bruijn. Just not this evening." She shot the detective a venomous glance.

John Hee nodded and, with a final glance at de Bruijn, walked toward the door, his rucksack over one shoulder.

Inez called to him, "If you would, please turn the sign to CLOSED."

He did, and the bell declared his departure with a soft clunk. Inez crossed her arms and said without preamble, "As you no doubt know, Mr. Gallagher came here earlier today and said what he intended to say. He was quite clear. Are you here to expand upon his demands?"

"I am not here about that. Although since you brought it up, I think it would be wise if you, Mrs. Sweet, and I met to coordinate our activities. Perhaps tomorrow morning at nine in the American Dining Room of the Palace Hotel? Breakfast courtesy of Mr. Gallagher, of course."

"I don't need Mr. Gallagher's charity," snapped Inez. "A free breakfast will hardly make up for him threatening to rip my life to shreds."

"True. But he has lost his son and now wishes us to work together to find out the who and why behind his son's death. We haven't much time. The least we can do is be efficient in our investigation and not duplicate efforts."

"Very well. Tomorrow morning at the Palace Hotel." Inez came out from behind the music box display case, aiming for the door. "I shall let you out."

De Bruijn shifted to block her path. "Excellent. However, I am here on another matter."

A prickle of wariness moved down her neck. "What then?"

"Antonia Gizzi."

The prickle became a chill. "Who *are* you?"

"Wolter Roeland de Bruijn," he repeated patiently. "I knew Antonia's mother, Drina Gizzi." For the first time, she detected a flicker of emotion, a slight compression of the lips, a flicker of the eyes, a tightening of the gloved hands over the handle. He added, "In Denver, before Leadville."

"You." Inez's heart pounded as if it would come right through the metal and satin stays. "You are Mr. Brown."

He raised his eyebrows.

"You are the one who abandoned them in Leadville. Antonia told me the story. Although she never met you face to face, she knew you visited her mother. You sent them away from Denver to a hotel in Leadville, with promises to take care of them and to support them. You promised Antonia's mother you would follow directly. But you didn't." She advanced toward him.

He didn't move, leaving them standing far closer than Inez preferred. They were nearly eye to eye, of equal height. She continued, "Instead, the monies stopped, and they were cast out into the street to make do however they could. You abandoned them."

"That isn't true," he said finally. "It is a long story. One that took time to unravel once I arrived in Leadville. I did send them funds. Every month. The funds were diverted at the hotel desk." A cold shadow crossed his face. "The desk clerk thought to enrich himself at Drina and Antonia's expense. He lost much more than coinage as a result."

Suppressing a shudder, Inez decided she would not pursue that particular line of questioning. "You told them you would join them soon. Half a year later, they were still waiting. Drina believed up to the end that you would come save them from the horror their lives had become. She never lost faith in you."

De Bruijn looked away. "I was detained. I explained it all in letters, which, along with the funds, never reached them. I came to Leadville shortly after you left. In fact, it could be we crossed paths at the train station—you leaving, me arriving."

With apparent effort, he dragged his gaze back to Inez, facing her suspicions, her open disdain. "It took me a long time to uncover what had happened to Drina and to determine Antonia was not in town. Although I eventually learned of your connection to the Gizzis, I did not know Antonia left with you. When I learned you were here, I hoped you might have information about Antonia. I did not dream she would be here as well. In any case, nothing excuses the fact that I promised but failed to protect and take care of Drina and Antonia. My failure led, in part, to Drina's death. There is nothing I can do now, except fulfill the promise to the daughter that I made to her mother."

Inez gave out a sharp laugh of surprise. "This is all very touching, but Antonia does not need your protection or your money or your…anything. She is my ward and my responsibility, a responsibility I take very seriously." *Granted, I am not doing the best of jobs right now, given I have no idea where she is and it is after dark.* Inez covered her flash of worry with indignation. "In fact, Mr. de Bruijn, I can assure you that any attempt to insert yourself into her life, or should I say *our* lives, would be most unwelcome."

"That," said de Bruijn, "is for Antonia to decide."

"Antonia doesn't know you from Adam. Her mother shielded her completely from any details about you. She thinks your surname is 'Brown' and your initials are WRB. We only know that because the letters are engraved on what I believe is your pistol."

He blinked, a hairline crack in the veneer of his composure. "You have the revolver I gave them for protection?"

The door squeaked open. The two of them turned to find Antonia standing in the doorway, her boots and skirts a wrinkled muddy mess, her coat half-buttoned, her bonnet hanging from its strings down her back. She looked defiant, tired, and scared, all at once.

She hesitated, looking from one to the other. "Uh, Mrs. Stannert, should I go upstairs? Wait for you there?" There was trepidation in her tone.

De Bruijn started toward her. "Antonia!"

Small lines of puzzlement pulled her eyebrows together. "Who're you?"

Damn it.

Inez seized de Bruijn's sleeve to halt his progress. "Wait here and keep your distance," she said under her breath. She approached Antonia, put an arm around her shoulders, and guided her forward to stand before de Bruijn.

Inez said, "We have much we need to discuss, Antonia, you and I. I'm certain you know what I mean. But first, there is this. In life, sometimes events pile up all at once and we must learn to deal with them as best we can." She took a deep breath and said, "Antonia, this is Mr. Brown."

The small, thin shoulder tightened under her hand.

She added, just to make it clear, "Your mother's Mr. Brown. WRB."

Antonia's knife was out in a heartbeat. She lunged for de Bruijn, slashing wildly. Inez, alerted by Antonia's tensing muscles, gripped her tightly, one arm wrapped around the girl's chest and the other around her waist.

"You! You're Worthless Rotten Brown!" Antonia screamed, struggling. "Why are you here? Go away! Go away before I kill you, you rotten bastard!"

"Antonia, stop!" Inez shouted. She shot an I-told-you-so look at de Bruijn as she restrained the writhing girl.

He had recoiled in concert with Antonia's lunge, his cane raised in defense.

Inez said, "Mr. de Bruijn, I think it best if you leave. Please shut the door behind you."

He didn't argue. Instead, he addressed Antonia. "Antonia Gizzi, I understand. And I am sorry. I hope later you will allow me to explain to you what happened. Perhaps you will forgive me, in time."

Antonia spat. The glob of saliva landed on one polished boot cap.

Giving Inez and her ward a wide berth, de Bruijn crossed the floor and let himself out. The bell stayed dumb.

Chapter Twenty

It had not been a good night for Inez.

First, there had been the long discussion at the kitchen table upstairs with Antonia. Inez had set aside her hairbrush along with her initial impulse to mete out punishment. Instead, she fixed Antonia some warm milk, and herself a cup of tea. Then, she sat down across from Antonia and began with the most difficult topic, de Bruijn's surprise appearance.

"I know meeting him was a shock, Antonia," Inez said. "In truth, when you first told me about this mysterious 'Mr. Brown,' who your mother said would show up and rescue you both, I doubted his existence. After all, you only heard of him and his visits from your mother and never actually met him. I thought perhaps she had invented him to give you hope of a better future as she struggled to make a life for the two of you. However, from what he told me just now, it sounds like he truly cared for your mother and had no idea the two of you had come to such a sad state of affairs in Leadville."

Antonia had stared into her mug, sloshing the liquid so it swirled inside.

Inez tried again. "Mr. de Bruijn says the letters and money he sent to your mother were never delivered. The hotel clerk where you initially stayed—"

"Stop!" Antonia clapped her hands to her ears. "I don't want to hear about it. I don't believe anything he says. He's a liar!

Why is he even here?"

Inez abandoned her tea to give Antonia a hug. After the girl calmed down Inez returned to her chair. "To answer your question, Mr. Gallagher hired him to find his son Robert Gallagher, the man we knew as Jamie Monroe."

Antonia cupped her hands around the mug. "What does Mr. Brown care what happened to Jamie? Who is he?"

"He's a…" Inez hesitated, "…a sort of detective."

"A policeman? But he doesn't wear a uniform."

"No, not a policeman." Inez hesitated again. "He works for private hire. Wealthy people such as Mr. Gallagher hire people like him to investigate, ferret out the truth, find things and people."

Antonia sniffed and wiped her nose on her sleeve. "Well, he must not be very good if he couldn't find me and Maman in Leadville, and if it took him this long to figure out that you and I came here." She glanced up at Inez. "You trust him?"

"He is invested in finding out what happened to Jamie. As long as our interests align, yes, I trust him."

"Some people will believe anything a con artist tells them," Antonia muttered.

Inez leaned over her cup of tea. "What did you say?"

"It's just when you're on the streets, like Maman and me were in Leadville, you learn not to believe everything you hear."

"I know a thing or two about confidence artists, cardsharpers, and flat-out liars," said Inez. "And yes, I trust him. To a point. Beyond that, well, we should reserve final judgment."

Antonia slumped in her chair. Inez placed a gentle hand on hers. "Antonia, long ago, I said I would take care of you, and I will. He cannot change that or anything else between us."

Antonia's clenched hand relaxed under Inez's fingers.

Inez continued, "However, you are to be civil to him. And no more cutting school, sneaking around, or eavesdropping. What possessed you to go directly to Mr. Gallagher with what you heard?"

Antonia squirmed. "You sounded like you were in a fix. Mrs. Sweet wasn't gonna help. I thought I could. I figured I'm just a kid, a girl. I figured Mr. Gallagher wasn't going to do anything to me." She looked down at her mug. "I guess it wasn't such a good idea."

"We are in agreement on that point. So, do I have your promise? No more truancy or eavesdropping?"

"I promise. I won't cut school, and I won't go listening at doors or peeking through keyholes."

Her earnestness only increased Inez's suspicions. She vowed to herself to watch what she said and check the various entrances and exits before holding any sensitive conversations in the back room.

Which raised another concern.

If she was going to put a considerable effort into finding out what had happened to the young Mr. Gallagher, she would have to be away from the store for portions of the day. Nico could not be counted on to cover for her. And John Hee, although he was quite knowledgeable about a variety of instruments and the various Oriental curiosities they had for sale, was strictly backroom. Most of the clientele had no issue with who might be behind the curtain doing repairs, but to have a man of Chinese extraction visible and acting as an expert or store manager would not do.

So, she needed to find someone to fill in for her, a temporary assistant manager, as it were. Someone trustworthy, who knew the musical world, preferably a pianist such as herself. Someone immediately available. Someone like Thomas Welles. Welles had a family to support. He didn't have a day job at the moment. And, a big plus, Nico knew and trusted him. She resolved to talk to Nico about it first thing in the morning.

Finally, there were the questions: Who had killed Robert Gallagher or, as she thought of him, Jamie Monroe? And why? Those questions, more than all the rest, kept her tossing on her feather bed and staring at the shadows on the wall.

Thus, the bells seemed particularly hellish when they erupted the next morning before sunrise. Inez dragged herself out of bed, completed her toilette in record time, and nudged Antonia through their morning routine. The girl looked as if she'd slept no better than Inez.

"Do I need to walk you to school this morning to be certain you arrive?" Inez asked pointedly.

"No'm." Antonia ducked her head over the morning porridge Inez had prepared.

"Good. I look forward to hearing how your lessons went today. I may be out when you come home, but will be back in time for us to go to Mrs. Nolan's for supper together." Inez added, "I am going to see if Mr. Donato will allow me to hire Mr. Welles for a week or so to mind the store."

Antonia paused, spoon hanging mid-air. "Why? Are you going to look for who killed Mr. Monroe?"

"First, I need to see where Mr. Monroe was found and see if I can determine where he died. The last may take some time." *But not too much time, I hope. We have none to spare.*

Antonia descended the stairs and Inez followed, intending to wait for Nico in the office. To her surprise, Nico and a laborer in a paint-splattered apron and peaked cap were standing out in front of the store. Nico, dressed in a stylish morning suit, was gesturing at the sign above the door. He spoke in rapid Italian to the painter, who was nodding vigorously and saying intermittently, "*Sì, sì*, Signore."

Nico broke off to say, "Ah! Signora Stannert. What do you think? Should our sign be in gold and black, same as on the window? Or should we try for something different? Perhaps blue? Or red? Or silver and gold?"

Inez realized that there was no reversing course now. Nico was bound and determined that "Donato and Stannert" should be emblazoned, varnished, and swinging in the breeze for all to see. *Oh, what does it matter? My efforts to stay anonymous are obviously for naught, at this point.* "Black and gold are much more elegant if we are trying to attract an upscale clientele."

"Of course, of course. You are right, as always." He addressed a few more fluid words to the painter. The man nodded, tugged on his cap deferentially, and said to Inez, "*Buon giorno, Signora,*" before hurrying away.

"Mr. Donato, may I have a word with you inside?"

"Of course, of course!"

As they walked toward the rear of the store, Inez began, "You have always said that I have complete management of the store in how it is run, correct?"

He looked at her curiously. "But of course. That is our agreement. And you have done marvelously, as I have said."

"Good. Because I would like to hire Mr. Welles for a short while, just about a week or so. I understand he is short of work right now. Having him stand in for me for part of the day would work to everyone's advantage and allow me the time I need to take care of some personal business."

Nico stopped walking, and Inez was forced to halt as well.

The puzzlement on his face was marred by caution and question. "You need an assistant?"

Inez continued in her most persuasive tone. "It would be good for the store as well to have a responsible person available. And you, well, you are so busy with all your appearances and so on. Welles, as a married family man and a pianist, would be a good choice. Perhaps we might even think of employing him permanently, half-time, if it works out as well as I think it will." She held her breath, waiting to see if he objected or demanded to know more.

Instead, he said in a peculiar tone, "Well. If you feel you must. As I said, you have complete management of the store. I trust you to do what is best. Thomas would be a good choice, as you say. May I ask, does this important business have to do with Signore Gallagher, the gentleman I met yesterday?"

She stared at him, wondering if he knew about Jamie Monroe being Harry's son.

"I understand you know each other from before. He told me he knew you from Colorado. He was at the Floods last night."

Inez held her breath. She now recalled suggesting to Harry that he show his son's photograph to Nico. If Nico mentioned this, or remarked on the resemblance of Robert Gallagher to Jamie Monroe, she would have to reconsider what to say to Nico about the entire situation and what to withhold. But if he did not mention it, neither would she.

The silence stretched between them until he added hastily, "*Scusatemi*, I do not mean to pry where it is none of my business."

She realized Nico was asking in a circumlocutory manner whether there might be a more "personal" connection between her and Harry. "No! It is not that at all. It's just..." Inez hesitated, wondering how much to divulge. She decided to err on the side of caution, even if it meant inventing excuses. "Mrs. Sweet has decided she wants her daughter taught at home. Others have expressed a similar interest in having me provide private lessons in their residences. This development could ultimately bring more business to our store. I thought it would be a reasonable avenue to explore, and since Mr. Welles is currently at loose ends..."

The tightness in Nico's face smoothed away. "Ah! That is most entrepreneurial of you, Signora Stannert. Certainly. One week, that is not much to ask, and as you say, will help Signore Welles and the store as well. Excellent idea."

"I am glad you agree that Mr. Welles is a satisfactory substitute for the time being. If I could ask a favor of you." She ventured to lay a hand on his sleeve. "I have no idea where Mr. Welles lives. Would you see if he is available to start today, or tomorrow at the latest? It would be such a help to me, if you would."

"*Certamente.* I will talk with him. I am sure he and I can come to an agreement."

Inez noted how smoothly he had slipped the responsibility of handling the arrangements out from under her, but decided, in this case, she would let it go. "Thank you, Mr. Donato." She gave his arm a small squeeze and withdrew her grasp.

"I am always available to help. You need only ask." He glanced toward the back of the store, somewhat wistfully, she thought, before adding, "I hope your morning brightens from here, Signora." He bowed and headed toward the exit.

She went into the back and stopped, staring about. Several big, bristling bouquets dotted the area. One sat on top of the student piano in the lesson room, another in the center of the large round table, and yet another perched in her office on a small black pedestal table, extracted as she recalled, from the showroom. No card, but it was clear to her that Nico was behind the ostentatious display.

What was he up to, that he felt it necessary to bury her in an avalanche of blossoms? She couldn't imagine that he was concerned that she might leave the business. Although, if he thought there might be a romantic possibility between her and Harry, and that Harry might lure her back to Colorado, that could account for the sudden effusiveness.

A knock at the back door brought her out of her musings, and she hurried to open it. Otto Klein stood on the other side, sweating and looking harassed. A cart, horse, and driver lingered in the alleyway behind him. "I am sorry to come calling at such an early hour, Frau Stannert, but I wondered if you could help me. Yet again. It has to do with Jamie Monroe."

The cart, she noticed, was piled with several trunks and musical cases. She also saw a music stand poking up out of the chaos. Otto continued, "You see, I have not been all truthful with you. Two weeks ago, Jamie and I had a falling out over the rent. I was having to foot the bill. A while ago, I said, 'No more'. Last night, Isaac Pérez told me there was a room to let in his boardinghouse. It is less expensive, with many of our friends there. I had to decide quickly. I paid the rent and I am moving out today. I have most things, one more trip. But you see, there is Jamie's trunk." He glanced at the cart. "He has not come back. I do not think it proper for me to take it with me. Perhaps you could keep it, until he returns? If he does."

Inez's mind was already working over the possibilities. If she could get into that trunk, who knows what she might find. "Certainly. You can put it upstairs, in the storage room."

"That would be wonderful!" He looked quite relieved.

Inez pointed to the seldom-used, outside staircase clinging to the backside of the two-story building. "That way would be best. I'll unlock the door at the top."

Otto and the driver struggled to pull a large trunk out of the cart and up the rickety stairs. Inez went up first, sorting through her keys until she found the one that fit the back door at the top of the stairs. She unlocked the door and entered, peering about the dim interior, finally pointing to the wall by the dusty window that overlooked the alley. "Right here would be best, where it is out of the way."

She frowned. The sash window was pulled up a couple of inches. Had it been that way for a while? She seldom came into the storage room and couldn't recall if perhaps she'd opened the window to air things out and forgot to close it.

Once the trunk was placed, the window closed, and the back door locked, they all headed down. Back in the alley, Inez asked Otto, "Do you recall anything about the longshoreman who knows Monroe and came to your boardinghouse? His name? Where he works?"

Otto mopped his brow. "Sven Borg. Said he worked the lumber trade on the docks."

She tucked the name away for future reference.

"He told you he recognized Jamie from his activities in the labor movement?" she asked.

Otto nodded, looking at the cart. The driver was whistling softly. "I believe so."

"She ventured another question. "Was Jamie working in that area? Do you know?"

"Ach." Otto looked distressed. "He has been working late nights into early mornings. Not so unusual. But he didn't like to talk about where. I think it was perhaps somewhere on the Barbary Coast. Or perhaps by the wharves at Mission Creek, where the body was found."

"It is not a good place down there at night," he added. "I hope you do not plan to go there looking for this Herr Borg, Mrs. Stannert."

Inez nodded, thinking back on what Jamie had written in his note to Carmella and what Carmella had said in the carriage. "I heard he had a new job lined up. Do you know anything about that? You say he hasn't been paying the rent. He doesn't have a source of regular income?"

"Ach. He is a musician. As with most of us, regular income is a dream. Why do you ask? Has someone identified the body? Is it Jamie?"

"I hope we will know soon." Inez was not ready to announce to the world that Jamie was the unfortunate victim. Not with things as tangled as they were. She would have to say something eventually, but not yet. Not now.

He looked as if he had more questions, but the driver called out, "Mr. Klein, if this hire takes longer than we agreed upon, it'll cost you more."

Inez walked Otto to the cart. "If you come up with anything that might help determine Jamie's whereabouts and activities, savory or unsavory, please let me know."

"Very well." He didn't sound happy. "But, Mrs. Stannert, there may be things that would not be fit for a lady's ears."

She smiled grimly. *And those are exactly the things that I need to hear.*

Chapter Twenty-one

De Bruijn looked across the table, littered with the remains of breakfast, at his two female dining companions. They could not have been more different in their attentiveness. Mrs. Stannert, who had arrived late, looking harried but determined, had closely attended to his each and every word. He also gathered she was watching him closely for signs of…pretense? Weakness? Her powers of perception had been remarked upon by Mr. Gallagher as well as by others in Leadville who knew her, so he was prepared to be on his guard when dealing with her face to face.

Mrs. Sweet, on the other hand, had barely seemed to register their conversation. Her wandering eye was more engaged in examining the dining room and casting appraising glances at the nearby men—solitary or otherwise, she did not seem to discriminate. Whereas Mrs. Stannert had eschewed all but coffee for breaking her fast, Mrs. Sweet had ordered widely from the menu and attacked the rolls and butter with the voracity of a laborer who expected it to be his only meal of the day.

The room was filled with hundreds of diners, and the ensuing din made conversation difficult. The clash of cutlery and china, mixed with the loud voices, was not conducive to meetings of a sensitive sort.

He leaned forward. "I propose that our next meeting take place elsewhere. Some place private."

"Up in the suite, perhaps?" suggested Flo, sending a flirtatious sideways glance to an impressively mustachioed gentleman two tables away who, de Bruijn noticed, didn't seem to mind in the least.

"I have to keep my time away from the store to a minimum," said Mrs. Stannert. "If you insist we meet daily—and given the paucity of time we have for our tasks, I agree we should—may I suggest the music store? I have an office area in back."

"Little pitchers have big ears," countered Flo. "Isn't that what got us into this mess to begin with?"

"Antonia will be at school all the rest of this week," said Mrs. Stannert. "Trust me, she won't be listening at the keyholes again."

De Bruijn found himself thinking that he hoped to see Antonia again. He hoped to have the opportunity to explain what had happened in Leadville and convince the girl he was only here to help her, and not destroy the life she and Mrs. Stannert had built together.

"Since you are the one with a schedule, then we shall meet as best works for you, Mrs. Stannert," said de Bruijn. "If anything of an immediate nature arises, you can send a messenger."

"She can call on the exchange," broke in Flo. "The hotel is on the telephone exchange and so is her store. Can you imagine? Why a music store? My boardinghouse in Leadville is on the exchange, but that makes perfect sense." She batted her eyelashes. "One never knows when there might be an urgent need for an expert trouser-serpent tamer."

Mrs. Stannert set her coffee cup down forcefully on the saucer. De Bruijn was intrigued that despite her proper appearance, she seemed familiar with the crude slang for unmentionable parts of the male anatomy.

De Bruijn folded his napkin and placed it beside his plate. "A busy day is ahead of us, then. Mrs. Stannert is going to try to find and talk with the longshoreman, Sven Borg. Mr. Borg recognized the body and seemed to know something of what the young Mr. Gallagher might have been up to. However, if the wharf environment proves too difficult to penetrate—"

Flo snickered. De Bruijn ignored her.

"—let me know as soon as possible, say, by this evening, and I will turn my attention in that direction. Meanwhile, Mrs. Sweet claims she can find a way into good graces of Mr. Poole, whose daughter was affianced to young Mr. Gallagher in Leadville before he came here to San Francisco."

Flo shrugged a shoulder, and dabbed at her lips daintily, before giving her napkin a little toss onto her crumb-scattered bread plate. "It should be easy. We know each other from Leadville. He knows I'm here. He and Harry almost had a pissing contest when they crossed paths at the hotel entrance when he arrived, and I was there to see it all. Poole has balls of brass, following Harry like that, and threatening him. In any case, with Harry gone, I'll arrange to call on Poole today. I'll weep a river about Harry's mistreatment and claim how I fear for my safety. He's always been a soft touch for a weepy woman or fainting female in distress." She rolled her eyes. "If he has anything to do with Robert's death, I'm certain I can pull it out of him." She wiggled her shoulders seductively, lest they misunderstand her meaning.

"I do not question your methods, Mrs. Sweet, if it is your choice to deploy them and you believe they will gain results," said de Bruijn. He glanced at Mrs. Stannert, who had folded her napkin and slipped it under her saucer and now empty cup. "As for me, I shall begin with the police. Mr. Gallagher has assured me he spoke with the police chief, and they will cooperate fully with me. I shall gain the coroner's report, see if the police intend on following up with an investigation. I will also make some inquiries as to whether Monroe had any brushes with the law."

De Bruijn noticed the waiter hovering, as if he was ready to pounce and clean their table. "Ladies," he stood, and they did as well. "It's time we begin our respective tasks. Wishing you the best with your endeavors, and I shall look forward to hearing from you at the end of the day."

He gazed at his co-investigators—a madam of an exclusive house of ill-repute and a saloon-owner-turned-music-store manager—and privately despaired. It would most likely fall upon his shoulders to solve the case while keeping Mrs. Sweet and Mrs. Stannert out of trouble and from harm's way. At least Miss O'Connell was available and willing to lend an expert hand if called upon. That was a saving grace.

Chapter Twenty-two

When Inez returned to the store, she found Nico and Thomas Welles in deep conversation. Nico turned to her and said, "Everything is settled. Thomas and I are working out the details. He will be here this afternoon. You are free for now." He waved her away and returned his attention to Welles.

"I may not be back until suppertime," she warned.

"No problem, no problem," said Nico, distracted.

Inez went upstairs to change into a well-worn, no-nonsense walking suit and a sturdy pair of boots. If she was to walk around the wharves by the Mission Creek canal, searching for Sven Borg, and visit the Mays at their laundry on Berry Street, which was just north of the waterfront, she didn't want to stand out from the working folks in the area.

As she dressed, she fumed at Nico's dismissiveness. When she had been trying to stay in the shadows, be anonymous, she didn't mind his occasional directives. At least, usually. And, he had pretty much let her run the store as she saw fit. But seeing Nico and Welles in close ranks, discussing the day-to-day operations of the store no doubt—*with no input from me!*—she felt quite shut out. Almost as if he had waved her off saying, "Go on about your business, little woman, you needn't worry about these matters."

She was overreacting, she knew. Things had been different at the Silver Queen Saloon in Leadville. There, she had been an equal owner. Here, it was a different story. *He is the owner, not me. And until I am an equal partner in the business, I must either accept his attitudes or find ways to work around them. Those are my choices.*

Still, it rankled her.

However, she now had time to investigate what had happened to Jamie Monroe.

At least, time for the next week or so. And she would have to keep in mind that she was, theoretically, giving piano lessons.

She walked down to Market and Third to catch a half-full horsecar and settled in for the short journey southward. They trundled down Third Street, two blocks away from Antonia's school on Fifth—Inez wondered if the girl had truly gone to class that day, or if she was again playing truant. They passed shops, grocery stores, and saloons, strategically located on the corners. Lodgings of various kinds occupied the second floors, while cross streets sported densely packed two-story row houses. A sharp right onto Berry Street, and Inez disembarked at Fourth and Berry, just before Long Bridge crossed the Mission Creek channel. During the day, lumber-burdened schooners and barkentines vied with hay scows riding low under towering bales for passage through the narrow channel. They plowed through excrement- and garbage-laden water the consistency of mud, their crews cursing the orders that had brought them to "Shit Creek." Those crews escaped as quickly as possible to the lowest of the low businesses lining the wharves or to the Barbary Coast.

Inez had been in this dockside area twice before, both times in daylight hours. Once to the music store's modest warehouse just off Third and Berry to examine a piano for a customer, and again to the Mays' laundry when she initially negotiated a loan with the two sisters. The laundry was in the opposite direction from the warehouse, so she started walking up Berry toward the higher street numbers.

As she passed Long Bridge, she wondered. What was Jamie

doing there? Had he simply stumbled into the wrong people or was his death more insidious?

Warehouses and receiving buildings large and small lined the water channel, partially hiding the various vessels and the piers that sent finger-like wooden platforms out into the garbage-filled water. On the opposite side of the street were the usual complement of establishments that depended upon the maritime environment and its workers. Several smithies, a wood turner, a couple of box manufactures, door and sash makers, a stair-builder. Proliferating among them were saloons, corner grocery stores, restaurants, and lodging houses, all of which offered liquor and wine for sale, either openly or behind back curtains. She recalled that the laundry was next to a shabby, westward-leaning nameless saloon that also offered lodging. The whole business looked suspiciously like a crimp house where a man who came for a drink or a place to lay his head ran the risk of being shanghaied.

It didn't take her long to reach the Mays' place. It was easily identified by the terse "Hand Laundry" sign above the door and a pile of bricks, stacked none too neat, against the new brick front. Random laundry implements were piled against an intact plank wall on the other side, including one scarred wooden tub and several badly dented metal tubs, and an impressively complicated but broken mangle that sheltered other smaller items under its shade. A murmur of voices inside assured her someone was at home. She knocked on the plank door, which shivered beneath her hand, and called out, "Hello? It's Mrs. Stannert."

There was a silence, then the door flew open under the hand of Bessie May, young Patrick's gray-haired, gray-eyed aunt.

When the building had burnt, it was Bessie who had stormed into Inez's office, still stinking of smoke, fire blazing from her eyes at the unfairness of the world. "As God is my witness, I stand here cursing Him for what He's done to us. We are ruined, Mrs. Stannert. Ruined! We bought bricks with the money you loaned us to build another drying room. The money is gone, and we will need to rebuild the entire structure in bricks. And us, without insurance, because no one would cover us, being as the building is wood."

Inez had said, "How much do you need?" She knew they would pay her back every penny plus interest owed. So far, her trust in the Mays had proved out; they had never been late with a payment.

Bessie gave her the eyeball. "We expected you earlier."

Inez did not take this abrupt greeting personally. It was just Bessie's way. Bessie, the elder of the two sisters, had seemed to have snatched up all the fierceness of spirit, kicking the more tender, tentative emotions to Molly.

"Business delay," said Inez.

Bessie apparently considered the equally terse reply as sufficient. "Well, come in then, out of the stink of the street. No doubt you'll be wanting to see that your money's been put to good use and not wasted."

The astringent smell of mint hit her almost like a physical slap as she stepped into the front room. A large stove, radiating heat, was positioned against the brick wall. Two laundry irons, which looked as if they must weigh ten pounds apiece, were coming to temperature on its broad surface.

Inez ducked under the lines of drying pillowcases, towels, shirts, sheets, and ladies unmentionables and nodded a greeting to Molly, who looked up from where she stood, bent over a sheet on a long table, another substantial iron in hand. A counter to her left held a pile of wrinkled sheets. A counter on her right contained a stack of folded bed linens, neatly pressed and creased. She lifted the iron and examined the sheet in front of her. Half of it had surrendered its crinkles, forming a smooth ivory plane. She straightened her hunched shoulders, tucked a strand of faded red hair behind her ear, and said, "Morning to you, Mrs. Stannert."

"And good morning to you," said Inez before Bessie peremptorily swept her away, to show her the back room, with its shiny new copper pots, and stainless-steel tub, and two stoves. This room had new brick walls on three sides. A single wood wall remained. "One more wall to go," said Bessie proudly, "and we'll be able to work on the rest of the ironing and drying room out front."

"What about your living quarters?" asked Inez. She knew they occupied a small set of rooms behind the laundry.

"That will be last, if at all." said Bessie. "The laundry first, so we won't get fined again. If not for you, we would have been thrown into the street. Two hundred dollars!"

Inez nodded. A city ordinance dictated that laundries not made of bricks were subject to fines up to a thousand dollars. Although Chinese laundries were the main target, that did not stop a local policeman from fining the Mays two hundred dollars for conducting their washing business in a frame building, even as the charred portion was still smoking.

"You have done as I suggested?" asked Inez.

"We pay the scum every week. He hasn't done but wink and look the other way, as you said he would." She spat on the floor and ground the phlegm into the board with a savage foot.

Inez nodded. She had figured that, just as in Leadville, paying a small "tax" to the local law would guarantee they would look the other way as the building underwent its transformation from planks to bricks.

"Patrick will be working on it this afternoon when the bricklayer arrives," added Bessie.

"Miss May, I am willing to advance you for more professional help. That would free Patrick for other chores," said Inez.

Bessie shook her head. "He has time for both. And he's learning a useful trade where the color of his skin won't matter a lick."

"But his music—"

Bessie bristled, and Inez knew she'd strayed onto a sore topic. "If left to himself, he would play the piano day and night. We didn't mind that he takes lessons from you on the occasional morning before deliveries, but now he's after us to let him work at that place next door. It's that old no-good drunken Irishman who runs the place, leading him on to play for pennies, when he could be learning a trade to make a decent living! I don't like it. And I like it even less that we are living here by the wharves, where he goes walking after dark. Oh, he thinks I don't know, but I do. It's a good way to get oneself killed." Her mouth tightened in disapproval. "We all agreed. Even Patrick. He's going to be a bricklayer."

Somehow, Inez doubted that Patrick had much to say about it. If Bessie had made up her mind he would be a bricklayer, her sister Molly would have agreed and that had probably been the end of the conversation.

The back door opened and Patrick entered, a bulging bag over one shoulder.

"More sheets from Mr. Henderson?" asked Bessie. At his nod, she pointed to a table laden with two similar bags. "Put them there. He should change his flea-ridden linens more often. You can tell him I said so."

Something Bessie had said set the gears turning in Inez's mind. "Thank you for the tour," she said. "You are all doing admirably. Let me know if you need more materials or, as I said, an extra set of hands to finish the work. Patrick, would you walk me out? I'd like to talk to you for a minute."

Patrick set down the bundle and turned to his diminutive aunt.

She waved a dismissal. "Go, boy. But don't dilly-dally once Mrs. Stannert is through with you."

Outside the building, Inez said, "Let's walk a little." She wanted to put some distance between them and the laundry, just to be sure they weren't overheard. They crossed the street and began strolling past the warehouses and receiving buildings. Inez said, "Being a bricklayer is a noble profession, but you have a talent. I'd like to see you get a chance to use it."

He looked down at his hands, turning them this way and that. "If I could convince Aunt Bessie that there's a living in it for someone like me, she might change her mind."

"I could perhaps help you find a position somewhere. At least, I could ask around." She scrutinized him. There was something about the way he glanced over at the saloon. Something furtive and guilty. "Your Aunt Bessie mentioned the establishment next door. You've been offered a position?"

"Uh." He was blushing.

She ventured a guess. "You are working there *now*?"

He caved. "Just an hour here or there. Late at night, when the regular pianist has to leave early. And only sometimes." He sounded desperate, pleading. "It's the only way I can practice. And Mr. Henderson, he don't mind the color of my skin. When he asked if I wanted to play more hours, I said sure."

"Your mother and aunt don't know?" Inez was astonished that the seemingly transparent young man could be so devious.

"I go for long walks at night." He hung his head. "I just don't tell them that I go to Henderson's first."

"The place is called Henderson's?"

"It hasn't got a name. Mostly folks call it Henderson's or sometimes Three Sheets. As in three sheets to the wind."

"No doubt appropriate," said Inez. "A question to you, then. Did you work there Sunday night?"

"No'm."

"Did you walk that evening down by the wharf?"

His gaze flitted left and right as if he was trying to decide what the correct answer might be, the answer that would get him in the least amount of trouble.

"You were." Inez confirmed. "Did you hear or see a disturbance? A fight or someone getting attacked?"

Even though they were walking, something inside him seemed to freeze. She stopped and said, "Patrick?"

He looked warily at her.

"A friend of mine was attacked on Sunday night. You might have heard. He was pulled from the channel the next morning, on Monday."

"Who was it?" There was a thread of fear in his voice.

"A pianist. Jamie Monroe."

Fear now drained his face.

She stared at him, incredulous. "You *knew* him?"

Patrick gulped. "Not much. Not really. He played at Henderson's." His words came out in a rush. "He worked late at night, and he's the one I sometimes stood in for. That was *him* they found by the bridge?"

Inez nodded.

Patrick shifted from one foot to another. He finally said, "I did hear something. I was walking around down by the hay pier. I thought it was just a couple of sailors. They sounded angry. I figured, late at night, they'd probably had too much to drink."

She held her breath. He didn't say anything more. "Did you see them?" she finally asked.

He shook his head.

Disappointment percolated through her. "Can you show me where this was?"

He nodded.

They crossed the street, continuing toward Long Bridge, and Patrick took her down a wide alley between two warehouses. "When they bring in the hay, it's hard to find your way around. Easy to get lost with all the bales, like walls."

He surveyed the wharf. Men were working on the far side, loading bales onto wagons. "This end still looks pretty much the same as it did Sunday. Best those men don't see us." He slid up next to a towering wall of bales, and Inez did the same. They followed the wall to a gap.

"Here," he said and slipped inside. The gap opened into a space, enclosed on three sides by bales and open to the water.

Inez looked around. "Here?"

"Yes'm."

She stood still a moment, trying to get a feel for the area. The stench from the water, gurgling beneath their feet under the pier, and from the vast garbage grounds up the street was overwhelming. She turned to Patrick. "Did you by chance tell the police about this? About what you heard?"

He recoiled. "No ma'am! It was none of my business."

So, if Jamie had a disagreement here, a fight, most likely the police have not been here looking around.

She began to walk the inside perimeter, keeping some feet away from the walls, scanning the ground.

"Ma'am?" He kept pace with her. "What are you doing?"

"Just looking, Patrick. Looking for anything unusual. Out of place."

"I don't see anything." He sounded nervous. "We shouldn't be here. Someone's going to find us, ask us what we're doing here, and tell us to leave."

"When they do, we will." She kept her eyes on the planks. They were filthy, scuffed, split, dark with years of use. Random clumps of moldy hay and clots of dirt appeared here and there, along with the detritus of months, years. She stopped, a cold rill running down her back. There, on the planks, a large red stain that stood out from the scuffed-in black mold. Next to it, there was a smaller stain. A handprint? In blood?

"We oughta leave." Now Patrick sounded panicked. "We shouldn't be here."

She glanced up at him. At six-four, he was an imposing figure. But his green eyes betrayed the fact that, inside, he was just a frightened boy.

"Soon," she said. She moved around the stain and the print, circling, then walked to the nearest hay bales. Something on the ground, nearly hidden by the lower edge of the bale, caught her eye. A container, small, dark brown. A little circular leather box, lying on its side, as if it had been tossed or kicked aside and had rolled up against the hay bale. She picked it up, freed a little brass hook, and opened it.

Inside was a velvet bed with an empty slot in the middle.

She knew what kind of box this was. What it was meant to hold.

Inez's mind flew to a distant time, ten-plus years past. Her soon-to-be husband, Mark Stannert, placed in her hand a little leather circular box, much like this one, and said, "We're two of a kind, I knew that the moment I saw you. You've stolen my heart, Inez, just slipped it out as neat as a light-fingered Sal. What do you say we make it official, Darlin'?" She remembered the exciting thrill that had run through her from the warmth of his touch and the promise in his eyes. Mark Stannert promised a future full of adventure and new horizons, an unbounded future very different from the one defined for her by her parents and her station. All of it, waiting for her to say yes, to open the little box and let him slide the gold ring inside onto her finger.

She fiercely willed the memory away. Aware of Patrick's anxious breathing beside her, Inez tilted the box to read what was printed on the satin lining inside the top—"Barnaby Jewelers, Market Street, San Francisco."

Chapter Twenty-three

Once Inez retrieved the box, Patrick succumbed to such panic that they were obliged to hustle out of the maze of bales and away from the hay wharf. "You won't tell Ma or Aunt Bessie about Henderson's and the wharf, will you?" he asked over and over.

She assured him over and over that she wouldn't. Before they went their separate ways, Inez asked him if he knew a Sven Borg. "A longshoreman who works with the lumber ships, I believe," she said. "He is the one who found the body by the bridge."

Patrick shook his head so emphatically that Inez thought he might lose his hat. But then he added, "You could try Johansson's lumber yard. Johansson is a Swede, and he mostly hires Swedes. Maybe he'd know." He pointed toward Long Bridge. "It's one of the smaller places on the docks. Between Sierra Lumber and the San Francisco Lumber Company."

With that, he headed back to the laundry, head ducked, hat pulled down, as fast as his long legs would take him.

Although it was little enough to go on, Inez took heart at the fact that there were three lumber companies in a row close to the bridge. Surely, this Sven would be found at one or the other of them. She started with Johansson's, hoping luck would make her search a short one. Her inquiry at the office turned up the fact that two Sven Borgs were employed at Johansson's: "One-eyed" Sven and "Broken-nose" Sven.

"I'm looking for the Sven who discovered the body by the bridge Monday morning," said Inez.

"Ah!" said the foreman. "That'd be Broken-nose Sven." He narrowed his eyes, suddenly suspicious. "Can I ask why you need to talk to him? We're very busy right now."

"I'm here on behalf of the family of the deceased," said Inez. Which was true.

"Wait here," he said and disappeared out onto the wharf. Inez cooled her heels for some minutes until the foreman reappeared with a stocky man, mid-thirties, blue workshirt, pants, waistcoat, and suspenders, silver-blond hair under his blue-and-gray checked cap, and a fulsome walrus mustache. The foreman turned to him and said, "Tell me when you're done so you can get back to work."

Inez introduced herself and noticed that this Sven Borg did indeed have a nose with a distinct tilt to the right.

"We talk outside, Mrs. Stannert? I just have a few minutes." His "vee" for "we," "yoost" for "just" and "haff" for "have" were all stamped with the typical Swedish melodic tones.

Once they emerged street-side, Borg leaned against the brick wall of the warehouse. "Do you mind if I smoke, Mrs. Stannert?"

"Not at all," she replied. "May I ask you a few questions?"

He nodded, pulled out a pouch of tobacco and some rolling papers.

"First, I want to thank you for going to Mr. Monroe's lodgings and notifying his roommate of your suspicions regarding the identity. You were correct. It was Mr. Monroe."

Borg had assembled a cigarette during her short explanation. He lit it, inhaled and exhaled the smoke reflectively, then looked at her with eyes as blue as his faded denim shirt. "May he go with God. Please tell his family for me."

"Of course. We are curious, how did you make his acquaintance? You are a longshoreman. He was a musician. What was your connection?"

"Ja. Well, I have been known to play a squeezebox sometimes." He squinted up at the sky. "Did his roommate, Herr Klein, tell you about the unions? About Frank Roney, the labor leader?"

"He mentioned it in passing," said Inez.

"Jamie—" he pronounced the name "Yamie"—"he was very interested in organizing the musicians. So, he came to the waterfront, to find others working for the labor cause. That is how I met him."

"Are there union meetings here? I apologize, I do not know much about the labor activities beyond what little Jamie told us."

Sven gave a half-smile beneath his mustache. "Ja, well, they are quiet meetings, not big as in the sandlots with the Workingmen's Party. The eight-hour day was a worthy cause. But in the end, the party was interested in helping the working class. The party is now gone, and good riddance. Their hate of the Chinamen, I did not understand. The party leaders, they said the Chinese steal jobs from honest workers, but I have seen they work hard too, in the factories, in the workshops, in their laundries. I have nothing against hard-working people. They are not on the docks stealing my job."

He sucked on the cigarette and exhaled, the smoke carried away in the light breeze. "Jamie, he felt the same. Do you know, there are Chinamen who are musicians? Jamie said he knew some. I think he had dreams that they should organize too."

Inez tried to think how to frame her next question. "Do you know of anyone in the movement, maybe someone from the old Workingmen's Party, who would have wanted to stop Jamie? Or wanted him dead?"

Borg's cigarette bobbed as he silently chuckled. "Jamie was a musician. Why would anyone care about a musician interested in learning more about labor organizing? No. No one. Jamie, he liked to argue. Sometimes, discussions were hot. But he only fought with words, not with his hands. He needed his hands to earn a living. Me?" He glanced at his own hand—strong, scarred, scraped, calloused, scabs on the knuckles, and closed his thick fingers into a fist. "As long as I can move the lumber from the ship to the wharf, that is good enough."

"Jamie came to meetings here, by the docks?" Inez asked.

"At a saloon, Henderson's," said Borg. "He played there some nights. He would come early, or sometimes stay late, after his time at the piano, and join me, Roney, others, to talk. Until Henderson wouldn't let Roney in anymore."

Inez stared. "At Three Sheets?"

He looked at her, bemused. "You know the place?"

"I have heard of it." Inez thought of what Patrick had told her and how threads formed between perfect strangers, forming a web of connections. Who else was connected, caught in the web?

"We were there Sunday evening." He tapped ash onto the ground. "There was one thing."

"What?" Overhead, a seagull screeched, then wheeled off toward the bay.

"Jamie, he told me he had some good news, and would tell me later. Something had happened to make him very cheery. But when Jamie was done playing, he and Henderson had words. I don't know about what. Jamie slammed the lid down on the piano, and walked out. Didn't stay to talk. I never found out what his good news was."

"Hmm." Inez tucked that away for later consideration. "Do you think his death was random? He was attacked on his way home or some such?"

Borg gave her a shrewd look. "He was down in this area many times. He was not a fool. He went after trouble sometimes, but it never caught him by surprise. Not that I saw."

"I have one more question," said Inez, adding, "I know you must get back to work."

"Ja, I do. In the office, they are counting the minutes I am out here. If I want to be paid for them, I will need to make up this little break." His cigarette was so short Inez feared for his mustache.

So, Inez asked the question she had been wondering about for some time. "How did you recognize him, at the bridge? His face was..."

"Beaten in." Borg dropped the remnant of his cigarette— no more than a paper sliver and a tiny tobacco shred—onto the boardwalk and ground it out with his boot. "His clothes. Sunday night, he wore a fancy waistcoat with flowers and a striped jacket. I remember, because he was so cheerful and his clothes were too. I recognized the vest and jacket when they pulled him out."

Chapter Twenty-four

De Bruijn absorbed what the police surgeon had told him. "So, he was beaten with a heavy object, but you are fairly certain it was not a blackjack or a billy club."

The physician raised tangled eyebrows. "Billy club? Surely you're not suggesting that one of San Francisco's finest, one of our own boys in blue was involved."

"Not at all," said de Bruijn, although the thought had crossed his mind. He knew full well, the law had no great love for union activists, given the sandlot riots of a few years previous in which members of the Workingmen's Party and various unemployed clashed with the police force. Memories would still burn bright concerning those times for those who had been involved.

He switched focus, broadening his thinking to encompass what heavy objects might be close to hand on a wharf late at night or easily carried from somewhere else. "Perhaps the weapon was a crowbar, a chain, a pike pole, or a bosun's cosh."

The police surgeon scratched his wiry gray beard, which could have done double duty as a bird's nest. "No, nothing like that. The object would have had a broad, flat surface but also fairly sharp edges. I considered a brick, perhaps."

He raised his hand, palm up, as if holding one. De Bruijn noted that although the physician's face was deeply lined, his hands were still smooth, the hands of a young man.

The surgeon continued, "There is a brick wharf in the area."

"Was he perhaps killed on the brick wharf?"

"Not necessarily. You look around any of those piers, and you'll find piles of bricks, pieces of lumber, various heavy metal objects on all of them. All I can say is since he was found by Long Bridge, he had to have been placed in the canal close to that vicinity or a bit upstream. The so-called 'water' in that channel is more of the nature of slow-moving sludge. He had not been in the water long, certainly not longer than one night. And he was dead before he went into the canal. I am certain of that. Absolutely no fluid in the lungs."

De Bruijn nodded. "Perhaps his attacker used a brick. A convenient weapon. Which means the attack would have occurred somewhere close to or on the brick wharf. The body would have been dragged or carried to the edge of the pier, or simply rolled off. I would imagine he was placed in the water close to wherever he was killed."

"That makes sense to me, but you best talk to a detective about your conjectures in those directions. I will say that he was hit not just once, but many times. Twice on the back of the head, many times on the face. If the point was to kill him, the blows to the crown would have sufficed. It's almost as if the attacker wanted to obliterate his face, his identity, so we would not be able to tell who he was."

Which was, de Bruijn thought, almost exactly what would have happened. Jamie Monroe's true identity as son of a wealthy capitalist might have remained hidden if not for Mrs. Sweet imparting information about the birthmark to Mrs. Stannert. The irony of the surgeon's remark did not escape de Bruijn. Young Gallagher had come to San Francisco to forge a new identity and divorce himself from who he had been. He had succeeded in doing so in life, and nearly so in death.

"It's a bit of a mystery," continued the physician. "I am sorry, Mr. de Bruijn, that I cannot offer more in the way of information to you or your client regarding the young man's death. At the time, we had no idea who he was and doubted we would be able to gain an identification, given the state of his body, so the autopsy was brief."

He clasped his hands behind his head and his focus wandered over de Bruijn's head to the wall of books and diplomas opposite. "At least, God, fate, or circumstances have made it possible for him to return home for a proper burial, as opposed to a final resting place in our pauper's cemetery." He stood, and de Bruijn did likewise. They shook hands, and the doctor added, "I hope you find out who brought this upon him."

"Thank you for your time." De Bruijn gathered his hat and walking stick. "I have spoken with the police chief. He referred me to Detective Lynch, who is handling the case. The detective was previously a patrolman in the area, so knows the area well. I shall talk with him next."

Privately, de Bruijn didn't think he would get much from the detective. For one thing, Harry Gallagher had made it plain he did not want the police pursuing the matter of his son's death and intimated that he had told the chief as well. De Bruijn and Gallagher had had some private words about that. De Bruijn feared that if the killer was made known to Gallagher, his client would exact his own personal justice, outside the law.

De Bruijn was not a fan of the vigilante approach and told Gallagher so. "We should cooperate with the police and allow them to do their job. They will be far more engaged, now that they know the victim is your son, and they have far more resources than I do."

"You have Mrs. Stannert and Mrs. Sweet," said Gallagher. "Do not underestimate either of them."

De Bruijn refrained from shaking his head. What sort of contributions could Gallagher imagine that a madam of a Leadville brothel and a businesswoman, astute though she may be, would offer to his investigation?

"And if you must employ others for tasks—this Pinkerton woman O'Connell you mentioned, ruffians, whoever—do so. You have a free rein. Money is no object. Timely results are."

And time was ticking away.

● ● ● ● ●

De Bruijn coughed and discreetly pulled out his handkerchief, the true purpose being to block, at least a little, the stench from the waterfront.

Detective Lynch grinned. "'Tis an almighty stink in this part of town. South of Market dumps its garbage just a few blocks upstream. Nearly three hundred wagons a day is the number I hear. Scavengers sift through it looking for rags, old bottles, scraps of iron, oyster shells, whatever might be useful. The rest is shoveled into the water. Although it seems a sin to call what flows here 'water.'"

De Bruijn tucked his handkerchief away. "So, this is where the body was found." He stood with the detective by the foot of Long Bridge, gazing into the listless brown murk that filled the canal.

"That's right," said the detective. "The officers who arrived first fished him out with pike poles. Quite the entertainment for the neighborhood's idlers and ne'er-do-wells, I wager."

De Bruijn could see that he would learn nothing from the scene. "Have you any notion who might have perpetrated the crime? I understand you were assigned to the case and have worked this area for a long time. I suspect you are better able to hazard an educated guess than the other detectives on the force."

The policeman smoothed his ginger mustache, attempting to look solemn but obviously gratified to be asked. He led de Bruijn away from the waterfront to Berry Street, saying, "True. I spent my early years walking these streets and still come 'round on occasion. I like to keep my face familiar to the folks who live and work here, and keep an eye on the hoodlums and scoundrels. Confidence games and swindles are part of city life, and not just in the Barbary Coast and the stock exchange."

De Bruijn gave a small smile, acknowledging the joke.

"You mentioned hoodlums. Do you think the young gentleman in question might have been laid upon and murdered by locals, by happenchance?"

"Well, there're also those who come and go on the waterfront, ye know. In this area, we have more 'coasting jacks,' the seamen who ply the coast and work both land and water. The deep-water jack tars, who come in on ships bound for the harbor at China Basin, are far more at the mercy of the Barbary Coast crimp houses and criminals than the seamen here on the channel. As for the local hoodlums, murder isn't their game. They'd just as soon use a blackjack to render a man unconscious, steal his purse and pocket watch, and leave him to wake with a bad headache and empty pockets."

He paused. "Now, I was made to understand I am to cooperate fully with you. I was also told the fellow we fished out wasn't your ordinary joe down on his luck but the son of a wealthy East Coast investor. Furthermore, I understand you, a private detective, are here to find out what happened to the poor lad, God rest his soul, and help bring to justice whatever criminal took his life away."

Lynch glanced at de Bruijn. "That last is *my* job, of course, but it's been a strange case from the start. First, I was told he was one of God's unknown creatures and we should not spend too much time on him when other cases were clamoring for our attention. Then he was identified as a penniless musician by two women claiming to be distant family. Finally, he is determined to be the son of a wealthy out-of-town investor of some influence."

"I can see where it would all be very disconcerting," said de Bruijn.

Lynch buried his hands in his pockets. De Bruijn could see them bunch into fists beneath the fabric and the muscles in his jaw working. "And then, I am told to take a strictly 'hands-off' policy on investigating, unless directed to do so. And to meet with you. All this, mind you, in rapid succession, over the space of a few days."

De Bruijn wished Gallagher had not been so heavy-handed in insisting that the chief shut down the police investigation. Detective Lynch was obviously sharp and well-connected in the neighborhood where the murder occurred. He would be a worthy ally in this endeavor. De Bruijn thought quickly. *Mr. Gallagher did say money is no object. Just results. And that I am authorized to "hire" anyone I chose.*

"I assure you that I, and by extension my client, are grateful for your time and insights. Furthermore, we would be most grateful for any information that would shed light on this heinous crime. I am prepared, with my client's full knowledge and blessing, to express that gratitude generously."

Detective Lynch stopped on the walkway and gave de Bruijn a sharp look. De Bruijn returned the glance blandly.

Lynch lifted his hat to pass a sleeve over his forehead. It was warm, but that was San Francisco—cool in the morning, not so, as the day progressed. He squinted up at the sky, as if taking note of the seagulls screeching above them. "And how, in general, might this gratitude be expressed?"

De Bruijn cast his eyes skyward as well. The birds wheeled toward the channel, no doubt searching for edibles in the floating garbage. "I believe I see an eagle."

Lynch nodded. The possibility of gaining a ten-dollar gold piece to talk about what he already knew seemed to reassure him and smooth his ruffled feathers. He replaced his hat and pointed across the street. "Henderson's saloon, The Three Sheets. Your man worked there on and off. It is also a gathering place for some who follow Frank Roney, organizer of the Seamen's Protective Union. Used to be, you could find Roney there as well, until he became persona non grata with Henderson for his talk. If you haven't considered the possibility that your man got involved with the union movements and got out of his element with the rough and tumble trades, I'd suggest that as a possible avenue of inquiry. Roney's an odd duck. Doesn't see the Chinaman as a threat to the lot of the common workingman." He didn't try to hide the bafflement in his voice. "If your man was of the same mind, there'd be those who'd take a dim view of that."

De Bruijn nodded. "The young man was indeed a vociferous defender of workingmen's rights. It sounds like a visit to Mr. Roney might prove insightful."

"And to Henderson," added Lynch. "He keeps an eye on everything that goes on in and near his den. If the victim crossed paths with a passing cutthroat, Henderson might know something of it. Now, speaking of ruffians, there are two others in particular who, shall we say, don't 'belong,' and who have drawn the watchful eye of the night patrolman. Enough so that he spoke to me about them after this most unfortunate death."

He gestured to the building next door to the saloon, which sported the sign "Hand Laundry." "Now, ye'd maybe think that business would be the province of a Chinaman. Instead, it's run by the May sisters and one a' them has," he hesitated, "a colored son. Big, strong young fella. The night patrolman has seen him walking around, late nights. Thinks he might be looking for trouble." He cocked an eyebrow.

De Bruijn nodded encouragingly.

The detective continued, "A block closer to the bay, there's a warehouse for some downtown music store. A Chinaman comes and goes, slips in and out at odd hours. The officer thinks he's up to no good but cannot say for certain. Problem is, he's in league with an Italian toff with a lot of pull, so it's hands off, no questions asked."

Sounds became sharper, vision clearer. De Bruijn said, "I'd like a closer look at the warehouse."

"Suit yourself," said Detective Lynch. "I need to get back to headquarters, but I'll show you where it is."

They crossed the street and walked up Berry, with de Bruijn taking note of the various businesses that lined the street. It was the usual sort one would expect by wharves that delivered lumber, bricks, and hay.

Lynch paused at the corner. "Halfway down the block. Brick warehouse." He leaned in close. "One more thing I happen to know because I've been here more years than I want to count. The Italian, he had the Chinaman on the payroll back in 1879, when it was illegal. I've always wondered what they are up to, besides selling pianos." He pursed his lips. "Also, in the pocket of the victim was a notice for the Chinese Theater in Chinatown. It struck me as odd that the victim, who was a musician, should have a program from the Chinese Theater, which employs Chinese musicians, and not a block away is the warehouse of a music store that employs a Chinaman." He shook his head. "It was something I thought to pursue, but," he gave de Bruijn a crooked smile, "other cases take precedence. Perhaps you'll find this information useful."

De Bruijn shook the patrolman's hand, pressing an eagle into it while he did so. "Thank you. I hope I can call on you again if questions arise that you might be able to shed light upon."

The coin vanished into a pocket in the dark blue uniform. "Happy to cooperate, as the captain ordered. If I hear of anything pertaining to your investigation, where could I find you?"

"Palace Hotel." De Bruijn handed him one of his business cards.

Lynch squinted at the simple card. "De Brew…?"

"Pronounced 'Brown,'" said de Bruijn, who had long ago given up on trying to correct the mangling of his name.

They parted ways, and de Bruijn continued up the block at a slower pace until he reached the front of the brick building. It was padlocked shut, silent, with dark dirt-caked windows that provided no clue as to what lay inside.

It would have been easy to keep on walking by without giving it a second glance. But de Bruijn was rooted to the spot, his gaze trained on the small brass plate affixed to the door. The words, etched in an ornate Italianate script, read "Donato's Music Goods and Curiosities. Store at the corner of Kearney & Pine."

Chapter Twenty-five

Antonia straggled alongside Copper Mick, who had started talking the minute he saw her after school and hadn't stopped. "Where were you yesterday? You missed an all-around muddle of a brawl in the schoolyard. Two ruffians from seventh—Red McCain is a basher likes t' terrorize all the little 'uns, stealin' their lunches and all, and Curly Lou sets trash fires by the fence after the bells ring and knocks the hats off anyone smaller 'n him— you know 'em? Well, they got to fisticatin' over something or other, and Curly Lou got snatched bald-headed by Red afore the principal came and pulled 'em apart. And then all of us boys in seventh got a lecture on how fightin's no way to settle differences. Ha! We boys got a good laugh on that one. I can just see me tryin' to talk a hoodlum outta mashing me to a pulp. Anyhow, I brought the new *Young Folks* magazine for you yesterday. It's got the next part of *Treasure Island*. Boy, that Captain North can really spin a yarn. Wait 'til you read what happens to Jim next."

"Don't tell me!" Antonia barked, then sneezed.

"Sounds like you're under the weather, matey." Copper Mick grinned. "Is that what had you locked below decks yesterday?"

"Yeah, I was sick, so I stayed home." She pulled out her handkerchief to blow her nose. "Mick, didn't you say your pa is a detective on the force?"

"Yup! Detective Lynch! That's him!" He fair puffed up with pride.

"Well, my aunt is in a real bind. We gotta help her. It has to do with a murder down by Long Bridge."

That did it. His eyes almost popped out of his head. "What?"

"Yeah, it's someone we know, uh, knew. Jamie Monroe. He played the piano and was really nice. And my aunt, Mrs. Stannert, but I call her Mrs. S, runs a music store, and we live above it, and Mr. Monroe, he was kinda sweet on the owner's sister, but, well, maybe kinda got tangled up with some bad sorts in the unions, or maybe he just got jumped by hoodlums or—"

Copper Mick stopped and pulled on the back of her book strap to make her stop too. "Whoa, slow down there. You're galloping like a runaway on a racetrack. Back up, and tell me what's going on. One thing at a time and take a breath once in a while. Let's just walk down Market a while, all right? Nice and slow."

So, they walked down Market and then turned around and walked up Market while Antonia spilled out the story of poor Jamie Monroe, who loved Carmella, and played the piano and sometimes teased her, but he was always nice, not mean about it. And how it turned out he wasn't Jamie Monroe at all but the son of a nasty toff named Gallagher who threatened to close the store, or ruin Mrs. S, or at least make life miserable for her, because he thought *she* knew all about how his son had taken up a different name.

Antonia didn't tell him how she'd heard all this by eavesdropping. She also passed over the part when she spilled the beans to Mr. Gallagher at the Palace Hotel. And she didn't mention Mrs. Sweet, because she wasn't sure what Mick would think about her "aunt" rubbing elbows with the madam of a Colorado whorehouse, even though it was a pretty high-class whorehouse. But she did tell him that Gallagher had hired a detective, a real Pinkerton-type sneaky guy, to find out who killed his son. Antonia added it was really, *really* important her aunt find out who did the deed before the sneaky private detective, who had a strange foreign name that sounded like Brown so that's what she called him, found out first.

"Criminy." Mick was impressed. "It's like a dime novel. Damsels in distress, a regular Simon Legree, a Pinkerton, and a mysterious murder."

"It's nothing like that," protested Antonia, somewhat stung. "This isn't some made-up story. It's real. And I need your help!"

"Sorry, sorry. So, what can I do?"

"Well, your pa's a police detective. Can you ask him about the murder by Long Bridge? Maybe there's police stuff that'll help us figure out who killed Mr. Monroe."

"Wow. I dunno. He talks about his cases sometimes. Not to my ma or sisters, of course, but with my brother Daniel. You met him the other day when we crossed Market. Daniel's a policeman too. And they let me hang around and listen, because I *do* want to join the force when I'm old enough, but I'm not supposed to say anything to anyone about what I hear. And, I dunno. It's one thing for me to listen, but if I actually ask him about a case? I dunno."

She wanted to stop and give him a shove, a little one, to make him shut up a minute.

"Look, Mick, just say that you heard some kids at school talking about how a body was found floating under Long Bridge just a couple days ago, and, and," her mind spun wildly, "and they're all scared about it, sayin' it was a young fellow, like your age, and he'd been grabbed by *pirates*, and they tried to shanghai him, and he must've fought back because they cut off his nose and his ears and—"

Copper Mick held up his hands. "All right! All right! Yeah, sure, something like that'd probably work. He doesn't like it when folks tell tall tales and spread rumors about police business, and he hates it when it's the kind of stuff that scares little 'uns. All right. I can do that."

"You have to do it tonight," said Antonia sternly. "Because, here's the other thing, we have to figure out who did this *really* fast. In less than a week. If we don't," she took a deep breath, "who knows? Maybe Mrs. S and I'll have to move away, because we'll get thrown out of where we live, and she won't be able to hold her head up in San Francisco anymore."

Antonia figured if he liked silly dime novels and damsels in distress, well, she'd give him a damsel in distress.

"Less than a week, huh?" They had reached the fountain where Antonia had seen Mrs. S and the lady with the veil just a couple days ago. Copper Mick leaned against it, staring at one of the lion's-head spigots, apparently thinking, then straightened up and tugged his cap down.

Antonia thought he looked older and just like an officer just then. All he needed was a blue suit and a star.

"We'll do it," he said. "I'll see you tomorrow after school and let you know what I find out. We'll find the bad guys and see justice done."

"Thanks, Mick." Antonia spat into her palm and held it out like she used to do with the Leadville newsies, back when she was one of them and they made deals and promises with each other. "Let's shake on it."

He hesitated, then spat into his own palm. They clasped hands. "Done!" he said.

A wave of happiness surged over Antonia. She had a friend in San Francisco. At last.

When she got home, she went straight to the store. But Mr. Welles was there instead of Mrs. S. "She had some business to attend to," he said. "I'm not certain when she will return."

He sounded busy in a "go away, I'm busy" sort of way, so Antonia went to the apartment instead. Taking the stairs two at a time, she wondered if there might be any leftover pastries from Carmella in the kitchen's pie safe. Once inside, she stopped.

Something was different.

A faint rustling sound drifted out from the back of the

building. A footfall, the sound of something heavy scraping along the floor. Antonia peeked down the hallway and saw the door to the storage room was open. Not a lot, but enough to show light from the window facing the alley.

Maybe it was because of the tall tale she'd spun for Copper Mick, but all she could think of was *Treasure Island*, with the buccaneer Billy Bones, his mysterious sea chest, and *pirates!* Antonia pulled out the knife her maman had used to protect them both in Leadville. She opened the blade, the little *ric-tic-tic* sound a comfort in the dim hallway. Her thumb pressed tightly along the back of the open, locked blade, she set one silent foot in front of the other. The rustling grew louder as she approached the door. She paused outside, listening. Finally, she heard a whispered "Damn!" and relaxed.

She knew that voice.

Pushing the door open with one foot, she said, "Mrs. S?"

Mrs. S whirled around. "Antonia! You surprised me."

She sounded kind of guilty. Like she'd been caught doing something she shouldn't've been doing.

Mrs. S stepped aside, brushing her skirts as if they were dusty. Behind her, close to the window, was a large trunk Antonia hadn't seen before. She knew every trunk and just about every box and crate in there from her secret times spent in the storage room with the dust, spider webs, and the occasional mouse.

Intrigued, Antonia ventured into the room. "I went into the store, and Mr. Welles was there. I guess you convinced him to help in the store?"

"That's right." Mrs. S looked down at the knife in Antonia's hand. Antonia hastily closed the blade and shoved it into her pocket.

Mrs. S just said, "Antonia, I could use your help. As I recall, you are fairly handy with a lock, am I right?"

Antonia now saw a hatpin and a couple of hairpins scattered on the planks in front of the mystery trunk. "Yes'm." She added virtuously, "But I haven't picked anything since Leadville," and crossed her fingers in the depth of her pocket.

"Well, see what you can do with this, if you would," Mrs. S pointed to the trunk.

Antonia moved closer, got down on her knees, and squinted at the lock. "Did you lose the key?" She knew it wasn't Mrs. Stannert's trunk but was curious what she would say.

"It's not mine," said Mrs. S stiffly. "It's Mr. Monroe's. Or young Mr. Gallagher's, if you will. In any case, it's being stored here until his father returns. I am hoping there might be something inside that might provide a clue as to what happened."

"Huh." Antonia looked at the hairpins on the floor and picked up two. "Can I bend one of these?"

"You may."

Ignoring the gentle grammatical rebuke, Antonia bent one of the pins, and said, "I'll need to break the other."

Mrs. S nodded.

Antonia inserted the head of the bent, two-pronged pin, and, using half of the broken pin, began to work the lock.

It didn't take long. A satisfying *snick* and she was able to swing the hinge plate open. She sat back on her heels, pleased with herself.

"Excellent!" said Mrs. S and actually clapped her hands. "Now come. It's time for supper. Mrs. Nolan will be most displeased if we are late."

"We're not going to look inside?" asked Antonia, disappointed.

Mrs. S took out her pocket watch and opened it. "No, we are not. We should leave now. I'll take care of that later."

Antonia started to grumble, but stopped herself. It didn't matter, because she could sneak into the room any old time and look for herself. Still, she grumbled just a little, because otherwise Mrs. S might get suspicious.

Mrs. S locked the room behind them. As she pocketed the key, she gave Antonia the sort of look that seemed to cut right through to every lie she'd ever made. "Have you been practicing on this door? You were very quick with those hairpins."

"No'm." Antonia crossed her fingers again, behind her back

this time, and quickly changed the subject. "D' you think Mrs. Nolan might have apple pie tonight? Or pumpkin? She makes pretty good pie."

"Well, we should hustle, because if there is pie tonight it will be gone in a hurry."

There was pie, along with chicken and dumplings, which was one of Antonia's favorites. Mrs. Nolan tut-tutted and fussed over them, saying, "Mrs. Stannert and Antonia! I've almost forgotten what you two look like. It seems like a month of Sundays since you've shown up for supper."

"We have been busy," said Mrs. S. The other boarders looked at her expectantly, but all she said after that was "I imagine none of your excellent cooking has gone to waste on account of us."

Mrs. Nolan seemed pleased at the comment and took to fussing at Antonia, asking how she was doing at school, had she made any friends, and was that a new dress she was wearing, before reminding her not to talk with her mouth full. It was hard to eat and answer questions at the same time, because Antonia was determined to get a second helping of dumplings if she could just shovel the food in fast enough.

She would've been happy to sit a while at the table afterwards, or in the boardinghouse parlor with its cheerful little stove, but Mrs. S hustled her right back out after promising Mrs. Nolan that they would be there for supper on the morrow.

When they got back to the store Mrs. S hustled Mr. Welles out the door as well, thanking him over and over for helping. Antonia also heard her say, "I need to talk to Jamie's friends, preferably all together. Do you think you might be able to round them all up tomorrow morning before the store opens?"

He hesitated. "I can try. Will you need me a full day tomorrow as well? Nico thought that might be the case."

"Yes, all day tomorrow. In fact, all this week, if you could, and possibly early next week."

"Sure. And I'll see if I can't bring the gang along, before

opening time." He cleared his throat. "I'm assuming whatever this is about, it isn't good."

"No. I'm afraid it's not." Mrs. S glanced at Antonia, who pretended to examine the music boxes but was really listening to everything. "I'll explain more tomorrow," she said and almost pushed him out the door. Then she looked at her pocket watch again. "Any minute now," she said.

"What's any minute now?" asked Antonia, curious.

"Mrs. Sweet and Mr. de Bruijn are coming. We have matters to discuss."

She wrinkled her nose. "Mr. Brown? Ugh. Is it about Jamie? Can I listen?"

"You most certainly cannot!" snapped Mrs. Stannert. "We have no idea what is going on here, and I don't want you involved in anything having to do with Mr. Monroe's death. And I warn you, should I catch you eavesdropping at the back door or some such, it will not go well for you."

"All right! I just wanted to help."

Mrs. S softened up at that. "I understand, Antonia, but this is something Mr. Brown, Mrs. Sweet, and I must do. You can help me best by doing your homework, going to school, and staying out of trouble. I don't need to be worrying about all of this and you too."

The front door opened. The little bell rattled like it was dying, and the private detective and the parlor hour madam came in.

"Well, hello there," sang out Mrs. Sweet. "It's the little newsie from Leadville. Antonia, right? Goodness, it's been a long time. And how you've grown."

Inez nudged Antonia, muttering, "Manners!"

Antonia managed a "Hello, Mrs. Sweet. How d'you do?"

"Just hunky-dory, child."

Mrs. Sweet sure seemed cheerful, Antonia thought, given they were all running around trying to find a killer. It made Antonia all the more determined to hear what they were going to talk about.

Mrs. S muttered "Manners!" again, and Antonia turned grudgingly to the detective. "Hullo, Mr. Brown." Another nudge. "I'm sorry I tried to stab you last night," Antonia said.

"You what?" Mrs. Sweet gave Antonia a wide-eyed stare. "Sounds like I missed some excitement."

"It was understandable," said the detective. "I would no doubt have wanted to do the same in your shoes."

"Antonia," said Mrs. S, "you have times tables to work on, I believe."

That was her signal to go. "G'night, everyone." She started toward the door, thinking that, if she moved fast, she could be in position over her knothole before they got settled.

"A minute if you please, Antonia," said Mr. Brown and turned to Mrs. Stannert. "May I talk with her privately? For just a moment."

Mrs. S frowned. Antonia could tell she didn't like that idea too much. Mrs. Sweet said, "I recall where you keep the good brandy, Mrs. Stannert. How about if I just go set things up and pour us all a jot?" and off she went, not even waiting for a nod.

Mrs. S finally said, "You and Antonia can talk by the front door, if you wish. However, I shall wait right here." She crossed her arms and stared at him.

He nodded and turned to Antonia. "I have something for you. Something your mother gave to me, which I want to give to you."

Antonia hated to hear him mention her maman. She wanted to slap the words from his mouth. But, something of hers? That she gave to him? "All right," she said grudgingly.

They walked over to the door, Mrs. S watching them like a hawk. Antonia felt all she had to do was glance her way and Mrs. S would come swooping down with claws bared to save her, if need be.

The detective crouched down, so he was at her level. "First, I want to say, Antonia, I am not here to take you away from Mrs. Stannert. I want to be certain you are well cared for, above all. That you are happy. Or at least, as happy as you can be."

"I'm. Fine," she managed to grind out between clenched teeth.

He gave her a sad little smile, which surprised her. She didn't think he could smile at all, much less like he really felt something. Then, he said, "Very well. Although I will say you don't look as if you feel particularly 'fine' right now. Maybe this will help."

He reached into his pocket and pulled out a thin, black braided cord attached to a small silver locket. He said, "I treasure this above everything else I have," and pushed on the catch. The little silver door sprung open, and inside was a photograph, about the size of his thumbnail. "This is a picture of your mother."

Antonia leaned forward, unable to believe her eyes. It was! It was Maman! Seeing the face she hadn't seen in over a year, except in dreams and memories, brought a deep pain to her heart. All she said was, "Maman never let her picture be taken. Never!"

"She allowed it once. For me. Because I asked her to." The detective then took Antonia's hand—very carefully and slowly, as if he wanted to give her every chance to yank it away—and put the locket in her palm. "The cord," he added, "is made from a lock of her hair."

Antonia saw the string was indeed a thin braid of dark, shining hair.

Mr. Brown continued, "She had beautiful hair, your mother, your Maman. Your hair is just like hers, Antonia. You are so clearly your mother's daughter, in appearance and in spirit. She had a bright spirit, independent, strong, and loved you a great deal."

Tears overflowed. She hated to blubber like a baby, but here she was. Everything was blurry, including Mr. Brown, and she couldn't be seeing very well because it almost looked like he was going to cry too.

He reached inside his pocket again, pulled out a card, and

put it on top of the locket in her hand. "This is my business card, with my name. W. R. de Bruijn. The W. R. stands for Wolter Roland. Sometime, whenever you wish, we could perhaps talk. You can ask me anything at all and I will do my best to answer. I am staying at the Palace Hotel. If you want to talk, or if you need my help, I will come immediately, without hesitation. At the hotel, give the hotelier this card. Otherwise, you can ask Mrs. Stannert to contact me. Bring Mrs. Stannert with you, too, if you would feel more comfortable having her there." He stood and brushed his hand over his mustache and beard, as if to stop himself from saying more.

"Th-thank you," blubbered Antonia.

All of a sudden, Mrs. Stannert was there, an arm around her shoulders, a hip to lean against. "Antonia?"

She snuffled and spluttered, "I'm fine. I've got to go w-work on my t-times tables now."

Clutching the locket tight, she dashed out the door of the music store. Cool, damp air surrounded her and seemed to add more tears to her face. She ran past the storefront, unlocked the door to the second-floor apartment with clumsy fingers, and pounded up the stairs.

It took two handkerchiefs to clear her nose. She threw each wadded piece of linen into the corner of her room. Finally, she took a clean one and wiped her face. After setting the locket on her bedside table, she used one finger to shut the tiny silver door on the image of her maman.

She sat on her bed for a little bit, sadness rocking her like waves on the ocean. Finally, after a long shuddering breath, Antonia removed her shoes, flexed her stockinged feet, and wrapped herself in one of Mrs. Stannert's old shawls she used as a coverlet on the bed. She picked up the two hairpins, one bent and one broken, and went down the hallway toward the back room and her listening post, whispering the times tables to herself as she went.

Chapter Twenty-six

As Inez and de Bruijn started toward the back of the store, she asked, "And what was that about?"

"A private business," said de Bruijn, courteously enough, but with a certain firmness that indicated the door to further discussion was closed.

Inez grabbed that implied door and wrenched it open. "Anything having to do with Antonia is my business. I don't know how much you heard about what happened to her and her mother in Leadville, but believe me when I say I have guarded her life with my own, doing things that could perhaps get me thrown in prison, should they become known. So." She gave him the eye. "Tell me. Now."

For a moment she thought he would not respond. Finally, he produced a small, almost indiscernible sigh and said, "I have been carrying a memento from her mother, Drina, since she left Denver with Antonia. Once I uncovered Drina's fate, I promised myself that I would deliver it to her daughter. That is all." He set the head of his cane against the passage door, adding, "Well, not quite all. I also gave Antonia my business card and told her she could call on me for aid at any time. No questions asked." He pushed the door open. "After you, Mrs. Stannert."

Inez stopped at the threshold. "She has me. I am well prepared and able to protect her from any dangers that may befall her."

"And if something should befall you? Not to be melodramatic, but that is possible, given the type of business we are dealing with here." He closed the door behind them.

"What kind of business is that?" said Flo brightly. She was sitting at the round table, an oil lamp in the middle casting a soft light on a bottle of brandy, close at hand and quite a bit emptier than Inez had seen it last.

De Bruijn removed his hat and set it on the table. "We were discussing the investigation."

A snifter with three fingers' worth of Inez's very best sat before the madam. Two additional goblets, only slightly less full, waited in front of chairs to either side of her.

Flo had thrown off her dark coat to display bare shoulders, milky pale in the lamplight, set off by a dress of sapphire blue and a necklace of pearls that suggested many oysters had given up their treasures to grace a generous décolletage that would make most men swoon.

"Excuse me," she said, fanning herself with a blue silk fan of the same hue. "I have an engagement directly after, and there would be no time to change. Mr. Phillip Poole is taking me to the theater and after-theater-supper at Maison Doree." She preened a little. "Have you heard of it, Mrs. Stannert? The most fashionable restaurant in the city. I expect we shall see many of the *beau monde* and *bon ton* there. It's the Delmonico of San Francisco. I mustn't be late in meeting him at the Palace Hotel."

Her eyes sparkled, with a gleam that some might attribute to anticipation or perhaps a previous helping of brandy, but Inez, long acquainted with Flo, recognized the brightness as the shine of a predator.

"On the hunt tonight, Mrs. Sweet?" Inez asked, sliding into the seat on one side, ignoring de Bruijn's pulled out proffered chair on the other.

"Happily for all of us, yes," said Mrs. Sweet. She bared her teeth in a smile.

"Would you wish to report first, then?" de Bruijn inquired.

Inez raised her hand—*wait*. She stood and crossed to the door leading to the alley. After half a beat, she yanked it open. Only darkness greeted her. Darkness and a cold breeze, which slithered in, curling around her boots and sliding up her stockings with a moist touch. She strode over to the passageway door and did the same thing. Nothing but empty silence.

"Brrrr!" Flo pulled up her coat. The shimmering blue dress disappeared in its dark folds. "Was that necessary, Mrs. Stannert?"

"Yes," said Inez. "And you know why." She turned to de Bruijn. "Antonia has been eavesdropping, most likely at the doors. Hence, the precautions."

She surveyed the back rooms, her gaze probing the dim corners. She couldn't help but feel those little eyes were peering at her still, but from where? Inez glanced at the ceiling. Its timbers were beyond the lamp's glow, lost in shadow. Aside from the table and the light, it was dark, and the only persons within earshot seemed to be the three of them, co-conspirators, bound together in the search for truth as to the death of the young musician Jamie Monroe, scion of silver baron Harry Gallagher.

"Well, I shall be quick." Flo touched the hair under the blue and pale pink hat—such a small and shiny object seemed hardly worthy of the name. "I am making excellent progress, given that I've only had a brief twenty-four hours to work my way into Mr. Poole's good graces. I can tell you, he hates Harry and his son like the very devil. He said he's glad the little bastard is dead, leaving Harry as alone as he is. I've seldom met a more thoroughly dislikable gent in a pair of trousers, but he's also charming in a scoundrel sort of way. He said he has nothing to do with the murder, and I believe him."

"You believe him?" Inez couldn't believe her ears. "Are you going soft, Flo?"

"Hardly." Those teeth gleamed again.

"We have very little time," Inez said. "You must get hard proof, one way or the other. Something we can follow up on."

"Oh, don't get your nose out of joint, Inez. Goodness, you are a nervous wreck. Don't worry. I am an *expert* at extracting *hard* proof." She gave de Bruijn a sly sidewise glance. "I'll find out where he was on Sunday night and let you know." She folded her fan and dropped it into her bejeweled reticule and pulled the coat tight around her. "Mr. de Bruijn, you asked the hack to wait outside, correct? Wonderful! Toodle-oo, all, I shall see you later. I'll turn the store sign to CLOSED for you, Mrs. Stannert, so you two aren't disturbed." And with that, she waltzed out. Her rapid footsteps tapped through the showroom fading into silence with the slam of the door.

Inez picked up her glass. "She certainly does not seem very concerned."

De Bruijn didn't touch his brandy. "Perhaps Mrs. Sweet thinks that by getting in Poole's good graces she can use him as a shield against Mr. Gallagher's threats. There is no love lost between the two men. I suspect Poole would welcome any chance to foil his plans."

Inez cradled the snifter in her hands. "I'm impressed! You can think like a woman, Mr. de Bruijn." She swirled the liquid gently, and brought it to her nose, inhaling the golden-brown scent. As always, the aroma brought back memories, both good and bad, of Leadville and the Silver Queen.

She jerked back to the present, listening to de Bruijn. "Today, I talked with the police surgeon who did the autopsy," he said, "and with the police detective who was nominally in charge of the investigation. This is what I found out." He outlined the autopsy findings and Detective Lynch's comments and theories.

When de Bruijn mentioned Patrick May, Inez tensed. She tensed further when de Bruijn said, "The second suspect Detective Lynch mentioned was the Chinese man who works here. Your store's warehouse is on the wharf close by." There was a small rebuke in his tone, as if he thought she had perhaps withheld this bit of information.

"John Hee?" Inez shook her head. "That sounds like so much blather to me. The sentiment against the Chinese in this town is heated. Any misdoing is laid at their doors."

"He was seen in the area late that night," De Bruijn pointed out. "So, from what I heard, we are still looking at possible involvement by the union and the two mentioned by Detective Lynch. We would be remiss not to follow up on all possibilities." He looked at her, with that wide-open, waiting gaze that she was coming to dread. "How well do you know, and trust Mr. Donato?"

She blinked, surprised at the turn of the conversation. "Why? Do you suspect…? Well, young Gallagher was courting Mr. Donato's sister. He apparently was not in favor of that, but he does not view any of the young musicians as proper potential suitors for Carmella. Ah!" She remembered the note from Jamie addressed to Carmella. "I do have something to show you."

She went to the desk and rummaged around until she found the note lying under the slit envelope, and handed it to him. "Jamie—that is, young Gallagher, I knew him as Jamie Monroe and that is how I think of him still—slipped this under my door to give to Carmella. He had to have done so the night before he died because I found it the next morning." She didn't offer any particular apology for opening the letter and de Bruijn didn't act as if he expected her to.

Inez returned to her chair and her brandy. "In it, he mentions the threats, or danger, involving his part in unnamed union activities."

He scanned the note. "May I keep this?"

She hesitated, then took a sip of her brandy, and waited while the warmth spread down her throat and across her breastbone. "I should give it to her eventually."

"Just until we are done with this investigation." He slipped the note into his pocket. "The detective also mentioned they found a notice for a Chinese theater in young Gallagher's possession. See the connections, Mrs. Stannert? Chinese theater—which has a strong musical component—musical warehouse for a store that employs a Chinaman for repairs and who is a musician himself…Yes, I heard the music when I came in last night to speak with you for the first time. I don't believe in coincidences. I should mention as well that Mr. Hee was illegally employed by Mr. Donato in 1879, when there was a law on the books prohibiting such."

"But it is certainly not illegal now!" Inez protested.

"It was then. No matter how you look at it, Mr. Donato was breaking the law, and I have to wonder why. I also wonder if it might have been a pressure point that young Gallagher could have used against Mr. Donato to press his suit." De Bruijn added, "I'm not saying this to argue with you, Mrs. Stannert. It's simply the facts."

"Well, let me tell you what I heard when I went to talk with Mr. Broken-nose Sven Borg, the longshoreman who iden-tified the body as being Jamie Monroe." She ran through her morning's exchange with him, ending with, "I believe there is a strong reason to look into Jamie's employment at this par-ticular establishment. We should ascertain the nature of the disagreement between him and the proprietor, Henderson. As well as any union connections."

She hesitated, debating whether to disclose her connection to Patrick and the May sisters. She finally decided that full dis-closure, or as near to it as she was willing to go, might take Patrick off de Bruijn's list of suspects. "I know Patrick May, the young man you mentioned. I am underwriting his mother and aunt's efforts to repair their laundry after a fire, and Patrick is a student of mine." She tipped her head, indicating the lesson room behind the glass pane. "He is quite gifted."

As she related all this, de Bruijn finally seemed to show a response, mostly by the ever-higher lifting of eyebrows and a tightening of the mouth.

Inez leaned forward. "Listen carefully to what he told me, and do not come to any judgment until you hear me through. Patrick told me straight out that he occasionally plays at the saloon late at night. His mother and aunt would not approve, so he has not told them. They think he is simply strolling about the wharves after dark. The night Jamie was murdered, Patrick was not at the saloon, but he did take a stroll. Down by the wharf where the hay is unloaded, he heard two men fighting. He did not see who it was, but retreated. He showed me where he heard the argument. It was amongst the stacked hay bales, which form something of a maze. He took me to the place, and I found this." She gave the ring box to de Bruijn, who examined it, and passed it back to her.

"I am thinking," Inez continued, "that perhaps Jamie bought a ring for Carmella. He was not paying his share of the rent, according to his roommate, so perhaps he used that money to help with the purchase. Given that note I gave you and certain remarks from Carmella, I do believe he meant to propose."

"Despite her brother's censure?"

"Young love," said Inez, somewhat cynically.

"I see." His eyes were now half-lidded, as he appeared to take that in.

She leaned back, thinking. Finally she said, "This is ridiculous. If we put together all of our suspicions, the list of suspects isn't shrinking, it's growing! And we have one day less to unravel the truth." The knot in her stomach returned. She picked up her glass and finished it off. The liquor eased the anxiety, but not as much as she had hoped. "So, what now?"

"We should make a plan," said de Bruijn, "one in which we will not be stumbling about and treading on each other's toes."

"Well, Mrs. Sweet is marching along to her own drummer. So I suppose we can leave Mr. Poole to her. Although, I am not certain I altogether trust that she will be giving 'her all' to uncovering the truth." Inez eyed the brandy bottle, gave in, and poured another measure into her glass. She offered the bottle to de Bruijn before realizing he had not even touched what he had before him.

He covered the glass with his hand and shook his head. "Thank you, but no. When on the job, I do not drink. And for this particular case, I need all my wits about me."

"I find my wits do not seem to mind a bit of *aqua vitae*, and indeed seem to perform better as a result." She forced herself to not snap at him. "As for tomorrow, I shall visit the jewelers with this box and see if Jamie Monroe purchased a ring. If so, that should fix the place of death, and maybe provide a few other clues. I would also like to chase down the local labor activist Frank Roney and ask him a few questions. Oh, yes, and first thing in the morning, I hope to meet with all of Jamie Monroe's friends and let them know of his passing."

"Are you going to reveal that Jamie is actually Robert Gallagher?"

"I believe I shall simply say his family has claimed his remains and he will be buried Back East somewhere." Her mouth dried, the lingering sweetness of brandy turned to dust. "In truth, I am not looking forward to telling them this. But perhaps one of them will have information that could prove useful."

"I would like to be present when you tell them."

"Absolutely not! Excuse me, but that is out of the question. With you there, they will be more inclined to hold their tongues."

De Bruijn lowered his eyes again, obviously a "tell" for when he was turning over information, making decisions. He nodded. "Very well. You know them better than I do."

"And I plan to try to find out what was going on at Henderson's that night."

"You intend to…what, walk right in?" He didn't try to hide his disbelief.

She looked him square in the eye. "Leave the hows and wherefores to me. I want to find out what they disagreed about. While I'm there, I'll see if I can find out more about Frank Roney's whereabouts and activities."

"A tall order," said de Bruijn.

"And you? What will you be doing?"

"I will attempt to find out from Mrs. Sweet if she has any concrete information I should attend to." De Bruijn paused. "I also do not trust she will be particularly attentive to her obligations on this matter, so I will look into Mr. Poole separately. As you said, our list of suspects is growing, and in some cases, we do not have any specific names. I would like to determine if Mr. Poole is on or off our list. Sooner rather than later. As for the union angle, I plan to delve further into that."

Inez leaned forward. "One person you might talk to is a newsman, Roger Haskell. The name of his newspaper, *The Workingman's Voice*, indicates where he stands on union matters. If he shows up, I could take him aside and let him know you might be wanting to talk with him."

Inez went to her desk, pulled a stack of business cards from one of the cubbyholes, and riffled through them until she found the one she wanted. She returned to the table and placed Haskell's card, with newspaper name and address, next to his untouched brandy.

"Thank you. I appreciate you paving the way for me." He picked up the card and tapped it on the table. "The other activity I have planned regards John Hee. He will be working here tomorrow?"

Inez nodded.

"When is his day over?"

"At six o'clock. He is very punctual in both arriving and leaving on time. Unless he and Nico…ah, Mr. Donato, are off on one of their errands."

"Hmmm."

That one non-remark caused Inez to examine him closely. "John Hee remains on your list?"

"Until I know more about him, I cannot discount that he has some part to play in all this. In any case, I intend to follow him tomorrow after work and see where he goes."

He smoothed his beard. Inez noted he had no rings and his cuff links and shirt studs were plain. With his still face, his nondescript clothes, Inez realized he would blend in, disappear in the busy city streets. At least, most of the streets. But not all.

"He lives in Chinatown," Inez said pointedly. "I should ask: have you been to San Francisco before? Do you know much about Chinatown?"

"I know enough."

He pulled out his pocket watch. "I should be leaving. You no doubt want to get on with your evening and take care of Antonia." He picked up his hat. "May tomorrow bring some revelations that strike some of the names off our list, and bring clarity to those areas where we, as yet, have no names." He touched the brandy glass with the handle of his cane. "Perhaps when all this is over, and we have discovered who committed this crime, I will take you up on your offer of a brandy, Mrs. Stannert." He actually smiled.

It was, Inez observed, a nice smile, and one couldn't help but smile in return. *He should do that more often.*

"I shall go out with you," said Inez. "Give me a minute to lock up."

After securing the brandy and the back door, she extinguished the light and locked the office door behind them, taking de Bruijn's untouched brandy with her. Once they had exited the store and she had closed and locked the front door, he said to her, "About Antonia. I did not mean to upset her as I did. I hope the token from her mother will comfort her, in the long run. If you would tell her I said so, I would be grateful."

Inez watched him walk away, thinking he was one of the most opaque persons she had met in this city by the bay. *I would not like to play a hand of high-stakes cards against him.* She walked the dozen or so steps to the door that led to the apartment. Back in their living quarters upstairs, she sought out Antonia, who was sitting on her bed curled up under one of Inez's old shawls. Inez sat beside her. "How do you feel?"

Antonia's nose whistled as she attempted to exhale.

"Is your throat sore?"

Antonia nodded.

"Try this." Inez offered her the brandy.

Antonia didn't move. "You're gonna let me drink that?"

"Just a few sips. It'll warm your throat and loosen up the congestion. Why don't you get ready for bed and I'll prepare a hot-water bottle for your feet and a cup of tea."

"That sounds good," said Antonia.

The gratefulness in the girl's voice did more to warm Inez's heart than an entire bottle of brandy.

She went back into the little kitchen and puttered, getting things ready for Antonia. When she came back, Antonia had on her nightclothes and nightcap, and had slipped into bed. The little bedside lamp shed a circle of light in the dark. When Inez slid the cloth-wrapped copper hot-water flask under the sheets, she brushed Antonia's feet and exclaimed in dismay. "Your feet are like ice! Did you take your stockings off when you came upstairs?"

The girl's eyes were already closing. "Cold…on the floor."

Inez looked at the braided rug on the bedroom floor and frowned. *What was she doing on the floor when she could have sat in the kitchen where it was warm?*

Children. There was sometimes no rationale behind their behavior.

Inez lingered for a moment, sitting on the edge of the bed, watching Antonia sleep, dark eyelashes still, her dark hair trying to escape the braids that neither of them had undone and combed out. Ah, well. No harm in not doing the fifty strokes with a hairbrush for one night. Her breath came slow and even. In, and out. The brandy seemed to have done its trick of loosening the cold and easing her into sleep. Inez looked at the little locket on the night table by the bed, and, with one eye on Antonia, picked it up and pushed on the little catch. The cover flew open, revealing the thumbnail photograph of Drina

Gizzi. Inez closed the locket and set it back on the table.

"He meant this to be a source of comfort, not sorrow," she said to the sleeping child. "When you are older, you will come to appreciate this gift from a man who was a stranger, but who cared for you and your mother deeply."

Leaving the tea on Antonia's nightstand in case she woke up later, Inez took the bedside lamp to the storage room, unlocked the door, and went in.

Jamie's trunk was just as she'd left it, by the window, unlocked. Inez wondered if the temptation had been too much for Antonia and she had snuck back in to see what the trunk held while Inez was busy downstairs with Flo and de Bruijn. If so, her little exploration would explain the icy feet. The room, unheated and a hallway removed from the kitchen with its stove, had a bite to it.

Inez set down the lamp, turned up the wick, and lifted the large trunk's heavy lid. The interior exhaled a mix of cedar, wool, and tobacco. Inez sifted through the top layers. There were clothes, of course. Several suits of fine wool Inez had never seen him wear. Dress coats and morning coats. Waistcoats. Fine linen handkerchiefs with the embroidered initials RHG. Expensive kid gloves. All attire from the privileged life he had cast aside.

She picked up a rectangular box, which had rested uppermost on the contents. About one foot long and half that deep, it held cuff links, shirt studs, coiled watch chains, and a few other male accouterments in an upper tray. Below the tray was a compartment holding a few cabinet cards and *cartes de visite*. An ambrotype in an ornate gold frame showed a close-up portrait of a woman, perhaps thirty-five or forty, with ash-blond hair, pale eyes, delicate features, and aristocratic bone structure. Definitely not the Leadville fiancée, Inez thought. Most likely his mother, Harry's deceased wife, whom Inez had never met.

First his wife, and now his son.

The losses had to be a heavy burden, she realized with a pang. She shook her head. Why pity him when he seemed intent on ruining her life?

Inez examined the box further as the cold crept through her skirts, petticoat, and stockings to freeze her knees. The shallowness of the inner compartment indicated there was yet another storage area beneath. But there was no lock, no little handle, no way to open the bottom drawer. It was secured tight. Inez spent several frustrating minutes pushing on the drawer's face and going over the exterior of the box, trying to find the "key" to disengaging whatever hidden mechanism held the drawer shut. About ready to give up for the night, she opened the box to replace the top tray. Only then did she spot the small brass button, positioned between the two hinges on the back edge. She pushed the button and the drawer popped open.

Inside the hidden compartment, she found a cache of letters, bound with a satin ribbon. Her heart wrenched when she recognized Carmella's letter-perfect penmanship. As she lifted out the letters, a folded piece of paper stuck to the bottom of the packet floated to the floor. Inez scooped up the paper and opened it. It was a receipt, stamped "PAID" from Barnaby Jewelers on Market Street, for a woman's gold ring engraved inside with "*Two but one heart till death us part.*"

Chapter Twenty-seven

The next morning felt almost normal to Inez.

Almost.

Antonia appeared on the mend, bouncing back with the incredible speed of the young from minor coughs and colds. Over breakfast, she rattled off her times tables at a lightning pace. She seemed anxious to get to school and banged out the door, leaving with considerably more energy than she had demonstrated over the past couple of days.

"Forward into the day," Inez said aloud, taking herself down the stairs and out into the street. She paused and took in the morning traffic from her vantage point on Kearney. She could see the busy to-and-fro of pedestrians, wagons, and horse-drawn street cars down toward Market, and up toward California, the warning clang of the cable-pulled street car, as it made its stop at the corner of Kearney and disgorged swarms of men, who hurried toward the big-board San Francisco Stock and Exchange and "new board" Pacific Stock Exchange on Montgomery.

Who were the souls who dabbled and dealt in stocks? Almost everyone, as far she could tell. Lawyers, doctors, preachers, bankers, merchants, clerks, bookkeepers, mechanics, and even women. No one, it seemed, was immune to stock mania. Inez allowed herself to consider what life might have been like if she, her then-husband Mark Stannert, and their business partner, Abe Jackson, had come all the way to San Francisco as originally planned. Perhaps they would have built a drinking and gaming establishment to capture some of the fortune from gambling fever that clutched the golden city.

But that was not what happened. Seduced by the possibilities in the silver mining boomtown of Leadville, they had lingered in the city in the clouds, then settled in.

She took a deep breath of the air. Cool, but not the piercing cold that sliced into the lungs in the Rocky Mountains this time of year.

Glancing up at the overcast sky, she wondered if she had made a mistake in not insisting that Antonia take an umbrella to school. "She at least has her bonnet," Inez said to herself.

She had just entered the store and was checking that the sign still displayed CLOSED when Otto Klein appeared and tapped on the glass of the door. She opened it and he squeezed inside, juggling a canvas bag and his cornet case. "I am sorry to be early, Frau Stannert, but glad you are here."

"I wanted to bring you this." He hefted the bag. "But first, I want to ask, is there news about Jamie? Herr Welles came by the boardinghouse last night, that is the house I moved into, where Pérez, the Ashes, and Laguardia also board. He said you wished to speak to everyone before the store opened today. I am assuming the worst."

Here it was.

Her first test.

Inez crossed her arms and steeled herself. "I am sorry to say, the longshoreman who came to see you was right. It was Jamie Monroe by the bridge."

"*Ach*." Otto's ruddy face paled. "I was afraid of that. *Mein Gott*. He did not deserve this. No one does."

An unexpected lump rose in her throat, originating from somewhere behind her breastbone. Otto pulled out his handkerchief and wiped his face, although Inez saw no sign of perspiration.

"You are right, Herr Klein, no one deserves such an end. I find it hard to believe that he is gone. All we can do is hope the police find who did this to him."

"What do we do now?" Otto pushed his handkerchief back into his pocket. "Should we start a collection for him, to have him buried properly?"

It was the perfect opening for the words she had prepared. "The authorities found his family. They are taking him home for burial."

There.

Short and sweet.

All true, provided she continued to skirt the details. No lies to trip her up later.

Just enough information to assure Jamie's friends that his body would not lie unclaimed, nor rolled into a pauper's plot. They would mourn, recover, and go on with their lives.

They had reached the back of the store, and Otto sank into a chair by the round table. "If possible, please pass along my condolences to his family." He set the bag carefully, respectfully, on the round table. "These are Jamie's and should go with his trunk. I finished emptying everything from the old room and found some of his clothes in the dresser."

It occurred to Inez that perhaps those clothes held further secrets or clues. "Did you check the pockets, perchance?"

"That would be disrespectful." Otto sounded horrified. "Prying."

She thought it would have been one of the first things she would have done, if the clothes belonged to a vanished room-mate who owed back-rent, but all she said was, "I shall make sure they are delivered along with the trunk."

"I also found two more items. This—" He handed her a brass key.

Inez blinked. Unless she missed her guess, it was the key to Jamie's trunk upstairs. "Thank you. And, the other?"

"This, it is strange. I found it under the mattress. On the

slats." He held out a sheaf of papers, folded in half, lined, creased, and somewhat the worse for wear.

At Inez's raised eyebrows, he had the grace to blush. "Sometimes, under the mattress, it is a little hiding place, you know. A good place for keeping things close, and requires no key."

Inez wondered what Otto had hidden on the slats under his mattress.

She sat down by Otto and unfolded the papers. "A list of names." She fanned the pages. "A lot of names."

"*Ja.*" Otto craned his head to view the list with Inez.

She skimmed the first couple of pages. Last name, followed by an initial, and a number. "These numbers look like they indicate amounts of money. So-many-dollars and cents." She frowned. "The first name has a checkmark by it, but none of the others do. Hmmm. And here, I cannot be certain, whoever wrote this had a terrible hand, but isn't this Nico? It must be, unless there is another 'Donato, N.' Or unless the last name is Darata, or Dorano, or some such. Goodness."

"I believe you are right, Frau Stannert. Yes. I think it is Donato."

More names marched down the other side as well in the small, crabbed script she did not recognize. "Who are these people?"

"I recognized only two names," said Otto, proving to Inez once and for all that, although he said he hadn't gone through his roommate's suit pockets, he'd had no qualms perusing a list concealed under his friend's mattress. "Donato, as you said. Now, go to the last page."

She flipped to the back. His finger glided down the list, stopping near the bottom. "Here."

Inez peered, wishing she had the spectacles she kept on the desk for close work. "What does it say? I can hardly read this writing."

"It says 'Welles.' With a 'T.' for Thomas."

She flipped the pages again, searching quickly for other

familiar names, but spotting none. "Thank you, Otto. For being so thorough and for entrusting this to me."

"Of course. I almost threw it out, but since Jamie thought it important enough to hide, and there was a chance he might show up, I thought I should give it to someone. I thought Nico, but I must be off for a job at a lunch counter this morning."

"I'll take care of this," said Inez. *After I've had a chance to ponder what it means.*

He chewed on his lower lip. "The others, you will tell them about Jamie?"

"I plan to tell them exactly what I told you just now."

His hunched-up shoulders eased down. He heaved a big sigh. "At least we know what happened to him. And as you say, I hope justice is found."

He picked up his cornet case and left.

With the help of her spectacles, Inez pondered the list, even as she organized the paperwork that she had neglected from the previous day. She now realized that the checkmark was done with pencil, while the writing was in ink. The pages appeared to have been torn from a ledger of some kind. So, what was it and what ledger did it come from? And why did Jamie have it and hide it?

She didn't have much time to ponder, because John Hee showed up, slipping in the back door. Inez followed him to his repair area and gave him a brief summation of the fate of Jamie Monroe. Given what de Bruijn had said, she watched Hee closely for any sign that this news was not new to him, any sign of guilt, nervousness, or mock dismay. But all she saw was sorrow.

Inez said, "Earlier, you told me that there were some who did not care for Jamie. Are you saying he brought this upon himself?"

Hee shook his head. "I cannot say."

Inez regarded him narrowly. *Or you* will *not say.*

She decided bluntness might at least have the element of

surprise, and provoke a response, perhaps cause him to let something slip. "You were seen at the waterfront that night. Someone, I do not know who, is casting suspicion upon you."

He paused in the act of raising the curtain to the alcove. Unfortunately, his back was to her, and she could not see his expression. Hee let the curtain drop, and faced her. He didn't act afraid, or angry. He seemed more amused than anything. "Am I suspected of murdering Mr. Monroe? Why? Because of who I am? Pig-tail. Coolie. The Chinese Must Go! Never trust a Chinaman. Because of this, and I am seen at night, on business for owner of this store, I am accused?" He shook his head. "Ask owner of this store, who makes life possible for me and you, too, Mrs. Stannert. Mr. Donato will tell you I was at warehouse and left after our business was done. I did not see Mr. Monroe. His ill fortune was his own making, not mine."

"A program for the Chinese Theater was found in his pocket."

"And eyes go to me? Mr. Monroe want to talk with Chinese musicians about unions. I work there, I told him, no interest in unions. He listen? Most like, no. He was a stubborn young man. Anything more, I do not know."

When she did not respond, he ducked under the curtain.

Inez backed away, returning to the office. She was not certain she believed him, but found his sincerity had struck a chord. She knew what it was like to be regarded with suspicion for being "different." Men in Leadville, who did not know her, assumed that any woman who ran a saloon sold more than liquor. How much worse it had to be for John Hee and the others of his kind who lived under constant harassment by hoodlums, the followers of the Workingmen's Party, and normal citizens alike. No wonder they keep to themselves in Chinatown. Strength came from numbers, at least Jamie and others had the truth of it there.

The tribe of musicians arrived shortly thereafter. They filed in the back door somberly, led by Welles. She said, "Gentlemen,

I have some sad news." She had set out shot glasses and a bottle of Scotch on the round table, thinking that, even though it was before noon, a little liquid courage would soothe the shock of what she had to say. "Jamie Monroe fell upon misfortune earlier this week. How it happened is as yet unknown, but on Monday, he was found in Mission Creek, by Long Bridge."

"Drowned?" asked William Ash horrified.

"No," said Inez, wishing someone else was delivering the information. "He was murdered."

Laguardia crossed himself, whispering "*Gesu, Guissepp'*..." Other exclamations of shock and sorrow rippled through the group of friends. They huddled closer, as if seeking comfort from each other. All except Welles, who held himself apart, arms crossed, head bowed, lips compressed.

"He needs a decent burial," said Laguardia. "If we all chip in, we could manage something. Surely Mr. Donato will contribute as well."

Now, for the rest. "The authorities found his family. They are taking him home to his final resting place. That is all I know." She hoped her brevity of explanation and denial of additional knowledge would forestall the natural flood of questions about "where" he was going and "who" was taking him.

She moved to the table and poured shots into each glass. "I wanted you all to know, and bringing you together to tell you seemed the best way. Otto was by earlier—he is working this morning—and I told him as well. I'll just add this. If you have any thoughts, insights, theories as to anyone who might have wished him ill, we could pass that information along. I know you all have your own lives to attend to." She hoped the vague "we" would encourage them to come specifically to her.

Walter Ash picked up a glass and turned to the rest. "We all came west to reinvent ourselves, right? To find new lives, new hope, here in San Francisco. And Jamie was one of us. Full of hope, looking to the future. And he cared, deeply. We may have shrugged off his passion for organizing, his insistence that we musicians should act together to better our lot, but we are surely all in agreement that he was a staunch friend and a good soul." He raised his glass. "To Jamie Monroe. May God rest his soul and help the authorities find the evil that brought an untimely end to his life."

With responses along the lines of "aye," "*absolutament,*" "hear hear!" the liquor was tossed down. A second, and then a third round was provided, along with more toasts. Inez, mindful of the visits she would have to make later that day, touched her lips to her glass but did not drink. She noticed that Welles, standing a little behind the group, did the same.

The young musicians scattered soon thereafter, promising to let Inez know if anything came to mind that might help.

Welles turned to Inez. "Does Nico know?"

"About Jamie? No. Not yet."

"Someone needs to tell him. I can let him know when he comes in this afternoon."

"Thank you." Inez was mightily relieved to avoid that task. She guessed Nico would not be put off by her vagueness and would push for more information.

Welles continued, "I'm sure he's going to want to be the one to break the news to Carmella."

Inez wanted to slap her forehead and curse. Of course Nico would want to tell Carmella. And Carmella, thinking Jamie's death was still a secret, would be caught completely off guard. Lies and secrets, they always complicated matters. She added another task to her day's activities: getting word to Carmella that the others knew of Jamie's death and that his body was taken care of. The rest of the story would have to come later.

Welles glanced toward the showroom. "I might as well open the store. How are the music lessons going?"

For a moment she couldn't figure out what he was talking about. Then she remembered. "Oh, very well, very well, indeed. I have more lined up this afternoon. Before you open, I'd like your help with something." She pulled out the folded list from her pocket and handed it to him. "Do you have any idea what this is?"

He took the list and held it up close and then further away, frowning. "The hand is atrocious. It is difficult to make heads or tails."

"I agree. But look, here is your name on the last page. And Nico is also listed."

Welles gave her a sharp glance. Inez realized she had inadvertently called Nico by his given name. Her face grew hot, and she said quickly, "They are the only names I recognize. Do any of the others seem familiar to you?"

Welles carried the papers over to the alley window, where the light was stronger. "Ah. Now I see. Hmmm. I can't be entirely certain, but this appears to be a list of the union members from the time we organized in the mid-70s. The numbers, though, look like dues paid or accounts." He pursed his lips and cut his eyes to Inez. "Where did you come by this?"

"Does it matter?" Inez shot back. She quickly retreated, injecting an apologetic overtone, "Otto found it in the room he had shared with Jamie. Any thoughts on who might have more information about this?"

"Try Haskell. He and the treasurer were friends from back then. I believe Haskell took all the books, records, and so on when the union dissolved. No one else had the space or desire to hang onto all that. Besides, as I'm sure you've heard, no one was all that keen on the stuff. Once the treasurer vamoosed with the funds, he was dead to us all."

"What was the treasurer's name?"

Welles hesitated for what seemed a long time before finally saying, "Greer. Eli Greer. I hate even saying his name. Brings it all back. Why do you ask?"

Inez folded the paper and tucked it into her pocket. "Curiosity, mostly. I have heard bits and pieces about the demise of the union, but not the full story."

Welles' face darkened, casting a chill shadow over Inez. He

said, "Sorry. It still gets my goat. If not for Nico, me and my family would've been out on the streets. I'd been counting on the return of my portion of the funds to make ends meet. It taught me a valuable lesson, though. Never count on the cash until it's in your pocket."

"It sounds as if it was a very painful time for those of you in the union. No wonder you were not particularly interested in Jamie's efforts to organize."

"It wasn't just that." Welles pressed his lips together in a slight grimace, as if he was trying to keep from blurting something out.

Inez waited, certain that he would eventually fill the silence between them.

He did.

"I hate to speak ill of the dead, but this particularly rankles. You see, Jamie was great at getting folks fired up, saying we musicians had to band together and stand firm, be comrades, arm-in-arm, and insist on better wages and working conditions. Then, not a week ago, he walked right in and underbid me on a position that I'd been counting on."

Up to this point, Welles' tone had been carefully controlled. Now, it became more intense. "It would've been long-term, steady. My kids are growing, we've got another on the way. I want to move us to a bigger place, but for that, I need a steady income. No more of this hand-to-mouth life. It's fine when you're young and single, but not when you're a family man with responsibilities. Anyhow, I'd told Jamie about it, telling him the job was as good as mine. So what does he do but go in and offer to do the job for less."

"That's awful!" Even as she exclaimed in sympathy, Inez thought of Jamie and his apparent financial woes. He'd bought a gold ring for Carmella. He'd promised they would wed, run away if need be. All that cost money. And he'd stopped paying his board, leaving it to Otto to make up the shortfall. She could understand the temptation. But to underbid a friend, one who needed the job just as much, if not more...

Welles bobbed his head, a jerk of agreement. "Not exactly comradely, is it? So, that's why I find it a little difficult to join in all the songs of praise for him, now that he's gone."

"Can't you get the job back?"

Welles almost sneered. "When a musician doesn't show, they yank in a replacement off the streets. There's always someone banging on the door, looking for work." He shook his head. "I'm just grateful Nico came when he did and asked if I was willing to help in the store. Trust me, Mrs. Stannert, I'll do whatever I can around here to make your life easier. Funny, isn't it? Nico has always been there for me, since the early days, and especially after the union went bust. Whenever he needed a pianist for a performance, and one wasn't already lined up, he'd bring me in. Threw jobs my way. Me and my family owe him everything."

Inez said, "It sounds like Mr. Donato has been a true friend to you." She turned to the nearest display case, ostensibly to examine a collection of odd little musical instruments— Oriental in nature, she suspected—but in reality to hide any suspicion betrayed in her expression. She'd seen just a flash of hot anger in him and wondered if that rage could turn murderous.

Someone had killed Jamie. And according to what de Bruijn said and she had seen, it was a brutal attack, which went far past a blow or two. It was an attack fueled by a passion of the most heinous sort. But Welles stood to lose much, if found out. Family, reputation, everything.

Would a family man do such a thing?

Look how much he's lost, not just last week, but also in the past. It can all add up, whispered that little voice inside of her.

Inez watched the pianist as he strode through the showroom to the entry door and stepped out into the street to greet one of their sheet-music suppliers. Would she now have to add Thomas Welles to her list of possible suspects? The list only seemed to grow, while the only thing growing shorter was time.

Chapter Twenty-eight

After leaving the store, Inez returned to the apartment to write a quick note to Carmella. She then tore it up. What could she say that wouldn't sound suspicious if found by Nico? Finally, she went to the corner where she had found the boy who had delivered the message to Flo. The boy was there, hands in pockets, whistling.

Inez approached him and said, "Do you remember me?"

He looked up, pulled on the brim of his cap, and said, "Sure. You're the lady with the message to Mrs. Florence Sweet at the Palace Hotel about hats. D'you have another message for her?"

"I have another message, yes, but not for Mrs. Sweet." She explained she wanted him to go to a private residence in the Western Addition—she gave him the address—and ask for Miss Donato. "If the door is answered by a gentleman, say you have the wrong house, apologize, and leave." She thought it unlikely Nico would be home. It was late enough in the day that by the time the messenger arrived, Nico would be on his way to the music store or already there.

The boy looked intrigued. "Crikey."

Inez continued, "If Miss Donato is home, tell her Mrs. Stannert says, 'Your friends know and your brother will know soon. Act accordingly. All is well, do not worry, I shall be by to see you in a few days.'"

"What if she has a message for you?"

Inez pointed down the street. "See the door next to the music store?"

"Sure."

"Have her write a note, seal it, address the envelope to Mrs. Stannert, and slide it under that door." She gave him two dimes, thinking the additional distance and time it would take to complete his task was worth it.

Next on her list: Haskell.

A short walk brought her to a three-story building. She paused inside the lobby, preparing herself for the climb up a staircase of narrow, steep stairs. Next to the wooden balustrade, which looked as if it could benefit from a good scrubbing and polishing, was a small sign pointing upward that said "The Workingman's Voice—Organize, unite, be heard!" Below, was the encouraging annotation "Third Floor," accompanied by an arrow.

Clutching her satchel and closed umbrella in one hand, Inez gripped the railing with the other and began her ascent.

A steady stream of men moved in the opposite direction. Many had the "air of the sea" about them while others appeared to be in league with the printing trade, if their ink-stained hands and clothes were any indication. All were unfailingly polite, saying variations of "Excuse me, ma'am," and stepping aside to let her pass.

She felt their eyes on her back and guessed that visitors of the female persuasion were few and far between at *The Workingman's Voice.* By the time she had made her way to the door of the newspaper office, she was beginning to think that perhaps she should have tried to catch Haskell at the end of the day.

Nothing to be done about it now. I am here, and I am not leaving without talking to Haskell himself. Too, there were other reasons. Welles had refused to say much. She hesitated to approach Nico directly. If dour Welles looked askance at her digging into the background of the early union, how would volatile Nico respond?

No, it was best to talk to Haskell, who, although an enthusiastic supporter and advocate of the labor unions and efforts in the city, had not been a member of the musicians union.

The door opened, emitting another fellow of the printing trade. He held it so Inez could enter. Inside was a cramped office space that included three desks, unoccupied except for the towering stacks of newspapers and other printed materials, and a fourth desk nearly hidden by a clutch of men. From the gravel voice and noxious cigar smoke that erupted from the epicenter, Inez guessed that Haskell himself sat at the desk. She heard him say, "The old guard from the Workingmen's Party was on the sandlot Sunday, but they've lost their fire, no surprise."

She cleared her throat and the huddle turned toward her. Conversation stopped dead, hats came off, and the group parted, revealing Haskell squinting through the tobacco-heavy miasma. He rose from his chair, adjusting his tie and tugging his waistcoat down from its rumpled advance upwards over a not-quite-white shirt. "Mrs. Stannert! This is a surprise! But we'll not look askance at a visit from the manager of one of the up-and-coming fine music stores of the city." He plucked the cigar from his mouth and grinned. "Welcome to *The Workingman's Voice*. You caught us doing what journalists do best—gossiping. So, what brings you to these parts?"

All those men staring at her made her uncomfortably aware of how unused she was of being the center of attention. She cleared her throat. "If I could take a few minutes of your time, I was hoping you could help me with some labor-related questions." Inez hesitated, eyeing the men who looked just as rumpled as Haskell. "I do apologize for the interruption. But it's important that I speak with you privately."

Haskell beamed. "No problem! Always happy to provide information on the labor activities of our fair city. 'Organize, agitate, educate, must be our war cry.'" He turned to his compatriots. "Any of you know who said that?"

"Henry George? Sounds like something out of his book *Progress and Poverty*," ventured one.

Haskell shook his head. "Susan B. Anthony. Goes to show, gentlemen, never underestimate the ladies." He balanced his half-smoked cigar on the edge of his desk, perilously close to a pile of what looked like trade circulars. "Shall we continue later? Give me some time to talk with Mrs. Stannert here and to digest the news, eh?"

The men, who, in absence of introduction, Inez surmised were reporters or scribblers of some stripe or other, filed out of the office, with one tossing over his shoulder, "See ya at the Parker House, Rog."

"You dined at the Parker House, Mrs. Stannert?" Haskell cleared off a chair for her, the process consisting of shifting a stack of newspapers off the seat and onto the floor. "Beans baked with green pepper, the best in the city. Highly recommended."

"I have not had the pleasure, but shall make an effort to try it some time." Inez sat, or rather perched, on the edge of the rickety chair. One of its legs was shorter than the others. Looking around, Inez realized her chair was in better shape than the others that she could see. She wondered if the state of Haskell's furniture was one reason all of the pressmen had been standing, then reined in her mind from idle speculation.

"I understand you have a vast knowledge of the labor activities and trade unions in town," she began.

He nodded. "I've been here a long time. Was a newsman on *The Call*, back when. Reported on the fight for a ten-hour day. Was there in March 1870, the day when a thousand men showed up for a hundred jobs to clear Yerba Buena Park. Listened to Henry George jawbone about the plight of the laboring man and the vanishing frontier, and proofed his *Progress and Poverty* back in 1875. That book ended up selling like hotcakes, too. The depression of 1877 was tough on workers here. I watched the Workingmen's Party of California rise and fall, the pick-handle brigade face off against the sandlot rioters. Now, we got Frank Roney, his Seamen's Protective Union, and the Trades Assembly. Gotta say, it's never dull." He raised his tangled eyebrows. "But I'm guessing you didn't come all this way to hear me pontificate. What can I do for you?"

"It has to do with the musicians union."

He laughed. "What union? The one that stuttered and collapsed back in '74? Or the one in young Monroe's imagination?"

"Ah." Inez realized Haskell didn't yet know about Jamie's fate.

After she explained, he sobered. "Apologies. I didn't mean to speak ill of the dead. A real shame about Monroe." He stared down at his desk blotter, his face sagging. "He had a lot of passion. Conviction. I actually thought he might pull it off, once he hit his stride. He reminded me of Roney." He blinked, then refocused on Inez. "At least the young fella is going home. Glad they found his family."

There it was. A natural opening for what she wanted to discuss.

"Otto brought Mr. Monroe's effects to me for safekeeping, just until they can be delivered to the family. I wanted to ask you about some papers that were in his possession." She pulled out the pages from her satchel and held them out to him. "Welles thought they might be from those union days."

He took the papers from her. "Oh, yeah. Monroe came and asked me all about the most recent go-round. D'you know, the musicians have been trying to organize for a long time around here. In 1850, when California became a state, they demanded a wage increase, saying they wouldn't play at the celebration unless they got one. Well, guess what? No music got played and I don't think anyone missed it. After that there were two attempts at unionizing. First one was in '69 and didn't get far. The second time was, like I said, in '74. They had better luck then, but it still didn't last."

"I understand you knew the treasurer from the most recent union? Welles told me his name was Greer."

"Yeah. I knew Eli Greer pretty well, or thought I did. A strange business, him disappearing when the union dissolved, taking off with the union funds. He sure didn't seem the type. I guess you never really know what a fellow's made of until he's faced with temptation."

"I wondered about that when you mentioned it the other night. Didn't anyone try to find him? Report him to the police?"

"Oh, sure. Not that our efforts amounted to anything. In fact, I spent some time trying to work out what happened to Eli myself. Talked to his wife, and some of his associates and friends. Even bought a drink or two for the detective looking into the matter. Nothing. It was like he'd vanished into thin air."

"Mr. Welles also said you 'inherited' some of the organization's records. Did Jamie look through them on one of his visits here? Could these papers be from them? " She surveyed the office, noting the stacks and boxes lining the walls and spilling out onto the floor. It was as if a paper army was gathering, preparing to launch itself upon the last vestiges of empty space.

"He did. He was curious as to why the union failed. I told him what I could. I also suggested he talk to some of the members from that time who are still around. Fellows like Welles, Donato, some of the others. He wanted to look through the records, and I said sure. No one else cared about them. They've been sitting there for years." Haskell nodded at a pile of boxes by the back window, listing dangerously to one side. "I pulled out what I had and left him to it."

The newspaperman focused on the pages from Inez, running a cursory eye over them. "I'm guessing this is a list of the members. I didn't know them all, but some of the names are familiar."

"You can read this?" Inez thought back to how both she and Welles had had trouble interpreting the crabbed scribbles.

"Oh, I come across worse than this in my job," he said. "Besides, I knew Greer and learned how to interpret his hieroglyphs. When you're a newsman, that sort of thing sticks with you."

"The numbers, could they be funds?"

"Most likely." He ran a finger down the column. "Largish amounts. Not typical monthly dues. I wonder. Maybe this is a record of the disbursements to be made when the union dissolved. The numbers are too large to be much of anything else. And original members would've received more, while those who joined later would've received less. That certainly tracks with what's here."

"Since this was in Mr. Monroe's possession, I am guessing he had some interest in what happened after the demise of the union. Perhaps he was trying to figure out what happened to Mr. Greer and the funds."

Haskell shrugged. "That's possible. But if so, that trail is long cold. You know, I felt pretty sorry for Eli's wife, and for the first year or so after he disappeared, I would re-visit things and ask around, just to see if anyone remembered anything as time went on."

"And?"

"Memory is a slippery thing, Mrs. Stannert, and the more time passes, the more imagination takes over where memory leaves off. It all eventually devolved into 'I might recollect something one guy heard from another guy.' One member thought he remembered Eli saying how if he ever got the chance, he'd head lickety-split for New York where there were more opportunities. Another thought maybe Eli joined the gold rush to Deadwood, up Dakota Territory way. Someone else thought maybe he once mentioned moving to Arizona Territory. When all those vague stories started being passed around, I knew it was a lost cause."

"If no one got their shares, it could have been enough to start over, if he was so inclined."

"True. Maybe the temptation was too great. Still, I would've thought he'd take the missus with him."

"Or maybe he was an easy mark for murder."

"True again."

Inez pondered on Mrs. Greer and what it must have been like for her. Perhaps her husband had kissed her good-bye one morning, promising to be home in time for dinner, and then… nothing. Much like what had happened to Inez the day her husband Mark had disappeared. "What happened to Mrs. Greer?"

"She stayed in town for a while, hoping he'd surface or that someone would eventually find him. Finally, she went Back East to her kin. I lost track of her then."

So much for talking to the wife, Inez thought resignedly. If there was anything to be found out about the vanished treasurer and funds, it would have to be through the list that Jamie Monroe had kept hidden under his mattress.

"What about the first name on this list?" Inez asked. "There's a checkmark by it, in pencil. The mark could have been original on the ledger, but looks more recent to me."

"Hmmm." Haskell squinted. "Abbott, S. I'll bet that's Stephen Abbott. I remember him. Lost use of his hands shortly before the union went bust. A musician who can't use his hands has it pretty tough. Haven't heard about him in years."

"Any thoughts on how I might find him, if he is still in the city?"

Haskell scratched his jaw. "There's the city directory, of course. But it doesn't catch everyone. You could try the Musical Protective Association. They assist sick and disabled members and families. Been around since '64 and reorganized in the mid-70s, right around the time the union went belly-up. They might know of him, or what happened to him."

"Where would I find this society?"

"They meet the second Tuesday of every month." He held up his hand at her exclamation of dismay. "Yeah, you just missed it. But if you're in a big hurry, and it seems you are, I'd say go talk to the secretary, John Baumann." Haskell broke off and snatched up his cigar, which was still smoldering on the edge of his desk.

Inez noted that the scarred wood was pocked with old burn marks and now a new one as well.

Haskell stuck the cigar in his mouth and mumbled around it, "Hold on a minute." He opened a drawer, extracted a battered copy of the city directory, and thumbed through it. "No Stephen Abbott. Let's try Baumann. Here we go. I'll write down the address for you." He turned to a tin can on his desk, bristling with sharpened pencils, took one, and neatly block-printed the address on the top page of the list.

He handed the papers back to her. "There. Now, are you going to tell me what all this is about?"

Inez sighed. "I wish I knew. I am trying to figure out what Jamie Monroe was doing the last few days of his life. This list was tucked away, hidden." She hesitated. "He had indicated, not directly to me but to someone else, that there was some... danger...coming from his activities in the labor movement. I'm trying to see if that perhaps had anything to do with his demise."

Haskell crossed his arms over his ample stomach and peered at Inez. "Seems more a job for the local law than the lady manager of a music store."

She thought briefly of her previous life and the many times—too many times—she had become entangled in murderous goings-on in Colorado. *I am not in Colorado now. I must be more circumspect.* "You are quite right, of course. But I can't stop thinking of Jamie, his family, the awfulness of the entire situation, and wishing I could do something, no matter how small, to shed light on what happened. I suppose it is human to want to make sense out of senseless violence. I am probably grasping at straws. Should I discover anything useful, I would of course go to the police." She mentally crossed her fingers.

Haskell nodded. "Good. See that you do. We'd miss those Monday night palavers over cards should something befall you." He gave her a small smile. "That was a joke, but not a good one. And we're not the only ones who'd miss your presence. Nico'd be lost without you. Dunno if he's made it clear to you, Mrs. Stannert, but he's real impressed with how you turned his business around. And in case you didn't know, he's a hard man to impress."

He put his elbows on the desk and leaned over it. "You didn't hear that from me. But seriously, if you're going to be nosing around the edges of Monroe's involvement with the local labor movements, be careful. There are some dangerous characters out there. Not the musicians, of course, but should you go farther afield in your queries as to his activities and associates..." He let that hang.

She tucked the list away in her satchel. "I promise you I will not put myself in a situation I cannot handle." She thought of her pocket revolver, safely secured in the drawer of her nightstand, loaded and ready for use.

"I'm sure you won't, Mrs. Stannert. You are a woman of common sense." Haskell glanced at the city directory. "My guess is Abbott is no longer with us. I'll do a little asking around for you, but I suspect if you do find an address for him, it'll probably be in Laurel Hill Cemetery."

"Perhaps." Inez picked up her umbrella and prepared to leave. *With luck, the cards will break my way and I will find out if any of this has anything to do with Jamie's death.*

Chapter Twenty-nine

Before Antonia had left for school that morning, Mrs. S had said, "Well, you are certainly cheerful today. Your catarrh nearly gone?"

"Uh-huh." She felt better, her head and nose hardly stuffy at all.

So she was in a good mood when she spotted Patrick May, the tall negro boy with reddish hair who delivered their laundry and was one of Mrs. Stannert's piano students. Mrs. S had let her hang around a few times during his lessons. He was really, *really* good. Mrs. S said so, and Antonia, after hearing him, thought so too.

He was walking ahead of her down Kearney, toward Market, hands in his pockets. She quickened her pace, calling, "Hey, Patrick!"

He turned around and looked kind of surprised to see her. He waited until she caught up then said, "Well, hello, Miss Gizzi."

"Well, hello, you can call me Antonia." She fell in step beside him. "Where you going?"

"Going to catch the horsecar on Market to get back to my ma and aunt's laundry. I have a brick wall to build. Where are you off to? School?"

"Yep. Lincoln School, the other side of Market. Is it all right if I walk with you a ways?" She was curious about him, and this was the first time she'd been able to talk with him.

He looked at her oddly. "You sure that's a good idea, Miss Gizzi?"

"I'm not Miss Gizzi, I'm Antonia. You keep calling me that and I'm gonna call you Mr. May. And sure I'm sure. It's just a little ways. Besides, I wanted to tell you," now she felt awkward, "you sure do play the piano nice. I wish I could do the same."

"Well, maybe you just need to ask your aunt to give you lessons."

"She's tried. I'm all thumbs and no music sense, she says." Then she said what popped into her mind. "Don't you go to school? There's a school for nig—" She stopped herself. Mrs. S had said niggers wasn't a good word to use, was like a slap in the face, no matter what she'd heard in the back alleys of Leadville. "For negroes?"

"Oh, I'm done with schooling. Learnt my ABCs and my numbers and that was it. Have to help my ma and aunt at the laundry. They need a man around to help out."

She looked at him doubtfully. He was big, really tall, and probably strong, but he sure wasn't no man yet. "So, where's your laundry?"

"Way south of Market on Berry Street. By the Mission Creek canal and the wharves. Where the schooners and such bring in lumber, bricks, and hay. Not a place you'd want to go, Miss Gizzi."

"Maybe, maybe not, Mr. May." She decided right then and there to ask Mrs. S to take her there someday. "What do you do at the laundry?"

"I do the heavy lifting, the deliveries. Fetch and carry." He grinned. "Whatever they tell me to do, basically."

"How do you practice your music? Do you have a piano?"

"No piano. Sometimes…"

"Sometimes what?"

"Well, next door, they sometimes let me use their piano. When no one else is."

She wanted to ask what this place was, but he looked so

uncomfortable she decided not to. Instead she asked, "D'you play by yourself? Or with others? D'you have any friends down there on the wharf?"

He laughed. "You are full of questions, aren't you? The piano, I usually play alone. Sometimes, though, I'll go see Black Bill and we'll play our mouth harps, when I have a little space of time."

She wrinkled her nose. "Black Bill?"

"'Cause of his skin, you know. He's like me."

She looked at him and said, "You're not black. You're more…tan."

"Well, I s'ppose most folks wouldn't make that fine distinction. They look and they see what they want to see."

She nodded, thinking back. "You know, where I used to live, there was Coffee Joe. He ran a, uh, saloon." She wasn't sure if he'd be shocked she'd know that, but then plunged on. "And at school, some of the kids call me a gypsy, 'cause of my skin. When I lived in Colorado, some of the boys gave me the nickname Deuce because of my eyes. But I didn't mind that. It wasn't like they were teasing."

"Your eyes?"

She pulled off her tinted spectacles and lifted her face so he could see her eyes from under the bonnet.

"Ha! First time I've seen someone with two different eyes like that. One blue and one brown. How'd that happen?"

She shrugged and put her spectacles back on. "My maman, that is, my ma, she had the same kind of eyes. People used to call her a witch, say she was cursed. All because of her eyes."

"Huh. Well, like I said. People look, and they see what they want to see. And then they don't look any further."

She nodded vigorously. "Say, I'd sure like to hear you and Black Bill sometime. Especially if you play the mouth harp as good as you play the piano."

He laughed. "The dump at Mission Creek is no place for someone like you, Miss Gizzi."

"The dump? He lives at the dump?"

"Yep. He's not quite all…" Patrick tapped his forehead. "He's a rag-picker, digs through the garbage lookin' for stuff to sell, and sometimes begs along the wharf. I sneak him a little food now and again, when my ma and aunt aren't looking. He has himself a little tent out in the dump, with a raggedy flag planted right outside. He fought in the war. Union side, of course. Says he paid his dues, and he claims that little spot of land on the dump as his rightful due payment from the U. S. of A. for services rendered. Well, he don't say it like that, but that's the idea."

So, this Black Bill fought in the war. That meant he was *old*.

"Do you have friends that live down there?"

"I'd say Black Bill is my only friend, actually. I'm too busy working, and there's not a lot of my kind down there."

She stopped. "Mr. May, I guess I'm not 'your kind' either, but we're both different, right? That's a kind of a kind. So, I'd be honored if you'd count me as your friend. I'll be your north of Market friend, and Black Bill can be your south of Market friend."

"That's good of you, Miss Gizzi." He sounded amused, like he was humoring her.

"I mean it." She insisted. "Copper Mick at school is the only friend I have. He's got red hair, that's why he's called that. Well, because his pa's in the force, too. Anyway, if we're friends now, that'll mean we both have two."

He grinned. "All right then."

"We're friends now, so you can call me Antonia."

"Well, all right then, Miss Antonia."

"And someday I want to hear you and Black Bill play the mouth harp."

"Maybe someday."

"Goodbye, Mr. Patrick."

Turning on Market, she headed toward school, happier than she'd been in a long time.

Two friends!
Maybe San Francisco wasn't so bad after all.

• ● ● ● •

After classes, Antonia hopped down the steps of Lincoln School, thinking her meeting Patrick May must've been a lucky thing, because the day had only gotten better from there. She couldn't wait to tell Mrs. S what Persnickety Pierce had said. Her teacher had actually complimented her! In front of the class!

Yep, things were definitely looking up. Now, if she could just help Mrs. S work out what happened to Jamie Monroe, everything would be hunky-dory.

A familiar voice behind her said, "There you are!" and next thing, Copper Mick was beside her, a big grin on his face. "I've got news for you," he announced.

"And me for you," said Antonia. "You first."

"Where are we walking?" He looked around. "This may take some time."

"Where do you live?"

"Down Third Street a bit. A few blocks."

"Can we walk over there so I can see your place? And then we can turn around and walk up toward the music store."

"Well, sure. I don't see why not. Except my sisters might make pests of themselves if they see us, so let's go down Fifth and take a side street."

They started walking, putting Lincoln School behind them.

Mick started. "Well, I did like you said, and asked my pa about the Long Bridge murder, kinda suggesting the little kids at school were talking about a boogeyman under the bridge had done it."

"And?" Antonia prompted.

"And he said, nah, it wasn't nothing of the sort. Just some poor bloke who was in the wrong place in the wrong time."

"What else?"

"And I asked if he was working the case to find who did it. He said he *had* been at first but was called off the case. Politics, he said. Which would explain why he was grumpy a couple days ago. Then he said things changed and he's now working it 'on the side.' He was even cheerful about it but warned me not to tell Ma because she'd have his hide."

"Anything else?" Antonia bounced on her toes a little, impatient to tell him her plan, as they stepped off the walkway to cross the street.

"Yep. You're gonna like this, I'll bet." Mick stuck his hands in his pockets, trying, Antonia guessed, to look casual, but obviously bursting to tell her something.

"Well?" she prodded.

"He said he's making progress and might even be making an arrest soon." The freckles on his face crinkled up with his smile. "He told me to keep it under my hat. So you gotta keep it under your bonnet as well, all right?" He reached out and tugged on her bonnet brim, dragging it down over her eyes and nearly dislodging her spectacles.

She pushed her hat back up and wished she was tall enough to yank down his cap in return. "Wow. I wonder who he thinks it is."

"He said he thinks a local. I suppose that could be almost anyone. Some hoodlum, or cutthroat, maybe a rag-picker or two-bit thug."

Antonia stopped dead in her tracks realizing something she hadn't thought of before. "Or maybe a Chinaman," she whispered. *John Hee.*

Mick had kept walking as he was talking but now stopped and backtracked. "A Chinaman? What made you think of that?"

"Remember I talked to you about Mr. Brown, the private detective who's trying to figure out who killed Mr. Monroe? Well, last night I heard," she hesitated, "*over*heard him and my aunt, Mrs. S, talking about who might've done it."

"Suspects!" Now Mick sounded really excited. "And they think a Chinaman did it?"

"Not Mrs. S, but the detective hinted around that he thought so." She took a deep breath. "The music store where we live and my aunt works. There's a Chinaman who works there, too. Repairing instruments and doing other stuff. His name is John Hee."

Mick looked confused. "This Mr. Brown suspects him? Does he live down by the wharves around Mission Creek? Why doesn't he live in Chinatown?"

"The music store has a warehouse down there. Anyhow, Mr. Brown was suggesting…" she was squirming a little now "… that maybe John Hee had something to do with Mr. Monroe's death. But I'm with Mrs. S on this. I don't think he did it."

Mick looked doubtful. "I dunno. The stories I hear about Chinatown, and the tongs, you don't want to get on the wrong side of them."

"Well, Mr. Brown said he's going to follow John Hee tonight and, I guess, try to find out more about him. So, Mick, you and me are going to follow them and see what's up."

"Into Chinatown?" He sounded really surprised now.

"Have you been there before?"

"Well, sure. The boys, you know, we go there sometimes on a bit of a dare. But you, you can't go, you're a girl." He stopped. "Sorry, Antonia. I don't mean no disrespect."

"I've got a way we can do this," she said, determined to say her piece. "And there'll be two of us, and you'll be with me, and no one will recognize me." She thought of the men's clothes she'd worn as a newsie in Leadville, when she pretended to be a boy. The clothes she'd snuck out of her storage room trunk and stuck under her bed to be ready for tonight.

She continued, "So, this is what we're gonna do. What's the name of your sister who's in my class?"

"Who's your teacher?"

"Persnickety Pierce." She bit her lip. "I mean, Miss Pierce."

He snorted. "Persnickety Pierce. That's a good one. Did you make that up?"

She nodded.

"That'd be Katie."

Antonia flashed on a redheaded girl with a face covered with freckles and two braids that always seemed about to unravel.

"She can be a bit of a prissy missy," he added. He slowed to a stop and pointed. "See that two-story house about half-way down across the street with two girls on the stoop? That's our place. My brother Daniel—he's the street patrolman you met—lives on the top floor, with his missus and baby, and my ma's sister and gran. The rest of us live on the bottom floor."

Antonia noticed the house had flower boxes along the bottom windows, and looked clean and nice. Mrs. S, if she ever saw it, would approve.

She said, "Now let's walk back toward the music store." They turned around and headed toward Market Street. Antonia continued, "I'm gonna tell Mrs. S that Katie invited me to your house for dinner tonight. One reason I want to see your place is so I can say I walked there with her after school and it's not far away."

"Uh, this might be hard to get Kate to agree to. She'll want to know what this is all about, and why you're coming over, and—"

"I won't be coming over," said Antonia. "It's a ruse." She liked how the word *ruse* sounded. It sure sounded better than saying they were going to lie.

"And," she continued, "you're going to tell your parents that one of your friends asked *you* over for dinner, and that you're gonna stay a while afterwards and help him with whatever you're studying now in class."

"Geography," said Mick absently, his eyebrows creased in a frown. "So, you won't be at my home having dinner, I won't really be helping a friend with homework, instead we'll be trailing a detective who's trailing a Chinaman?"

"Right!" Antonia was proud of herself for coming up with this devious plan. "And since John Hee leaves work at six, you better come over at, say, five-thirty to walk me to your home for dinner."

"Oh yeah?" He looked a little taken aback at that. "Why?"

"Well, Mrs. S isn't gonna let me just waltz around downtown on my own after dark. But if she meets you—and I just know you can do all the 'hello, ma'am, nice to meet you, ma'am' proper talk—she won't mind."

"I can do that." He looked down at his school garb. "If we're going to be sneaking around Chinatown, I can't wear this."

"I have it worked out. Bring a rucksack with the kind of clothes you want to wear. If she asks, you can say it's books or last minute groceries for dinner or something. But I don't think she'll ask you. Once we leave, I know a place right close by where you can change clothes. No one will know."

"And what about you?" He looked her up and down, from her ruffled bonnet and lace collar to her plaid skirt and proper boots. "What are you going to do?"

She grinned. "Don't worry about me. Once you're changed, I'll do the same. You'll see."

Once they got close, Antonia showed him the door next to the store, the one that led up to where they lived. "Just ring the bell. But don't be later than five-thirty."

Mick nodded and glanced up at the sky. "I'd better skedaddle then. I sure hope you know what we're doing here. I don't like lying to my parents. My da, he's got a nose for liars."

"Well, look at it this way. You *are* helping a friend...me! And it's even with geography of a sort. You're going to get us around Chinatown, and that's something I sure couldn't do on my own. It'll be an adventure, Mick. And we'll be helping my aunt, and maybe helping find a killer, or at least narrowing the suspects, because it's not John Hee. He's innocent, I'm sure."

Mick left at a trot, and Antonia continued to the door leading upstairs after glancing in the store window. Mr. Donato was there, talking with Mr. Welles, who was frowning. He was one sourpuss, that Mr. Welles. But when she'd said that to Mrs. S, Mrs. S had just said he was a family man with a lot of responsibilities, which he took very seriously. "Unlike some men I've known," Mrs. S had muttered under her breath, and Antonia had wondered if maybe she was thinking about Mr. Stannert back in Leadville.

Just then, John Hee came out from the repair room. It looked like he was showing Mr. Donato a strange, almost-a-violin-but-not-quite sort of instrument. Not wanting to be caught staring through the window, Antonia scooted off to the living quarters.

She was a little disappointed that Mrs. S wasn't there, as she wanted to blather out her story, her ruse, while it was all still fresh in her mind. What would she do if Mrs. S didn't come back in time to meet Copper Mick? She'd have to write a note, leave, and hope for the best, hope that Mrs. S wouldn't be mad that she, Antonia, had gone off without checking with her first.

At least she had some time to prepare.

Antonia pulled the worn and tattered men's clothes out from under her bed. Off came her school clothes and petticoats, and on went the trousers and shirt. She struggled back into her dress, rolled up the pant cuffs so they didn't show, and stuffed the cuffs of the too-big shirt up into the dress sleeves. The old waistcoat wouldn't fit underneath, and there was also the ratty jacket and the faded red cap, as well as the too-large shoes with a dime-size hole in the left sole. She bundled up everything in the jacket, hurried down the hall, through the storage room, out the door, and down the rickety steps, keeping an eye out and an ear cocked in case someone stepped out the back of the music store.

Luckily, no one did, which allowed her to sidle past the back entrance to the old outhouse in the alley leaning hard against the rear wall. Antonia silently thanked her lucky stars they had a water closet and she didn't have to use the musty little wooden shack. Someone had put a lock on it, but not a very good one, because Antonia was able to remove it in a jiffy. She'd explored the outhouse before. It wasn't too bad. And it had a high shelf off to the side, perfect for stuffing her rolled-up jacket and its contents. Once that was done, she rehung the lock, but didn't close it, and hurried up the rickety stairs to the storage room.

It was almost sunset when Mrs. S came home. She looked tired, distracted, but the first question out of her mouth was, "How was school?"

Antonia was happy she actually had some good news to report. "Great! Miss Pierce complimented me on my times tables memorization. And I solved all the problems she put up on the blackboard, faster than anyone else in class. And I got all the oral problems right, too!"

Mrs. S nodded. "See what happens when you apply yourself?"

Antonia wasn't sure if it was because she had "applied" anything. The answers just seemed to "be there," without her hardly thinking. Even the new multiplication problems today had not been hard. Although her classmates seemed to think they were.

"Oh! And I was asked over to dinner tonight by one of the girls in my class, Katie Lynch."

Mrs. S raised her eyebrows in that way that told Antonia she'd better sound convincing when she told her story. So, she did. And it sure helped that the downstairs bell rang before Mrs. S could start asking a bunch of questions.

"That must be Katie's older brother, Michael," said Antonia brightly. "Katie said he'd walk me to their house on Third and walk me home after. He's in seventh grade. He wants to be a policeman, like his father. That's what Katie told me."

Mrs. Stannert's eyebrows rose higher at that. But once she answered the door, and Copper Mick whipped off his cap and started with his "Good evening, ma'am," and "Pleased to meet you, ma'am," and "Sure glad my little sister's finally found a friend at school," and other such blarney-blather, Mrs. S seemed to warm up. After Mick gave Mrs. S his address, she sent Antonia and him off, with the stern warning that Antonia should be home no later than nine o'clock.

"I may not be here," she said, "but I expect you to act responsibly and get yourself to bed at a reasonable hour."

"Yes'm, I will."

They hurried down the block until Antonia nudged Mick into a narrow slot between two buildings. "Turn here!"

"Where are we going?"

"You'll see. Hurry! We don't have much time!"

When she finally showed him the old outhouse, he balked. "I'm not going in there. I'd rather change right here in the alley."

"Suit yourself," said Antonia. "I'll use it then. I'm gonna be quick, and you'd better be quicker, that's all I've got to say."

She went in, closed the door, and shucked off her dress. After pulling on the rest of her disguise, she turned the dress inside out and rolled it up, so it wouldn't gather any dust, and stuffed her dress, coat, bonnet, and shoes up on the shelf. Then she put her spectacles up there too. The last thing she wanted to do was lose those and somehow have to explain to Mrs. S. She clutched at the locket with her maman's photograph, hanging under the men's shirt and her camisole. She'd forgotten to take it off inside her room. *I'm not leaving it in this shithouse.* The locket on the braided hair chain would stay where it was, hidden and safe.

Cap pulled low and tight to her ears, she slammed out through the rickety door to find Copper Mick, a bundle of clothes in his arms, standing there looking uncertain. His eyes widened in the near-dusk light. "Antonia? Is that you? Mother of—" He checked himself. "If I hadn't seen you go in, I'd never guess that was you coming out."

"Thanks." She added, "If you gotta call me by name, call me Tony, all right?"

"Sure." He looked at the yawning outhouse, said, "If you

can do it, I can do it," and plunged inside. She heard him rustling around in there, and a grumble or two emerged. "It's dark in here. Don't want to fall down the hole or drop a shoe or…" followed by "Stinks too. But not as bad as I thought it would."

"Shush," she whispered. "Just hurry!"

More shuffling and mumbling and eventually Mick tumbled out, disheveled and breathless, stuffing his good jacket into his knapsack.

Antonia looked at him admiringly. "You look like a real hoodlum, Mick."

He glanced down at his worn trousers, nearly out at the knees. "Not sure that's a good thing for Chinatown."

"C'mon, the six o'clock bells are going to ring soon. We need to be where we can watch the front door." She led him out of the alley and to the corner of Kearney and Pine. They stopped short of the pool of lamplight and pushed themselves against the side of the building. The evening church bells started, and Antonia said, "Watch."

Sure enough, the door to the music store opened before the last echo died away. John Hee, with his wide-brimmed hat and a long, narrow sack slung over his back, started walking west. Mick sucked in his breath. "He's headed toward Chinatown," he whispered.

Antonia shook his sleeve. "Over there. Across the street."

They watched a shadow detach from the gloom under a store awning. The shadow passed under a streetlamp and briefly became an unassuming man with a small beard and mustache, almost invisible in his dark coat and derby. "That's him!" said Antonia. "The detective. Mr. Brown."

They watched him walk in the same direction as John Hee, staying on the opposite side of the street, blending in with all the other men in their dark suits and coats.

Antonia tugged on Copper Mick's sleeve again. "Come on!"

Shadows following shadows, the two joined the thin stream of pedestrians and blended into the approaching night.

Chapter Thirty

Following Mr. Hee proved simple.

He proceeded without evasion to Chinatown while de Bruijn lingered a modest distance behind, keeping an eye on the Chinese violin Hee conveniently had slung across his back. The stringed instrument, an erhu, was inside a long sack with its distinctive head and tuning pegs protruding from the top. As he slowed his pace to match Hee's, the detective pondered what he'd uncovered about Hee and Donato earlier that day.

The warehouse had been the focus of his interest. When he had first learned of its existence, he had wondered if some kind of smuggling might be involved. Opium, of course, was his first thought. But there were other possibilities. Artifacts and items of historical, artistic, or economic significance, for instance. It was an easy scenario to build: a ship from the Orient would arrive, carrying certain illegally obtained goods. An intermediary would be necessary to bridge the Celestial and Occidental worlds—in other words, John Hee. The goods could be stored in the warehouse and eventually displayed and sold as "curiosities" at Donato's store. Perhaps some were spirited straight to the homes and private museums of personal collectors, willing to pay dearly for them.

Nothing would be easier.

The more de Bruijn had considered it and inquired amongst those he knew in the shadowy world of antiquities collectors, the more he became convinced that his scenario had merit. Too, there was the matter of Donato's elevated standard of living and affluence. His ascendance to the top of recognized musical talent could account for some of his prosperity, but not all. First, he bought the store. Then, the warehouse. And most recently, the house where he lived with his sister. And he did not skimp on his wardrobe, being a regular customer at the most exclusive tailors and haberdasheries in the city, nor his priceless collection of stringed instruments.

And he never ran a tab but paid in cash.

For everything.

There was also Mr. Donato's personal life, which seemed chock-full of intrigues and liaisons with women primarily from the higher levels of society. His charm was legendary, which gave de Bruijn pause when he thought of Mrs. Stannert and Donato working in close proximity. Surely she wouldn't inadvertently let slip that the violinist was considered a suspect in young Gallagher's death. But as de Bruijn knew, even the most intimate of secrets fell victim to the heat of passion or the magnetism of charisma.

De Bruijn gave himself a mental shake and refocused on Hee, who was moving through the shifting pedestrian traffic on the opposite side of the street.

Chinatown lay just ahead. It was time to narrow the distance between himself and his target.

Once they stepped over the invisible border into Chinatown, the streets and lanes would become more crowded, more difficult to navigate, more shadowed, more dangerous. Although de Bruijn was no stranger to this neighborhood, it had been many years since his last foray. Even though police patrolled regularly and armed officers accompanying curious visitors touring the quarter, he had to stay on his guard.

He was alone.

De Bruijn crossed the street and entered foreign territory.

The lighting, the language, the scents, the buildings, the

very air and ground—all shifted. The surge of pedestrians intensified, while the individuals parted around him as water around the bow of a ship. Groups huddled in the doorways and on the boardwalks, moved in and out of buildings. He passed laundries, pawnbrokers, gambling halls, clothing stores, apothecaries, and businesses with display windows crammed with miscellaneous wares, all packed as tightly as the streets.

Between buildings, narrow, dark alleys displayed the white ghosts of garments hung to dry on invisible clotheslines. Signboards in gilt, black, and red—over doors, on window-frames, and on door-facings and on walls—exhibited the fluid slashes of Chinese calligraphy and, in some instances, the familiar English letters. Large Chinese lanterns suspended from the small, street-facing balconies of restaurants cast dim pools of light on the walkways.

A pungent fish aroma punctuated by roast duck wafted from one eatery, soon vanquished by the sickly sweet scent of garbage and rotten-egg odor of stagnant water wafting from a narrow passage just beyond. That in turn was washed away by a cloud of warm steam carrying the biting scent of lye from a laundry. This constantly shifting olfactory kaleidoscope was blanketed with the inevitable scent of sweat and unwashed bodies accompanied by the waxing and waning floral notes of opium and incense.

For de Bruijn, the sensory assault was a siren song, breathing life into memories he preferred stayed buried. The detective dragged his attention back to the erhu, which bobbed along as its owner wove his way through the crowd. De Bruijn slid past a group of gawkers, their guide saying, "This here sign reads *Hang Hi*, but means not what you might think. Instead, it is the Chinaman's sign for prosperity." The rest of the lesson was lost to de Bruijn as he moved on, his gaze fixed on Hee's large-brimmed hat and musical instrument.

An intense knot of people blocked the sidewalk ahead. Hee stepped to the side and vanished. De Bruijn hurried to the spot to find his quarry had gone into a narrow alley.

A *dark*, narrow alley.

Luckily, it appeared short and uninhabited.

De Bruijn hesitated. Peering into the alley, he twisted the handle of his walking stick and pulled, revealing the blade hidden in the shaft of the cane.

A shadow detached from the gloom, and John Hee's distinctive silhouette emerged from the other end. Determined not to lose sight of his quarry, de Bruijn gripped the handle more firmly and dashed into the alley. The detective was nearly out the other side when Hee crossed Washington Street, heading toward the Chinese Theater.

He only had time to think, *ah, that explains the erhu*, before a hand from behind gripped his sword arm. He tried to turn, block and parry…

Darkness.

A piercing screech was his route back to consciousness. That, and a voice. A child's voice saying, "Copper Mick! Stop that! You already scared 'em away with that thing!"

"It's a police whistle," said another voice, older-sounding, somehow. "We need the police."

He was falling, back into a dream, with no sound, no vision, only pressing pain.

"Mr. Brown! Are you dead? Wake up! Mr. Brown!" The child's words—he knew that voice—blasted through the mist.

The other person said, "Look, if he's dead, he sure isn't gonna be able to say so, right?"

Now a third voice chimed in, softer, older, foreign. "What happen here?"

"John Hee! Am I glad to see you!" The child sounded relieved. "It's me, Antonia. You gotta help us. This here is Mr. Brown, he's a detective, and he was following you, and we were following him, and he was attacked in the alley. Mick scared 'em off with his police whistle, but that scared off everyone else too. We can't lift him, and he won't wake up. Look at all the blood! D' you think he's dead?"

Antonia. John Hee.

The names scrabbled through the dark of his muddled mind, reaching for the light.

De Bruijn opened his eyes to a world he could not, for the life of him, bring into focus. A world he couldn't even remember.

Where am I? What am I doing here?

The ground beneath his back was hard, lumpy, cobbled. Dampness ran around his shoulder blades. His head throbbed with a dull ache.

Three blurry faces peered down at him. Two boys and a Celestial.

The youngest boy yipped. "His eyes are open! Mr. Brown, I'm sorry, your cane is gone. They took it when they scarpered."

Who?

He must have said it aloud, because the older boy said, "Dunno who. Muggers. Hoodlums. Cutthroats. Lucky for you all they did was bash you in the head and take your walking stick."

"Who are you?" He heard his own voice, thick, distant. He felt as if he had slept a long time and awakened in a strange land.

"I'm Antonia! Antonia Gizzi!" said the young boy, no, the girl, yes, Antonia, of course. She pulled something out from under the layers of jacket and shirt.

A locket.

"Remember?" She swung it in his face. "You gave this to me. It was from Maman. Mr. Brown, don't you remember anything? Did they steal your wits too?"

It was as if his thoughts struggled through gauze, red, red as blood, embroidered over all, the finest Chinese silk gauze.

Chinese.

John Hee. Chinatown. San Francisco. Gallagher.

"Ah." The exclamation came out as a grunt. Memories returned. Where he was and what he had been doing. Following this man, this John Hee. The very man who was now holding out his hand, offering to help him up. De Bruijn lifted his head. Pain exploded in his skull. He grabbed his head with both hands, then pulled them away. They were slick with blood.

"Come," said John Hee. "You must go. Rest. See doctor. Where you stay?"

De Bruijn, focused on not vomiting and keeping his head from flying off his body, could not answer.

Antonia piped up, "He's staying at the Palace Hotel."

John Hee looked from her to the boy Mick. "I cannot go there. I must go to the theater soon, for performance. It is final act."

"The final act?" Antonia sounded confused.

Mick said, "Don'tcha know, Antonia? The Chinese theater puts on plays that go on for nights and nights and sometimes months and months."

"I didn't know," she snapped, then looked down at de Bruijn. "Mick, we can't carry him, just the two of us. We need John's help. John? Can you help us get him to the music store? Up the stairs to where we live? It's just a few blocks. He can rest on my bed until Mrs. S gets home, and then maybe she can call a doctor." Antonia bit her lip. "I'm gonna catch holy heck for this."

John Hee said, "You two save his life with the whistle and shouting. If Mrs. Stannert give you heck, I explain, if that help." Hee pulled a strap over his head and handed Antonia the sack at the other end.

The erhu. For the theater. Of course.

"I carry him to store, then go."

De Bruijn wanted to say *Stop!* John Hee, of no large stature, could not pick him up and carry him. They should find an officer instead.

Hee turned to Mick. "Belt, please?"

Mick unfastened and handed over his belt, holding his pants up with one hand. "I shoulda worn braces."

"No. This good." Hee wrapped and buckled the belt around de Bruijn's waist, over his trousers but under his jacket. De Bruijn, who realized he had somehow come up to sitting during all this, only wanted to close his eyes. Every jolt caused another wave of dizziness and pain.

"Now, stand," said Hee.

Mick got to one side of de Bruijn, John Hee on the other. "On knees, Mr. Brown?"

De Bruijn slowly got to his knees, the steady pull of the belt steadying him.

Mick and Hee increased the tension on the belt and brought him to his feet. Through the fog that slowed his thinking, de Bruijn realized Antonia, hovering, was dressed in men's clothes. They were ridiculously oversized, cuffs dragging in the filth of the alley.

"Now," said John Hee. "Walk. One foot, other foot, Mr. Brown. We help."

They headed to the main streets of Chinatown. When they were stopped once and questioned by an officer, Mick was quick to speak up. "Poor fella is a friend of the family. Our man John is helping me get him home. Too much to drink, an' we are just takin' a shortcut, because who wants to carry him up and down hills, right?"

De Bruijn thought it as good a story as any. Certainly better than anything his addled brain might produce. The officer let them go, admonishing, "This is no quarter for young'uns like yourselves, nor for a gennulman like him there."

Antonia muttered to Mick, "We're lucky he didn't recognize you, what with your pa bein' a detective and on the force and all."

"Aw, he probably knows my da, but not me. Besides, it's dark, and I'm not exactly dressed like a policeman's son."

The hardest part was at the end, at the stairs.

De Bruijn would have been willing to crawl up the stairs on hands and knees, or rather curl up in the entryway and sleep, but they would have none of it.

"You gotta go up. The. Stairs," huffed Antonia behind him, shoving him on a most undignified portion of his anatomy.

But it was John Hee, his hand wrapped firmly in the belt around de Bruijn's waist, who supplied the muscle needed to propel him up the stairs and finally onto Antonia's little bed.

"Need doctor." John Hee had lost control of certain articles of speech during the ordeal.

Mick said, "There's Dr. McGee. My ma says he's good. Should I fetch him?"

"He's gonna want to be paid, right?" Antonia sounded nervous. "I know where Mrs. S keeps the household pin money. I suppose Mr. Brown'll pay her back."

They looked at him. He closed his eyes and floated.

From a distance, John Hee said, "I go now. Everyone be fine. No worry."

Mick said, "Dr. McGee's a good 'un. Don't worry about the money. He'd probably even put it on a bill for you. Are you gonna be all right here, just you and him?"

"Of course I will." She sounded indignant. "I'll just sit and make sure he keeps breathing."

Multiple footsteps pounded away, in time to the beating of his heart, and the throbbing of his head.

He floated.

A small, icy hand slid into his and squeezed. He tried to squeeze back, to open his eyes, but couldn't. The hammering in his head thrummed through his whole body, sapped his strength.

Before he slipped into dreamless sleep, he heard Antonia whisper, "I just wish I knew where Mrs. S was. She'd know what to do."

Chapter Thirty-one

After seeing Haskell, Inez went directly to the residence of the San Francisco Musical Protective Association's secretary only to be told by his frazzled housekeeper that he was away "across the bay" on a job. Furthermore, he would not be able to see her until the next morning and he then would be gone the rest of the day. Inez thanked her and promised to return before noon.

"It's important," she added, "and I cannot wait until the meeting next month. I must talk to him as soon as possible."

The housekeeper sighed, not moved by Inez's urgency, and tucked a strand of limp brown hair behind her ear. "It's alwus 'as soon as possible.' When they's get sick, when something bad happens, they's alwus need their money wi'out delay."

This statement perplexed Inez until she realized that the housekeeper probably thought she was the wife of some poor, deathly ill member of the society, desperate for the funds needed to pay the grocer, the rent, and the doctor. Inez did nothing to dissuade the woman from her assumption. *Let her think whatever she wants, as long as she passes the message along that I have an urgent need to talk with him.*

When Inez arrived home she avoided the store, not wanting to be questioned about the private piano lessons she was supposedly giving. She was beginning to wish she'd simply said she had private business to attend to. Her lies just complicated an already complicated situation.

Upon unlocking the door and letting herself in, Inez discovered an envelope just inside the threshold. Noting the partial boot print on the cream-colored stock, she marveled that Antonia had somehow failed to spot the envelope even though she'd trod upon it. Inside was a simple "Thank you" in Carmella's fine script, proof that Inez's message had been received and acknowledged.

Another silver lining brightened her day when Antonia announced a classmate, Katie Lynch, had invited her to dinner. Inez was pleasantly surprised. It was the first time since moving to San Francisco that the girl had mentioned making a friend. When the girl's brother, Michael, showed up to walk Antonia to the Lynch's home on Third Street, Inez was surprised yet again.

The boy seemed nice enough. Certainly polite and knew his manners. However, she had detected a certain nervousness in him as he held his hat, smiled and bobbed his head, and answered all her questions. She wondered what it was he wasn't telling her. Although, if the number of words spoken was an indication of his sincerity, he was entirely guileless. In fact, he ran off at the mouth a bit, which, again, could just be nerves. But Inez had noted his gaze dart around as if looking for an escape when he described the many members of his family, particularly Katie.

Until he mentioned his father the police detective.

That gave Inez pause. Could this be the same Detective Lynch who de Bruijn had met? The Detective Lynch who was "nominally" in charge of investigating the Long Bridge murder? It would be quite the coincidence, but life was nothing if not filled with coincidences and serendipitous twists of fate.

As she mulled this development, Michael chatted on about his father, visibly more relaxed and beaming with pride, saying, "Once I'm out of school I'm going to join the force like my da and my brother Daniel. He's a patrolman now."

So, a policeman's son, planning to become a policeman

himself someday. One might conclude that an aspiration to join law enforcement argued for qualities of honesty and integrity, but such had not always been Inez's experience.

Inez shook her head. Surely she was reading too much into this.

Inez watched Antonia interact with Michael, or as she called him, Mick. They chattered with an air of familiarity. Inez wondered if the friend who had invited Antonia to sup with the Lynches that evening might not have been the aforementioned younger sister Katie, but perhaps Mick himself.

From the little she saw, Mick treated Antonia with respect and the sort of boyish good nature that didn't indicate anything but a genuine fondness. And Antonia was still young. She evinced none of the girlish blushing and batting of eyelashes that would indicate she thought of the young Irish lad as anything more than as a friend. *Ah, but give her a few more years.* Inez was not looking forward to those times, given Antonia's stubborn will, which rivaled Inez's own.

At least Mick had given her his address. And since Inez's evening's plans included taking the horsecar down Third to the Mission Creek waterfront, she would be going right by the house. With a little luck she might spot Antonia with Katie or Mick. That would certainly clear up any lingering suspicions regarding Antonia's true whereabouts.

Once Antonia and Mick departed, she headed for the storage room to prepare for her expedition to Henderson's Three Sheets. Inez hunted down one of several trunks she had brought with her from Leadville, set her lamp atop a nearby tin hat box, and opened the trunk. She drew in a deep breath, inhaling the clean aroma of cedar accompanied by undertones of wood smoke and an indefinable scent that brought back memories of the high mountain boomtown she had once called home.

The yawning trunk beckoned her to pause, to sift through its contents slowly, to remember the place, its people, her life.

Anxious to shut the container and shut away the past,

Inez pushed aside soft silk petticoats, fine linen lace-bedecked camisoles, satin-lined corsets, and patterned silk stockings, all swathed in tissue to protect them from time. Close to the bottom, she uncovered the trappings for her transformation, including black trousers, dark shirt, and black waistcoat. She set aside a black frock coat, deeming it too meticulous for where she would be, and opted for a somber sackcoat of similar midnight hue. Slouch hat, celluloid collar, necktie, and a long wind of linen to bind her breasts flat. Finally, she hauled out an old pair of Mark's boots wrapped in plain brown paper.

She slammed the trunk shut, picked up the clothing items and the lamp, and hastened out of the room as if the ghosts of all her past misdeeds were on her heels.

It had been some time since she had dressed the part she planned to play. Her hair was longer now, having grown out from that time two years ago when she had chopped it all off in a desperate bid to blend in anonymously with a certain male milieu. This evening, she would fall back on her old tricks from years earlier, tucking her braided hair under her collar and wearing her hat low. No one ever took their hats off in the various gin mills she had occasion to frequent in her past life. She suspected it would be no different in San Francisco.

She changed quickly in her bedroom and examined the results in the mirror over the washstand, with the lamp turned low. The lighting at The Three Sheets would be smoky and inadequate if the place was anything like the Barbary Coast dives the musicians occasionally discussed. "It will do," she said to her shadowed reflection.

Two more items were required.

She opened the drawer in her nightstand and extracted her pocket revolver, a Remington Number Two Smoot's Patent. Loaded and ready, but unused since she arrived in San Francisco. She did not expect to discharge it tonight. Still, given where she was going and the hour, it would be prudent to take it with her and foolhardy to leave it behind. She checked the revolver quickly, but thoroughly, before placing it in her jacket pocket.

Finally, she reached into the back of the drawer for the business card she had recently obtained. The simple card, as free of embellishment as the man it introduced, stated:

W. R. de Bruijn.

Private detective. Inquiry agent.

Finder of the lost.

"Let us see what we can find at The Three Sheets," Inez said to the card. She then tucked it into her waistcoat pocket before dousing the lamp and heading out to the street to catch the Third Street horsecar to the Mission Creek wharf district.

•• • ••

A gaggle of redheaded girls sat on the porch of what Inez surmised was the Lynch house as the horsecar rolled past. A young, dark-haired matron sat with them, a baby on her knee. Inez did not spot Antonia. *She could be inside.* Wherever she was, the girl was sensible. Intelligent. Although impulsive. Surely after their last talk she would avoid any escapades that would land her in hot water. At least, Inez hoped so. She sighed and pushed worries of Antonia aside.

Inez slouched down on her bench in the horsecar and pulled her hat brim lower over her face to indicate she was not open to casual conversation. Many of the laborers and seamen who crowded the car disembarked with her at the Long Bridge stop. Inez lengthened her stride, enjoying the freedom of movement of trousers. She reflected that if bloomers were not such an outré fashion, she would be sorely tempted to adopt them in her daily life.

Carmella, Inez thought, would be intrigued.

Nico would be scandalized.

When she was opposite Henderson's Three Sheets, she stopped for a good hard look. Two stories high, brick-fortified, it clearly wasn't just in the firewater business. She recalled her music pupil Patrick mentioning that, above the saloon, Henderson rented boarding rooms for sailors. Her scrutiny traveled to the second-story windows where light from candles or oil lamps wavered behind ragged and torn roller shades. A prickle of unease whispered over her skin.

Inez was familiar with the stories involving crimping and shanghaiing. One would have to lead a very sheltered life in San Francisco to not have at least heard the terms. The musicians, some of whom claimed to have seen shanghaiiers in action while working one or another low-class dive, loved to tell tales over the Monday night card games. Such tales usually involved sailors, come ashore for a "little relaxation" in the city's various unsavory establishments, who were drugged with laced Pisco punch or dropped with a blackjack. These hapless souls invariably awoke on board an ocean-going vessel the next morning to be told they were now members of the crew, bound for parts north to the Bering Sea or south around Cape Horn.

The street level had no windows at all. The only thing breaking the brick façade was a door below a barely legible sign. Inez hunched her shoulders as a chill breeze drove the damp beneath the wool of her jacket, and considered.

No windows meant she would be going in blind.

Was I a fool to not take de Bruijn's suggestion and let him tackle this?

Even as the question crossed her mind, she knew the answer didn't matter. She was not turning back now.

Inez slid her right hand into her pocket and was comforted by the touch of her pistol. She set her jaw, walked across the street, pushed the door open, and entered.

Chapter Thirty-two

The first thing that struck Inez was the noise.

Conversation carried on at the level of a shout. An ill-tuned piano sprayed notes from an upbeat tune, attempting, but failing, to lift above the roar. Smoke from pipes, hand-rolled cigarettes, and cheap cigars hung thick and heavy, besting the most opaque of San Francisco's ground-level mists. Only no fog ever boasted such a throat-closing combination of aromas—a clash of tobaccos mixed with the odor of unwashed, sour bodies packed close together. Fumes from the spillage of alcoholic beverages of unknown toxicity joined the fray. She paused just inside the door, staying in the shadow of the dimly lit bar, trying to get a bead on the place before venturing farther into the murky interior. The saloon was full of small tables, all occupied. The tops were littered with glasses, bottles, chipped plates, and what appeared to be a few games of dice and cards.

To the left was the bar, a nothing-fancy business-like affair. Beyond it, toward the back wall, was the piano, an upright. The piano player had his back to her, his face hidden from her sight. Nonetheless, his imposing size and hunched posture over the keyboard was familiar, much to Inez's dismay. Part of her was tempted to walk up behind him—for it had to be Patrick laboring over the ivories—poke him in the back, and hiss, "Sit up straight!"

Rather, she kept to the gloom and hoped Patrick wouldn't

catch sight of her. Not that she thought he would recognize her, in this place, dressed as she was in men's attire. Besides, what could he see through the impenetrable fug that hung between them? Still, best not to tempt fate by moving too close to the music.

She stepped to the near end of the bar where the bartender, a man with an eye patch, conversed with a sharp-looking fellow in a natty derby. Leaning an arm on the surface, she rapped on the wood with her knuckles.

The bartender switched his attention to her. "Aye? And wha'll be your poison, sir?" The burr of Scotland rolled from his tongue.

Before she could say anything, the man in the derby said, "Allow me, eh? Always good to see a new face around The Three Sheets." Sharp eyes flashed to the bartender and back to Inez. An unspoken signal had passed between them, she was certain. The derby-hatted man gave her a quick up and down, taking her measure with practiced ease.

A warning shiver ran down her limbs, and her toes clenched inside her boots as if to prepare her to run.

She pitched her voice low. "Kind of you," she said, deciding to keep her responses short. She needn't have bothered, because the fellow with the derby turned out to be the loquacious sort. "Looks like you're ready to do the town, all cleaned up for the ladies, eh? Can't do better'n the Paris of the West for that, eh? Been around town before, or is this your first time in the magic city? If you're looking for bunk, board, and no questions asked, you've found the right place, right here."

He pulled a coin from his pocket, and tapped it on the liquor-soaked counter, grinning. "Fancy a little game of chance? Call heads or tails. Loser pays the next round of drinks. I'll pick up this one."

Inez narrowed her eyes. He'd not given her a breath of space nor asked her name. Not that an exchange of names was a given in such places. But such over-eagerness put her on her guard.

A nudge at her elbow caused her to look away from the derby-hatted fellow. The one-eyed bartender had set a shot glass by her arm. "Donovan speaks the truth. Henderson's the name, mate." He held out a paw for Inez to shake. His hand swallowed hers. Her knuckles popped as his grip bore down briefly, then released. "We like to give newcomers a little something on the house, encourage them to come back, ye ken?"

He handed a glass of equal measure to derby-hatted Donovan and kept a third in front of himself. "No mariner, then, are ye? I recognize the ones that spend time in the rigging. A steward, I'm guessing? No matter, to your health. And here's to wives and sweethearts. May they never meet!"

Inez automatically lifted her glass and stopped, the rim hovering at her lips. The stinging scent of cheap whiskey rose into her nose, smelling of danger and nightmares. Donovan had downed his drink and was watching her, eyes gleaming, face hungry as a ferret's. She glanced at Henderson, who watched her as well. His own glass waited before him, untouched.

In one rapid move, she set her glass down by Henderson with one hand, while picking up his with the other. He jerked, his attempt to grab it back proof enough for her. She tossed the liquor down, its rawness burning her throat, and said, "To your health as well, gentlemen."

Henderson bristled, balled his hands into fists, and banged them on the counter. "Just who are ye?" He leaned over the stained wood, speaking softly but with menace. "One a' Roney's cronies? Out t'break the backs of the likes of us who are helpin' the seamen find their next jobs? Or are ye one'a the new lads on the force? If the latter, ye be barkin' up the wrong tree. I've paid your taxes and I've paid your fees many times over to the regular patrol, so don't be lookin' to me to line your pockets."

Holding up her hand to stop the torrent of words and flying spit, Inez said, "I'm none of the above. Furthermore, I care not what you do here. *Either* of you."

She glanced toward Donovan. He had melted away, leaving his spot at the bar empty.

Refocusing on Henderson, she continued, "I have questions, and I can make it worth your while if you answer." She pulled out de Bruijn's card, wiped the counter with her sleeve, and set it face-up for him to read. He peered at it. "De B—, de Br—What is this? Inquiry agent? Finder of the lost?" He glared at her with his one eye.

"Call me Mr. Brown. As to what I do, that should be plain. I find what is lost. I inquire until the truth comes out. And I show my appreciation for cooperation." Locking her gaze with his so he would not assume violence on her part, she reached slowly into her inner pocket, withdrew a two-dollar bill, and pinned it to the surface of the bar.

Now that she was offering to pay him and not demanding payment, his shoulders came down from up around his ears and his fists relaxed. "What d'ye want to know?"

"I want to know what happened between you and Jamie Monroe Sunday night."

When he glanced toward the piano, she knew she had it right.

Something had occurred.

"There's naught to say." The belligerent tone was back.

"You argued. He left. What happened?"

"What's it to ye?"

So, you want to play it like that, do you? She directed a smile at him, but it was not a friendly one. "You've heard about the Long Bridge corpse."

He scratched one stubbled cheek, cautious. "Aye, of course. It's been all the talk along the canal, a matter for speculation and wager. Naught know who it is, bein' his features was obliterated."

Now it was her turn to lean over the counter, into his face. "Oh, his name is known. It's Jamie Monroe. And the last place he was seen alive was here. In The Three Sheets."

Shock poured over his face. He licked his lips and glanced around. "I had nae to do w' that."

She repeated, "You and Monroe argued the night he died. What about?"

"I'm tellin' ye, that had nae to do wi' anything that happened to him."

Stifling a sigh, Inez reached into her pocket again. Another two-dollar bill joined the first on the counter. "I am only looking for answers for his grieving family. I work for them. Not the police. Nor Roney and his ilk either, if that's what's got you worried."

He laughed. A deep bark. "Worried! Me? More like they should keep their distance from The Three Sheets. That's what I told Roney last time he came in here preachin' t' the customers about the Seamen's Protective Union." A shout went up from the other end of the bar. "Wait here. There's some who've run dry."

Inez waited, listening to Patrick's lively rendition of "Darling Nelly Gray" and watching Henderson efficiently refill glasses and take in change. He returned and jerked his thumb toward Patrick. "Hear him? The half-breed? He's good. So, I'll tell ye what I told Jamie Monroe: I found a replacement who'd play for less. Strictly business, I told him. Why should I pay more when I can get nimble fingers for less?"

"That someone being...?" She inclined her head toward Patrick.

"Aye. He'd be happy playin' for free and was willin' to kiss my boots for a few pennies a night plus whatever he gets from the punters. I told Jamie, ye agree to work for what the half-breed's willin' to take, ye can keep the job."

"I'm guessing he did not take that well."

Henderson looked grim.

She hazarded another step out, verbalizing her guess at what might have caused the situation to escalate. "And Monroe knew what you do here. You and Donovan. Shanghaiing, crimping."

He shrugged. "No law against it. Go t' the Barbary Coast. 'Tis everywhere you'll find it."

"Kidnapping is illegal," Inez pointed out. "Perhaps he threatened to go to the authorities or mention it to the seamen's champion, Frank Roney, who'd take actions against you or your business."

He shook his head. "Roney talks, he agitates, but he's more a nuisance than a threat to me."

She didn't reply. But she didn't release the money either.

He continued, "Look, if I thought Monroe'd do something that would hurt me or the business, I'd would've set Donovan on him and he'd be halfway to China by now, tyin' sailor's knots."

She squinted, letting her disbelief show.

"I'm nae murderer! On my mother's grave. On the family Bible." Then he blurted, "There's nae profit in it."

That, finally, she believed.

Inez released the bills and he slid them into his apron pocket.

"Any thoughts on possible enemies? He was killed shortly after he left here. It had to be someone in the area." She pulled out a quarter eagle and tapped it idly on the scarred surface.

He leaned on the bar again, this time with the air of a co-conspirator. "Talk to Roney, that's my advice to ye, Mr. Brown. Monroe was strong on labor. Everyone knew that. It wasn't safe for him, especially around here, with the Whitehall boatmen seein' the unions as a threat to their livelihoods. I warned him many a time to watch his talk. Maybe Roney knows something."

The tapping ceased, but Inez held onto the gold coin. "Where would I find Frank Roney?"

"He's not to be found in The Three Sheets anymore, that's all I know."

Inez nodded, thinking Sven Borg could probably tell her. "Anyone else come to mind who might've had it in for Jamie Monroe?"

Henderson hesitated.

She waited.

Finally he said, "Donovan's a cold-blooded sort."

Throws his mate overboard to draw the sharks away.

Inez pushed the coin across the bar and nodded toward Patrick. "The lad. Young. Strong. Surprised you and Donovan didn't offer him a drink, throw him in a boat, and send him off on one of the ships in need of men."

The coin vanished. Henderson said, "Eh. His mother does my laundry. Besides, where'd I find anyone else who'd play for near free, and be grateful for it?"

Inez touched the brim of her hat in thanks and left. Once outside, she inhaled deeply, filling her lungs, and let it all out with a whoosh. She headed toward Long Bridge to pick up the horsecar, thinking about what Henderson had told her. It all made sense, and although she didn't like or trust Henderson, she believed him when he said he had nothing to do with Jamie's death. His statement that there was "no profit in murder" rang true. However, her visit to The Three Sheets had done nothing to shorten the list of people who might have wished Jamie ill, and could have perhaps been desperate enough to kill him.

Might. Could have. Perhaps.

There were still too many equivocations and possibilities, and not enough absolutes.

Berry Street was quiet, although she heard distant voices off in the direction of the piers. The moon shone down cold, aloof. The air brushed her face, a damp caress. Her footsteps sounded loud, seeming the only ones for blocks.

As she passed by an alley, something stirred in the darkness, at the periphery of her vision. If not for that, and the fact that she was alert and stone-cold sober, she would have had no warning at all.

As it was, she was mid-turn when Donovan came at her, leather sap raised, mouth grimacing. She shouted "Stop!" at the top of her lungs, not disguising the timbre of her voice. His eyes widened as he realized he was about to attack a woman.

His momentary loss of focus gave Inez the split second she needed. She sidestepped and his momentum carried him past her. His arm arced downwards, still aiming at the spot where she had been. Inez pushed his wrist through the curve of his attack, sweeping his arm down and back. Off balance, he began falling forward. Inez slammed his unprotected nose, which gave with a satisfying pop. With a yelp of pain, he tumbled hard onto the ground.

Out came the revolver from her pocket. Donovan found himself staring at a woman dressed in men's clothing pointing the business end of a no-nonsense handgun at his head. Her hat had tumbled off, and she brushed away strands of long hair that had escaped from beneath her collar.

Leather sap abandoned, Donovan sat up, covering his nose. Blood gushed down and over his shirt. "Jesus!" he cried out. "Fucking Mother of God! You broke my nose!"

"And you tried to knock me senseless," Inez snarled, gun trained on his forehead.

He moaned and rocked back and forth, sitting on the pavement. "My nose."

Inez had run out of patience. "Jamie Monroe. You know him?"

"I fucking knew him. Yeah."

"Knew." Past tense. "So, you are aware he's dead."

"Yes. Jesus! Yes."

"You killed him." She figured the direct attack was best. Enough with the subtleties.

"No! Why would I do that? Christ Almighty."

"Because he was about to destroy your livelihood? Tell the law that you were shanghaiing reluctant seamen and perhaps the odd accountant or warehouse worker who was unlucky enough to stop in at The Three Sheets?"

"Augh!" His voice was muffled behind his hands and the blood. "If I thought he was going to squeal on me, I'd've shanghaied him myself. Put him on a ship bound far away."

"Like you planned to do with me, I assume."

No response.

"Who would've wanted him dead?"

A mumble from Donovan, then he said louder, "Henderson's a hot-headed cocky bastard. If he thought Monroe might spill the beans to someone with clout, able to shut him down, I wouldn't put it past him."

Chapter Thirty-three

Inez kept her gun in hand and visible until the uptown-bound horsecar appeared. The trip back home seemed to take a lot longer than it did going down to the wharves. Inez dragged herself to the door leading to her apartment. While digging in her pocket for the key, she looked up at the windows. No lights. Perhaps Antonia was abed and asleep. That would be a good thing. She could continued straight to her own bedroom, shuck off her reeking disguise, clean up, tumble into the bedclothes, and sink into sleep.

Her feather bed had never beckoned so seductively.

She made her way up the stairs to the small landing. Boots in hand, she opened the door and stepped into the darkened apartment, stocking-footed and silent until she hit a loose board that gave out a small creak.

"Mrs. S?" Antonia, sounding not at all sleepy. "Come here, quick!"

Alarmed by the urgency in Antonia's voice, Inez dashed to Antonia's room, still wearing her trousers, sack jacket, hat, and all. At the doorway, she stopped and stared. The roller shade was up and the corner streetlamp shed its full light upon a perplexing tableau.

De Bruijn lay in Antonia's small bed, in his shirtsleeves, a wide bandage wrapped around his head. He appeared to be asleep. Antonia sat by his side on one of the kitchen chairs.

She, too, was dressed in male attire. In fact, unless Inez missed her guess, it was the same suit of clothing Antonia had worn in Leadville when she'd been a street urchin passing as a newsboy and selling copies of the local paper. Antonia looked as if she wanted to jump up and give Inez a hug but didn't want to let go of de Bruijn's limp hand.

Just inside the door, a crumpled cloth was wadded on the floor. Inez nudged it with her foot. It appeared to be a blood-soaked pillowcase.

"The doctor says Mr. Brown's gonna be all right," said Antonia.

Inez looked at her ward. A flood of exclamations, imprecations, and interrogations clamored to be voiced, but Inez kept her peace, walked over to the girl and gave her a hug. Antonia wrapped her free arm around Inez's trousered legs and buried her face in Inez's jacket. After a moment, Inez gently pulled herself away, went to the kitchen, retrieved the second chair, and brought it back into the bedroom. She set the chair next to Antonia's, sat down, and said, "Tell me. Everything."

Antonia explained to Inez how she had concocted a plan to follow the detective and then twisted Mick's arm into accompanying her, and how John Hee had headed to Chinatown and de Bruijn had followed him and she and Mick had followed de Bruijn. She emphasized how Mick had "acted the proper copper," blowing his whistle and scaring away the thugs that tried to roll the detective. John Hee also emerged a hero in the tale, coming back to help carry de Bruijn to the store. "He couldn't go to the Palace Hotel, he said, and he's a musician, Mrs. Stannert. He plays one of those Chinese violins with the long neck at the Chinese Theater in Chinatown. I don't know why Mr. Brown thinks he's a bad guy."

Mick had gone off to get a doctor, she added. Once he'd returned with Dr. McGee, Mick'd vanished again because as he said, he was going to get "holy heck" if he didn't get home right away. Antonia then confessed that, to pay the physician for the visit and the syrupy medicine he'd left for the detective, she had raided the household fund—hidden not very cleverly by Inez in an English biscuit tin on the kitchen shelf. At this point, Antonia stopped her narrative to complain she didn't understand why the Brits called the contents *biscuits* when they were clearly *cookies*.

Prodded back to her story, Antonia finished by saying the doctor had shooed her out of the room while examining de Bruijn. Afterwards he'd told her to tell her aunt that the gentleman friend of the family had a mild concussion and should be on the mend in a few days. "He said Mr. Brown needs to rest." Antonia looked over at the detective, whose eyelids had begun to flicker. "Mr. Brown didn't like that at all."

"I can imagine," said Inez drily.

De Bruijn's eyes flew open. He appeared remarkably alert for someone whose head was swathed with gauze. "Toss out that patent medicine," he said very distinctly. "It's nothing but laudanum cut with a large quantity of alcohol."

It took five minutes of arguing with a woozy but determined de Bruijn before Inez reluctantly accepted he would not stay. "The doctor will be coming to see me in the morning. See how I am faring. I told him I would be at the Palace Hotel." He had Inez fish around in his waistcoat pocket for a business card for a carriage company and asked her if she would call them on the store's telephone.

The card read *Telephone Cab and Carriage Company, Joseph Lynch, prop.*

She raised her eyebrows. "Lynch, as in the detective?"

"Martin Lynch is the police detective, and this is his cousin. Or second cousin. In any case, they have a telephone. Detective Lynch said should I require transportation any time I am in the city, all I had to do was call, mention his name, and service would be efficient and forthcoming."

First the detective, then his son, and now his cousin. The Lynches were popping up everywhere, it seemed.

De Bruijn had managed to get himself into his waistcoat and was struggling with his jacket. He froze, his eyes narrowing as if he was trying to bring Inez into focus. "Mrs. Stannert, your clothes." His gaze wandered over to Antonia. "And you, Antonia. What are you two doing in that apparel?"

"I'll explain tomorrow," she said shortly. "I fully intend to visit and check on your condition. If you are up to it, we can discuss where we stand and where to go from here."

The carriage arrived promptly with Joseph Lynch himself in the driver's box. He tipped his hat, keeping his gaze studiously directed at Inez's face. She gave him points for not glancing even once at her trousered legs and for treating her with all the deference that might be due to one of San Francisco's elite. After he'd helped de Bruijn down the stairs and into the cab, Inez paid the driver what she adjudged to be a handsome fee for his efforts. She instructed him to accompany de Bruijn to his rooms, notify the hotel staff that his passenger was suffering from a concussion, and explain a physician would be by in the morning. "May I have another of your cards for the gentleman?" she asked.

Joseph Lynch produced one, and she leaned into the carriage, pulled de Bruijn's jacket open, and tucked the card in his waistcoat pocket. "Don't lose this, Mr. de Bruijn."

Once the carriage was off and clattering down Kearney, Inez returned upstairs. Antonia was already in her nightclothes and in bed. Inez fetched a clean case for the pillow and debated how to proceed.

While listening to Antonia's story, Inez had been alarmed on many fronts. That Antonia had undertaken a nighttime journey into a dangerous part of town, never mind that she was not alone. That she had somehow managed to convince Mick, who seemed the upright sort, to go with her was a blessing but also a concern. That she had somehow managed to insinuate herself wholeheartedly into the investigation of Jamie Monroe's murder. Such investigations, Inez knew from her own experience, could recoil violently onto those whose only crime was searching out the truth.

Inez finally settled on the topic most easily dealt with: the fact that, despite all of her precautions the previous evening, her ward had still managed to eavesdrop. Covering Antonia's hand with her own, Inez began, "You and Mick probably saved Mr. de Bruijn's life. A good deed and no small thing. However…"

Even in the dark, she saw Antonia stiffen at the word.

"You obviously listened in on the discussion between me, Mr. de Bruijn, and Mrs. Sweet. I checked the doors before we began. No one was there. Tell me how you did it."

Antonia chewed her lip, then turned her head away with a sigh that sounded like it came from the depths of her soul. "I was on the stairs in the alley, the ones that go up to the storage room." She twisted under the covers to face Inez, tucking her free hand under the pillow. "I still had the hairpins I'd used to open the trunk for you. So, I unlocked the room, and went out the back door. I went down the stairs just far enough so's I could hear everyone through the window. I saw you open the door, but I stayed very still and you didn't see me."

Inez was impressed with Antonia's tenacity but opted for a slight frown of disapproval. "I am disappointed that you went against my express order not to eavesdrop. You put yourself and your friend Mick in a very dangerous position. However, I understand. You were worried and wanted to help. So, I am willing to let this pass, given the circumstances."

"I'm sorry."

And she indeed looked contrite, with her eyes wide and shining, and her lower lip trembling. Inez had to settle for that and hope Antonia wasn't pulling the wool over her eyes. *For if she is lying to me about this, in whole or part, what else is she not telling me?*

The next morning, Inez tried to keep a semblance of normalcy to their routine. Antonia complained about the staleness of the bread and asked when Carmella might be by with more *zeppole* or *cornetti alla marmellata.* "I don't know, but I shall pay her a visit if she does not come by today or tomorrow and let her know we miss her presence and pastries," Inez assured her.

As Antonia prepared to leave, Inez stayed the door with a firm hand. "What will you do as soon as school is out?"

Antonia's face was hidden by the bonnet and its brim, but her response was clear enough, if a little sullen. "I'll come home."

"Good." Inez opened the door to the outside world.

Antonia lingered, "I was thinking," she said, "maybe I could see Mr. Brown on my way home and make sure he's all right."

Inez put a hand on her shoulder. "I am visiting him this morning and will share your concerns." She gave Antonia a little push, encouraging her on her way.

Antonia took a step, then two, then stopped. "He didn't have to give me Maman's locket. She gave it to him. Not me." Without waiting for an answer, she trudged away.

Inez leaned against the doorjamb and watched the girl disappear down the street, book bag swinging from its strap.

Was I so contrary at her age?

She didn't really have to pose the question to herself. She had been all that and more. If not for her own iron will and contrariness, she would not have escaped the stifling, pre-determined future prepared for her by her parents. She would have certainly ended up a proper New York matron, married to someone of her father's choosing and languishing in Newport or Saratoga Springs during the summer season. Instead, here she was, for better or for worse, with no one to blame for her fate but herself.

And Inez would have had it no other way.

She went to the store with the idea of glancing at any paperwork, invoices, bills, that might have accumulated. Too, if John Hee was there and she could catch a few minutes alone with him, she thought she would quiz him about the previous night's events. Instead, she found Nico, once again uncharacteristically early, in deep conversation with Welles as they poured over some sheet music. Or rather, Nico was holding forth while Welles nodded and said, "Yes. I've got it, Nico."

Inez glimpsed the word *Sonaten* on the copy Nico was waving around. He said with characteristic intensity, "First, *adagio sostenuto*." He drew the words out in a slow, loving fashion, sweeping his sheet music across in a long arc. "And then *presto!* *Presto*! *Presto*!" The sheet music flapped energetically up and down.

"Yes, Nico, yes. I've got it. I've got it." Welles' voice held a trace of impatience.

"Passion, Thomas! Start and end with passion!" Coda completed, Nico turned to Inez and bowed. He abandoned Welles and strode toward her, expression and tone still intense from his fervent lecture. "Signora Stannert! I hoped to see you this morning. Come! Come! *Sbrigati*, please!" He hustled her toward the back of the store. As they passed Welles, Inez caught his gaze. The pianist rolled his eyes, just enough for her to see.

Nico almost pushed her into the office, exclaiming, "*Ecco!*" and slamming the door behind them.

Inez gaped. *He has gone overboard this time.* The office area was a veritable floral jungle, awash with flowers spilling out of vases on every available surface, their competing fragrances an olfactory jumble.

"Nico, what is this?" She had trouble forming a complete sentence.

"Before you left to give piano lessons and do whatever takes up so much of your time, I wanted to express my appreciation." He was directing his stream of zeal toward her now. "These past few days, I have realized how much I have come to depend and count on you. Signor Welles, he is of course adequate, but he cannot replace you. He cannot!"

"Thank you. You are most kind." *And most unnerving.* She

had begun to contemplate whether it would be possible to bring Welles in permanently as assistant manager. That way, once she was legally half owner, she could devote more time to lessons and to cultivating her investments and extracurricular business arrangements.

"All this is…most beautiful." She could not figure out what to say.

"It cannot begin to express the depth of the appreciation, the respect, the admiration I have for you!"

Things felt as if they were beginning to get out of hand. Inez took a step back and tried to inject a warm distance to her response. "Mr. Donato, I am overwhelmed by your generosity. I don't know quite what to say. I am happy you appreciate the work I do on behalf of the business."

"Furthermore, it is my sincere wish you will be my guest tonight at a recital Thomas and I are to give at the Palace Hotel."

"Ah." Inez frantically tried to form a plausible excuse that would allow her to stay in Nico's good graces and not offend him.

He continued, "It will be…" He kissed his fingertips and gestured upward as if tossing glittering superlatives into the air. "The event is a private party, a soirée being given by a visitor to our fair city, Signore Phillip Poole. Thomas and I will perform the Kreutzer sonata. Beethoven, yes? And some Mozart. You will see, it will leave them all dazzled!"

At the mention of Poole's name, Inez's mind stopped searching for ways to escape and began racing. "Mr. Poole, you said?"

He beamed. "Sì! He heard me play and asked for a reprise! I told him rather than doing the same pieces with a quartet I would bring Signore Welles—who is a very accomplished classical pianist, not just a noodler of low-class ditties—and we would play something truly extraordinary. Beethoven's Violin Sonata Number 9, Opus 47, the *Kreutzer Sonata*. He agreed."

Phillip Poole. Father of the young woman in Leadville who had killed herself in despair over having been jilted by Jamie when he was in his previous incarnation as Robert Gallagher.

Phillip Poole. The one concrete murder suspect Inez had not had a chance to meet or evaluate. Yes, Flo was theoretically doing so, but still. Inez suspected once Flo had decided Poole was innocent, she had stopped digging.

This is my chance. Time is short. I will not have another opportunity to observe him or perhaps to even talk with him.

Shifting her approach, Inez cast her eyes down modestly and brought her fingers to her lips, as if thinking. "Oh, I am so honored! I would love to attend. My hesitation comes from being not entirely certain I have anything appropriate to wear."

Nico seized her hand. "Whatever you wear, you will surpass the *belle* of Nob Hill and, indeed, the flowers themselves in grace and elegance."

His touch sent an unexpected heat racing from her hand to the pit of her stomach. Alarmed and fearing she may have fanned a flame she had not intended to ignite, Inez slipped her hand from his eager grasp and said, "I suppose I could find something amongst the gowns I brought with me from Colorado."

"*Eccellente!* I will pick you up at eight this evening and promise to have you back well before midnight. I know you do not like to leave Antonia alone long after dark. I promise you, it will be an evening to remember, Signora Stannert. And Phillip Poole is also from Colorado, you are—how do you say?— *compatrioti.* Compatriots! I will introduce you."

"How serendipitous," exclaimed Inez matching her enthusiasm to his. "But what I look forward to the most is seeing you perform. And Mr. Welles, of course."

He beamed. "You will not be disappointed, I promise."

She smiled back. *I will make certain of that. With luck, I shall meet Mr. Poole myself and perhaps determine what part he had to play, if any, in Jamie's death.*

Chapter Thirty-four

Time was trickling away.

Inez could see it in her mind—an hourglass, with the preponderant amount of sand now weighting the bottom.

Gallagher would be back in a few days. Today was disappearing, and she had much to do.

First, see de Bruijn. She had promised both him and Antonia she would do so. While she was at the Palace Hotel, she would try to corner Flo and see what she had accomplished the previous day. If anything. Next, a quick trip to the waterfront, yet again, to find Broken-nose Sven and ask him where she might find organizer Frank Roney. Afterwards, talk to Roney, inquire about his connection with Jamie, and see if he had any insights into the union "danger" Jamie had referred to in his letter to Carmella.

Return to the home of the Musicians Protective Association's secretary for the address of Stephen Abbott, the first name on Jamie's list and the only one who had warranted a checkmark. If she was correct in her thinking, the list was important since Jamie had removed it from the union's records and hidden it. Why did Jamie take it? Did he talk to Stephen Abbot? If so, did Abbott know something connected to the so-called danger that Jamie tried to warn, and then reassure Carmella about?

Finally, she had to be back in time to meet Antonia for supper—she dare not let the girl down again—and be ready for Nico at eight.

Grain by grain, more sand sifted into the bottom of the hourglass.

The physician was in de Bruijn's hotel room on the seventh floor when Inez arrived. She waited in the open corridor dotted with tropical plants and classical statuary, cooling her heels.

When the doctor emerged, she pounced, bombarding him with questions about de Bruijn's condition and prognosis until he unbent far enough to say, "He received a nasty blow to the head, but is recovering. I'd advise a few days of bedrest. Two or three, at the least. I suggested a nurse, but he declined vociferously. I will have the hotel staff check on him routinely and notify me if he seems worse. The curtains must stay drawn. He is fairly coherent right now. Tires easily, so keep your visit short."

Inez thanked him and entered the room, which seemed vast in the gloom. A small lamp guttered on the nightstand. De Bruijn was propped up in bed, surrounded by a mountain of pillows. He was dressed in a clean shirt, sans collar, and a paisley dressing gown. His waistcoat and jacket hung over the back of an overstuffed chair by the heavily curtained window. His hat waited on the seat, his shoes on the floor. All in all, he seemed prepared to jump up and throw on his attire the moment he was able.

"Mrs. Stannert. Good. I need you to tell me what happened last night. Much of it has vanished from my memory."

As best she could, she recreated the events as Antonia had related them, finishing with, "I don't believe John Hee is in any way connected with the murder."

"Maybe not murder," he muttered. "But, there's something."

"What?"

He opened and closed his mouth, took a deep breath and slowly released it. "I cannot recall. Only that I had some certainty of misdoings. Illegalities."

"Well, until you can recall what it is, I suggest we set John Hee aside as a suspect. I have made some progress on delving into Jamie's union activities. I also discovered he had a set-to with a previous employer, a Mr. Henderson, who owns a crimp house and saloon called The Three Sheets."

"Henderson," muttered de Bruijn. "The name is familiar."

Inez recounted what she had found out, beginning with Otto's discovery of the hidden list of names and her subsequent visit to *The Workman's Voice*. "I believe Jamie was interested in the previous union's dissolution—the reasons for it and so on—and also was perhaps looking into the disappearance of the union's funds. The common consensus seems to be the union treasurer, Eli Greer, made off with the money. Haskell and others apparently tried to unearth what happened, without success. I'm wondering if Jamie might have uncovered anything in that direction."

"And?"

She shook her head. "Nothing. All my queries so far are coming up empty."

"When would this have occurred?"

"Seven years ago."

"A very cold trail."

"So it appears. But I can't help but think this list is significant and worth following up on."

The doubt on de Bruijn's face was plain. "Anything else?"

Inez moved on to The Three Sheets, explaining that Jamie had lost his position when another musician offered to play for less and skirting how she obtained the information. "Today," she finished, "I'm off to track down this Stephen Abbott from the list and to see if I can't find Frank Roney as well. Oh! I would like a couple more of your business cards, if I may."

She had been focused on the wavering lamp flame during her report. When silence greeted her request, she glanced over to find de Bruijn with his eyes closed. Hating to wake him, but needing to clear up one last point, she cleared her throat. His eyes flew open and he said, "Yes?"

"Have you seen or heard from Mrs. Sweet?"

His brows drew together and he lifted a hand as if to run it through his hair, only to wince when he touched the bandage. "I don't think so." The uncertainty in his voice was new to Inez. He added, "I am almost certain I have not seen her since our last meeting."

"Well then, I shall have to run her to ground." Inez rose, studying him. Even in the dim light, he looked wan, his face etched in pain or perhaps exhaustion. "Can I get you anything before I go?"

"Unless you have a magic powder to make this infernal headache disappear, I am afraid not."

Inez smiled. "Alas, I do not."

"Well then." He closed his eyes. "Let me know what you find out. This evening, I think I should be better. Once I rest. We need reinforcements. I must consider." The words were coming slower, tinted with a slightly foreign cadence and an inflection Inez had not detected previously in his speech. For the first time, she wondered if de Bruijn originally hailed from the Continent.

She moved to go, and he stirred. "The Italian, a philanderer. He, the Chinaman, be careful." he murmured, then lapsed again into unconsciousness.

Inez frowned.

The Italian? As in Nico? If so, de Bruijn wasn't telling her anything she hadn't ascertained about Nico's proclivities.

And did de Bruijn mean "he" as in "the Italian," or "he" as in "John Hee"? John had nothing to do with the murder, she felt certain. But de Bruijn indicated other activities, illegal perhaps, were afoot. She wanted to ask him more, but it was clear he was not in a state to respond lucidly, if at all. Then, she remembered he hadn't responded to her request for business cards.

As Inez debated whether to wake him yet again, he turned a little in the bed, a small snore escaping. That decided it. Loathe to wake him, she tiptoed to the overstuffed chair and proceeded to rifle his pockets with impunity. His waistcoat yielded what she sought: his business cards. Inez took two, then one more for good measure.

Now, for Flo.

Inez returned to the front desk only to learn Mrs. Sweet's room was two doors away from de Bruijn's. Curbing her impatience, she rode the elevator back to the seventh floor. She knocked softly, then firmly upon the designated door, with no results. No rustling inside, no imprecations hurled at the unexpected visitor, or shoe thrown in a temper against the paneled wood.

Flo was not an early riser, which led Inez to just one conclusion. Flo appeared to have fled. Inez wagered with herself the madam had either returned to Leadville or decamped to Poole's rooms. She was betting on the latter. She didn't think Flo would leave town without at least sending a message to her. But who could say?

From there, it was time to catch the horsecar back to the Mission Creek waterfront. Inez chafed silently as the driver stopped at what seemed like every single corner on the way. By the time she made her way to Johansson's lumber wharf, it was noon. She stopped two men carrying their tin lunch buckets and was directed to the foreman, who said, "If you're looking for Broken-nose Sven, you'll find him on the pier with the others."

She headed in the direction he was pointing. The day had warmed, and the stench of the waterway was all-encompassing. She spotted a group of men sitting on a stack of lumber, their lunch pails open. If it had been her, she would have preferred to sup far from the foul waters sluggishly lapping at the pillars beneath the pier. The men's animated conversation, in a language Inez guessed was Swedish, came to a halt, and they watched her approach, curious. Broken-nose Sven, wearing the same blue-and-gray checked cap as previously, stood and with a remark that was unintelligible to Inez—she theorized he might have said something like "Here is the crazy lady again"— approached her.

He removed his cap. "Mrs. Stannert, good day."

"Hello again, Mr. Borg. My apologies, but I have one last question of some urgency for you."

"Ja?"

"Where could I find Frank Roney? I must speak with him today."

"Well." The word came out *vell*. "He is an iron molder. You will have to talk to him after work."

He threw what sounded like a question to his lunchmates and received a torrent of responses in a foreign tongue.

Sven turned back to Inez. "Tonight, he will be at the sandlots, where the new city hall is being built. He is there first, and after the men gather, they go to Meiggs wharf to talk to the sailors. To warn them of the crimp houses and tell them about the Seamen's Protective Union, ya know."

"About what time would he be at the sandlots?"

He scratched one end of his walrus mustache. "After work. Five-thirty. Six o'clock."

Six o'clock.

The sun was now overhead, demonstrating how warm San Francisco could become mid-day as fall turned to winter. A trickle of sweat ran down the back of her neck and disappeared between her shoulder blades.

She would have to be prompt with the rest of her tasks or she would miss her chance to talk to the labor activist. There would be neither time nor opportunity for her to skulk around North Beach and the wharves up there looking for Roney. Besides, after her nighttime foray into the wharf area by the Mission Creek canal, she had no desire to "test the waters" at the Barbary Coast after dark.

She thanked him and hurried off, using her umbrella as a makeshift parasol. Next stop was Baumann, the Musical Protective Association's secretary. Inez prayed he would be home, even though she was coming well after the morning hours. The same housekeeper, with her hair more neatly pinned, answered the door. Her first words were "You said you'd be here by noon."

"My apologies. I was unavoidably detained. Is Mr. Baumann in?"

"No, he's not. He waited until noon then left."

"Hell!" Inez said under her breath.

The housekeeper stiffened. "Excuse me?"

Inez back-pedaled. "I said, 'Help!' I really must talk with him today, soon as possible. Is there no way you can help me? Can you tell me where he is?"

The housekeeper relaxed. "I don't alwus know where he goes, he only tells me when it's overnight. But I'll tell him you came by after noon. Tomorrow, come back before noon." She shut the door.

Chapter Thirty-five

Inez stood at the closed door and briefly rested her forehead against the unyielding plank.

Tomorrow morning.

Another day gone. One day less to figure out who killed Harry Gallagher's son.

It seemed an impossible task.

Inez returned to her quarters and, mindful of the clock, proceeded to rifle through the large, upright wardrobe trunk holding her finery from her days in Leadville. Back then, she regularly dressed formally for Saturday evenings, the better to distract her players from their cards. There were also the various balls, formal events, and soirées she had attended, first with her husband Mark Stannert, later with Reverend Sands. Inez caressed the fine fabrics—satin, silk, velvet, cashmere, brocade. They whispered of times past, desires which waxed and waned. Her hand hovered over one dress, a mix of greens, satin insets on a dark green velvet overdress, lace tracing the décolletage, flowing in a soft waterfall down the front of the bodice. It was the dress she had worn nearly two years ago when she attended Leadville's Silver Soirée with Reverend Sands. Her fingers stroked the fabric, the touch bringing back a flood of feelings and memories of what had occurred after the dancing was done.

Unbidden, Nico's fervent and sudden handclasp replayed in her mind, how it had shocked her senses in a way she had not anticipated. Inez shoved the green dress aside. She did not want to wear something next to her skin that had borne witness to past volatile passions. A dress of midnight blue beckoned.

"This one," she said to herself. As Carmella had pointed out earlier, her six-month period of half-mourning for her "dear and departed" husband was over. The dark blue princess-style dress was an appropriate choice. Soothing, calm in its coloration, with a touch of gold for warmth and ivory lace on the three-quarters-length sleeves, it would complement her olive complexion and brunette hair. The square neckline was not daring, yet reasonably stylish for an exclusive private party at the Palace Hotel. The gown was not the latest fashion, but then who would expect her to be dressed *à la mode?* Certainly not Nico.

With this dress, she would not glitter, but neither would she fade into the shadows.

Inez gathered the necessary accouterments from the trunk's drawers: shoes, stockings, gloves, brooch, a fan, petticoat, camisole, satin-covered corset, two gold bangles for her wrist, a satin-and-cashmere manteau to wear over all. She carried the lot to her bedroom, arranged the dress and the rest on the coverlet, and stepped back to survey her ensemble. Satisfied it was complete and she would not be racing around at the last moment searching for forgotten items, Inez checked her pocket watch. Downstairs, the door slammed.

She met Antonia in the kitchen. Antonia seemed surprised. "You're here!"

"I said I would be."

Antonia nodded, looking unconvinced.

Inez continued, "We shall have to take dinner early."

"Why?"

"I have several things I must take care of this evening."

"Like what?" Antonia dropped her book bag on the kitchen table, sat in the kitchen chair, and pulled off her bonnet and spectacles.

"I am going to talk to someone about Jamie's union involvement. I'm not certain if I'll gain any useful information, but we cannot afford to leave any stone unturned. Later tonight, I am to attend a concert at the Palace Hotel given by a man who had no great love for Mr. Monroe."

"There's only a few days to figure out what happened, right?" A note of anxiety crept into Antonia's voice.

Inez tried to sound reassuring. "That is what Mr. Gallagher indicated before he left, but he was grieving and most likely did not mean everything he said. Perhaps when he returns he will be more inclined to listen to reason. After all, it is a tall order to try to find the perpetrator of such a crime, and none of us are professionals in this respect."

"Mr. Brown is," said Antonia. "He's a finder of the lost. It says so on his card. If the killer is hiding, he'll find him."

"If Mr. de Bruijn weren't currently recovering from his unfortunate expedition to Chinatown, that might be true. But he will not be able to help for a while."

"What about Frisco Flo, uh, Mrs. Sweet? Isn't she looking for the killer, too?"

"Supposedly," said Inez.

Antonia stared at her. "So, it's just you. You're the one who's got to figure it all out in time to tell Mr. Gallagher when he comes back to town."

Inez didn't reply.

Antonia sighed and bent down to unbutton her boots. "At least Mr. Brown knows John Hee didn't do it."

Inez kept de Bruijn's reservations about John Hee to herself. "By the way, I visited Mr. de Bruijn this morning. He is improving. The doctor says he must rest for now."

Antonia nodded, obviously not listening.

"What is it, Antonia?"

She looked up. "Will Mr. Gallagher really be able to ruin our lives? Make us leave again and start over somewhere else?" A narrow furrow of worry divided her brows.

Inez pondered how to respond. She finally decided to be as truthful as possible without causing alarm. "I don't know. He moves among the well-to-do and high society set. Men such as he wield a certain power that comes with wealth and position. But what are we to people such as they? I think the danger lies in Mr. Donato deciding I am a liability to the business." *Or to his reputation.* "Should it come to that, I shall do my utmost to convince him otherwise." The memory of Nico's warm fingers on hers rose, unbidden. An answering heat flowed outward from the pit of her stomach, sending a flush to her face and a tingle to her fingertips.

She shook her head, irritated with her traitorous body. "I am pursuing a couple of lines of inquiry which may yield useful information. If we can demonstrate to Mr. Gallagher we have done our utmost on his behalf, he may be satisfied and willing to turn to the police for assistance in solving the mystery of his son's death. But enough of ifs, perhaps, and maybes. We must leave for Mrs. Nolan's and convince her to feed us an early dinner."

Mrs. Nolan was nonplussed to have her usually tardy boarders actually arrive to sup before the dining hour. Her ruffled feathers were soothed by copious apologies from Inez and grateful exclamations over the cold mutton and ham, cornbread, and stewed fruit she put before them. She popped out of the kitchen as they were finishing to say, "Well now, I'm just sorry you won't be around for the rice pudding I'm making for dessert."

Antonia dropped her fork on her plate and looked pleadingly at Inez.

Inez asked her, "Do you want to stay and wait for dessert? You'll need to walk back on your own."

"It's not far. I'll be careful," Antonia promised. "And I won't go through Chinatown, I promise."

"Well! I should hope you would not!" said the scandalized Mrs. Nolan. "That is no place for a proper young girl such as yourself or for any proper person of any age. In fact, why don't you stay and help me clear the table after the boarders are done and I'll walk you back myself?"

"Thank you, Mrs. Nolan," Inez said before Antonia could demur. *At least this way she will not get into any trouble and will arrive home safely.*

Grateful to have one less person to worry about, Inez walked to where the new city hall was being built. It was a bit of a trudge down Market Street, but she didn't trust public transportation to get her there by six o'clock. By the time she reached the sandlots, the sun had set in earnest. Gas streetlamps shed pools of bright, hissing light. Out of breath and hat askew, Inez spotted a knot of men just beyond reach of the lamplight. The dome of the new city hall loomed behind them. Eleven years after breaking ground, the city center buildings were still under construction. Their skeletal columns and ribs rose like ghostly ruins of a bygone empire.

Inez picked up her pace, reaching the men just as they started to move purposefully away from their meeting site. "Mr. Roney?" she called plaintively. "May I speak with you?"

A figure detached itself from the group and approached her—a man of middling height, dark hair, full and lengthy beard, and solemn eyes. "Ma'am? Have we met?"

"No, we haven't. I am Mrs. Stannert. It's about Jamie Monroe, a pianist. I have been told he was a comrade of yours or perhaps a follower."

He frowned. For a moment Inez was afraid he would say he knew of no such person, but then his brow cleared. "Monroe, yes. Working to resurrect the musicians union." She caught the Irish intonation, an uplift at the end of his statement, which made it sound almost a question.

"Roney?" one of the men called. "Are you coming?"

"May I walk with you?" Inez interjected. "I don't want to keep you from your evening's activities. I understand you are heading to the waterfront. I am going that direction myself. At least partway."

He waved at the huddle of men. "Go ahead," he called to them. "I'll be following, while I answer the lady's questions." The group began walking up Market with Inez and Roney trailing behind.

"I haven't seen Monroe this week," said Roney. "I hope he isn't ill. Working, perhaps?"

Inez braced herself. "I'm sorry to tell you he's passed. Was murdered down by the Mission Creek wharves."

Roney stopped on the walkway. "A tragedy! Murdered, you say?"

"Sadly, yes. The family, to whom I am close, believes his union involvements may have led to his death. I am trying to find out if there is any truth to this." She hoped the vague explanation would suffice for her presence and her questions. "I was told by Mr. Haskell and others you might know more. You might know whether he was in any danger."

"The poor lad. And his family." He shook his head.

They started walking again. Inez waited for him to say something more. He finally said, "D'you know, organizing and agitating for workers' rights is not a safe occupation, and on occasion turns violent. However, I have yet to see musicians throwing brickbats or taking up pick-handles. Monroe's desire for his comrades to join him and form a trade union was not met with much success or interest."

They passed under a streetlamp and the yellow light splashed across his face, making him look jaundiced. He continued, "Those who own and run the music halls, theaters, restaurants, and so on who hire musicians may be 'thieving capitalists,' but I have not seen the players of trumpets and keyboards rising up in concert against them." He smiled briefly at his own wordplay. "And I don't see those who do the hiring turning violent against Monroe. There would be no reason."

"But wasn't he also trying to organize the Chinese musicians, build bridges to those who provide musical entertainment? Perhaps his efforts in that direction drew the ire of those who view the Chinese as, ah, a class beneath."

Roney had started shaking his head at the first mention of "Chinese." He said, "Ah, Mrs. Stannert, t'was such a notion of his, no one took it seriously when he spoke of it. We all know, the Celestials live in a world apart. Not beneath, but apart. They take care of their own and have no wish to join our efforts. We have common goals, we are all men trying to make a living, put a roof over our heads, and bring food to the table. But our common goals end there. Young Monroe was perhaps ahead of his time in this regard. But no one took him seriously, and I cannot see anyone taking his life for his foolishness."

"So, you don't know of any reasons, any possible persons, who might have wished him harm as a result of his desire to organize those of his profession?" Inez saw the list of suspects shrinking before her eyes.

"I assure you, Mrs. Stannert, no one of my acquaintance nor anything he confided to me indicated danger from such quarters. I know he was trying to determine what brought the previous efforts to unionize to failure, but beyond mutterings of past misdoings of a fiduciary sort, he didn't say much."

The hidden list of names flared up in her consciousness. "Along those lines, do the names Eli Greer, Stephen Abbott, Thomas Welles, or Nico Donato mean anything? Did he talk about any of them in connection with the past union efforts?"

"I'm sorry, Mrs. Stannert. Those names mean nothing to me."

They had reached Kearney Street. "Thank you, Mr. Roney, but this is where we part ways. I appreciate your time and your patience in answering my questions."

"Please pass along my condolences to young Monroe's family, if you think the sentiments of a trade unionist would be welcome. I'll add, I believe you are chasing ghosts, Mrs. Stannert. The city can be a dangerous place; he ran afoul of the fates. His family should mourn him and be proud for him taking a stand against the capitalists who bleed us dry."

She nodded, thinking Harry Gallagher would probably

not welcome the sympathies of a dyed-in-wool union man. On impulse, she added, "I wish you well with your efforts on behalf of the workingman and woman. Workingwomen need the help of men such as yourself all the more. They have no vote, no voice, and also labor for others under difficult and dangerous circumstances."

"That they do, Mrs. Stannert. And thank you."

Walking up Kearney, Inez thought over what Roney had told her. She trusted his knowledge and intuition regarding the labor activities and attitudes in the city. After all, Roney was certainly more in tune with such than either she or de Bruijn. Roney's remarks had only served to put aside some of the possibilities she and de Bruijn had been pursuing.

She sighed, frustrated. Perhaps tonight would be different. If she had a chance to meet Poole, she could take the measure of the man and gain some insights into whether he might have orchestrated Jamie's murder. *After all, who would have better reason for murderous intent than the father of a daughter who was jilted and shamed in the public sphere into taking her own life?*

Chapter Thirty-six

His head hurt like the devil, but that wasn't the worst of it.

The worst of it was the fact he had been caught flat-footed, as if he were an amateur.

He had too many distractions, de Bruijn decided. Distractions which had pulled his concentration and focus from the investigation.

Concerns about Antonia. Trying to keep track of what Mrs. Stannert was doing. Plus wondering where Mrs. Sweet had vanished to. He suspected Mrs. Sweet had moved lock, stock, and barrel into Poole's suite. But as things stood, he could hardly go down to the front desk and put forth the necessarily discreet inquiries. Standing up, dressing, and moving from the bedroom to the parlor had been enough to set his head spinning. It felt as though the sharp edge of an axe was trying to split the back of his skull wide open.

And, of course, there was the investigation into the murder of his client's son. The threads he had so carefully gathered up and followed. At least, *had* been following, up to the moment he ignored his best instincts and had dashed into that damnable alley in Chinatown.

His current circumstances had forced him to acknowledge he needed someone who could act in his stead, who had the skills and abilities to do what needed to be done. What *he* should have been doing.

Which was why, having placed a call and received a positive response, he now sat in the overstuffed chair in the parlor of his rooms at the Palace Hotel. Waiting, with the curtains mostly closed, because he still could not handle full daylight.

A light knock at the door prompted him to say, "Enter" in a voice which sounded like thunder to his own ears.

Elizabeth O'Connell came in and he tried to rise.

"No need, Mr. de Bruijn. Stay as you are."

He settled back. She cocked her head, inspecting him as she removed her gloves. "I must say, that is not your best look."

His hand rose to the bandage cushioning the crown of his head. "A nuisance, at the very least." He indicated the chair facing his own.

"How many days before you can be out and about again?" She sat and positioned her satchel on her lap.

He halved the number of days the physician had advised. "Perhaps two. In the meantime, events are in motion, and I need your assistance."

"Of course."

He handed her a folded sheet of paper on which he had penned his instructions, a process which had taken him a ridiculously long time to complete. "This is what I want you to do."

Miss O'Connell opened and scanned the page. "A fair list. I cannot split myself into three, obviously. I will need assistance. I have authorization to hire associates? They come with the most impeccable credentials and are circumspect, of course."

"Of course." He was having trouble forming the words.

"Do you have a preference as to where I should start?"

Normally, he would have been able to respond thus-and-so is the first priority, such-and-such is the second. But his head was throbbing and felt filled with water. He heard and understood her words as if from a great distance. He swam to the surface long enough to say, "I suggest you start with the third item. The gentleman."

Miss O'Connell folded the paper into quarters and slid

it into her satchel. "I shall get busy and report when I have something concrete. Mr. Gallagher is due in the city, when, precisely?"

"It could be Monday, but best to have this business concluded by Sunday, if possible." He closed his eyes. The throbbing slowed.

"Very well," she said from the other side, where the light still lurked. "Mr. Gallagher will have nothing to complain of when he returns."

"Remember, what we need is proof."

"I am aware of the objectives and the desired results. You can count on me, Mr. de Bruijn."

"Good." Her skirts rustled through the fatigue threatening to drag him into sleep. A few moments later the door hissed open and shut over the thick carpet, leaving him in blessed silence, the memory of her departing words a balm: *you can count on me.*

Chapter Thirty-seven

The bell downstairs rang promptly at eight, and Inez descended, pulling her satin-and-cashmere manteau about her shoulders. She opened the door to Nico, dressed in his evening finery.

"Signora Stannert, you are *squisito*, exquisite!" He doffed his top hat with a flourish and an admiring glance. "You have been hiding your light under a bushel all this time. You outshine the stars."

Inez wanted to roll her eyes. Instead she smiled and said, "Thank you, Mr. Donato."

He looks different, somehow.

Nico offered her his arm. "Please. Allow me. Signore Welles is coming with us. For a recital, I always make certain to gather the musicians together in one carriage. It is my way of assuring we all arrive or none of us do." He escorted her to the waiting hack.

Inez ducked into the carriage and, with a rustle of satin, sat opposite Thomas Welles, also in black formal evening wear. "Glad you could join us, Mrs. Stannert," said Welles. "It'll be quite the crowd in attendance, I understand." He held Nico's violin case in his white-gloved hands.

The carriage bounced lightly on its springs as Nico entered and sat next to Thomas. He retrieved his violin, remarking, "And we shall do our best to entertain and enthrall, as only Mozart and Beethoven's music can."

Welles rapped on the wall, and the carriage began to move. Nico set his case on the seat. As they passed a streetlamp and turned onto Market, Inez realized what was different about Nico. "Mr. Donato, where is your magnificent cloak?"

Instead of the fine wool overgarment with the distinctive ermine collar he always wore, he had on a black cloak with a luxurious dark fur collar.

"Ah. It is out of fashion. This," he stroked the dark fur collar as if it were a living creature, "is new. Just this season. Elegant, yes?"

Welles shifted, one white glove rising to hold his top hat as he turned his head toward Nico. "I thought you told me your kingly cape had been ruined."

"Ah," said Nico dismissively. "One and the same. Ruined by the fickle turn of *la mode*. When in the public eye, one must be in vogue, *si*?"

Light poured into the carriage windows as the vehicle pulled into the circular driveway of the central court of the Palace Hotel and squeaked to a halt. The musicians exited first and helped Inez down. They crossed the marble-paved floor beset with potted trees and plants. Far above, the glass-encased dome was opaque with the night sky.

Inez recalled being up at the seventh-floor gallery arcade only that morning and looking down onto the carriage court. From seven floors up, the greenery had appeared little more than shrubs. Down at floor level, it seemed a veritable forest.

As the trio proceeded to the elevators, Welles engaged Inez, inquiring politely about Antonia, how she was doing, whether she was enjoying school. His eldest, he confided, was in third grade and finding it challenging. As she chatted with Welles, Inez registered Nico was scanning the reception area as if hoping to recognize some of the elite and powerful of the city. Or perhaps, she thought, he was hoping the elite and powerful would recognize *him*.

The elevator operator whisked them up to the second floor.

"We will be in one of the grand parlors," said Nico. "We have performed there before, Thomas and I."

Welles nodded. "The hotel keeps their pianos well-tuned. A pleasure to play."

Inez could hear the swell of voices grow as they approached a set of tall doors. Bright as the gaslight in the open corridor was, the light spilling from beyond the doors shone all the brighter. They paused at a cloak room where Inez shed her manteau, Nico his new cloak, and Welles his overcoat, before entering one of the Palace Hotel's public "parlor rooms," which had about as much in common with the humble residential parlor room as the ordinary two-story room-and-board residences had in common with the mansions of the city elite.

The parlor, decorated in a French Rococo style, was of outsized dimensions and glamor, much like the hotel itself. The grand room easily accommodated the hundred or so Inez estimated were in attendance. Massive bronze and gilt chandeliers holding constellations of gaslights shed their brilliant yellow light over the guests. Most of the women were dressed bright as peacocks, while the men were uniformly dark and somber in their eveningwear. Their fans aflutter, the women glided about in form-fitting attire of silk, tulle, taffeta, brocade, and satin on the arms of their male companions. Meanwhile, dark knots of single men clustered here and there, like murders of crows, cigar smoke curling above their heads in languid eddies.

Discomfited, Inez halted inside and snapped her fan open. It had been a long time since she had attended a soirée. There had been balls and fetes in Leadville, to be sure. Yet, this "small concert gathering" was a whole different elevation of entertainment entirely, more akin to the half-remembered balls and parties she attended as a New York City debutante or the elegant gatherings in London and Paris whispered about amongst the girls in her long-ago boarding school.

A waiter approached them with a silver tray, offering champagne. Nico waved him away. "After the performance," he said as he scanned the room.

Inez determined to slip away at the first opportunity—surely the musicians would need to prepare for their performance—and hunt down one of those bobbing trays circulating the room. As she longingly watched the waiter retreat into the crowd, she noted the young and not-so-young women in their vicinity were directing sidelong glances or boldly open gazes of interest their way. Well, not at *her*, that was certain. Clearly Nico was the one drawing their interest and stirring their fans into a quickened tempo.

"Ah! And there is Signore Poole," said Nico. "Come." Escorting Inez and trailed by Welles, Nico moved through the crowd. Many of the guests acknowledged Nico with a nod or bow, and more than one called out, "Signore Donato!" or "Looking forward to your performance, Maestro!" In the case of the ladies, who by etiquette remained mute, they communicated with smiles demure and not-so-demure. Nico returned all with nods, bows, and smiles of his own, sprinkled with remarks such as "Ah! Signore Walton! Good to see you and the lovely Signora," and "The concert, you will not be disappointed!" and "Signore Welles and I, we have been hard at work, turning the score into music fit for the angels."

Inez lost track of what else he said because dead ahead, in the direction Nico was leading her and Welles, was Frisco Flo standing with a cluster of men.

Flo had her back to Inez, but there was no missing or mistaking her. Attired in an orange and crimson confection of bows, ruches, lace, drapes, pleats, and puffs, and with her blond curls caught up with a flowered and befeathered ornament, Mrs. Sweet locked arms with her escort in a manner bordering on scandalous. As for the gentleman, who was middling in height and impressive in girth, his identity was quickly made clear when Nico said to Inez, under his breath and with an air of perplexity, "Is that not Signora Sweet with Mr. Poole?"

Poole turned toward the Leadville madam, saying something. She threw back her head and emitted a tinkling laugh in response.

Inez discarded any thought of trying to deny Flo's identity to Nico. "I do believe it is," she said, cheerily determined.

"How does she even know him?" Nico sounded baffled.

"It's a small world, I suppose," said Inez, attempting to sound offhand.

Poole must have seen them approaching, for he turned to greet Nico with a welcoming smile. At least, Inez surmised it was a smile, given the crinkling around his eyes, as his "friendly muttonchops" served as a thicket to hide his mouth from view. "Mr. Donato, you have arrived!" His voice was surprisingly deep and sonorous. "I was afraid we would run out of champagne and conversation before your concert was to begin. And who is your lovely companion?" He was now staring at Inez in a manner she found very disconcerting and, even worse, vaguely familiar.

Those muttonchops. That voice. I know him.

Flo looked around when Poole began speaking. The madam's expression reflected the same horror and trepidation now welling up inside Inez.

Nico said, "Signore Poole, may I introduce you to Signora Stannert, and here is my accompanist for the evening, the esteemed pianist Signore Thomas Welles."

Poole stepped out of the knot of men, pulling Flo with him. He seemed hardly to acknowledge Welles beyond an absent nod. All of his attention was focused on Inez. "Mrs. Stannert, you say? An honor to meet you, ma'am." He hesitated. "Have we met before?"

Inez sucked in her breath, and along with the ambient scent of tobacco, a memory formed, as it were, out of the smoke. The venue was one of her former husband Mark Stannert's infamous poker gatherings, upstairs in the exclusive card room of Leadville's Silver Queen Saloon. An evening of high-stakes games peopled by high-rollers, silver mine investors and owners, Colorado capitalists and entrepreneurs. She was now certain one of the players, seen once and never again, had been the man now giving her a piercing once-over.

Flo quickly interposed herself between Poole and Inez, blocking his view. She sent her fan to fluttering and directed her baby-blue gaze along with her considerable charm at Nico. "Why, Mr. Donato, here you are! And not a moment too soon. As I was telling Mr. Poole, I am so excited you will be playing for us tonight!" She clasped her hands together in girlish anticipation, allowing the fan to swing from one shapely wrist. "I absolutely must have a seat in the front row! I do not want to miss a single note."

She looked over her shoulder at Poole, pouting slightly, head atilt, her décolletage deepening, thanks to her bent arms and bosom-level clasped hands. In this single pose, she somehow managed to be beguiling, pleading, and commanding, all at once. "With Mr. Donato and Mr. Welles here, we should begin, don't you think?"

Poole, his attention re-focused onto Flo, said indulgently, "Of course, Mrs. Sweet, your wish is my command." He crooked his arm for her, but she waved him off. "I need another moment with Mrs. Stannert." With a final glance at Inez, Poole proceeded to the far end of the room where rows of chairs faced a grand piano.

Welles said, "Sounds like our cue, Nico. Ladies, shall we escort you to the front row?"

"Thank you," said Inez, "but Mrs. Sweet and I will make our way there in a moment."

Welles bowed and headed toward the piano. Nico captured Flo's gloved hand and bowed. "Signora Sweet, such happenstance! We shall play for you and Signora Stannert."

Flo simpered.

Nico turned to Inez and, taking her hand, performed the same gesture. "My music is my gift to the two most beautiful women in the room."

Inez said, "I am looking forward to it."

As Nico hurried off, Flo snapped open her fan and, using it to shield the lower part of her face, she whispered to Inez, "What the *hell* are you doing here?"

Inez opened her fan with a flick of the wrist and fanned herself slowly. "The invitation was extended by Mr. Donato. I could hardly say no. Especially when I heard Mr. Poole had requested the concert. I thought I would ask him a few questions. But now, that does not seem like a good idea. And what are you doing here? Why haven't you been in touch?"

"Because," she hissed, "there is nothing further to tell you! I already *told* you Phillip Poole had nothing to do with our problem."

"What makes you so certain?"

Flo actually snorted, but quietly. "First of all, I know on Sunday night he was, shall we say, 'fully occupied' at Diamond Carrie Maclay's brothel."

"He could have hired someone to do his dirty work," Inez muttered from behind her fan.

Flo's fan fluttered faster. "Phillip arrived the same time as Harry—"

"Phillip. On a first-name basis now, are we?" Inez murmured.

Ignoring her comment, Flo continued, "And just like Harry, he had no idea where to look and had no idea Robert had taken on the name of Jamie Monroe. Nobody did. He was completely shocked when I told him Robert was dead. Then, he said, 'Good riddance,' and said he wished he could've challenged Robert to a duel and shot him himself. It's all bluster, though. The kind of violence he does is in the boardroom, not on the streets."

A few arpeggios and scales floated from the direction of the piano. Nico began tuning his violin. "Ladies, gentlemen," called Poole, "please take your seats."

Inez and Flo drifted toward the chairs arranged in semicircular rows facing the musicians.

"If you are done with that line of investigation, why haven't you contacted us?" Inez whispered. "De Bruijn was attacked in Chinatown. He's recovering, but I could use your help. There are only a couple of days left."

"I *am* helping," said Flo in an aggrieved but subdued tone. "I'm helping us both. Listen Inez, the gold rush may be over, but there are still opportunities aplenty to make money in San Francisco. I'm working to make sure neither of us ends up in the gutter as a result of this affair. You know and I know, we'll never find the killer. We've been running in circles and nothing has turned up, right?"

"There's still a chance we can identify a reasonable suspect."

"In two days? Look, we're going to end up telling Harry his son was probably killed by some unknown thug or cutthroat down on the wharf. Harry won't like it, so I'm making sure to get some 'protection' from Poole against Harry's wrath. Harry is a big gun in Leadville. If he is determined to shut me down there, maybe he could. But San Francisco is a big city and his influence probably isn't as strong here."

"He was able to shut down the police investigation into his son's death," Inez pointed out. "I still don't understand why. They have the resources to deal with this. Why turn to us?"

Flo gave her fan an irritated little flit. "Doesn't matter. The point is, he's limited in what he can do here. As for the police, they are the same all over. Pay their extra fees and taxes and they look the other way. Anyhow, I've had my eyes open for local business opportunities. And trust me, there are plenty of opportunities!"

"In the flesh trade?" asked Inez, not believing her ears.

"Of course in the flesh trade. I'm not going to open a candy store! And I want you to be my partner. If Harry decides to tar you with the same brush, you might as well be damned for a sinner than for a saint."

"I can't believe this," muttered Inez, shaking her head at both Flo's machinations and her muddled turn of phrase. They had reached the front rows. Nico and Poole were in deep discussion while Welles warmed up on the piano. Nico glanced at the two women and with a slight smile gestured with his violin bow to two empty chairs front and center. Flo beamed at him then turned to Inez, closing her fan as she did so.

"I hope they're not talking about us," she murmured. "It could get awkward. You should have stayed out of this."

Inez lifted her eyebrows, smiling pleasantly. "And how was I to know Mr. Poole would recognize me?"

Flo wiggled into her seat and tapped her closed fan on her lap. "Leave him to me. But you'll have to handle the charming signore yourself. Just remember what I said about business opportunities, should he decide to give you the heave-ho."

Once everyone was seated, Nico stepped forward and the coughing and rustling subsided. "*Benvenuto e buonasera.* And thank you to this evening's host, Signore Poole, for providing such an elegant setting for us to offer our modest musical talents for your entertainment."

Inez heard several of the nearby women sigh when Nico rolled out the words with what seemed a stronger than usual accent. Nico gazed around the assemblage. "I see many I recognize," he began, "but some new faces as well. For those who do not know me, may I introduce myself? I am Signore Nico Donato, and my accompanist is Mr. Thomas Welles."

Inez could hear the rapid flip and flitter of fans behind her and on either side, accompanied by feminine whispers. She was certain if she turned around she would see batting eyes, modest blushes, and eloquent smiles, all directed at the signore with the violin.

Thomas half rose and bowed perfunctorily.

This was clearly Nico's show.

"Shall we begin with a little Mozart?" Nico raised his violin into position, he and Welles exchanged a glance and nod, and they launched into a series of perfectly executed Mozart sonatas.

Inez was impressed both by their individual virtuosity and the perfectly timed, invisible communication between them. Nico and Thomas Welles made it seem effortless, seamless, a musical conversation handed back and forth. But Inez knew how difficult it was, how much work went into making it look so very easy. She allowed herself to float on the music while observing their styles of playing. Welles seemed to disappear into the flow of music, much as she did, except for the times when he and Nico, as if by previous agreement, would exchange a look, a nod. Nico, she had to admit, knew how to play to the crowd, bringing the song out of the instrument and the emotional intensities hidden in the sonatas. When the musicians finished, Inez let out a sigh and was surprised to hear a surrounding chorus of feminine sighs echo her own. Flo gave a little start, and Inez realized the madam had been half-dozing.

Under the cover of muffled clapping from gloved hands, Flo opened her fan, leaned toward Inez, and murmured, "Are they done?"

"One more piece," said Inez, joining the applause.

With a "Huh!" Flo closed her fan before applying three fingers of one hand to the palm of the other in lukewarm praise.

The second piece was the promised Beethoven Sonata Number 9, *The Kreutzer Sonata.* The performance, a transcendental union of music and musicians, pulled her into an embrace which did not release until the final perfect notes fell and faded into silence.

The guests all rose to applaud with enthusiasm. Flo stood and tugged at her overskirt, remarking, "A bit excessive, wasn't it?"

"It was marvelous!" said Inez.

Flo lifted a shoulder and looked around. "Where did those waiters go?"

Women of all ages surrounded and engulfed the musicians. Inez turned away, resigned that she would not be able to leave immediately.

Flo brightened. "Ah! There is the champagne and I am dying of thirst. I'll be right back. I'll bring you some, too." She took off across the room.

Inez moved over to one of the shrouded bay windows and pulled a corner back on one of the ornate brocade curtains to peek at the cityscape. A masculine, "Ahem," behind her caused her to drop the heavy fabric back into place and whirl around. Poole stood there, skewering her with his penetrating gaze. "Did you enjoy the concert, Mrs. Stannert?"

"Indeed. It was remarkable." She surveyed the room over his head, hoping to catch sight of Frisco Flo with the promised champagne or of Nico breaking away from his admirers. Poole swiveled around to see what caught her eye.

"If you will excuse me, Mr. Poole." She circled around him, ready to escape.

"A word, Mrs. Stannert, before you go."

She could hardly run away in the face of such a direct request. Reluctantly, she faced him. "Yes, Mr. Poole? What about?" Inez hoped it would be about an innocuous topic. Such as her opinion of Mozart.

"Come come, I believe you know. And I am certain you would prefer we talk here, where we have a bit of privacy."

Taking some cold comfort from the fact she was taller than he by several inches, Inez pulled out her fan to give her hands something to do and decided the best plan of attack was to be blunt. "I understand you are here in San Francisco on personal business, Mr. Poole. The business of revenge."

Poole's head snapped back, and he regarded her narrowly. "You wish to get to the point, Mrs. Stannert? I can appreciate that. Very well, we shall be direct with each other. Yes, I came to find the man who drove my daughter to her shame and her death. Robert Gallagher. When Harry made sudden plans to head this way, I knew the game must be afoot. He had his investigator on the trail, and all I needed to do was follow along, let my fellow follow his fellow, and then be first to jump when the bastard who destroyed her was rooted out."

Inez crossed her arms, tapping her fan on one sleeve. "You wanted him dead."

"Of course I did," he said through gritted teeth, then made a visible effort to unclench his jaws. "I'm glad he died and so viciously. God's will was done."

"I doubt God had anything to do with it."

"Then justice was done, if you prefer. The kind of justice man brings to man, when the courts are useless. He would never pay legally for what he did to my little girl. This, his murder, was far more satisfying. To make Harry suffer as I have." He broke off and brushed a sideburn with one hand, a nervous tic, Inez surmised, when he was overwrought.

He continued, "I'd not be sad to see Harry's empire fall into ashes as well. Once I'm shut of him and our agreements, I'll not do business with him again."

"You claim you had nothing to do with his death? You didn't set 'your fellow who followed the other fellow' to cut off young Gallagher mid-tune?"

She waited to see that unconscious hand rise up and brush the sideburn again, but it didn't. Instead, his face turned red and he balled his fists. Then, apparently aware of the picture he must present to the room at large, stretched his fingers out and flexed them. Almost as if he wished he held her throat in his hands. "You are right in one regard. I could have hired some thug to do the dirty work. If I'd been able to find him first, I would have. But I did not. I swear on my daughter's grave."

"Then, I believe our conversation is over," said Inez calmly and made to move aside and let him pass.

But Poole wasn't done. "Last time we met, Mrs. Stannert, was in Leadville while you were still married and owned a saloon in a not-so-esteemed part of town. Imagine my astonishment upon seeing you here and learning you are now in charge of a respectable, well-regarded music store. It seems Robert Gallagher was not the only one looking to bury his past in San Francisco, eh?"

Inez felt the blood drain from her face.

He leered, triumphant. "Just keep in mind, Mrs. Stannert. Things buried eventually come to light and stink and rot."

Chapter Thirty-eight

"Rot? What rot?"

Inez turned to see Flo with Nico by her side. They each held two glasses of champagne. Flo wrinkled her nose, perplexed.

"Nothing, nothing at all, my dear Mrs. Sweet," said Poole. "Mrs. Stannert and I were just chatting about old times. The air in Leadville, you know. The odious smell of sulfur and whatnot."

"Old times?" Flo shot a nervous glance at Inez. "Oh, I think we should just focus on the here and now, don't you agree?"

"*Assolutamente*," said Nico handing Inez a glass. "Signora Sweet and I, we thought we should all toast to a successful evening, yes?" He raised his own and said, "Signore Poole, thank you for your patronage. I hope when you are next in our fair city, you will consider doing this again."

"Why not?" said Poole amiably. "It's been a profitable trip, all around. Quite satisfying. I shall be certain to employ your and Mr. Welles' considerable talents when I return."

Inez raised her flute along with the rest, sick inside. When the champagne hit her tongue, the fizz and overwhelming sweetness only intensified her nausea. "Is it not to your taste?" Nico inquired, gesturing to her glass.

"I suspect I am simply tired," said Inez.

"Ah! And I promised to have you back early." Nico swept up her glass and turned to Poole and Flo. "It's been an honor,

Signore Poole. Signora Sweet, please do visit the store again sometime. We could show you some of our finer pianos, for your daughter, perhaps? How is she doing with her lessons?"

"I shall make it a point to drop by," Flo chirped, twisting one blond curl around her finger. Her eyes shifted from Nico to Poole and back again.

As Nico and Inez turned to go, Inez heard Poole say, "I had no idea you were interested in the finer points of music-making, Mrs. Sweet. And what's this about a daughter?"

Inez left it to Flo to work her way out of the situation. Inez had her own future to ponder. She suspected Poole had not been chary in telling Nico about her past, which meant she would have to "face the music" with Nico probably sooner rather than later. As they prepared to leave, Inez asked, "What about Mr. Welles?"

"He has his own way home," said Nico. At the cloakroom, he helped her on with her manteau before shrugging into his new cloak. "Going back, it will be just us two."

Which meant the reckoning could be sooner.

In the carriage, after he was sure Inez was settled on the bench across, Nico set his violin case on the seat beside him and sat back, gazing thoughtfully at Inez. The carriage squeaked into motion.

"So. I understand you are not a widow, Signora Stannert. Is this true?"

Damn it. How am I to keep this from coming down around my ears.

Inez looked out the window, grateful they had left the brightly lit central court of the Palace Hotel and rolled into the dim streets where he could not read her expression. "True, unless you count being a 'grass widow' as being a widow, which I do. My former husband is dead to me. As dead as if he lay six feet underground."

A silence stretched between them, then Nico said, "Your husband. What did he do to earn such disgust from you?"

Inez regarded him, surprised at the personal turn of question. She had steeled herself, expecting questions about the saloon, demands about her part in its running, speculations about her social standing, and perhaps an interrogation into her familial lineage. Or even, God forbid, pointed inquiries about Reverend Sands, as it was possible Poole had somehow gained knowledge of her affair with the reverend. All of these topics she was prepared to dodge, if possible, or answer with shaded truths, if pressed.

But she was not expecting or prepared for this.

Still, it would be easy to answer, although not pleasant to say. "Well, if you must. I suppose I owe you that much, Mr. Donato, given how you no doubt feel I have deceived you, or at least led you astray in some respect as to my status and past. To be brief, he lied to me in one of the most heinous ways a husband can lie to a wife. He disappeared, without a trace, for more than a year. Then he returned, wanting to continue as if nothing at all had happened. I was tempted to do so until I found out he had been living as husband and wife with another woman, and this woman—" Inez took a deep breath to brace herself against the words—"was with child. His child. She came to town, confronted him and me in a very public location, and demanded he set me aside for her." As she spoke, tears welled up.

She blinked them away, but Nico must have seen them or heard them in her voice. He handed her his handkerchief. "I am sorry. It is no matter. As Signora Sweet said, it is better to think of the present and the future. The past is gone. I care not what went before in your life. Although I was taken by surprise when Signore Poole told me."

"What else did he tell you?" Inez was determined to hear it all, so she knew how much damage was done and how she might, if possible, repair it.

"It does not matter what else was said." The carriage squeaked to a stop, and Nico looked out the window. "Ah. We are at the store. Will you indulge me for a few minutes before you return to your lodgings and Antonia?"

Inez acquiesced, glad there would be no more questions. Still, she wondered what Nico knew and what, more immediately, he had in mind.

Nico unlocked the store and ushered her in. He went over to the grand piano, remarking, "I have a request, Signora. I realized tonight you and I, we have not played together. In fact, am I right in thinking this was the first time I have performed for you?"

"Well, Mr. Donato, I would not presume you performed for *me* tonight. You and Mr. Welles enchanted everyone in the room, as I'm sure you know. However, you are correct. I'll admit I also thought how strange it was, that in all these months, this was the first time I heard you play."

"Since I practice at home and not at the store, it makes sense. But it does not excuse this lapse on my part. I have only heard you on the piano once, when you first visited my store. I was impressed, even then. I remember, you had such a light, sensitive touch. So. Tonight, I am decided. We will remedy this deficiency *immediatamente*."

"Now?" She watched, bemused and intrigued, as he set his violin case on a small, round table of oriental design and opened the grand piano lid.

"Now." He held out the chair for her.

She hesitated, but only briefly. *After all, what harm can come of this?*

Besides, her fingers had been aching for the coolness of ivory and ebony keys for some time. She had not sat at the piano for the past week, what with all that had been going on. Even before then, she played intermittently. The situation here was not like in Colorado, where she could turn to her parlor grand in her own home for solace, for reflection, whenever she pleased.

"Very well." She took the chair and lifted the fallboard, exposing the keys.

He pulled out his violin. "What shall we play? *The Kreutzer Sonata?* Would you enjoy that? The piano score is here in the store, I know."

"Perhaps another time. I would need to practice so as to not embarrass myself or frustrate you," said Inez, a little horrified at the thought of attacking the involved Beethoven sonata cold, in the semi-dark, with Nico.

She glanced up at the ceiling, considering, and realized Antonia's bedroom was directly above. "Antonia loves Beethoven's Bagatelle Number 25 in A Minor, *Für Elise*. I usually play it at least once a week for her. But I've sadly neglected my duty lately."

"Well then, it is decided!" Nico smiled down at her.

Inez smiled back. She now understood why he was pursued by so many of the feminine persuasion. He could be exceedingly charming. And when he looked at her like that…

She redirected her focus to the piano and ran her gloved fingertips lightly over the tops of the keys.

Nico said, "Play it once, solo. Then again, and I will join you."

Inez nodded. She pulled off her gloves, set them aside, and touched the cool keys. She could almost hear herself reminding her students: *wrists relaxed and level with the hand, fingertips on the surface of the keys.*

She closed her eyes, blocking out all but the piano, letting the quiet fill her until she was ready to replace the silence with music. She launched into the short piece, letting the familiar melody and theme carry her away, playing at the slower tempo she had adopted for Antonia. When she finished and circled back to the beginning, the notes of the violin wound in and around her own, pulling her out of the music. As the two instruments joined together, blending their individual styles and tones to form a deeper, richer whole, Inez relaxed again, able to let the harmony and melody flow over and through her.

They played it twice together. At the end, Inez left her hands rest in final position and allowed echoes of their performance to slowly die away.

"*Bellissimo*," said Nico, somewhere above her. In the dream state playing sometimes brought to her, his voice almost seemed a continuation of the music.

"Why did we wait so long?" He took her hand, and Inez thought he only meant to help her to her feet. But as she rose, he pulled her closer, and she realized that was not his intent at all. Time seemed to slow, even as her mind and her heart began racing faster.

Her first thought: *why not?*

It had been a long time since a man had been so attentive, so admiring. A long time since she had been touched in this way, buried, as she was, in work, in worry, in care for Antonia. She had purposely stayed in the shadows to protect them both, for it had seemed that only by being anonymous and unnoticed would they be able to create new lives in this new city.

Her second thought: *why not Nico?*

He was charming. He was attractive. He was desirable. With all this, and endowed with the gift of musical talent and sensitivity as well, it was easy to understand why women swooned and dropped their gloves and signaled with their fans and laughed with that lighter-than-air breathless expectancy when he appeared.

Besides, she was curious.

Curious to taste the unknown.

So, she let him guide her to her feet, pull her close and closer until there was no space between them, then touch his lips to hers. First, a light kiss. Then, a second, more lingering. And a third....

Inez, eyes closed, responded as harmony spoke to melody, left hand to right. She allowed long-dismissed passion to uncurl inside her, warming her with pleasure and inducing a growing longing. Her hands and arms had, of their own volition it seemed, pulled his head down to her throat. There, in the dark, in the silence, he was faceless. He could be anyone.

He kissed her neck, brushed her ear with his whisper, "Why did we wait so long?"

The trancelike moment shattered and awareness rippled through her.

What am I doing?

This isn't just anyone. This is Nico.

It was as if someone had switched on the bright gaslights in the darkened room, blasting insubstantial dreams into hard-angled reality. If she needed to satisfy her thirst for intimacy, Nico was probably her worst possible choice.

Inez cleared her throat and untangled her fingers from his hair. She slid her arms from around his neck, her hands slipping over the soft fur collar of his cloak. "Mr. Donato, we must stop."

"Surely we are past the point of Mr. this and Signora that." He sounded mystified and even a little affronted.

Inez realized she had to tread carefully. "Please, this is all very sudden. I mean, perhaps not sudden, but...I need time to think."

"Thinking can come later." He began to pull her back into the embrace.

"There is much at stake." Realizing that might sound cold and calculating, she added hastily, "It is not just you and I. There is Antonia to consider." She hated offering up her ward as an excuse. It felt as if she was hiding behind the girl's skirts.

"I thought..." He truly was bewildered, Inez realized. He might not have had a woman refuse his advances before, in which case the possibility of injured male vanity made the situation even more fraught.

"Nico." She capitulated as far as using his first name and tried to turn the word into a caress. "You have me at a disadvantage, surely you see that. Surely you can give me the space, the time, I need to think over this change in our relationship."

He released her and retreated. "Very well." But it didn't sound like he thought it was well at all. "It is late. I have kept you from Antonia." His words and tone also retreated into formality, politeness.

He turned and put his violin away. Inez closed the fallboard and wrapped her arms around herself to ward off the sudden chill in the room. They walked out of the store together. After locking up, Nico turned to her and said, "Please, Signora Stannert." His voice held a tinge of desperate determination. "For very long, I thought you still in mourning and did not want to presume. My intentions toward you are honorable, I swear it."

"I see." And she did—but not in the way he probably intended her to see. Inez now realized what particular Pandora had been released when Nico had discovered she was not a widow but a divorcée. Perhaps his intentions had once been "honorable," but that would no longer be the case. In Nico's world, and indeed throughout most of society, a widow was a decent woman worthy of respect. A divorcée was not. Nico's assertions about his intentions could be nothing but an outright lie. Knowing her real status, he did not step back but instead reconsidered his options. She suspected such thinking had been the catalyst for his attempted seduction. Furthermore, she was willing to bet that being rebuffed by an "immoral" woman was unfathomable to him.

Unable to think of anything to add that would neither encourage further attempts nor instigate possible repercussions, Inez said, "Thank you for a beautiful evening. The concert, everything. And it was such an honor to play with you."

He bowed, a little less stiffly. "I look forward to doing so again very soon." Before she could respond he grabbed her hand, kissed her fingers, and then let her go, and walked away, back toward Market.

Shuddering, Inez unlocked the door to the apartment, a sanctuary from the mess she'd just sidestepped. The bottle of high-end whiskey she kept in the bottom drawer of her nightstand was the only company she craved in her bed that night. She hurried up the stairs and went to check on Antonia, expecting to find her nestled under her blankets with her nightcap pulled down over her eyes.

Antonia was not asleep.

She sat in bed facing the door, her dark hair tousled, her countenance stormy, chin resting on her pulled-up knees, nightgown clamped tight around her feet. The flannel nightcap lay crumpled on the pillow as if she'd yanked it off and thrown it there.

Inez stepped inside the room, questions dying on her lips. Antonia glared at her, almost vibrating with anger. "You played *our* song with him. Yours and mine! Why?" She threw herself down on the bed, still curled in a ball, and jammed the nightcap back on, pulling it down over her eyes and nose and nearly to her mouth.

Inez couldn't come up with any explanation or response besides "I'm sorry," which seemed ridiculous given the crime she was being accused of. Finally she said, "I thought you would like it, Antonia. I did it for you."

The nightcap material covering Antonia's nose whuffled in and out with her sniff.

Inez tried to hold onto her temper. She was tired. The girl was tired. Inez just wanted quiet to think, space to drink, and time to sleep. "Get some rest," she said. "Tomorrow is Saturday. No need to rise early." She closed the door.

Pondering her next day's tasks, Inez paused in their little kitchen on her way to her room. The roller shade was up, and the yellow light from the streetlamp outside made the two chairs, the small table, and the simple stove look very stark.

A single cup sat on the table from the morning's breakfast, unwashed, alone.

She crossed her arms, staring at the cup and thinking. De Bruijn was recovering. Flo was off on her own mission to protect herself from any repercussions from the failed investigations.

If any progress was to be made in finding out who killed Jamie, Inez realized, she would have to make it.

Chapter Thirty-nine

Inez awoke with a dull headache. She couldn't accuse the champagne since she had only had a sip at the recital, so the whiskey would have to stand alone, guilty as charged. It had only been two fingers' worth three times over, but she felt as if she had guzzled the entire bottle and had gone down to the store's office for more.

Thinking of the office and the store brought the previous evening back full force. Inez set the heels of her palms against her eye sockets and groaned. Things were getting entirely too complicated. Nico now probably had certain expectations as to how their interactions would "evolve." And heaven knows, when Nico had expectations, it took a lot of fancy footwork and careful maneuvering to nudge him off target. She would have to be on guard and distant, but not too distant, whenever he was around. She thought of all the flowers and the bouquets he had showered on her in the past, culminating in yesterday's sudden, almost desperate avalanche of blooms.

Of course, that was all before he found out she was no widow, but a divorcée.

Why now? Of all times? While she was still trying to figure out the union list, trying to see if what had happened in the past had anything to do with what was going on in the present.

It should have been enough to make her bolt out of bed. Instead, she lay for a while longer, nursing her aching head. She would have to dress for a long day of trudging about the city. First, to the Musical Protective Association's secretary. There she hoped to obtain Stephen Abbott's address, and perhaps ask a question or two about Eli Greer. Next, she would go to Abbott, find out whether Jamie had visited him, and, if so, what they had discussed. She only hoped Abbott lived in the city, not across the bay or at some even more remote location, or, as Haskell had surmised, was dead and buried.

And, at some point during the day, she supposed she should talk to de Bruijn.

Uneasy on several fronts, Inez toyed with the idea of bringing her pocket revolver with her. Who knew where Abbott lived and where their conversation might lead her from there? Or perhaps de Bruijn would have insights and that would require her to traipse about in unsavory areas of the city.

Two days until Harry's return.

Was he already on his way? Had he, perhaps, banked the flames of his anger and desire for revenge with sorrow and acceptance? He might then be more likely to listen to reason, if they failed, and accept that they had tried, she and de Bruijn and Flo, to uncover the killer but had only managed to eliminate suspects.

Inez sat up in bed. "What am I doing?" she said aloud. All of her thoughts, all of her concerns and worries since she had awakened had to do with the men, who suddenly loomed large in her life. Harry. Nico. Even the association secretary and Abbott. All of a sudden, what they thought, what they did, seemed crucial to her very survival.

Inez threw back the covers and got dressed. Once she was properly attired except for footwear, hat, and coat, she picked up her walking boot, weighing it in her hand as if it were the sum of her sudden awareness.

In Leadville, she had been in charge of her own destiny, the face of the Silver Queen saloon. The regulars and others had joked how she was the "Silver Queen" herself. "All hail the queen!" they'd say and raise their glasses and hats to her. She had been their equal in drinking, in poker, in facing down danger, and stepping up to protect those she loved.

Coming to San Francisco had been her decision. She had not been following in the wake of some man's dream. Indeed, one of the things she loved about Reverend Sands was he recognized her independence, her strength, and her determination, and he accepted her as a partner, accepted her as she was. Even when she chose a different path from his.

Inez jammed her foot into the boot and grabbed the boot hook tight. "That does it," she said aloud. If she had to stand her ground with Harry, stare his rage in the face, so be it. If he threatened to expose her past history in an attempt to sully her reputation in San Francisco, she would not deny it, not slink away, but stand tall on all the good she had done for the women she had helped in her brief time here.

She would fight.

And if, once all was said and done, she lost her claim on the music store, she would not beg. She now had to admit that claim was as flimsy as the paper their agreement was written on. Her eventual half-ownership of the store rested entirely on the whims of the man who owned it, and she suspected Nico would now insist she become his "mistress of convenience" as the price. If so, she would thumb her nose at him and walk away.

It would be his loss, after all.

She would find other opportunities.

Another life to live for Antonia and herself. Whether in San Francisco or elsewhere.

The world was a big place.

No sooner had Inez finished with boots and hat than the doorbell downstairs began ringing. She headed toward the stairs. Antonia popped her head out of her bedroom, a frown creasing her tired face. "Who's that?"

"I'm not expecting anyone," said Inez, opening the door

onto the landing. Downstairs, the ringing stopped and the pounding began, joined by high, frantic female voices.

The May sisters.

Inez's first thought: What on earth were the laundresses doing here, breaking down her door, on a Saturday morning?

Words emerged from the general hubbub as Inez hurried down the stairs.

"Mrs. Stannert! Are you there? Answer the door!" That was Bessie.

"Oh, please dear Lord, ma'am, please you must be there!" That was Molly.

Inez opened the door to find them both, out of breath, hair in disarray, and no hats or gloves. "What's wrong?" Inez asked, because it was very clear something had the women in the extremity of distress.

"The police," wheezed Bessie, and lurched forward to grip the doorjamb with her wash-worn hand, "they came for Patrick!"

"What?" Inez tried to grasp what she was saying.

"He's no murderer!" wept Molly. "My sweet boy, he's no murderer. How could anyone think that? Ah, the Lord God has turned his back on us!"

Bessie gaped at her distraught sister, who had thrown the skirt of her apron over her face and was sobbing hysterically. "Molly! Blaspheming will not bring him back."

"My darling boy," wailed Molly, a cry from the heart. "He's payin' for my sins."

Inez drew them into the tiny entryway. "Patrick's been arrested for murder?"

It was left to Bessie to explain. "They came to the laundry. Nearly broke the door down. Dragged us outside, Molly and me. They were throwin' our bricks around, the bricks we paid good money for! And then one, he holds up a brick, sayin' 'Here 'tis!' and we see, it's foul and bloody. At least, that's what they say, 'We've found the foul and bloody brick, that's proof enough that the boy did it,' they say."

"Proof of what? Murder? Murder of whom?" And the light went on as soon as the words left her mouth.

Bessie confirmed Inez's suspicions, by saying, "The dead one they found by Long Bridge. He was a musician, playin' for Henderson next door. And we didn't know this, but after he was killed, Patrick stepped into his shoes. So, they think he killed the poor lad for the job. And we didn't even know! Patrick, he sleeps on the back porch, and he was sneakin' over at night, after good people are asleep, and playin' for that good-for-nothing drunken crimp." Bessie spat. "When I get my hands on that boy, he's going to wish he never saw a piano in his life nor set a foot in that vile and vulgar place."

"The police didn't arrest Patrick," said Inez, catching up at last.

"He vanished." Bessie said. "Went out the back way, most like, when he heard the voices. Which of course, makes him look guilty as sin. So, the one who used to be an officer and was always friendly to us, he's now a detective, Lynch is his name, curse his eyes, he turns to us and says, 'Now, Bessie, Molly, where's your boy?' He says, 'It's no good hidin' him. We'll find him sooner or later, and it'll be the worse for him if it's later.'"

Molly emerged from beneath the apron, eyes red and raw. "You have to help us! You have to find Patrick! He can go to the police and explain, tell them he was nowhere near the place on Sunday night."

Bessie crossed her arms. "Molly, it's the devil or the deep blue sea. They won't believe him." She turned to Inez, eyes intent. "It's either turn himself in or vanish for good. I think his best chance is to leave." She had to lift her voice to be heard above Molly's wail of anguish. "Leave and never come back. But first, we have to find him."

A small sound up on the landing made Inez and the Mays look up. Antonia was gazing down, still in her nightclothes, a stricken expression on her face. "Patrick's in trouble? They think he killed Jamie Monroe?"

Inez pointed up at her. "Back inside, Antonia."

Without a word, Antonia retreated.

"Monroe? That's the name Lynch gave the lad they pulled from under the bridge." Bessie stared at Inez. "You knew him."

"I did." Inez's mind raced frantically. Suddenly, her day was complicated many times over. "I will do what I can. The best way to clear Patrick is to find the real killer."

"Ah!" exclaimed Molly in despair. "The police, they're not looking for anyone but Patrick. D'you mean me and Bessie have to find the murderer? How are we to do that?"

Inez looked from sister to sister and finally said, "Not you. Me."

Chapter Forty

Inez grabbed her reticule from the stand by the door, pulled out a few coins, and gave them to the sisters. "Take these. Give them to Patrick if he shows up. He will need to be careful, but perhaps he can take a ferry across the bay, make his way to Sacramento. They won't look for him there. He must manage for just a while until I straighten this out. Then he can return."

Molly promised through her sobs that if Patrick should reappear, she would insist he disappear again.

After the sisters left, Inez rummaged in her handbag, checking for the business cards she had lifted from de Bruijn's waistcoat. Assured they were still there, she returned upstairs and added her pocket revolver to the bag. She headed out, calling, "Antonia, I am leaving. Fix yourself breakfast and work on your school assignments while I'm gone. I have a lot to do today, but I'll be back in time for dinner."

A muffled "All right," emerged from behind the closed bedroom door as she left.

Once outside, Inez glanced toward the store. It was before noon, so Welles had yet to arrive. *What about Nico?* whispered a little voice inside. Inez silenced the voice. She had other, more important worries on her mind today.

Pulling out Jamie's list, she read again the address Haskell had neatly printed out for her. She walked around the corner onto Kearney and hailed a passing hack. It was Saturday and surely early enough to catch Baumann, the Musical Protective Association's secretary, at home.

When she approached the secretary's house, she was pleasantly surprised to see a gentleman tending to a rosebush in the tiny pocket garden. "Mr. Baumann?" she inquired.

He turned around, spectacles perched on the end of his nose, shears in hand. "Yes?"

"I was here yesterday and the day before. My apologies to you and your housekeeper for being late yesterday." She held out her hand.

He removed his gardening glove and they shook. "Ah, yes," he said. "About the association. First, may I offer condolences if they are in order, Mrs....?"

Inez allowed herself a brief smile and said, "Again, my apologies. I did not explain my business as it was a sensitive matter, and I did not want to disclose it to anyone but you."

She fished out one of de Bruijn's business cards from her reticule and handed it to him. "Mrs. Wilhelmina de Bruijn."

He took the card, read it, and raised his eyebrows. "A female private investigator? First time I've met one. And what does this 'finder of the lost' mean?"

"Well, Mr. Baumann, in this case, it means I am looking for the whereabouts of one of your members who is due to come into a bit of money. Unfortunately, he is not listed in the city directory."

Baumann adjusted his spectacles and said, "This sounds like good news for a change. Most of the visits I receive on association business are sad affairs. Please, come in."

Once they were inside, his housekeeper magically appeared, barking, "Shoes! Dirt! I just cleaned the floors!" and then, just as mysteriously, vanished into the back of the house.

Baumann set his shears, cap, and heavy gloves aside, removed his shoes, and slipped on what looked like an exceedingly comfortable pair of velvet carpet slippers. Inez admired their finely beaded roses while he noted, "Martha's bark is worse than her bite. I'm quite used to it, but she sometimes terrorizes the visitors." He showed Inez to the parlor, asking, "What is the name of the gentleman in question?"

"Stephen Abbott."

Baumann nodded and shuffled across the hall to a small office. She watched him go behind a desk, pull out an oversized record book, and turn the large pages. She held her breath, hoping he would not slam it shut and declare Abbott not on the roles. When she saw him pick up a pen, dip it in a bottle of ink, and draw a piece of paper toward himself, she inwardly rejoiced.

After scratching on the paper, he closed the heavy book and returned to her, waving the scrap to dry the ink. "Yes, Mr. Abbott is one of our members, and has been receiving assistance for some years now. A sad case, according to my records. He has moved around frequently. If you are not familiar with San Francisco, I should warn you, Mrs. de Bruijn, to be prepared. He does not live in the best part of town presently."

Inez took the paper and examined the address. "Am I correct in thinking this is in the Barbary Coast area?"

"Indeed." He removed his glasses and cleaned them on his waistcoat. "If you have a male associate, you may want to bring him along for that particular visit."

"I shall keep your suggestion in mind," said Inez. "I have one more question, about a different person. An Eli Greer."

He blinked, looking a little unfocused without his spectacles. "He was the treasurer of the previous musicians union."

"Yes, that's right. I was wondering if you two ever crossed paths."

"And what has this to do with Mr. Abbott or your inquiries?"

"Well," she cast about for a reason, any reason, for her questions. "I understand the funds from the previous union disappeared and Mr. Greer with them. I imagine that left Mrs. Greer in a financially compromised situation. Was your association able to help her? Was Mr. Greer ever found? As an investigator, I have a professional curiosity in such matters."

He settled his glasses back on his face. "If 'finding the lost' is your expertise, Mrs. de Bruijn, it is too bad for Mrs. Greer's sake that you were not around in those earlier times. What you say is true. Mr. Greer, for all intents and purposes, disappeared without a trace. I did not know him, personally, but I did know Mrs. Greer, as she applied for relief to the association. However, since no one could say for certain whether her husband was alive or dead, we were not able to offer much in the way of assistance. Unfortunately."

"Thank you for your help."

"Not at all, Mrs. de Bruijn. As I said, it gladdens me to hear that Mr. Abbott, one of our less fortunate members, will be receiving some good news to brighten his day."

Baumann's last remarks only served to prick Inez's conscience as she walked to the nearest corner and waited for the horsecar that would bring her closer to the center of town.

She debated. Talk to de Bruijn first? Or track down Mr. Abbott? With a start, she realized she had, for a little while, completely forgotten about Patrick May.

That decided it. A quick visit to de Bruijn. Perhaps, with his connections, he could call off the police hunt for the boy and save his frantic family much grief.

De Bruijn listened closely to Inez's tale of the Mays and finally said, "I agree, the young man is not the murderer."

Inez sat back with a sigh. "Good. I'm hoping you can convince Detective Lynch of the same."

They sat in the parlor room of his suite, de Bruijn in an easy chair, Inez on a nearby settee. The heavy curtains were partly drawn away from the large bay window, allowing light to filter through the inner lace curtain.

"I am afraid you overestimate my influence," said de Bruijn. "Finding the person who is responsible, or at least a more convincing suspect, is the only way we will be able to stop their search." He shook his head, then winced, and touched the crown of his head gingerly. "Think, Mrs. Stannert. What kind of motive are we looking at here? Look at the brutality of the murder. One blow, two, would have sufficed to kill. Yet the killer went at him, again and again, past the point of reason or logic. I believe this was a crime of passion—unplanned, unpremeditated. I cannot see such a murder occurring over the loss of a job."

Inez chewed her lip. "Unless…"

"Unless what?"

"You say you cannot imagine such a killing occurring over work. But Jamie, that is, young Gallagher, had just accepted a day job. Carmella told me he was planning on keeping the night one as well, counting on them both to make ends meet. Anyhow, this new position was one that another pianist, a colleague of his named Thomas Welles, had thought was promised to him. Welles has a family, a growing one. He is under a lot of pressure. He's a moody sort, prone to dark turns of mind and seems to nurse grudges for a long time. He is still smarting over the loss of income from the collapse of the previous union. Might he have confronted Jamie?"

"Who has the most to gain with his death?" De Bruijn countered. "And what else was he up to his last few days? I can't help but think this murder was impulsive, the violence taking him by surprise. What he was doing in those days before his death might well have set the wheels in motion."

Inez pulled the list out of her purse. "I am following up on this list I told you about earlier, the one Jamie had hidden under his mattress. It appears to be names of previous union members, and perhaps the amounts of money owed to them after the union disbanded. There is only one name checked off, the first: Stephen Abbott. I know you think it a very long shot, but the list was apparently important enough to Jamie that he squirreled it away from casual eyes. It involved the unionization of musicians, and there were obviously some strange goings-on back then. In any case, I plan to go talk with Mr. Abbott as soon as I leave here."

"I should go with you," de Bruijn made as if to rise.

"Absolutely not. You are not fully recovered yet, certainly not enough for a carriage ride and an interview. I will let you know what happens. Besides, I'm guessing Mr. Abbott will be more inclined to confide in an attentive woman than a man who looks as if he recently lost a fight on the streets."

De Bruijn settled back in his chair, resigned. "How did you find him?"

Inez debated, then decided she was done with prevaricating. "I went to visit the secretary of the Musical Protective Association. I pretended to be you, and the secretary gave me Abbott's address."

"You what?"

Inez pulled out de Bruijn's card. "Wilhelmina de Bruijn, private investigator."

De Bruijn frowned.

"Look at it this way, I simply acted as your proxy. If you were recovered, you would have been the one to visit him."

"That I doubt," grumbled de Bruijn. Almost as an after-thought, he added, "I received a telegram from Mr. Gallagher."

Her stomach clenched. "And?"

"He expects to be here the day after tomorrow."

● ● ● ● ●

"Are you sure you want to do this?" Hack driver Joseph Lynch, Detective Lynch's cousin or second cousin—Inez couldn't recall which—stood by the half-open carriage door as if to block Inez from disembarking onto Battery Street.

"I am certain. I was warned this was not the best part of

town." Inez scooted over on the bench and leaned on the door, pushing it open.

Joseph Lynch seemed disinclined to relinquish the door to his passenger. "How about I go with you?"

"And leave your rig unattended? Absolutely not. This will not take long, I promise. Just wait here, as we discussed."

The slant of sun was beginning to cast long shadows across the street. Inez had no desire to be out and about after or even close to dusk. The names of some of the Barbary Coast's bloodier quarters whispered through her mind—*Murders' Corner. Deadman's Alley.*

She had prepared herself for the day's activities by wearing sensible boots and walking skirts, and she had her pocket revolver. She was alert, wary, but not afraid of setting foot on the Coast.

According to Baumann's scrap of paper, Stephen Abbott lived on the second floor of the disintegrating building before her, above what appeared to be a concert saloon or dance-house of the lowest kind. Music of a sort leaked from behind the crooked closed door and shuttered windows. A man and a woman lurched from a nearby alley and made for the door. The woman turned to glance at Inez, who caught a glimpse of empty eyes and a vacant face, abundantly painted and powdered. The woman's male companion pulled her roughly into the dim interior of the establishment. Inez registered flickering light and darting shadows before the door slammed shut.

It was all reminiscent of Leadville's red-light district. Inez recalled the times she had ventured into its most desperate areas—Tiger Alley, where gamblers gathered to "buck the tiger" at disreputable gambling dens, and Stillborn Alley, named after the unwanted infants of prostitutes plying their trade in the district. *Then, as now, I must be careful, be on my guard. But I must also remember: Most of the people here are destitute, lost, desperate. The devils that lurk and look to harm will not be out and about until dark has enveloped all.*

She had already transferred money from her purse into her

skirt pocket along with the list of names. Her gun was in her coat pocket within easy reach.

At least there appeared to be a separate door to the second floor, so she would not need to venture into the warren below. She hastened to the door, which opened readily without key or latch. The stench of urine and vomit assaulted her senses. She left the door ajar to bring light into the gloomy interior, stepped around a puddle of uncertain origin, and headed up the stairs.

A small window on the landing presented her with three unpainted doors, all closed. Which one was Abbott's? She walked the small hallway, barely wide enough to accommodate a single person. Two of the doors yielded no clues as to their occupants. The third, at the very end of the hall, sported a brass doorknocker of a cherub blowing a trumpet. Taking a gamble that this was the musician's door, Inez knocked.

There was some scrabbling inside followed by the trembling voice of an elderly man. "Who's there? I've got a shotgun. I'll blow you t'pieces if you try to come through the door."

Inez pulled out her revolver and flattened herself against the wall, away from the door. "Mr. Abbott," she called back. "I was given your address by Mr. Baumann, from the Musical Protective Association. I need to talk to you. I can make it worth your while."

"Who are you?" the voice was still suspicious, despite her invocation of Baumann's name.

"Mrs. Wilhemina de Bruijn. A private investigator. I have a card, if you would like to see it."

"Slip it under the door, face-up."

Inez did as she was told. And waited.

Finally, she heard the scrape of a lock being pulled back. The door creaked open. "Come in," said the voice behind the door.

Inez tightened her grip on her revolver, put her finger on the trigger, and slowly pushed the door open wider so she could enter. Once inside, she swung about.

The door creaked shut behind her revealing an elderly man,

nearly bent double, a few strands of gray hair crossing the top of his head. He craned his head upwards to view her. He held no shotgun, and indeed, Inez could not see how he could have picked one up, much less held it. The finger joints of his empty hands were contracted with knotted protuberances, the fingers themselves bent and crooked, overlapping and curling. He must have caught her staring, for he held up his hands and said, "Y'see, I must be careful about who's on the other side of the door. No more trumpet-playing for me, either. Hasn't been for a long time now." He nudged the business card with his foot. "Ye can pick up your card, Mrs. de Bruijn, if ye wouldn't mind."

Subdued, Inez did as he suggested.

He said, "What business d'ye have that would be 'worth my while' to hear ye?" With a slow and crooked wobble, he headed to a straight-backed chair, gesturing with an elbow to the only other chair in the room. Inez sat and looked around. Two candles burned on a small table that leaned perilously. The curtains were in tatters. A small warming stove held nothing warm upon it. Inez wondered what he did for meals, how he cooked, how he took care of himself.

He leaned forward in his chair. "It's a lucky thing for me I used to work for the proprietor of this august establishment, back in the day. He takes pity on me and brings me what's left once the customers downstairs are done with the eating and are only interested in the drinking."

He sat back. "Yes, I'm a lucky man. And it sounds as if you are bringing more luck my way, Mrs. de Bruijn. What can I do for you?"

Inez focused on her task. "I have some questions regarding the previous union, the one that foundered in the mid-70s."

"Aye?" his voice sharpened, the tremble lessened. "Troubled times. I recollect well."

His body was frail, but Inez guessed he still possessed his wits, which was what she needed.

She slid Jamie's folded list from her pocket, and said, "I

believe you were visited by a young man recently, name of Monroe. Although I am not entirely certain he would have called himself so."

"Yes, young Monroe." That was all he said, forcing her to continue.

She held up the folded papers. "I suspect he showed you this. I believe it is a list of the union members and the amounts they were to receive back once the union ceased to be. I am guessing that Mr. Monroe came and asked you some questions about that time."

"Oh, yes, you have that right, Mrs. de Bruijn. All of it." His gaze held hers.

Inez waited. Finally, she said, "I wonder if you would tell me what you told him."

"Why not ask him yourself? Since you have the list, you must know him."

"Alas, I would, but I cannot. You see, young Mr. Monroe died this past Sunday night. Brutally murdered."

At that, Abbott lowered his eyes at last. "How? Who?" The question was barely audible.

She told him the story, adding, "I am investigating for his father, who is understandably grief-stricken and wants to know what happened and why. The local law has been less than help-ful."

"Aye, the police have their own priorities, and a poor musi-cian in the wrong part of town would not be high on their list, I wager."

"Can you help us? What did you and Mr. Monroe talk about?"

He nodded and hid his curled, deformed hands in his lap. "I remember when the union failed. We were heartsick, those of us who had fought hard to make it happen. As is only right, the funds collected were to be returned to the members. I had a wife, children. We needed that money. I was home and waiting the evening the treasurer arrived with his case."

"The treasurer was Eli Greer?"

Abbott nodded again.

"He brought the funds in cash?"

"Paper money. I didn't think any more about it after I got my share. Until I started hearing that the other fellows hadn't got the same visit. Eli, he'd disappeared. Took off with the rest of the money. Oh, those were dark times."

Inez tried to ignore the scent of old despair in the air between them. "You didn't say anything to them?"

He shrugged. "What good would it have done to say I'd been paid when no one else received theirs? Would they think I had done something to Eli, since I was the only one to see him alive, him and his case of money? Besides, I needed the money. I had a family to feed. I kept quiet, all these years. And after a while the memories faded and went away, just as old friends and family do."

"Did Mr. Greer seem the sort who would abscond with the funds?"

"No. That was the strange thing. At least, strange to me then. But, as I've learned over my long time on this Earth and in all my years in this city, you never really know what lies in the heart of a man or what he's made of, until the desperate times. Or a woman, for that matter. Why, you probably think the fellow who runs the dance hall is a villain. But he has been like a son to me, gave me a roof over my head, food to eat, and his girls, they help me when I cannot help myself. While my friends, all of them, have long gone or drifted away. I told young Monroe that. I told him, if he was to start up a union again, to be sharp as to who they voted in as treasurer. Keep an eye on the one who guards the money."

A silence hung between them until he said, "But ye've not asked the question he asked me at the end. Surely you, a lady private investigator, would have the same question."

Inez reined in the urge to jump up, grab him by the front of his worn, stained shirt and yell, "Just tell me!" *He's toying with me, like the sphinx, "guess the answer to this riddle."* How often did he have company? He probably spent days, weeks, essentially alone.

Alone.

Inez asked, "Was there someone with Mr. Greer when he came to see you?"

His lined face creased into a smile. "Ah, you're a quick one! Monroe asked that, too. It just took him longer to get there. Yes, a young fellow was with Eli. One of the junior members."

"Who?" Her heart pounded so loudly in her ears she could hardly hear him speak.

He shook his head. "The names, I never remembered the names. They were all young, and I was old, even then. I remember he was ambitious. He had dark hair. Was the thin and hungry type."

Welles. The description fit. She thought of the pianist, his black moods, the anger and resentments he nursed.

He claimed he hadn't received any money back when the union collapsed. But could he have lied?

After all, Abbott had lied through silence. Abbott's words came back to her: you never really know what lies in the heart of a man or what he's made of, until the desperate times.

Could Welles have lied, all these years?

He claimed to have managed through those times because Nico had helped him.

Nico.

Suddenly she couldn't breathe.

She almost missed it when Abbott added, "I never remembered their names, but I knew which instruments they played. The one who was with Eli that night, he played the violin, like the angels."

Chapter Forty-one

That morning, Antonia heard the doorbell ringing and Mrs. S pounding down the stairs, but what really brought her bolt upright was the screaming and shouting that followed. Antonia got out of bed and went to the open door at the top of stairs in time to hear the talk about Patrick, Jamie's body by Long Bridge, and a bloody brick. She couldn't believe what she was hearing. Patrick? The boy who played piano and was her friend?

She must've made a sound because the two women—one must've been Patrick's maman because she was all in hysterics—turned to look at her, and Mrs. S ordered her back to her room. She'd heard enough to know that Patrick had disappeared when the police showed up, and no one knew where he was.

But she knew.

Once Mrs. S had left, after telling her to do her homework and adding that she'd be back in time for dinner, Antonia reached under her bed and dragged out the stinky clothes she'd worn to Chinatown just a couple days ago. They were pretty filthy, but that was perfect for where she was headed: the dump by Mission Creek, to see if Patrick was hiding out with his friend Black Bill.

She had to talk to Patrick, find out what happened, and see if she could help. Maybe she could learn something from Patrick to prove it wasn't him, and maybe she could convince him to talk to Mrs. S.

Antonia threw on the menswear, wrinkling her nose as she did so. Well, at least she'd look and smell like she fit right in with the rag-pickers and garbage-sorters. She grabbed her maman's folding knife, checked the locking blade, and stuffed it in her trouser pocket.

It didn't take long to walk there. The only parts of her journey that set her nerves on edge were slipping out of the apartment—she hoped no one she knew, like Mr. Welles or Mr. Donato or Mrs. S, happened to come by just as she slid out and locked the door—and walking past Copper Mick's home. She supposed she didn't have to walk that way, she could've gone down a different street. But she half hoped maybe he'd be outside, and she could talk him into joining her on an adventure to Dumpville. Then again, after their adventure in Chinatown, maybe he'd not be keen on tracking down someone who the police pegged a killer. And his pa was a detective. So, all in all, she was glad when she didn't see him as she slouched past on the other side of the street, her cap pulled low.

When she reached Berry, she turned right and kept walking. The farther she walked, the more invisible and more comfortable she felt in her shabby, dirty clothes. And once she reached the first garbage wagon unloading its trash onto the ground, she fit right in. The dumps were bigger than she expected. Humps and hillocks of reeking garbage stretched out along the water, going on for at least a block, maybe two or three, with more full wagons lining up to get rid of their loads. She dodged the wagons and their fresh leavings, skirted the men and the few women who were wielding pitchforks, sticks, and shovels, poking each reeking load as if hunting for buried treasure. The sort of treasure that Antonia saw them pounce on included not only old bottles, scraps of iron, old sacks, bricks, and rags, but also bruised and decaying fruits and vegetables.

Antonia thought back to when she and her maman lived in Leadville's Stillborn Alley. They didn't have much food then, but Antonia'd managed to bring hard-boiled eggs, bread, and cheese home from some of the work she picked up cleaning the saloons late at night, back when she'd worn the same clothes as she wore now and called herself "Tony."

But…this stuff.

Did people really get so hungry they'd eat a head of cabbage that was all brown? Or did they sell the food? If this was what the rag-pickers had for supper, no wonder Patrick brought food when he came to visit them.

Antonia finally gave up and asked a woman, who was adding to her apron full of oyster shells, where Black Bill might be.

"Over yonder." She pointed away from the waterfront. "In a tent wi' a little flag."

Antonia thanked her and headed in that direction. Farther away from the channel, the garbage lessened and a welter of tents and shacks took the place of trash piles and heaps. She was glad to spot a canvas shelter, sides bowed in and flapping in the breeze, with a small stars and stripes flag on a short stick stuck outside in the dirt. She went up cautiously and called at the closed entrance, "Is this Black Bill's place?"

The tied-down flaps twitched a bit. "Who wants to know?" asked a growly voice.

"I'm looking for Patrick May." She hoped she wasn't going to get in trouble for asking for Patrick by name.

The flaps parted, displaying the head of a man with a long cottony beard and a face dark and glowering as his name. "That don't answer the question of who you are or what you want."

"I'm a friend of his. I know he's in danger and I'm here to help." She raised her voice, but not too much. "Patrick, are you there? It's Antonia. I've got to talk to you."

"Antonia?" Patrick's voice came out of the darkened interior. Black Bill's face disappeared at the entrance and some shuffling around sounded inside. "It's all right, Bill," said Patrick. "I know her."

"Ain't a 'her' out there," growled Black Bill.

Patrick poked his head out between the flaps. His eyes widened. "Antonia?"

She nodded.

He pulled back one of the canvas wings and settled cross-legged in the entrance. "I'm sure glad to see you. Hardly recognize you, though. I was tryin' to figure out a way to get word to Mrs. Stannert, and here you are. As my ma would say, 'A blessing.'" He added, "I'm not gonna stand, because I don't want anyone to see me. I'm not going out until nighttime. Safer that way." His voice broke into a squawk. "The police, I heard them say they think I killed Jamie Monroe. I didn't! So, I figured I'd best sneak out the back way. I wasn't going to wait for them to walk in and put me in jail."

Antonia squatted down. "I know you didn't kill anybody. But they found a bloody brick at the laundry. Did you know that?"

He shook his head.

"Your ma and aunt came to see Mrs. S and I heard them talking. Mrs. S, she's trying to track the real killer. I came here to see if I can help you. Maybe I could bring Mrs. S out here and you and her could talk."

"No!" he sounded alarmed. "But if she's looking for who did it, I have something I want you to take back to her. Maybe it'll help."

He crawled back into the tent. Antonia heard him say, "Where'd you put it? The fancy collar I gave you."

"You're not gonna give it to that girl-boy?" demanded Black Bill. "I can get a lot for that one. At least a dollar. Maybe more."

"Look, I trust Antonia. She'll make sure you'll get paid for it."

"Well, since you gave it to me in the first place…" Some more inarticulate mumbling ensued and eventually Patrick reappeared, a bedraggled something clasped in one hand.

He held it out to her. "Carry this someplace really safe."

Antonia stared at the item dangling from his large hand. It was limp, like a dead animal. Then Antonia realized it was a fur collar, once white with black fur slashes. It would've been regal, if not matted with dirt, brown gunk, and blobs of dried… something.

There was only one person she'd ever seen wearing a collar like this.

A little faint and a lot queasy, she asked, "Where'd you get this?"

"Tell Mrs. Stannert I found it the night of the murder in the spot I showed her. Tell her that on that night, after the ruckus died down and everyone left, I went back and found it there. Tell her I'm sorry I didn't mention it before. I didn't say anything to her because I didn't know it meant anything. I just thought it was a rag that might be worth something to Black Bill."

"Oh, it's worth more'n the dollar Black Bill talked about," said Antonia, gingerly taking the fur—was that dried blood all over it?—and stuffing it into her oversized jacket pocket. "This here rag is worth your life, Patrick. It's gonna prove you didn't kill Jamie Monroe."

Chapter Forty-two

It was getting toward dusk, but Inez had one more stop to make.

She had to be sure that her growing suspicion had some basis. That there was motive. *To kill a young man because he is enamored of your sister, is that enough?* Penny-dreadful novels might be littered with even more improbable tales, but this was a real murder. Inez thought such a motive was pretty thin. There were many ways to discredit a penniless musician and drive him out of town. All Nico would have had to do was whisper to people he knew, and doors would slam in Jamie's face. It just seemed if Nico was the killer, there had to be something more.

So that is why she directed the hack driver, Joseph Lynch, to Carmella and Nico's home out in the newly minted Western Addition. An elegant three-story, it sat cheek-by-jowl with neighbors to either side without losing its dignity. Inez paid the driver, thanked him for his time, and made certain to add a generous tip for the Barbary Coast portion of the journey. She mounted the steps and rang the bell, fervently hoping Nico would not be in.

If, God forbid, he was, and they ended up face to face, it would be an exceedingly awkward meeting on several levels. However, she at least had a ready explanation for her unannounced visit. Since Welles had volunteered that he would tell

Nico of Jamie's death and Nico would then tell Carmella, Inez guessed Carmella would have been "informed" by her brother by now. This provided the rationale for Inez to drop by and see how Carmella was faring.

The door flew open. Much to Inez's relief, Carmella stood there, an apron over her housedress, flour up to her wrists. White splotches along a cheekbone revealed where she must have absent-mindedly rubbed the back of her hand.

Carmella grabbed both of Inez's hands, effectively powdering her kid gloves. "Oh, Mrs. Stannert! I am so glad to see you! Come!" She pulled Inez inside. "I sent the housemaid and cook home early today. They have been hovering and driving me mad. This means we can talk without worrying about their overhearing."

She led Inez past a formal parlor to the right and a music room to the left, its bay window facing the street. In the music room Inez glimpsed a parlor grand piano, comfortable chairs, a cluster of music stands holding sheet music, and a few paintings on the walls, before she was whisked further into the house.

"Thank you so much for your message," Carmella added, herding her toward the rear of the house. "The boy was very precise. He obviously thought it was a strange warning to deliver, but he was very polite and waited for me to pen a response to you. Did you get it?"

"Yes, I did. I take it that Nico told you of Jamie's death?"

"Ah, *sì*. And hearing it broke my heart all over again. It was terrible. I couldn't say anything, I just cried. I think Nico now feels sorry for how he treated Jamie in the past."

Sorry or guilty? Inez wondered grimly. "Well, thank you for sending a note back. Otherwise I would have been on pins and needles, worrying about you being taken by surprise."

"And I've been on pins and needles myself, wanting to know how last night went. Nico left early this morning, before I was even awake, or I would have asked him."

Inez, startled, wanted to pursue this pronouncement, but

Carmella hurried ahead. The aroma of fresh baked pastries and bread in the oven grew stronger until Carmella pushed a door open and ushered Inez into a warm and homey kitchen.

"Sit! Sit!" She grabbed a cloth and whisked it across a wooden chair by a table burdened down with what looked like a full day's worth of baking.

Inez sat, surveying the edibles. "So, this is what you did today?"

Carmella flitted about, making tea. "Yesterday and today. I could not go out and about. I just could not."

She collapsed into the chair next to Inez. "All I can think of is Jamie. Baking has been my solace. And I am so glad you came! Now, tell me everything. What did he say? How did he say it?" She sat back, bright with anticipation.

"How who said what?" Inez wondered if she meant Nico's invitation to attend the previous night's performance. It was the only connection she could make.

Carmella's face began to dim. "He didn't…Nico said he would…He didn't propose?"

It was Inez's turn to stare. "Propose? Gracious, no! He escorted me to a concert last night, a performance in the Palace Hotel." The scene in the music store flashed through her mind, but Inez added, "That was all."

Now Carmella began to blush. Her flour-covered fingers rose to her cheeks. "Oh. He promised."

"What is this about?" Now Inez was getting irritated, firstly, because it sounded as if there had been a certain amount of plotting going on behind her back, and, secondly, because the conversation was veering in directions that had nothing to do with her current visit.

Carmella looked away, as if unwilling to meet Inez's eyes. "Nico has been saying forever that I should be more willing to consider the young men he shoves under my nose and not encourage the ones who, as he says, are 'destitute dreamers, nobodies without a future.' And *I* tell him he should turn away from those women who fall all over him, the married women who throw their husbands aside to chase after him, the loose women who keep him out all night, the debutantes he flirts with and who he risks ruining. I tell him he should be considering eligible, appropriate women who are under his nose. One in particular." Now, those fingers moved to cover her mouth.

Inez sat for a moment, examining her own slightly bruised pride. Had the invitation and the jungle of flowers been nothing more than Nico's attempts to assuage his sister's sadness, or perhaps add Inez as an appropriate "cover" for any affairs he had going on? But she had approached him the same way, with a certain amount of cynical manipulation. And of course, any chance of a legal union between them had disappeared once her former marital status was exposed.

She shook her head. The tangled webs of emotional motive behind last night's embrace were inconsequential. There were other matters to discuss far more important than her wounded vanity. Inez lifted the teapot lid, and the scent of bergamot assailed her. "I believe the tea is ready." She poured for them both, saying. "Carmella, I am flattered you think me a worthy partner for your brother."

Although I would argue that I am not to be shoved around like a chip in a game of cards.

She kept that thought to herself, continuing, "But nothing of the sort has transpired. I came here for two reasons. One, to see how you were doing after this week's sad events." Inez glanced at the table of baked goods. "And two, I wanted to ask you some questions about the time of the previous musicians union."

Without mentioning Nico, Inez explained how Jamie had been interested in what brought down the union and transpired after that. "I wonder if his inquiries in that direction had anything to do with his death. I am grasping at straws, I know."

Carmella drew a finger through a scattering of flour on the table, frowning. "I was about Antonia's age when the union dissolved. Nico would be the one to ask."

And he is exactly the one I do not want to ask. "But I am curious as to what you recall. What was life like for you and Nico back then?"

"Oh. I remember that." She crossed her arms, hugging herself. "Our parents had died about four years before. I was so little. It was just Nico and me, and he had to take care of me. He was about the age I am now. Our father had wanted him to become a fruit peddler, like himself. Nico always wanted to be a musician, play his violin. They fought about it. After our parents passed, Nico threw himself into music. But it did not go well, for a long time. We moved again and again, each place worse than the one before, as he tried to make a living." She lowered her eyes. "It was bad. But even then he insisted I continue my schooling."

"What was it like when the union collapsed?" Inez held her breath.

Carmella unfolded her arms and picked up her teacup. She looked at Inez. "Do you want sugar?"

Inez shook her head.

Carmella sipped some of the fragrant black tea. "It was a crazy time. Nico was gone frequently. Sometimes he brought me with him, if it was a meeting with others. I remember them saying the money had disappeared. Everyone was afraid and angry. 'How could the treasurer do this?' they asked over and over. No one had any answers, except that the money was gone and the treasurer with it."

Inez nodded. So far, she had heard nothing new. "But luck finally turned your way, did it not? I am sure it was a relief to you. When did things begin to improve?"

"It was a while after the union was gone. I remember, because Nico came home one day, very excited. He had an opportunity, he said, to play for someone important. I asked who, and he teased me, saying it was a private party, one that little girls had no business knowing about. I wondered at the time, but now I believe it must have been for a wealthy man who was entertaining 'friends' of a certain sort." She shrugged. "I've not asked Nico. It was long ago and doesn't matter. I do remember he immediately went out and bought a new suit of clothes to wear for the performance, including the cape he likes so much, the one with the ermine collar."

"And after that?"

"Oh, after that, it was as you said, fortune smiled. Nico was gone most evenings but always came home smiling. He finally began talking about some of his performances. We moved to better and better places. It was like a dream. I had no idea one could make so much money from music! Papa would have been astonished and proud, if he had been here to see his son."

The timing was right, Inez thought. What Carmella and Abbott had told her wasn't hard proof, but maybe enough. She felt a modicum of guilt for leading Carmella in this direction, inadvertently betraying her brother, as it were. But then, Carmella had clearly been doing some maneuvering of her own, so Inez shushed the small voice of conscience, finished her tea, and stood.

"Thank you, Carmella. I should go. I promised Antonia that I would be home in time to take her to dinner." Inez added, "I have always thought of you as a friend, Carmella." The words just popped out, and Inez realized that even given all that had occurred, she still had a soft spot for the young woman. "So, your brother hasn't been home today?"

She shook her head. "He came in late last night, I think, but was gone when I woke up. I've not seen him all day. If he is in the store, please send him home."

Inez nodded, a tickle of worry worming its way inside.

Carmella walked her to the door and Inez paused. "One last question. I almost forgot. I noticed Nico had a new cloak last night. Very handsome, but not as 'kingly' as his previous one. What happened to the lovely one with the unusual collar, do you know? It was such a mark of distinction."

Carmella leaned on the doorframe, absently wiping her

hands on her apron. "I was sad when he lost it. He told me he accidently left it in a hack early this week. He tried to track down the carriage and recover it, but alas, it was long gone. The new one is nice, but no replacement for the old. Clothes make the man, yes?"

● ● ● ● ●

In this case, thought Inez grimly, clothes might *un*make the man. Particularly, Nico's various lies to different people about the fate of his trademark cloak. As she made her way home, she thought long and hard about what she'd learned that day. A man of impulse, Nico wasn't keeping his stories straight. But perhaps he thought it of no consequence. Certainly, by itself, a missing cloak meant nothing. However, the timing was suspicious.

And the fact that Nico had accompanied the union treasurer Eli Greer on his fateful rounds—or, who knows, perhaps Nico just happened upon him and offered to go with him— was not damning in itself. But she could imagine what might have happened. Perhaps once Nico saw the case of money he was...what?...overcome by temptation? Saw a quick way to pull himself and Carmella out of the downward spiral they were in?

There was no way to know unless she asked him directly, which she was not about to do. She wondered if Jamie Monroe had wandered down a similar path, only in his case, perhaps he met Nico, late one night, and, in a bid to win Carmella's hand, threatened to disclose certain "suspicious coincidences" of timing.

A shrewd and levelheaded man would have pooh-poohed the whole thing. Who would believe such a story, so full of holes and half-guesses? And how could it be proved? But, someone more impulsive, like Nico—who was obsessed with his reputation and appearance—just might in a fit of rage or fear take the most direct route to putting such tales to rest.

Shooting the messenger, Inez thought, always led to disaster.

All the hacks rolling past were occupied, and in any case, her available money had gone to Abbott and the driver Joseph Lynch. Deciding to walk, Inez allowed her feet to pick the route home. She headed up Bush, the cool evening air brushing her over-warm cheeks, one hand resting on the grip of her Smoot, just in case. The street rose gently ahead of her. She paused once at the corner of Jones, gazing up the steeper grade toward Russian Hill and the undertaker's, where she had identified Robert Gallagher only to have Carmella claim him as Jamie Monroe. If she had known where all this would lead, would she still have made that trip with Carmella or would she have insisted on going alone?

The rest of the way home, Inez pondered how she was going to present her findings to de Bruijn and ultimately to Harry. Harry had threatened to destroy her life and livelihood in San Francisco. Having mulled his threats for a week now, she was doubting he could do all he claimed. But if Nico turned out to be guilty of murdering young Gallagher, wouldn't the results be the same? If it all went public, Nico jailed and charged, the store would not recover. The musicians who hung on his every word and gave life to the business would disappear. As would the customers.

And what would happen to Carmella?

Arriving back at the building, Inez glanced first into the depths of the store, shuttered and dark.

No one. Not even a flicker of light in the back office.

Good.

She did not want to face Nico without knowing what her path forward would be. At the least, she would continue acting "normally," so as not to rouse his suspicions.

A hack stood at the corner, the driver wrapped in an overcoat, wide-brimmed hat pulled down, looking for all the world like he was catching a quick snooze in the box. Perhaps she could hire him for the short journey to the Palace once she replenished her coin supply. She unlocked the door to her living quarters, anxious to get Antonia, head to the hotel, meet de Bruijn, and discuss their next steps. After her evening walk up Bush, the air inside was like a hothouse. She shed her coat and hung it on a peg before ascending the stairs, calling, "Antonia?"

Inside the kitchen, she paused. The table held Antonia's schoolbook, splayed facedown. A flickering light leaked down the hallway. She heard a light footstep, then two, the clatter of something hitting the floor. Inez stifled a sigh. Apparently, Antonia's curiosity about Jamie's trunk had gotten the better of her. Inez could picture how it happened: Antonia, spending the day wandering down to the music store and back, staring out the window, working on her recitations and numbers. Eventually, getting restless, she thinks of the off-limits trunk and grabs her hairpin lockpicks…

Inez walked toward the storage room. "Antonia? I've told you not to go back there. Come, it's time for dinner. We will go to the Palace Hotel. Perhaps Mr. de Bruijn will join us."

She walked through the doorway and saw a lamp turned low on the floor by Monroe's trunk. Her mind tried to take in the chaos she was seeing. Close by, her wardrobe trunk was open, with her stockings, shoes, fine dresses, and underthings strewn around. Jamie's trunk also yawned, its contents tossed about the floor: shoes, shirts, trousers, papers, the box that had held cuff links and letters, framed photographs—

The door slammed shut behind her and she jumped. She whirled around, just in time to see Nico struggling to pull a revolver from his jacket pocket. Her hand automatically went to her empty skirt pocket and she cursed herself. Her gun was in her coat, downstairs. Nico finally yanked his gun out, dislodging a small object from his pocket as well. Small, circular, gold, brilliant, it pinged on the wood planks and rolled toward Inez. She captured it with a foot and swooped it up.

A gold ring.

Engraved inside were words just barely visible in the lamplight: *Two but one heart till death us part.*

Chapter Forty-three

Inez held up the ring Jamie Monroe had bought to give Carmella. The ring that belonged in the jewelry box Inez had found on the hay wharf. The ring that Inez had found the receipt for in Jamie's trunk. She held it up toward Nico as if it was a talisman against the revolver in his shaking hand.

"Ah, Signora Stannert, why could you not leave well enough alone?" said Nico, sounding close to despair.

"You are a murderer." Her words were flat, cold. "That is not something 'well enough,' to be ignored and left alone."

She stepped toward him, closing the ring in her fist. "Where is Antonia? What have you done with her?"

"I would not hurt the girl. She is not here. Gone to dinner, to the boardinghouse, I expect, which is where you also should have been."

Thank God she's not here.

Relief calmed sharp fear and shaped it into resolve.

"You would not hurt her, but you threaten me, her guardian and the only one standing between her and a life in the streets, with a gun." She took another step, approaching him at an angle, hoping he would perhaps back away from her accusations, away from the door.

She had never seen him with a gun, so she was taking a chance. Perhaps he didn't know how to use one. He certainly acted as if he had never held one before.

That could be to her advantage, or disadvantage. He could shoot intentionally and miss, or inadvertently pull the trigger and hit her by accident. She continued, "Do you mean to kill me too, then?"

He retreated a step. "No! That is, I do not want to. I am not that kind of man."

"Ah, but you are. You killed Jamie Monroe. Do you know his real name was Robert Gallagher? Harry Gallagher's son, and you killed him. My God, Nico. What a mess you are in."

He flared. "I only wanted to talk to him. He sent me a note, asking to meet. We met on the wharf, after his work, after my business at the warehouse. He asked for Carmella's hand in marriage. I told him he would marry her over my dead body. He said," he licked his lips, "other things. It got…out of hand. And then, when it was over, I thought if I could make him disappear, eventually Carmella and everyone else would believe he left, moved away. But the tide didn't take him away, not like—" He stopped.

"Not like the previous time," Inez finished.

His eyes widened.

"And Jamie found out, didn't he?" she said. "All your good fortune happened after the last union failed, but it wasn't luck, was it? You killed Eli Greer, the treasurer who was distributing the union funds back to the members. You killed him after he visited Stephen Abbott, and then you kept the money that belonged to the others. You stole from your friends, your colleagues. You built a life with wealth that wasn't yours and claimed it was talent and luck. But the acclaim came later, after you built your life on a lie." She took another step toward him, hoping to force him farther away from the door so she could throw it open, slam it into him, and escape.

This time, he didn't retreat.

Instead, he stepped forward and whipped the gun barrel at her face.

She blocked the blow, crying out as the barrel cracked into

her forearm. Pain shot like lightning up her arm. The ring flew from her grasp, bouncing and rolling out of sight.

Nico grabbed her shoulder, pivoting her, and smashed her face-first into the door panel. Stars exploded in her vision. His voice seemed distant.

"Do you know what his last words were? 'Not my hands.' He was dying, and he begged me not to hurt his hands."

Dizzy with pain, Inez tried to twist sideways from his grasp.

Nico shoved her into the door again, hard. The panel rattled, the rough surface tore at her cheek like sharp fingernails. "I am sorry, Signora. This is not what I wanted, what I hoped, for you and me. But you brought it on yourself. On us."

He then wrenched her away and spun her around so she faced the window overlooking the alley. The hard muzzle of the gun jammed into the base of her neck.

Time stood still.

Her vision blackened at the edges, until all she saw was Jamie's gaping trunk and the dark-paned window above. She felt hot, then very, very cold. *Not this way. It cannot end this way.*

"Nico, stop. Don't do this," she whispered.

"Hands behind your back, Signora."

She complied, and he locked her wrists together with his long fingers. "If you do not want to end up dead, you must do as I say." He twisted her wrists and she bit back a scream, sure her arm was broken.

The pressure of the muzzle lifted, and she went limp with relief. Before she could move or say anything more, a silky rope snaked around her wrists and tightened. One of her stockings? She guessed so, but since it was behind her back, she couldn't tell for certain.

"I do not want to kill you," he said under his breath. "I just need time. Later, when Antonia returns from dinner, she will wonder where you are and will find you. Eventually. By then, I'll be gone."

"What are you doing?" She meant this in a wider sense—what have you done to your life?—but he answered in the specific.

"I will take a page from Signore Monroe's book, disappear, and re-invent myself, far away from here."

What about Carmella? Was she going with him? Was he abandoning her? Inez opened her mouth to ask and a wad of silky material—another of her good stockings?—stopped her words.

He continued, "If only Signore Monroe had told me who he really was. Yes, I saw the photograph. Signore Gallagher showed me, asked me if I knew him. Son of a rich man, well-placed. If he hadn't pretended to be someone he was not, this would not have happened. I would happily have allowed him to court Carmella, and he wouldn't have gone digging up the past. It would all have been so different." He sounded sad, and angry, as if the turn of events was due to Jamie, due to Inez, due to everyone but himself.

Regaining her wits, Inez tried to spit out the gag.

"No, no. You must stay quiet for now, Signora." A length of material—a sash?—looped across her mouth and nose. He tied a knot at the back of her head. Pulled it tight. She held still. If he pulled much more she would not be able to breathe at all, and that would be the end of her, although not immediately, and certainly most unpleasantly.

He pushed her toward Monroe's open trunk. "Forgive the mess. I had to look for anything else you or he might have had that might tie his death or the past to me. Nothing. Signore Welles told me about the list of names. I knew you were getting close to the truth. I'll not bother you for those papers now. What you do with them, I do not care. I will not be here. You can prove nothing. All you can do is tell stories, and who will believe you? Besides, I will be gone."

His tone intensified. "You would not want to hurt Carmella further, would you? She will be bewildered, frantic, and wonder what happened to me. She will need you. I have arranged to leave the store to you and to her—yes, you will finally have your half-ownership—and everything else is left to her. She is the only one I regret leaving now." The sorrow in his voice was genuine, but brief.

Then he was all business again. "Get in."

Inez stared at the trunk. Surely he wasn't going to lock her inside Jamie's trunk.

When she didn't move, Nico shoved her over the side. She tumbled in, hitting her shoulder hard on the wood-ribbed bottom. She lashed out at him with a foot. He grabbed her ankle and held it.

For one brief moment, she saw his face. His jaw was set, determined, eyes hollowed in the lamplight, his usually well-groomed hair a wild, curly mop. He looked nothing like the talented musician Inez thought she knew, the one who captivated San Francisco's high society and seduced all with his charm and his music.

He looked a monster.

"The only reason I do not kill you as I killed Signore Monroe is because Carmella will need you. Do not fail her." He shoved her foot inside and slammed the lid, shutting Inez into complete darkness.

Inez heard the latch click, the key turn and lock. She heard him say, "Good-bye, Signora."

Footsteps retreated across the floor. A door opened, then shut.

She lay on her side in the trunk, head forced down between her shoulders, knees bent, walking skirt and petticoat twisted around her legs. Her injured arm was pinned beneath her, screaming to be released. Inez attempted to shift onto her back and breathe shallowly through the satin encasing her nose. She kicked the wall of the trunk behind her to test its strength.

She had never been in such complete, saturated dark.

The walls at front, back, above, below, seemed to constrict, shrink around her. It was like being buried alive.

She tried to calm her breathing. What if the air in the trunk was all she had? How long would it be before Antonia found her? *Please don't let her come back while he is still here.*

Time seemed to stretch eternal as Inez strained to hear. Would she hear the door open downstairs? Would Antonia call out for her?

Sounds, outside the trunk. Inez kicked harder. There was a footfall, followed by a scraping at the keyhole and Antonia's urgent whisper through the walls of the trunk. "Stop it, Mrs. S! He's gone, down the stairs. I'm hurrying."

The lock sprung open and the lid creaked up, revealing Antonia's frightened face.

After the darkness in the trunk, the storage room with its one window on the night felt like coming into the dawn. Antonia pulled the tie and gag from Inez's face. Inez sat up, gasping for air and against the pain, finally sputtering, "You were here, hiding?"

Antonia moved behind Inez. "I was waiting for you so we could go to dinner. I heard the doorbell ring and I peeked out my window."

Inez heard the clickety-click as Antonia opened her folding knife.

"It was Mr. Donato," she continued, "so I didn't answer. But then, he opened the door. He had a key! To our place!"

Inez realized, as owner of the building, of course Nico had a key. He had never mentioned it, and it had not occurred to Inez until then that he could come and go as he pleased in their quarters.

Antonia's sharp knife sliced through the silky rope, freeing Inez's hands. Cradling her injured arm, Inez climbed out of the trunk. "Quick, to your room. The window," she said.

They could not stop him, Inez thought, but if he had gone to the store after leaving their apartment, perhaps he was still around. In that case, they could watch which way he went and call the police. Inez was past debating the pros and cons of turning Nico over to the law. Harry Gallagher might want to deliver his own private brand of justice, but the time for such things had passed. Now, the focus was to keep Nico from disappearing, taking some ship, train, or ferry out of the city and vanishing into the world beyond.

Inez and Antonia hurried to the bedroom window in time to see Nico emerge from the music store below. Carrying a satchel and his violin, Nico walked to the corner where the hack that Inez had noticed earlier waited by a streetlamp.

Nico talked to the driver, then opened the carriage door and climbed in.

"Dammit!" whispered Inez, partly from pain, partly from frustration.

"I'll follow him," offered Antonia.

Before Inez could respond, a muffled crack sounded from the carriage, followed by two more so close together they almost sounded as one.

The horse lurched forward in his harness until the driver, seemingly heedless of the shots inside, tightened the reins.

The door of the carriage flew open and Nico fell out into the gutter.

Inez and Antonia gasped.

Nico got to his hands and knees, swaying, then crumpled to the cobblestones.

The driver cracked the reins and the hack sped off, careening around the corner.

"Quick!" said Inez.

She and Antonia raced down the stairs. Inez grabbed the store keys from the hook on the way out, intending to give them to Antonia and tell her to use the telephone to call the police.

She hurried to Nico, lying facedown, and knelt. With her good arm, she pulled him onto his back. He had been shot once in the head, another time in the throat, and a third time in the chest. His face was covered with blood, his collar and waistcoat blood-soaked.

His eyes were open. At first, she thought he stared at her, but then she realized his gaze went far beyond her, up to the light and beyond into the clouded evening sky.

He wasn't breathing.

Another carriage approached from the opposite direction, hoofs and wheels clattering. Inez struggled to a stand and retreated to the sidewalk, shielding Antonia behind her. The carriage stopped, and de Bruijn stepped out, his face nearly as pale as the bandage under his hat. His eyes locked first with Inez's before sliding past her to Antonia. Relief washed over his countenance. He hastened over to Nico, and, as Inez had done, knelt to examine him.

"It happened a few minutes ago. Someone was in the carriage when he got in," said Inez. She put her good arm around Antonia, hugging her shoulders. "They shot him three times. He either was pushed or fell out of the hack. The driver then took off down Kearney, toward Market."

De Bruijn nodded, stood up, and advanced to the corner, looking in the direction Inez indicated. He shook his head and came back to them.

He said bleakly, "Gone," adding, "I am too late."

Inez gazed at what had once been Nico Donato, a gifted, passionate musician, a fiercely protective brother, and thought of all that had transpired to bring him here. The first long-ago murder had gifted him with the means he needed to build a comfortable life for himself and Carmella. That one killing, when it threatened to surface, had eventually led him to kill again. This time, his victim was his sister's suitor, a man he thought inconsequential and penniless who turned out to be anything but. Robert Gallagher, alias Jamie Monroe, had been another young man who, wanting to create a new life, had turned his back on his past, his deeds, and misdeeds. Like Nico, Jamie had sought to build a life of his own making, based on lies.

Nico had sought to keep his lies alive and bury the truth,

until he could do so no longer. He finally tried to flee a life in which truth was as insubstantial as the fog. A life which, in the end, he could not outrun.

She said, "We were, all of us, too late."

Chapter Forty-four

At six in the morning on a Sunday, the Palace Hotel dining room was nearly empty. A few families, most likely headed for mass or some other church services after breakfast, were scattered throughout the immense room, the clink of tableware and murmur of voices subdued by thick carpet and distance from his corner table. Public, neutral, but also discreet.

Which was precisely the sort of venue de Bruijn had decided he required for his conversation with Miss O'Connell.

He had determined that it would be best not to meet with her in private, concerned he would not be able to contain his temper if it was just the two of them.

He had no more than five minutes to review what he planned to say to her before she slipped into place across the table from him. She was dressed as any proper, young woman might for a morning church service—a fine outfit of alternating grays and a matching hat that somehow managed to highlight the subdued red of her hair. She gave him a small smile, her face otherwise watchful, wary.

The waiter rushed over to pour her coffee from the silver coffeepot. She shook her head at the proffered sugar, then placed her large gray handbag on the table, near at hand. De Bruijn eyed it, remembering the handgun he'd glimpsed inside a different handbag at their previous meeting.

"On your way to early confession, Miss O'Connell?" The

words slipped out, unbidden, unexamined, not part of the script he had fashioned beforehand.

She picked up her cup and studied him over the rim. "How are you, Mr. de Bruijn? Recovering from your very unfortunate accident?"

"I am improving, thank you. As you know, I have had much time to ponder and have found myself wondering: just how accidental was it, Miss O'Connell? Being that it was unfortunate for me but not for you?"

She set her cup down on the saucer so gently, it made not the slightest sound. "Forgive me for stating the obvious, Mr. de Bruijn, but it seems you are slipping. You would never have been caught in such a situation back when we first made our professional acquaintance. What has happened to you since then?"

She was right. And he knew exactly what had happened to change him, to cause his focus in this investigation to falter. Drina happened. And Antonia.

But he refused to be sidetracked in the conversation he'd prepared. "When did Mr. Gallagher hire you? Was it before he left? Or after, through telegram?"

She toyed with the drawstring on her bag. "I am always open to freelance opportunities. You know that, Mr. de Bruijn. I saw no conflict with a parallel request to provide support to your efforts."

"I instructed you to *follow* Mrs. Stannert, Mr. Hee, and Mr. Donato," de Bruijn said through gritted teeth. "Not to *kill* anyone."

"Mr. Gallagher's instructions were quite clear, Mr. de Bruijn. I would think you'd be pleased with the results."

"Pleased that you set a trap and murdered Donato in cold blood? You do me no honor." He sat back, glared at her.

"Temper, temper, Mr. de Bruijn." She lifted her napkin from her lap, refolded it into its original configuration, and set it by her half-empty cup.

"Before you leave, you owe me something."

She raised her eyebrows.

"A report, Miss O'Connell. On your activities." He kept his voice as hard and cold as steel.

"I reported to the client, as is proper. Honestly, Mr. de Bruijn, I cannot believe you have not worked out the full scope of my actions. But as you wish." She folded her hands on top of her bag, an exasperated schoolteacher forced to explain a simple arithmetic problem to a deliberately obtuse student.

"You authorized me to hire associates to help me carry out my tasks. I did so. I assigned them to watch Mr. Hee and Mr. Donato, and report on their findings. I kept Mrs. Stannert for myself. Mr. Hee spent most of his time in the warehouse, in his room in Chinatown, and at the store. Nothing to report of note there. Mr. Donato, on the other hand, was very busy. He bought a one-way ticket on a ship bound for Paris." She added, "France."

"I know my geography, Miss O'Connell."

"He also visited his bank, his lawyer, and the warehouse. He had a large trunk sent to the ship. Meanwhile, I trailed around after Mrs. Stannert, who made stops connected with the past union. That was her idea, you know, that young Gallagher's interest in the disbanded musicians union was somehow tied to his demise. You and I were wrong in thinking the illegal trade in artifacts was the key. But that is water under the bridge now." She shifted in her chair. "At the end of the day, she went home. You can imagine my surprise when I saw the associate I had hired to follow Mr. Donato outside the building. He explained that at that very moment, Mr. Donato was also in the apartment."

She unfolded her hands and straightened a glove seam. "I sent him up to reconnoiter while I waited in the street. He overheard Mr. Donato confess to Mrs. Stannert. The words used were unambiguous. Mr. Donato exited the apartment and entered the store. My associate exited soon thereafter and told me what he had heard. I believe you can deduce the rest. Have you any questions?"

"No questions, but an observation." He leaned forward, giving weight and emphasis to his next words. "Mrs. Stannert and Antonia were inside that building. He could have killed them both."

She didn't flinch or change her expression. "He could have. But he did not."

De Bruijn realized she had thought of the possibility, taken it into consideration, and decided it was worth the risk.

His hand clenched on the tablecloth.

Her matter-of-fact tone did not waver in the least as she added, "I was given a job, and I did it. Robert Gallagher's killer was identified and dealt with. Mr. Gallagher is satisfied that justice was served. You will be paid. I will be paid. It is over."

"Not over for Mr. Donato's sister. Not over for the young man who has been falsely accused of Jamie's—" he shook his head, distressed at the slip— "Robert's murder. What of him?"

"Oh, it will all work out. And now, I have an observation for you, Mr. de Bruijn. You underestimated Mrs. Stannert completely. She determined the who and why for this case. She put the pieces together, and all I had to do was follow her lead. You should thank her for all her hard work. Speaking of work," she checked her pendant watch, "I must be going. Mass to attend. A certain gentleman has doubts of his wife's fidelity and believes they pass messages during mass."

She rose, and he did as well.

Miss O'Connell touched her hat, giving it a slight nudge. "Will you soon be returning to Colorado or points east, now that the case is finished?"

All he said was "No doubt our paths will cross again, Miss O'Connell. I'll remember this."

"Oh pish-posh." She picked up her reticule. "I will put your words down to the dreadful knock on the head in the alleyway. I am certain once you are yourself again, you will forget this unpleasant affair, come to see that what I said was true, and we will resume our mutually beneficial business relationship."

De Bruijn watched her walk away, taking the shortest path to the door and blending, as she always did, effortlessly into the setting. None of the families nor the few single men breaking fast early gave her more than a cursory glance. She was good, one of the best, he acknowledged that. But, she could be wrong.

And she was wrong about one thing: He would never forget, nor forgive, the violence she had done to what was right—legally and morally—here, this November, in San Francisco.

Chapter Forty-five

Luncheon time on Monday afternoon in the Palace Hotel's magnificent dining room was loud, noisy, and exuberant. At their table in the corner, Inez leaned in toward Flo and de Bruijn, the better to separate their words from the random conversations at nearby tables.

De Bruijn asked Flo, "You are leaving?"

"This evening. Mr. Poole has reserved a private car for our return to Colorado." She was wearing her travel clothes, which although properly dark, were aflutter with fringe, bows, and pleats. "I've been gone too long, and can only hope the girls and clients haven't burned the place down in my absence." She turned to Inez, "I'll be back, though. There's gold to be mined in these city hills," and winked.

Inez knew what she meant—Flo had mentioned a local madam she knew was getting married and giving up the trade. Flo could hardly contain her excitement at the prospect of buying the business, and was twisting Inez's unbroken arm to back her offer. "We don't even have to be involved, except at arm's length. I'll hire someone to manage the house," she'd said.

Inez shifted the sling to ease the ache in her arm, thinking two, three months would be a long time to play one-handed piano and depend on Antonia's help to dress.

Flo tut-tutted, sympathetic. "Shall I butter your bread for you?" Without waiting for an answer, she seized Inez's butter knife and slathered a thick layer on the slice resting on Inez's bread plate. "And have I told you how glad I am to see you out of those dreary clothes you were wearing when I first arrived? That maroon is so much more attractive!"

Inez turned to de Bruijn. "And you? What are your plans?"

"I will be staying. For now. I have already had inquiries from a number of people." He smoothed his small beard. "Including from a few who are inquiring whether my 'wife,' Mrs. Wilhemina de Bruijn, is also available to offer her investigative services."

Flo snorted, privy to the reference. "Fat chance. Inez is going to have her hands full now that the music store is all hers."

"*Half* mine. The other half belongs to Carmella." Inez thought of the exhausting hours she had spent with Carmella yesterday. After reassuring Carmella that the broken arm was due to a misstep on the apartment stairs, Inez had stayed with her in the Donatos' parlor. Antonia had disappeared into the kitchen to eat *svogliatella* and rearrange the baked goods to make room for the food that would appear from neighbors and churchwomen, once Nico's death became widely known.

"I knew this would happen!" Carmella had wailed. "It was just a matter of time!"

Inez had decided to tread carefully. "You knew what, exactly, would happen?"

"Oh, Mrs. Stannert, it is so clear. I warned him time and again that someday a jealous husband or angry father or brother would be the death of him. Nico, he was no fighter, he knew nothing of guns, of violence."

Inez elected not to respond, simply letting the young woman sob on her good shoulder. "What will I do now, without him?" Carmella pulled back, wiping her red-rimmed eyes.

"First, you will mourn," said Inez. "You will let those around you fuss and take care of you. And then, Carmella, you can do whatever you want. Help in the store. Hire on with the lady printers, the Fleurys." Inez saw the possibilities open an expanse as exciting and vast as the central plains she had glimpsed through a train window, years ago. "Open your own bakery. I will help you."

"But...this house. This was Nico's dream. It is too big for just me."

"Stay in the house and rent out rooms to boarders," suggested Inez. "Or if you prefer, move into accommodations for proper young women such as yourself, and rent the house as a whole, or sell it. You can do anything, Carmella, when the time is right, and you know your own mind."

At the last, Inez gave Carmella the packet of letters from Jamie's trunk and the gold ring, saying simply they had been in his effects. "I am sure he would want you to have them," said Inez. That had brought on a renewed storm of tears. Inez had debated revealing Jamie's true identity, but finally decided against it. Like brother, like lover—the two most important men in Carmella's life had both had their secrets. What good would come of telling Carmella that her fiancé was not the person she believed him to be?

Inez blinked, bringing herself back to the Palace Hotel and to de Bruijn saying, "Do you and Miss Donato have plans for the store, Mrs. Stannert?"

With a nod of thanks to Flo, Inez picked up her bread. "Miss Donato is leaving it entirely in my hands. So, to begin with, I am hiring Welles full-time to help with the daily management. I also asked John Hee if he would continue providing repair services and take charge of obtaining and maintaining the 'curiosities.' But to avoid black market items." She meant that as a reassurance to de Bruijn.

He nodded.

"I shall spend more time with Antonia," Inez added. The future was already looking brighter for her ward, with a new friend at school and her renewed interest in her studies.

Inez continued, "I shall continue to explore investment opportunities, once I have more time. Offer piano lessons, perhaps teaching less fortunate students for free as I am doing for Patrick May. I still have hopes for him. Music frees the soul, you know."

"Speaking of Mr. May, has he come out of hiding?" de Bruijn inquired.

Inez nodded. In her concluding conversation with Harry, she had made it clear she wanted no "payment" for her part in solving the murder, other than for him to clear Patrick's name. "With Mr. Donato dead, there is no proof as to who committed the murder," she explained. "Only Antonia and I heard what he said. All the evidence is circumstantial, and there's not much of it. We have the collar from Mr. Donato's cloak, but cannot prove that it was found on the scene. So, although we know who killed your son, we are the only ones. We need your influence with the police to free Patrick May. He is innocent."

Harry, with a black band of mourning encircling his sleeve and looking more tired and worn than she had ever seen him, had just nodded. However, he had been true to his unspoken promise, and Inez had received a joyous visit from Bessie and Molly May, relieved that Patrick was freed and no longer a suspect. Inez had been surprised that Harry wasn't more surprised when she had given her short report on Nico. She finally surmised he had already heard as much from de Bruijn. But still.

"Patrick May? Who's he? And what's this about a black market? Is that for Chinese vases and whatnot?" Flo looked from one to the other, blank. "Goodness, you two were busy while I was otherwise occupied." Her gaze traveled from de Bruijn's wrapped head to Inez's broken arm. "I'm glad I stayed out of whatever it was you two were up to."

Inez set her bread down, untouched. "I cannot stop thinking that, despite everything we did and all we uncovered, we failed in the end. We know Nico killed Harry's son. But who killed Nico?"

Flo lifted a shoulder in a shrug. "It doesn't matter. You gave Harry what he wanted: the name of his son's killer."

Inez continued, "I know you think that's enough, Mrs. Sweet, and nothing more is to be done. Mr. Gallagher seems likewise inclined. Perhaps he believes that, in a larger sense, justice has been served. But I do not. Surely, Mr. de Bruijn, you feel as I do. It seems to me our work is not yet done. Does Mr. Donato's murder have anything to do with our investigation? Or could the perpetrator be, as his sister thinks, a jealous husband? Will we ever know?"

Through Inez and Flo's exchange and Inez's final comments, de Bruijn's face had grown increasingly troubled. He finally removed his napkin, folded it neatly, and placed it beneath his plate. "Our investigation is ended, Mrs. Stannert. Mr. Donato's business in stolen antiquities alone would have made him many dangerous enemies, men who are as invisible as they are violent. I doubt the perpetrator will ever be found."

She met his straightforward gaze. His dark brown eyes were noncommittal, yet Inez could swear he was concealing something with his studied neutrality, just as his plate now concealed his napkin.

He knows something about this, but he will not tell.

If that was the case, Inez thought, perhaps it was for the best. For if she knew the whys and wherefores of Nico's murder, would she have to keep that from Carmella as well, storing it away with all her other secrets?

Meanwhile, Flo's attention had wandered off and away, roaming around the dining room. She brightened. "There is Mr. Poole! He promised to take me on a drive to the Cliff House before we leave San Francisco." She rose, bestowing a brilliant smile on de Bruijn and Inez. "The bill for luncheon goes to Mr. Gallagher, correct? Tell him thank you. Well, no, tell him to go to hell, what with all he put me through. The three of us, we shall all meet again, I hope? Under better circumstances?" She retrieved her parasol and beaded bag. After fluttering her fingers at them with a "Toodle-oo," she threaded her way to the dining room entrance where Inez espied the stocky figure of Poole, waiting.

De Bruijn, who had risen when Flo did, sat back down. "Well, Mrs. Stannert, now that we can count this particular episode as closed. I have one other matter I would like to discuss with you. If it is possible and not an intrusion, I hope you might consider allowing me to call on you and Antonia now and again. Informally."

Inez hesitated. "I shall need to speak to Antonia before I can give you an answer."

"Of course."

Inez thought it was very likely that if de Bruijn hadn't offered to keep in touch, Antonia would have insisted *they* visit *him*. She gathered her purse. "Will you be staying on in the hotel?"

"For now. They have any number of full-time residents. It seems like a reasonable location for me to set up my business."

"Hmmm." Inez inspected the detective, his somber dress, his somber mood. She reflected on how, once he had somehow managed to put it all together from his sickbed, he had dragged himself out to try and right a situation that he suspected was about to go terribly wrong. "You said you are taking on clients. Of all kinds?"

He settled his hat gingerly atop his head, picked up his cane—not as fine a one as was stolen, but fine enough. "Of all kinds. Finding what is lost continues to be my specialty. Disappeared spouses, stolen inheritances, reputations unjustly ruined, as well as the mundane misplaced family jewelry and purloined accounts."

Inez considered the women she knew through her business dealings. All hard-working, without exception. She thought how some, through their own ignorance or blind emotions, were taken sad advantage of. They came to her, sobbing, tricked by slick sellers of goods and services never delivered, wronged by previous business associates, stolen from by loved ones including husbands, brothers, grown children—familial perfidy knew no bounds when it came to money.

She smiled. "Mr. de Bruijn, I daresay we shall find ourselves working together again soon."

Author's Note

Warning: spoilers lurk in these final ruminations, so beware.

In *A Dying Note*, my Silver Rush protagonist Inez Stannert and I make our first foray into 1881 San Francisco, after five previous books set in 1880 Colorado. New venue, new times, new almost everything for us both.

First, a quick look at what is "real" and what is the result of my fervid imagination. The D&S House of Music and Curiosities, Henderson's Three Sheets, and the Mays' laundry are all fictional, for instance. The Palace Hotel (with its millions of bricks) is real, as is Lotta's Fountain, the Lincoln public school, and other landmarks. The waterfront along the Mission Creek channel and into China Basin/Mission Bay is real. However, depending what you read, the name of this shallow, busy waterway between Berry Street and Hooper Street varied in the 1880s: Mission Creek, Mission Creek canal (or channel), Channel Street canal, China Basin canal, and, more colloquially, Shit Creek. As I rumbled and wrote my way around this area, I found Nancy Olmsted's book on the subject especially useful: *Vanished Waters: A History of San Francisco's Mission Bay.*

Chinatown and the Barbary Coast existed, although some of the streets have changed names or spelling over time (for instance, Dupont Street is now Grant Street, and Kearney Street is now Kearny). In those cases, I elected to use the names and spellings of the times. There are some wonderful maps of San Francisco to peruse and play with on the internet, including the David Rumsey Map Collection and OldSF.org. The latter site ties the San Francisco city map to images from the San Francisco Public Library's San Francisco Historical Photograph Collection. Maps of the times always end up teaching me things I didn't know before and setting me straight on things I *thought* I knew. For instance, in nineteenth-century accounts of San Francisco, I read about folks going to Point Lobos for an afternoon picnic and so on. As a native Californian, I'm a little embarrassed to admit that the only Point Lobos I knew was the one outside of Monterey, California. Definitely not close enough to San Francisco for an afternoon's jaunt in a buggy! The 1880s maps helped me realize that San Francisco's Point Lobos is essentially the area now called "Lands End."

The initial impetus for this book—the "spark," if you will—was the labor activities and formation of unions in San Francisco. From what I've gleaned, 1881 was a fairly quiet time for the labor movement, which gave me room to maneuver my characters and their fictional shenanigans. Information was sparse about pre-1885 labor efforts in the San Francisco musical world. In 1850, San Francisco's musicians demanded a wage increase, which was ignored. In 1869, they attempted to organize a union, which failed, and again in 1874, which again failed. Finally in 1885, they succeeded in forming the Musician's Mutual Protective Union, Local 10, which was chartered by the National League of Musicians. Eventually this organization would become the current day Musicians Local 6.

According to the paper *A History of the Musicians Union Local 6, American Federation of Musicians*, by Steven Meicke, when the 1874 union disbanded, "[its] failure was attributed to political competition among the potential leaders of a would-be musicians union. It was believed that the 'abortive efforts of various rival organizations' thwarted the formation of a legitimate union, and that some of the leaders sought to 'obtain control for the furtherance of private and selfish ends.'" (In this quote, Meicke references an April 29, 1917, article in the *San Francisco Chronicle* titled "Musicians' Local, No. 6, Has Had Years of Activity Advance Cause of Good Music; Beginnings in 1885.")

Hmmmm… intriguing!

Meicke also noted that when the union disbanded, the money in the treasury went back to its members. This is where fact and fiction parted ways and my musings took over: suppose those fund didn't make it back to the members?

If you are curious about the labor movement in San Francisco, there are many resources and books out there—an avalanche, actually. One of my favorites for an overview is *A History of the Labor Movement in California* by Ira B. Cross. It has a very nice discussion (and photograph) of Frank Roney, a union organizer who makes a cameo appearance in the story. Roney was deeply involved in the Seamen's Protective Union and was a leader in the early days of the Workingmen's Party of California. As Cross notes, "Night after night found him under the light of some friendly street-lamp along the water front talking to small groups of seamen… [W]hen the steamship sailors and firemen gathered to discuss their grievances, he was among the first to advocate the organization of a union." In September 1880, Roney helped form the Seamen's Protective Union, which survived until early 1882. In July 1881, Roney became president of the Representative Assembly of Trades and Labor Unions of the Pacific Coast.

For those who are wondering, Susan B. Anthony really did say, "Organize, agitate, educate, must be our war cry." However, she said it about a decade later, in the early 1890s. It is such a great quote, I simply could not resist including it in my story.

The inclusion of women in unions and the organization of "women's work" was still a long way off in 1881. For insights into what women were up to, I recommend *Like a Machine or an Animal: Working Women of the Late Nineteenth-Century Urban Far West, in San Francisco, Portland, and Los Angeles* by Mary Lou Locke, Ph.D. thesis, 1982 (Locke writes the Victorian San Francisco Mystery Series under the name M. Louisa Locke); and *Capital Intentions: Female Proprietors in San Francisco*, 1850-1920, by Edith Sparks.

For an eye-opening journey into San Francisco in this general timeframe, you can find and download this 1876 book from the internet: *Lights and Shades in San Francisco*, by B. E. Lloyd. A sizeable section of the book—100 pages—delves into Chinatown and its occupants, providing a fascinating but cringeworthy window into the perspectives of the day. Chinatown and the Barbary Coast are also the subjects of *The Barbary Coast: An Informal History of the San Francisco Underworld*, by Herbert Asbury, published in 1933.

A couple of great websites to find out more about almost any San Francisco-related topic or luminary are "FoundSF" and "The Virtual Museum of the City of San Francisco." "Calisphere," a project of the University of California Libraries, provides "free access to unique and historically important artifacts for research, teaching, and curious explorations." Well, that just about covers everything, doesn't it! I can attest that one can easily lose track of time exploring the photographs and other materials on this site. Finally, I'm going to throw open the metaphorical trunk and yank out some other books I found particularly useful. Note: these are all over the (San Francisco) map:

• *The San Francisco Irish 1848–1880*, by R. A. Burchell

• *Bonanza Inn: America's First Luxury Hotel*, by Oscar Lewis and Carroll D. Hall (This is all about San Francisco's Palace Hotel)

• *Shanghaied in San Francisco*, by Bill Pickelhaupt

• *More San Francisco Memoirs, 1852-1899: The ripening years*, complied and introduced by Malcolm E. Barker

• *Methods of Teaching*, by John Sweet, Principal of the San Francisco Girls' High School and Normal Class (copyright 1880)

• *Making San Francisco American: Cultural Frontiers in the Urban West, 1846-1906*, by Barbara Berglund

There are many more, but I'll save them for another story.

For those who are new to the series and might be wondering "What the heck is Leadville?" my early books also include author's notes with plenty of references. Enjoy!

To see more Poisoned Pen Press titles:

Visit our website:
poisonedpenpress.com
Request a digital catalog:
info@poisonedpenpress.com